STOLEN BY SHADOW BEASTS

THE COMPLETE COLLECTION

LACEY CARTER ANDERSEN

DEDICATION

To my kids- Always remember that you're never too old for excitement and adventure.

WANT MORE FROM LACEY CARTER ANDERSEN?

Want to be part of the writing process? Maybe even get a taste of my sense of humor? Teasers for my new releases? And more? Join Lacey's Realm on Facebook!

FAE SECRETS

STOLEN BY SHADOW BEASTS: PREQUEL

ONE

Ann

It's dark on campus as I limp among the headstones in the graveyard, hissing through my teeth when I take too deep of a breath, then trying to calm my racing heart as the pain slowly dulls back to tolerable. I press a hand to my side and lean on a headstone, taking a brief break before continuing forward.

All around me it's silent, other than the night animals and the stirring of the wind. Students and faculty have long since gone to bed. There aren't even guards in this area of campus. Because, why would there be? No one would expect a light fae to be out at this time, wandering between graves, lost in thought.

But most of my kind don't have dark secrets that could destroy them.

Keeping so many secrets makes me restless. Unable to sleep.

Out here I can also limp instead of concealing it. I can walk around like every inch of my body is hurting, instead of forcing myself to move about like a "proper lady." And that's strangely freeing in itself.

"More secrets I don't have to keep out here in the dark," I whisper.

Only a night owl answers my words as if to say, *you've never been as good at hiding your injuries as you think you are.*

I scowl, glaring at the owl on the branch of a tree. *I'm doing my best, you judgmental bird...*

And I was. But, unfortunately for me, the night before I was sent off to Royal Fae Academy was one of the bad moments for my stepfather. My "godparents" had dropped me off, after taking me out to a celebratory dinner before I left for the semester, and my stepfather *hated* Daniel and Blake.

Daniel had a brief romance with my mother when she was single, before he came out as gay. But despite the fact that their romance didn't work out, they became the best of friends. And when she got pregnant by a human, Daniel claimed me as his own so no one would know I wasn't a full light fae. But then to further protect me, my mother quickly married another fae who was far below her status and decided we would all play the part of a happy family.

I honestly think my mom was coming from a good place. But she had no idea how much my stepfather would hate raising another man's child. Something he reminded me about over and over again with his fists. And she, being a traditional light fae, had no idea how to handle such an angry man with such a bad temper. She had pushed herself hard to make me prettier. To sew better dresses for me and make sure my manners were perfect. Everything she did was to try to make him like me, but even as a young girl, I knew that no matter what I did, he'd hate me.

Because I was a daily reminder that my mother had loved someone else and that my stepfather had gained wealth and position only through necessity for my mother. It burned inside of him, twisting in his gut like a blade. He thought he deserved our life and could have it, if not for me.

The fool couldn't even seem to understand that my mother never would've chosen him in the first place, if not for me. Not that I'd ever tell him so.

"I'm a light fae, not a moron," I murmur.

That night just a few days ago, I'd tried my best to escape my stepfather, knowing that me seeing my father would put him in a bad mood. But he'd been waiting for me in my room, drunk as hell, and more pissed off than I'd ever seen him.

I'd tried to fight back. I *always* tried. But in the end, I'd ended up in a ball on the floor while he kicked me over and over again. All I could manage to do was try to protect the already badly injured parts of my body that his fists had bruised and broken.

When he'd finally spit on me and called me a bitch, all I could taste was my own blood. And beyond the pain, all I felt was a strange sense of gratitude that I'd be leaving the next morning and finally get a break from him, even if I was only going to another place where I would feel like an unwanted outsider.

So now, days later, I'm feeling better, at least physically. Being a fae means that I heal quickly, but not as quickly as a full-blooded fae. And yet, I still hurt. I still ache when I breathe too deeply, and one of my legs feels sore, like I'd been running for days.

Yet walking around with my aching body is better than sitting in my dorm bed, consumed by dark thoughts.

Thoughts of who I wish I was. Thoughts of how I wish I could be myself, even if for just a moment.

"What are you doing out here?"

I stiffen as the husky voice of an unfamiliar male rolls down my spine. Slowly, I turn around to face the man. He's cloaked in shadows, but he's tall and radiates a confidence that makes me uncertain if I should be running to him or away from him.

"Taking a stroll," I answer, trying to keep the curt note from my voice...and failing.

"A stroll at midnight in a graveyard?" I'm not sure if he sounds amused or doubtful.

"What's it to you?" I counter back, suddenly irritated that at the one time I should be left in peace, some jerk has shown up to ruin it. And yet, I never have an attitude. No, normally *I'm sweet as pie*, like the other light fae.

Apparently, I'm in a mood.

He cocks his head and comes closer.

I instinctually take a step back.

He laughs. The sound is low, almost sexual. "I have to admit, it's been a while since a woman tried to get away from me."

My voice trembles a little as I answer him. "I can't decide if you're bragging about your sexual prowess, or if you're some kind of serial killer."

He freezes. "Am I scaring you?"

"You're not making me feel comfortable," I tell him honestly, wondering if that's the wrong move.

If he's here to kill me, shouldn't I be trying to sound more confident?

"Fuck," he mutters, almost to himself. "I'm sorry. I've been so distracted lately I think I might have forgotten basic fae manners."

He clicks on a flashlight that lights up his face, and my breath catches. This man is undoubtedly the most beautiful man I've ever seen. Even though most people look creepy with a flashlight held up to their faces like that, he doesn't. He looks like some kind of bad-boy angel. His hair is light brown, left a little long on top, and his eyes are blue. But not the pale blue of most fae, more like a dark blue the same shade as the depths of the ocean, a color I've never seen before in my life in a person's eyes. The lines of his face are pleasant too, and his dark brows arch over expressive eyes.

I have to remind myself to breathe. I've never had this kind of instant attraction to anyone before. Certainly not a random man in a graveyard. It's as unsettling as it is strangely appealing. I've been so bored playing the good little fae. This feels like something dangerous. Like something I've been craving with my whole being.

"I'm Rayne, by the way. Rayne Bloodmore."

"Fuck," I whisper, then press my knuckles to my mouth in embarrassment. Light fae don't swear. But then, hadn't he? Hadn't Rayne, of one of the most powerful fae houses, just sworn?

"H-Hi," I stutter out.

"And who are you?" he asks, suddenly turning the flashlight onto me.

"Mary Ann Hart, but I go by Ann. I mean, my friends call me Ann. Not that I have a lot of friends, or that the ones I'm friendly with know me well enough to know I hate the name Mary Ann." I close my mouth, realizing I'm babbling.

"Ann." He says my name in a breathless way, then comes closer.

The light is drawn away from my face, and then he's inches from me. To my surprise, he reaches out and touches my face, cautiously, like he's afraid I might break. And up close, under the moonlight, he's even more handsome. I feel like I'm caught in a whirlwind, and there's only him and I inside of it.

"I'm trying to do something," he says, almost as if he's in awe. "I want to change the world."

I just stare, not sure how to answer.

"I want to focus on it completely. I don't want any distractions. But then, you..."

"Me?" *Is he feeling this strange connection to?*

"You're my mate. Aren't you?"

I shake my head in denial. I'm only twenty-three. It's too soon to find my mate. Maybe not for everyone, but it is for me. And my family isn't all-powerful, like his. We're barely royals. And what's more, I'm not a pure-blood fae. There's no way I'm the mate to Rayne Bloodmore.

And then, he leans forward and kisses me.

Whatever doubts I had fall away, and the spark that's between us grows until it feels like it might consume me. His lips go from soft and gentle, like they're testing my reaction, to hard and possessive. It isn't like a light fae. They're always gentle. Always smiling like painted dolls. But, no, Rayne doesn't kiss me the way I've been kissed a hundred times before. His lips awaken a need inside of me that changes something deep in my soul.

When his tongue slips inside of my mouth, I moan. My hands clutch the front of his shirt, drawing him closer. One of his hands digs deeply into my long hair, while the other pulls my hip to him until I can feel the hard evidence of his arousal.

I'm a light fae. We move slowly. We date. We get to know each other.

But mates are different. I've heard that a million times. Even so, this isn't what I expected. This need to have him here and now. To let the entire world burn if it means keeping him and I trapped in this moment forever.

And then he pulls back.

A whimper escapes my lips, and I stand on my tiptoes, offering him more.

He's breathing hard. "This isn't the time for a mate."

And the way he says mate seems to echo through me. "For me either," I tell him, still on my tiptoes, still wanting more.

He leans down and begins to kiss my neck, speaking softly. "I have so much to do. I can't offer you everything you deserve right now. Love. Unconditionally. My full attention. My everything. Not yet. Not when I'm so close."

"Close to what?" I whisper.

He pulls back from me, ever-so-slightly. "It doesn't matter, does it? Not the timing. Not that we're not ready. We're mates. And if we're mates, you're the one person I can't lie to. You're the one person who needs to know everything too."

"Everything about what?" I ask, trembling as his lips suck the juncture of my throat and neck.

He stops and then takes a small step back from me. His expression unreadable. "What if I told you that the dark fae aren't as evil as we've been led to believe and that light and dark fae aren't so different from each other? That this idea that purebred light fae are somehow better than anyone and anything else is all a lie?"

What would I say? Dark fae have always frightened me a little because of their terrifying powers. And yet, they are so rare they're almost like nightmares to scare children, rather than living, breathing people. But I'm not a pure light fae myself, so the notion that this man might feel we aren't inferior to him excites me. Perhaps there is a reason he's my mate.

"Ann?" He practically purrs my name.

I jerk, realizing I hadn't answered. "I'd want to learn more," I tell him honestly.

His lips curl into a smile, and he takes my hand. "Do you trust me?"

"I barely know you," I say, an unexpected laugh exploding from my lips.

"But do you trust me?"

I realize he isn't joking. Normally, I'm not the least bit trusting. I try to come across as naive and maybe a bit dumb, but deep inside I hold everyone at a distance, fearing if they get too close they might learn my secrets. But when I search inside of myself, I'm startled to realize I do trust him.

Maybe it's the mate bond. Maybe it's because my body is still tingling from his touch. I don't know. But the words come easily. "Yes. Yes, I do."

He squeezes my hand lightly for a second, then turns and begins jogging out of the graveyard, pulling me along with him. And I work damn hard, once again, not to limp. Not to show I'm injured in any way. Because that isn't a secret I'm ready to share with anyone yet, not even him.

My thoughts race as I try not to focus on how good his hand feels curled around mine. What do I know about Rayne and his family? His father is technically an impossibly rare dark fae, but it's been accepted by all fae that Rayne is purely of his mother's blood. His poor sister, on the other hand, is said to be purely a light fae by her family, but no one really believes it. Everyone who meets her whispers that she takes after her father, although no one is foolish enough to actually speak out against them.

They are powerful. So powerful that they could have

been kings and queens a long time ago. Technically, we are all lords and ladies, all of a similar rank, and yet, everyone knows where each family falls in line. What's more, Rayne's family has close ties with the other most powerful families. My parents will be ecstatic that he's my mate.

Only, none of that really matters. Not really. If the powers that be had determined we are mates, then I need to know him. Not his family. Not the legend of him. But *him*.

And, I guess, wherever he is taking me now might actually tell me something about him.

I never dive into things without thinking. I've never just raced off with a man into the darkness. But that's only the person I pretend to be: quiet, a careful thinker, a planner, and completely boring in every way. Maybe tonight I have a chance to actually figure out who I am when I'm not pretending.

Can Ann be brave? Can Ann follow her heart instead of her head?

Maybe, my thoughts whisper back.

We stop at a dark, stout building with vines all over it, tucked into a lonely corner of campus.

"What's that?" I ask, a little breathless.

"This is a secret no one wants us to know about. A way to get under the school and explore the tunnels concealed beneath."

I look at him, wondering if he's serious, then realize he is. "You want to show me something in the dark tunnels under the school?"

He surprises me by turning around and closing the distance between us. "I'm doing this all wrong. Finding my mate has fried my brain. I'm not thinking clearly." He releases a slow breath. "You and I are meant to be together. One day, we'll get married, probably have children, and I'll ensure that you never want for anything. Not money. Not anything you ever want, including love and affection. But I need to know...do you want Rayne, the powerful son of a ruling house? Do you want to just see me the way everyone sees me? Because I have secrets, Ann, and I wonder if you'll regret learning them."

This man...can he read my mind? Can he see inside the deepest parts of me? Because his words seem to echo my own thoughts. I have secrets too. And if he finds out I'm a half-breed, he'll still marry me, but will he hate me? Should I tell him the truth or continue letting this burn inside of me forever?

"I have secrets too," I finally admit.

His eyes widen as they run over me. "I want to know what they are. I want to know everything about you."

"I want to know the real you too," I answer with a smile.

So, there would be no secrets between us. But will we regret this moment? This promise between mates?

A strange wail comes from somewhere behind us. Perhaps from the graveyard. I turn around and stare, seeing a dark shape hunched and creeping between the headstones.

"Fucking hell," Rayne whispers, and there's fear in his voice. "This wasn't supposed to happen, but now we need to get you out of here. To somewhere safe."

"What's not supposed to happen?" I whisper right back.

He turns to me, his expression grave. "We're being hunted."

TWO

Rayne

A fucking monster is hunting us. Not the kind my sister loves so much, but the kind that will slit our throats and drink our blood without an ounce of regret. You see, this monster isn't just the kind who lives its life, searching out prey, like a lion who hunts a gazelle. Hunting just to survive.

No, this is something else. Because to this monster, I'm not normally its prey. This is a creature commanded to seek me out. And that's bad, really bad.

My enemies are getting bolder. They don't just want to scare me off any longer.

They want me *dead*.

At any other time, I'd consider their bullshit flattering. It'd mean I must be getting so close to the truth that they worry I'll destroy them. Which means I need to keep going, keep searching for the truth, and deal with the monster when it finds me.

And learn to use the powers I know about in theory only.

At any other time.

But tonight, I'm holding the hand of my mate, and that changes everything. She has to be my priority. My soul is screaming as much. And for a man who rarely felt fear, it's worrisome how much I fear anything happening to my Ann.

So, I lead her down into the tunnels beneath the school knowing that there I'll be on even footing with the beast. Technically, these tunnels are filled with other monsters, dangerous creatures, and an enemy who has seemed content to just play with me so far, but I know all these challenges well enough to protect her here. I don't have the same confidence about taking that thing on head-to-head in the open.

Clutching her much smaller hand, it feels like my world has been turned upside down. This is no longer just about my obsessions. It's about keeping her alive.

And that scares me.

I've never had to be responsible for anyone but myself.

But then I think of her, standing there in the night. She has long blonde hair, like most of the light fae, and pale blue eyes. I'd always thought the light fae blended together. That none of the women were particularly beautiful or particularly interesting. But Ann...she's both beautiful and interesting.

Her eyes are wide, as if permanently curious about the world, and she has the darkest, longest lashes I've ever seen. Her brows arch over those big eyes, giving her an innocence that is oddly appealing. And her lips? Gods, I can't resist them. They are so full, a shade darker than pink, but not quite red. And they are as soft as they looked. So entirely soft that I thought of nothing else when I touched her.

I shudder, arousal uncurling inside of me. This is not

the time to think of such things. Not with an enemy on our heels, and not with my sweet mate being dragged behind me.

Of all the ways I imagined meeting my mate, this scenario never even occurred to me.

And yet, if it brought her to me, it's hard to feel anything but pleasure about it.

"What's going on? What's hunting us?" she puffs behind me.

I slow, wondering if I'm pushing her too hard. She sounds far too out of breath given the situation. Or maybe being out of breath with a monster chasing you is normal? I'm not sure...

But before I can answer her questions, there's another strange wail that echoes down the tunnels. So, it'd seen us? Or sensed us? Either way, it isn't far behind.

I draw the dagger from my belt and grit my teeth, not sure how much to say. "I have enemies, Ann. Enemies who don't like what I'm researching."

"What are you researching?"

For someone being dragged through the darkness with a man she barely knows, Ann is handling this better than I could've imagined. Most light fae would've taken off running the second I walked into that graveyard. Most light fae wouldn't believe me when I told them we were being hunted.

I'm impressed. And more than a little turned on by both her bravery and her natural curiosity.

I'd been accused of being far too curious for my own good more times than I could count.

"I'm researching things that a deadly group would rather I didn't."

When I get her to safety, I will tell her all about my obsession. About the day my sister was born. About the day she first showed that she had the power to kill with a thought, and I knew for certain she was a dark fae. I loved her. I loved her as much as any brother could love his little sister. And the idea that the world would be cruel to her if they knew the truth had eaten me alive, even as a boy.

Yes, my father is a dark fae, and like most he can be cruel. He wears his darkness like a cape, keeping us at arm's length. Keeping everyone but my mother away.

He is exactly like the dark fae people fear.

But Esmeray was never that way. She has a beautiful laugh, a wonderful smile, and a kindness deep in her soul that any light fae would envy. Her existence taught me that what we understand of dark fae is wrong, and I'm determined to show the world something that will get them to see that life isn't so simple. That the dark fae can't all be bad, and the light fae all good.

I researched. I obsessed. And all roads led me to the Royal Fae Academy. Here I knew I would learn the truth. And I did. Once I had it all organized, I would prove to the world what I know in my gut and dark fae will no longer be treated like second-class citizens.

Yes, I'd explain it all to my mate. Not about Esmeray. Not yet. That secret was one I had thought to take to my grave. But everything else my mate would learn.

There's scraping in the tunnel behind us. I pick up speed, even though my Ann is slowing.

Whatever the secret society had sent after me...I have a feeling it has the power to kill a fae, or else they never would have sent it. As much as I want to turn around and fight it, the risk to my mate isn't worth it.

I scoot to one side, resheath my dagger, and pick Ann

up. A slight gasp of surprise leaves her lips and then I sit down, dangle my feet off the edge of the secret area, and jump down.

She stifles a scream that comes out as a wheeze and I keep running.

In the dark, it's impossible to see the many hidden passageways and the dangers around us, but I don't need my eyes. I know these tunnels all too well.

I stop and press a button on the wall. It's soundless as it draws open, and then I climb in and close it behind me. I do this for three more walls, knowing it will be impossible for the beast to track us here. There's no way it knows this place the way I do, even though it took me far too long to learn all these secrets.

At last, I set Ann down and push open the final wall. I gently steer her forward, then close the wall behind her. Grabbing the matches from where I keep them, I light the candles in the walls and turn to face my mate.

Her eyes are wide as she stares around my secret room. At the makeshift bed on the floor. At the food and water jugs lining the wall. At the desk with its piles of books and papers that I'd taken from around these tunnels to learn the secrets the society guarded so carefully.

"What is this place?" she whispers.

I lift my arms. "This is where I do my research. I know all of this is strange. I understand if you're thinking that you must have the wrong mate." I drop my hands, almost choking on the last words. The thought that she might not want me slams into me, and it feels like it takes effort not to crumble to my knees and beg her to reconsider.

Her gaze moves about the room, then falls back on me. "I want to know more. I want to know everything."

I lick my lips, feeling uncertain. "Are you sure? Once you know, there's no going back."

She squares her small shoulders and her gaze meets mine. "I think it's already too late."

I release a slow breath. Okay. Here we go. "Everything you know is a lie…"

THREE

Ann

I just stare dumbfounded at the man in front of me. I'm not sure how many hours we've been talking, but it feels like nothing will ever be the same for me again. Rayne honestly believes that not only are dark and light fae equals, but that any fae is capable of learning the powers of the other type of fae. That, to me, is unbelievable. He says that it's harder to learn the dark fae's powers for us, but not impossible, and he's been practicing.

"So one day you might be able to kill with just a thought?" I ask, making sure I understand him correctly.

He nods.

A small laugh of disbelief escapes my lips. "But light fae feed on joy and happiness, all the good emotions. Good emotions make us feel strong. They make us feel connected. How would we possibly be able to use their ability if we can't feed on negative emotions like they can?"

"I think...I think we should be able to."

I shake my head. "I've never once sensed someone's jealousy. I've never once...drained someone of their negative emotions, like a damned vampire, and felt stronger. If I could do it, wouldn't I be able to?"

He gives a small smile. "Think about it like watching an incredible athlete win a race. You might say that you could never do that. But, technically, our bodies are made to do some incredible things. With the right training, maybe not everyone could win a race, but it's possible."

I frown and stare down at the ancient book on his table and the scribbling of notes on a paper beside it. "So with all your practicing, you haven't been able to prove you can use their powers yet?"

He sighs. "Not yet. But I think I'm close. And I think the order has realized that I've stolen texts that could prove who they are and that they've purposely set out to make the world believe that dark and light fae are different."

I turn away from the desk and stare at this man. This incredible man. I'm not sure I can ever believe that a light fae can learn the powers of a dark fae. But the thing is, I believe that *he* believes it. And for some reason, that's enough for me.

He moves closer to me and tucks my hair behind my ear.

A shudder moves through my body in response, and I feel myself leaning into him. It's strange. I'm not a virgin, but I'm also not the kind of woman who feels this comfortable with a man so quickly. I usually prefer a bit of a personal bubble until I get to know someone. But it's like with him, we already know each other on some deep, profound level. Now, we just need to learn the surface things.

"What do you think, my Ann? Am I a fool? Is this quest of mine doomed to fail?"

I look up into those dark blue eyes of his, and my breath

catches. In his face, I can see that this is not something he can walk away from. And realizing that makes something else hit me. This *is* personal to him. Technically, he takes after his mother. But does his sister? Are the rumors about her true? Is that what this is all about? Saving a young woman?

My heart aches.

"You wouldn't ever abandon this, even if I begged you to, because it impacts someone you love. Right?"

His hand drops, as does his gaze.

I cup his chin and force him to look at me. "You don't have to say it. You never have to admit it. But it's okay. I won't ask you to stop this quest. All I ask is that you include me in it. If we're mates, and this is important to you, then it's important to me too."

To my surprise, he reached behind his neck, unclasps a chain, and lifts a stone from under his shirt. A gasp catches in the back of my throat. It's the largest, most exquisite blood stone I've ever seen in my life. These gems are only found on the lands owned by the Bloodmores, and they're considered rare and precious.

"I want you to have this."

I feel my eyes widen, and I'm already shaking my head. That stone could buy an island. It could buy things my family could never even imagine. "I can't. Someone like me would look ridiculous wearing something so rare and precious."

Thunder seems to crash over his face. "Someone like *you*? What the hell does that mean?"

I struggle to find the words. Does he really not know? He must. But I'll explain the truth if he wants me to. "I'm plain, Rayne. I'm not the smartest or the prettiest. I don't come from some amazing family. People would laugh seeing me wear something that beautiful."

His movements are oddly well controlled as he fastens the chain around my neck. "Let's get something straight right here and now. There is nothing plain about you. The blood stone pales in comparison to not only your beauty but also your good heart. If anyone says a word otherwise, they will see why the Bloodmores have been feared for so long."

I swallow hard. Maybe I should be worried as the heavy stone falls on my chest. With any other man this might feel like a collar around my throat. But with Rayne, it feels like he's given me wings. Like he's just given me permission to be exactly who I am, like that's enough for him, and that he'll protect me in a way I've never been protected before.

I draw in a deep breath and move to close the distance between us, but something about the twist of my hip and drawing a deep breath at the same time makes pain shoot from my ribs. Instead of kissing him and showing him just how much I valued his words, I'm suddenly gasping and gripping my side.

"What is it?" His arms are around me in an instant.

Shaking my head, I close my eyes. I'm embarrassed. I want this man to know me, everything about me, but not this weakness. Not yet.

Before I can stop him, he lifts my shirt to reveal my stomach, and it feels as if the room drops several degrees. "What happened?" he asks, and there's shock and barely controlled fury in his voice.

I open my eyes and stare at his horrified expression, then down at my horribly bruised and battered body. "It's nothing."

"It's not."

For some reason, tears gather in my eyes. "My stepfather just gets angry sometimes."

He's silent for a long minute. "Is this the worst of it?"

I can't even answer him, because no, it's not. My whole body looks like this right now, and I'm mortified that he now knows. This man I'm supposed to marry, to love for eternity. He knows that someone treated me like a worthless punching bag.

"I want to see all of you," he says softly.

I meet his gaze. "It's bad," is all I can manage.

His lips curl up into a smile, but there's fury in his eyes. "I'm going to get naked. I'm going to show you every scar on my body, and I'll tell you all about them. I'm not going to make you get undressed. Someone clearly has treated you like property. Worse than property. They've taken and taken from you, and I never want to do that to you. Between us, everything will be your choice. You never have to feel like you have to do something. Do you understand me? You'll only ever do what you want."

Gods damn it. "Okay," I whisper.

Rayne stands back from me and pulls his black t-shirt off, dropping it to the floor. I had expected this godlike man to be muscular, but somehow, to also be perfect. It surprises me when I see the scars all over his body. I gravitate toward him, like we're magnetically charged, and run my fingers along one particularly bad scar on his shoulder.

"How did you get this?"

He smiles. "That was actually from a beast down here. He caught me off-guard. And then, because I couldn't let anyone know what I'd done, I stitched it up myself. Not well."

"And this one?" I point to a smaller one on his arm.

This time, he laughs. "My best friends and I used to

practice our swordplay a lot. Usually, I was the one to accidentally leave a few scars for them, but Dwade managed that one on me."

Unable to help myself, I lean down and kiss it. "I like your scars. I feel like they all have a story, and they're helping me learn about you."

His gaze is kind as he reaches for the button on his pants. And then, he draws his boots, socks, and pants off, standing only in his dark boxers. I see more scars, all over his body, but my feelings remain the same.

"You're so beautiful."

"So are you," he whispers.

And I realize that he thinks that now, but will he think that when he sees me? *Really* sees me? For some reason, I need to know. I need to see the look on his face and know if he can accept this about me too.

I reach for the hem of my shirt and slowly pull it off and over my head. Then, taking a deep breath, I throw the dress on top of his clothes, then follow with my pants. Forcing my gaze to meet his, I'm surprised when I see tears in his eyes.

"Is it that bad?" I ask.

He's there in an instant, pulling me into his arms. His voice comes low into my ear. "The Bloodmores aren't like the other light fae. We don't tolerate anyone hurting the people we love. Before the week is out, I swear that your stepfather will drown in his own blood."

I shiver, but only cling tighter to him. Can this man really kill a monster like my stepfather?

And maybe I have some dark fae in me, because I hope so.

He draws back from me, and then I'm in his arms. He carries me to the bed, lays me down more gently than I ever imagined a man as big as him could, and then he curls up behind me, covering me with a blanket against the chill.

I swear, I've never felt safer. Never in all my life.

When I turn to tell him as much, his breath comes out sharply. "Why are you crying? Did I scare you? Did I hurt you?"

I brush my cheek and find moisture. "No. I--I've just never felt safe like this. Like I've found a real home."

He begins to wipe my tears and whispers, "You'll always be home in my arms."

When he kisses away my tears, I lean into him, glorying in this feeling. I stroke my hands over his shoulders and down his chest, memorizing every scar, every line, every part of him. Our lips meet, and I know he'd meant it to be a soft kiss, but I deepen it instantly. I don't just want his comfort.

I want him.

My tongue tangles into his mouth, and he groans as I rub myself against him. I want to reach for those tiny boxers of his and draw them down, to see all of him, but his hands catch mine, and he pulls back.

"If we don't stop..." He shudders.

"I don't want to stop," I tell him, my voice husky.

He shakes his head. "I'll hurt you. And I will never willingly hurt you."

His words are perfect.

I push him onto his back and smile. "Then, allow me?"

He hesitates, his gaze sliding over the black and blue bruises that cover my body. "Okay, but don't do anything to make your injuries worse."

"Yes, sir," I say with a smile, then reach forward and draw down his boxers.

His hard cock springs forward, and my gaze greedily

drinks him in. Rayne is blessed in all ways. Not just his family. Not just his good looks and good personality. But this man is large and thick. Unlike anyone I've been with before.

I trail a finger over his erection and he gasps, his hips jerking up. It's strangely erotic as I continue to touch him, watching him seem to fight for control with every ounce of his being. Precum beads his tip, and I can sense the tension in his muscles as his hips continue to jerk, but he keeps himself from touching me.

It makes me feel even safer with him, and I hadn't thought that was possible.

As I reach for the clasp at the front of my bra, his gaze jerks to my breasts. When I flick my bra open and pull it off, his mouth forms into an O, and his eyes darken. Next, I slide my underwear off, and he reaches out, then drops his hand, as if afraid to touch me.

I crawl over him, so that I'm straddling his upper thighs, and his cock is just in front of me.

"Ann," he whispers my name.

I grab his wrist and guide his hand between us. "Just touch me."

And then, I lean forward and kiss him again. To my surprise, he obeys, his big fingers sinking lower and brushing my mound. Yes, I'd asked him to touch me, but it seems he's gentler in all ways, more than I expect. It takes him a ridiculously long time to part my lower lips, and even longer to begin to stroke my inner folds. I'm restless, my hands running all over him, kissing him harder and harder as I bounce against his fingers, wanting more. Needing more.

And then, one finger plunges inside of me, and I gasp against his lips.

"Is that good?" he asks, a mixture of concern and arousal.

I shudder. "So good."

My words seem to encourage him, and he continues to gently plunge in and out of me, working my body, preparing me for him, even though I'm already soaking wet. At last, I push his hand aside and then inch up his body, positioning the tip of his cock at my opening.

"Fucking hell," he groans, as I slide myself inch by inch down onto his body.

But I disagree. This isn't hell. It's heaven. His big cock filling me, awakening nerves inside of my body I never even knew existed. It feels so oddly tight, but also so satisfying that it's like I'm coming apart.

When I reach his hilt, we're both breathing hard. I give myself a moment to get used to the sheer size of him inside of me, and then I rise up, instantly missing his length inside of me, and slam back down.

He gasps my name, and I'm nearly swept away with my desire. I begin to ride him, harder and harder, faster and faster, when his hands lightly land on my hips. I want him to touch me everywhere, but for now, it's enough just to have him inside of me.

I feel my orgasm building higher than I ever imagined possible as my inner muscles clench and squeeze him, trying desperately to milk him of his desire. And then I come crashing over the edge.

We're both shouting together. The world is gone around us, nothing but the two of us existing.

He comes inside of me, his hot seed slick within my channel. And to my surprise, knowing that I brought him to the edge sends me over it again, and I continue to ride him until I collapse from my second orgasm.

Lying on top of him, breathing wildly, I swear I've never felt so alive. Something about Rayne is so dangerous, so unexpected, and also a safe haven away from the world.

I can't quite explain it, but I know this is where I belong, for the first time in my life.

And then, we hear something behind us. I turn in time to see the wall being pushed open. A creature like nothing I've ever imagined wails, throws back its scaled head, and then focuses red eyes on us.

My blood runs cold. Now that it's closer, I can sense the iron demon's powers deep in whatever this is. It isn't a pure iron demon, but it doesn't matter. Iron demons are our greatest weakness. Deadly sworn enemies to the fae that have a thirst for our blood.

If it gets close to us, we're doomed.

Rayne pushes me to the side and I fall into the blankets. His gaze goes to his dagger, still on his belt under our pile of clothing, too far away to reach in time.

The creature snarls and Rayne climbs slowly to his feet.

It lunges at him, and I scream. Already I can feel the burning from being close to the iron demon, and as it crashes into Rayne, I know that he can only survive for minutes with it touching him.

Leaping to my feet, I scramble for the dagger. Rayne is rolling around with the demon, and I pull the blade free and drive it into the demon's back.

The bastard doesn't even react, and my skin is burning like it's on fire.

"Run!" Rayne shouts. "Get out of here!"

And somehow I know he doesn't believe he'll survive this.

Like hell I'll let that happen. I just found my mate; I'm not about to lose him.

Gritting my teeth, I grab the hilt and pull the dagger out of its back, then I start to stab it over and over again. The creature snarls and suddenly springs off of Rayne and onto me.

Rayne shouts my name, and it feels like a scalding blanket is on top of me. It's hard to breathe. Hard even to fight. I don't know how Rayne was still struggling against this thing, but I'm already starting to slow.

And then the demon's eyes widen, and it collapses on top of me. Rayne shoves it off, and he's there in a second, pulling me to his chest. We're both breathing hard, staring at the demon that almost killed us both.

"How did you stop it?" I finally manage, my voice terrified.

After a minute, he whispers, "With my mind."

I look up at him, and he stares down at me. Rayne just used the powers of a dark fae. Whatever this secret order was afraid of, by sending this creature after us, they'd unlocked it. If Rayne could use this power, after establishing that the history of the dark fae isn't what everyone has been led to believe, it'll change our world.

"So, this is done?" I ask, the words coming out shaky.

He looks back at the demon. "No, I'm afraid it's all just beginning."

I think of my stepfather. "Teach me," I whisper. "Teach me to kill."

MONTHS LATER, as a prisoner of the shadow beasts, I'll think back to this moment over and over again. I'll wonder how one minute I had my mate and was on the cusp of something incredible, and the next I'd lost everything.

SHIFTERS' FAE CAPTIVE

STOLEN BY SHADOW BEASTS: BOOK ONE

ONE

Ann

I'VE NEVER WANTED to kill anyone more than I want to kill my kidnappers. My fists have continued to beat on the back of the shadow beast that carries me for most of the night, but he seems as untroubled by my assault as I would be by the soft touch of sheets against my legs. I don't know if the creature can even feel, or if he's not reacting because he's a huge being of nothing but muscles, but it makes the desperation inside of me grow.

"Asshole!" I shout, but my voice is ragged from all my screaming already.

The woods around us are a blur. I spot the other shadow beasts occasionally when the light from the moon illuminates them for the briefest of moments, and I see the shapes of trees, but that's it. It's as if I stepped out of a world of fire and screaming and battle into a different kind of nightmare.

All I know for sure is that I'm being taken further and

further from the Royal Fae Academy. From my friends. From the only place my family will know to look for me.

And I'm scared.

In my twenty-three years, I've never experienced anything like this. Secrets I know my fair share of. Shame... I know that emotion even better. But true fear? Fear for my life? That emotion is still new to me. It creeps past all the happy emotions light fae are supposed to surround themselves with. And I know how it all started.

With Rayne.

With my mate.

A man who was murdered.

I thump the back of the shadow beast once more, harder, and I shout, but the sound is cut off by a sob I didn't even know was building. My life before Rayne was boring. I was an average-looking light fae, born to an average family, and sent to the Royal Fae Academy like all royal light fae. I never felt special. I never felt excited about, well, almost anything.

Meeting Rayne and finding my mate was like suddenly seeing colors for the first time. He brought so much joy and love and mystery into my life. Soon, we were creeping together beneath the tunnels of the school, searching for the answers to secrets that only Rayne really understood.

But now I know what he had been doing. He had been trying to save his sister and all the other dark fae. *He was too good for this world.*

He never lived to see what followed all his efforts, but I'm proud to be part of the battle to help save the dark fae. I'm even prouder that I stood against the shadow beasts and rescued my mate's sister.

But now? Now I no longer feel like a brave warrior. I feel like a prisoner to beings that are terrifying and dangerous. As much as I try not to think about what they want with me, the question keeps popping back into my head.

Why did the shadow beasts take me?

Another sob escapes my lips, and the shadow beast that carries me slows for the briefest moment.

He makes a sound. It's almost as if he's speaking to the other shadow beasts, but I don't understand his words if he is. I think I heard him speak English during the battle, but it could've just been my mind playing tricks on me because he doesn't seem to understand me now or have the ability to communicate with me.

I don't even know for sure if these creatures are intelligent enough to communicate with each other in *any* language. *Are they more man or beast?* I think about them wearing those collars during the battle. It was clear they were prisoners then, but now what are they?

And when we get to wherever they're taking me, will they hurt me?

"Just release me," I say, loud enough that my words feel too loud in the dark night.

But the beast that carries me doesn't respond or react. He just keeps running.

Time continues to fly by, but I'm not sure how many hours have passed until we come out into a clearing and I see that the moon is hanging low in the sky. It seems these creatures have been running most of the night. The beasts seem to speed up, and I glance around and realize just how fast we're going. Faster than any fae can move. If we'd been traveling this fast all night, I have a feeling we're already days away from the academy.

My stomach sinks.

"Just release me! Put me down!" I beg again, my voice cracking.

None of them slow. They just keep going. More time passes, and then we suddenly stop.

The shadow beast that carries me lets me drop gently to the ground. But for some reason, my legs don't seem to want to hold me, and I collapse onto the ground before him. My gaze moves from the hulking beast above me, his dark hair concealing most of his face, to the area around us. This area could be any other place in the woods, except I see a ring of stones and the evidence of wood having been burned in the center of the stones and a river.

Why have they brought me here? What is this place?

There's another noise from one of the shadow beasts. A string of sounds, like a low, husky song, or a language unlike any I've heard before. The shadow beast emerges from the darkness beneath the trees and comes closer to me. This one, I think, has blonde hair. But it's long like the man who carried me, tangled, and filthy.

They're all filthy. But if they were prisoners to our enemies, then that would explain it. Unless, of course, they were just always this gross.

The third shadow beast is suddenly at my other side, and I shriek, cowering back. Part of me recalls the bad-ass bitch I'd been just a short time ago and wants to slap me for shrieking. But when he kneels down and peers at me from beneath the strands of his dark hair, all the fight goes out of me, and I actually feel my body go cold and numb. These things could tear me in half. I'm sure of it.

I also still have no clue what they want from me, and I have a feeling staying quiet and not moving might be my best bet. Yeah, it feels a little like playing dead, but I just sit still, staring into his oddly pale blue eyes until he stands again and begins to speak in that odd language again while moving his hands. His hand gestures are oddly similar to sign language. I'd learned some of it in high school and almost feel like I pick out a couple of words.

"Girl."

"Bad."

"Mistake."

They're definitely communicating. I guess they are more man than beast. But I'm still not sure if I'm correctly interpreting any of the words, or if I'm just trying to apply meaning to the gestures.

As their discussion grows heated, I eye the trees behind me. Maybe, if I'm fast enough, I can make a break for it when they get distracted. Play dead, then run for it.

It's the best plan I can come up with at the moment. So, I hold my breath and wait.

The trio moves a little away from me and toward a big thicket of tangled vines and shrubs that cover, what appears to be, the side of a small hill or mountain. Licking my lips, I shift my legs around, trying to get the blood pumping through them, then tense and slowly move to my feet.

When none of them look back at me, I feel a surge of relief and turn around.

Only to come face to face with a nightmare.

The creature behind me is five or six times the size of the shadow beasts. It's all darkness, like the deep shadows beneath a tree. And it's built like a wall. Huge arms, huge shoulders, but a short frame. Small tusks curl over its upper lip, and silver eyes fix on me as if I'm the root of all its problems.

Fuck...

I take a slow step back, my heart racing, and it opens its mouth in what seems to be a threat, but could be a smile. Either way, I know I'm in trouble. Taking another step back, my legs suddenly crumble from under me, and I reach my fingers back until they connect with a branch. I draw the branch in front of me, clenching it like a bat, and decide if I'm going to go down, I'll go down swinging.

A soft growl escapes its lips.

And then, the shadow beasts are on it. A scream tears from my lips as they knock it to the ground. The world is filled with growls from the men and screams of pain from the thing, and then it grows silent.

I don't release my branch as the shadow beasts climb off of the thing. They're covered in blood. Their nails are long, and their expressions enraged. The thing that had terrified me so terribly a moment ago has been sliced to pieces, and its head is tilted at an angle no head should be able to tilt.

They shuffle around it, but I can't quite figure out what they're doing, when suddenly the thing is on fire. A gasp slips from my lips, and I scoot back a little further, holding the branch more tightly. The fire releases a horrible scent like rotting flesh, and then the body collapses into ash.

Shit.

If that's what the shadow beasts can do to that huge creature, I was wrong to be scared of the hulking creature. I should've been running like hell from the shadow beasts the second they were distracted.

But as they close in on me, I know it's already too late.

TWO

Ann

THE SHADOW BEASTS LIGHT A FIRE. I watch them beneath my lashes, sitting near enough to the flames that I hope they think I'm behaving, but I'm secretly trying to figure them out. As they move around, gathering wood and talking in their strange language while gesturing and glancing at me, I try hard not to look like a threat, or like prey. They definitely look wild, like men raised by wolves rather than humans, but they're not quite as mysterious as I thought they were in the beginning.

I've also decided to name them. The one who seems to be in charge is Daddy. He has the longest, darkest hair of the three and green eyes. Not a pale green either. It's a green so deep that it's eerie as the gems peer out beneath the strands of his hair like a painting, or a wild animal, rather than a human. Fluffy is the smallest of the three, both in height and width. His hair is long, and perhaps just a touch paler than Daddy's, but his eyes are an ice blue rather than green. Tiny is the one with long, blond hair. He is the largest of the three, both in height and general size. While Daddy is built like a warrior, Tiny is built like a warrior's protector. He's so thickly corded that it actually seems impossible that he's real.

But even though Fluffy is the smallest, they're all big. I feel like a fairy near giants. It's no wonder Daddy wasn't affected by my fist against his back. I probably couldn't have bothered him with a hammer.

Yeah, I'm in trouble.

"So, can you guys speak English?"

They look toward me, then focus back on their tasks. Okay, no English. But also no anger directed at me. Not the worst-case scenario.

"And are you guys going to tell me what you want from me?"

This time they just seem to completely ignore me.

"Okay, that's fine. I don't need to be understood. I don't need to be talked to. But I do want you to know that I think you're a bunch of assholes to steal a woman. No matter what you plan to do with me, that's a dick move, right from the start. I don't know how you'll come back from that without just being forever the dick trio."

None of them react. For some reason, a little of the tension I've been carrying eases. If they don't react to being called assholes and dicks, they probably won't react to much. And if they don't care about me talking to myself, then hopefully that means they aren't just looking for a reason to hurt me.

All good signs.

"Also, I named all of you. What do you think of that? You, Mr. Green Eyes, are now officially Daddy, since you seem to be in charge of this bunch. The smallest of you giant weirdos is now officially Fluffy. And you, the biggest dude of them all, are Tiny." I laugh to myself, and Daddy looks over at me through his hair, his expression unreadable.

Oh boy, maybe it's time to shut up. If I find my own voice annoying, chances are I shouldn't push it with these three.

I sigh, then lean back a little, even though it doesn't make the ground any more comfortable. I'd been given no indication of how long this abduction of mine would last, so my best bet is probably to just learn as much as I can about these guys and where I am, so if the opportunity to run comes, I might actually have a chance at getting back home.

So, I narrow my eyes and focus.

At first, I'm staring at them because I want information from them, even nonverbal information. But eventually, things change, and then I'm watching them because I *can't* seem to stop watching, because even in their bulkiness, there's a finesse that mesmerizes me, a grace that's equally spine-chilling and elegant. Whatever they are, I could watch them move all day if not for the strange fear watching them brings. It's like one part of my brain admires them, and the other part can't stop thinking about what men this large and this graceful could do to me if I piss them off. I can't even tell myself that I'm smaller and faster, because I'm pretty sure they're as agile as they are powerful.

At last, the one I've named Daddy kneels down in front of me. He gestures to the river and then to me.

"Uh. No, thanks. Hard pass." There's no way I'm going into that river. Not a chance.

His brows draw together, and again he gestures between me and the water.

I shake my head, then mouth the word, "No!"

He looks back at the others.

I swear the biggest of the three rolls his eyes. He stomps across the clearing, and a scream catches in my throat before he picks me up, tossing me over his shoulder. Now, I do scream. And to my shock, he gives my ass a hard smack that silences me.

Then, I'm dumped into the frigid river. I gasp in a breath that's just water, then surface, spitting out water and coughing. It's cold. Not just a little bit, but *shockingly* cold.

"What the hell is wrong with you?" I scream at the huge man.

It looks like the other two are mad at him. But after a minute, they all reach for the small cloths covering their cocks and untie the sides.

My cheeks burn. *Oh my God, are they really going to get naked and jump in this river with me?*

I don't have time to wonder further, because they sink into the water with me, and I wrap my arms around myself, chattering. At first, I just stare at the moon, but then I can't help myself; I glance over at them. They've washed their loincloths, and now they're bathing themselves.

My jaw drops open, and I know damn well that I'm staring. But I can't help it. The thick layers of filth on their bodies are coming off in the water, and hard muscles glisten beneath the moon and the stars. It feels like I'm caught in some strange world that's somewhere between a nightmare and a really hot porn video.

Not that I find these guys sexy. Not at all. They're my captors after all.

Oh, fuck, am I getting that weird condition? Stockholm Syndrome? In a few days will I think these shadow beasts are my best friends?

I swallow hard as Daddy goes under the water, then resurfaces, scrubbing his long, tangled hair. The one I call

Fluffy goes to the river edge, climbing out of the water just enough that I can see the top of his well-defined ass. My mouth goes dry, and I don't realize what he's doing until he turns around, holding a bunch of yellow flowers. He hands them to the other guys, keeping some for himself, then hands some to me.

"Uh, thanks," I say.

They all begin to scrub the flowers in their hair and over their bodies. Okay, so, I guess, they're using the flowers like soap? I crumble the flowers in my hand and breathe in their scent. I'm shocked that the flowers don't smell...flowery. More like wood or something I can't quite name.

Ah, damn. Are these guys saying I smell? Okay, I can't exactly smell *great* after the battle at Royal Fae Academy. So, even though I'm freezing and not happy about it, I rub the flowers over my skin. I undo my braid, rub the flowers through my hair, and then rinse my hair out underwater.

When I come to the surface, the guys are all staring at me. "What?"

My word seems to snap them back to focusing on their own little baths, and I glare at them as I rebraid my hair. *That's right, jerks, I used the flowers and actually took a bath. Not for you though. Because I don't like smelling.*

Daddy climbs out of the river, and I suddenly forget what I was mad about. His ass is *fine*, not just nice, but fucking perfect. Even so, I find my neck straining to spot his cock. If he turns around just a little I could see it, but he's got his little loincloth retied within seconds, and I try not to feel disappointed.

The smallest of the shadow beasts makes a sound, and I turn to him. He gestures that it's time to get out, and the big guy comes toward me with narrowed eyes. I almost shriek again. There's no way I want Tiny carrying me back out of the river. *Naked.*

My cheeks heat and I scramble out. Unfortunately, the night is even colder out of the water, and I rush to the fire's edge, kind of wishing that I'd taken off my clothes, so at least they'd be dry. I put my hands to the fire, and my teeth chatter.

A second later, I sense motion, and I remember that Tiny and Fluffy are probably getting out of the water, and every inch of them should be on full display.

Even though these guys kidnapped me and I find them irritating, I turn a little and glance at them. Unfortunately, they already have their loincloths on. I know my lips are pouting, but when I glance up at their faces, Fluffy is looking at me, and I think there might be a little smile behind his dark hair.

Oh, man. I did not *want to get caught checking out these guys.*

From that point forward, I try to remind myself that these guys are my enemies, and that my goal is to stay warm and stay safe, *not* ogle them. But as they move closer to the fire, letting the beads of water dry from their almost naked bodies, I feel like I've developed a permanent blush.

It's going to be a long night.

The fire burns through the late hours of the night, tended by one beast or another. I know because I don't sleep. I can't. As tired as I am, as desperately as I need sleep, I'm too scared about what could happen if I let my guard down. I still have no idea what these men want from me, but I keep hoping to see something in their actions or words that explains why they took me. Yet, even though I stare at them until my eyes hurt, I still don't have any answers.

They continue to communicate with words and

gestures, though I can't understand. But my urge to kill them has decreased. Thinking back to everything that's happened so far, and even watching them, they seem strong, but they don't seem...cruel. Yeah, I could be wrong. They could be like sharks that suddenly turn around and bite, but some small voice inside of me says that whatever they brought me here for, they've had many opportunities to hurt me already and haven't.

Despite all my apprehension, I feel...safe. Maybe not *safe* exactly, but not in imminent danger. They protected me from that weird creature after all, and I get the sense that maybe they would do it again, even though I hope we don't have to find out.

Or maybe they just killed it for fun, and haven't killed me yet because they're busy, and I'm just coming up with reasons not to pee my pants and run screaming through the woods. Because, yeah, that instinct is definitely there, behind all the attempts at applying logic to this illogical situation.

Before the sun is up, we're on the move again through the woods. There's no trail marked, but I'm sandwiched between Daddy and Fluffy while Tiny walks behind me. I can't stop wondering about them--whether they have names, what they are, why they want me.

Can they even talk? Are they like those kids who were raised by wolves that could never acclimate back to the human world?

I didn't have a clue.

"So, when you guys make those sounds to each other, are you talking?"

No answer.

"I think it *is* some kind of language, but I don't under-stand what it could be or why you wouldn't know English.

Here, all supernaturals speak English in order to be able to blend in with the humans. But, I guess, you guys don't really have that problem, do you? With the whole barely any clothes thing and the lack of showers, I bet you don't exactly mingle with humanity much. Still, it's strange you're just hiding out here in these woods. I know this territory is protected, and that part of it owned by the Royal Fae Academy while part of it a nature reserve, but even out here I imagine you have to come across the occasional supernatural or human." I frown, that thought lingering. "Which means it's probably safe to say we might run into someone else eventually. *Humm*, but I guess no one really knew you guys existed until the battle with the fae, so maybe you *have* been able to hide out here undisturbed by people of any kind."

Is that even possible? Hell, that actually makes the most sense. Which, of course, gets me thinking for a little while before I focus back on what we're doing.

The terrain was much less treacherous for me when I was being carried. I definitely stumble more than I'm proud of now, but the shadow beasts are always close, catching me and releasing me before I can fall on my ass. Even though I feel clumsy and awkward, I prefer being on my own two feet. While walking on my own, the scent of plants, of earth, and of life comfort and soothe something deep in my soul. Something I never expected.

I breathe in deep, filling my lungs with the perfumed air. It's almost as if I'm surrounded by a beautiful world untouched by mankind and supernaturals alike. I think I'd almost like it here.

If I wasn't, you know, a prisoner and all.

We eventually stop. This area of the woods looks like any other, but Daddy cups his hands and makes a strange sound, like a bird I'm sure I've never heard before. Then, the guys nod to each other and move forward slowly, while looking all around. Tiny kneels down and gestures forward. I stare at him in confusion, and he lifts a brow, before sliding through the moss beneath the huge tree.

They end up leading me to an underground cave I would've never seen if not for them. But now that I know it's there--camouflaged in that moss between a thousand-year-old oak and a lush hill--it's something I won't likely forget.

The cave is dark and dank until Tiny manages to light a torch that's secured to the wall. The flames dance, spreading light to chase away the dark shadows. The walls are smooth and clay-like, and the air chills me, cooler and damper than outside. It's an underground kind of dampness and I shiver, but I don't try to leave. I wait because I don't know why they've brought me here, and I know damn well if I try to run for it now, I'll be caught quickly, and any kind of trust we've built will be gone.

I'm not willing to risk that. I sure as hell plan to run away, but I can wait. If there's one thing I'm known for, it's my patience. My fathers told me that over and over again every time they visited my mom when I was young. They'd hug me tightly, lavish me with gifts, and tell me I was the gentlest, most patient child they'd ever met.

Which always confused me. Every time my stepfather beat the shit out of me, he said it was because I was a bad kid. So, was I awesome or bad? I never really knew.

I still don't.

A shiver rolls through me again, and I wrap my arms around myself. My teeth start chattering, and I try to push away the image of my stepfather's face. I have enough going on right now. The last thing I need to do is think about the only monster I've ever been soul-deep terrified of.

Trying my best to ignore my dark thoughts, I take it all in. I look left and right, but it just seems to be like any other cave. Until I see light above and the temperature of the cave gets noticeably warmer. Our group moves a little faster, weaving around the path until we come out into a huge room.

My jaw drops open. There are at least a dozen shadow beasts prowling throughout the cave. In the center of the mountainous cavern, a waterfall tumbles down into a big pool where two shadow beasts are bathing naked. Steam rises up from the water and seems to hover in the room, warming an otherwise cold place.

I feel my cheeks heat and look away. My gaze catches with Tiny's dark eyes, and I avoid his gaze. *Did he see me staring at the naked men?* Another shadow beast is weaving a basket near a huge fire. Two others are sharpening their blades, speaking to each other in low voices.

Suddenly, two shadow beasts separate from the walls beside us. Daddy speaks to them in a low voice, using the same strange language I don't understand. The two new shadow beasts keep staring at me, and they don't look happy, but they eventually hug Daddy, Fluffy, and Tiny.

Within minutes, at least two dozen shadow beasts have surrounded the three I know. There's a lot of talking in their strange language, and a lot of gesturing with hands. My guys are hugged a bunch, and there's a general sense of celebration. But every time anyone looks in my direction, they don't seem as welcoming. I can't tell if they're curious about me, annoyed, or angry. Either way, it isn't a good response.

Do they think I want to be here?

"Nice to meet you too," I grumble.

None of them react. They just continue staring at me with those gazes filled with unhappy emotions. In fact, if I try, I can feel the unhappy emotions coming off of them. I close my eyes and sense resentment, exhaustion, and anger. Then, I open my eyes and glare right back at them.

"I hope one day you get that stick out of your asses," I grumble.

And then it hits me: the three who had taken me were prisoners of the light fae. Do these shadow beasts think I was involved with keeping their friends prisoner? That would be...bad. *Really* bad. We can't even understand each other well enough for me to explain that I had nothing to do with what happened to them.

Is that why they took me? The thought makes my stomach turn, so I push it away.

Most light fae are good at seeming happy and relaxed all the time. From a young age, we practice keeping smiles on our faces and meditating. It's looked down upon for us to get angry, jealous, or any other of the darker emotions connected with the dark fae.

I practiced more than most other light fae so I could cover up my mom's secret and seem normal, but it was never a natural thing to me. Sarcasm and anger came more easily. It wasn't until Rayne that I realized that maybe I had to show one face to the world, but it was okay if I wasn't that person deep down.

Now though, it feels like there's no reason to pretend to be anything except myself, and it's...oddly nice.

Daddy weaves through the crowd and grabs my arm, hauling me through the huge cavern. Little crystals glow on all the walls, illuminating a light that has the same softness as moonlight. It's almost delicate, but somehow gives almost as much light as the huge fire in the center of the room.

As we go deeper into the cavern, I realize that along the walls steps have been carved into the stone. As I glance up, I see that nestled into the walls of glowing crystals are little caves. It almost looks like seeing the side of a beehive...well, for bees that can't fly. There has to be twenty or thirty little caves, and based on the light radiating from them and the curtains covering most of the entrances, I get a sense this is where the beasts live.

"Cool," I whisper under my breath.

Fluffy lightly touches my arm and gestures with his head to keep going. Where he touches me, it feels strangely warm. I look down, blinking at his fingers so lightly pressed against me.

He draws his hand back in a rush, as if I was bothered by his touch.

The truth is, I'm not sure if I was. But I *am* confused. *His touch was almost...nice.*

I push the thought away with anger. Rayne was my mate. My only mate. And he's dead. No other man will ever make me feel the way he did. I will die alone, clinging to the love I feel for him, just like most fae who lose their mates.

My shadow beasts move forward in the direction Fluffy had indicated. We walk around the shadow beasts near the fire, all gazes drifting to me as their strange language goes silent. My beasts take me to a tunnel lined with more of the crystals on the walls, and this time they're hurrying a bit ahead of me.

They probably know this is the last place I'm going to try to escape from. And they're not wrong. I try to keep up with them until they lead us past a cave, and then I pause near the entrance and stare inside. There's a man lying on the ground under a blanket woven from vines. He's a warrior, big with long hair the color of honey and a body like the oak outside. Tall. Big. Broad. Unconscious. He's not simply sleeping, but I don't know why I'm so sure. His breaths come slow, not fatigued or labored, but not natural either. Maybe like he's in a trance.

"Magic? A spell?" I whisper the questions to myself.

Tiny comes back to me and lifts a brow.

"Follow you, got it, got it," I say with a sigh.

He leads me to a seat near, but not quite beside, the man's head. I can look at him, and I'm close enough to touch him, but I keep my hands curled at my side. My gaze moves over the room. This looks almost like an archaic hospital room. There are shelves all over the room with little glass bottles filled with different herbs and liquids. And the scent in the room is definitely herbal too.

Daddy goes to one of the shelves and pulls several bottles down. He pours little bits from different bottles, then takes a stick and smashes them all together in a shell, before adding a small amount of liquid to the mixture. He carries the shell over to the fire, and sets in on a rock in the center. Within seconds, the liquid starts to smoke. The others move, and they form the points of a triangle around the large seashell before Daddy picks it back up.

Isn't it hot? And why the hell is it smoking?

I can't see the inside of the shell, but their heads bow over it, and they appear to be in deep thought or prayer to whatever deity they pray to.

It's strange. At that moment, I'm absolutely fascinated by them, this place, and the unconscious man. This all feels like a puzzle I can't quite figure out, but I'm determined to solve. So even if they weren't between me and the door, I still wouldn't have run. I'm invested now. I have to see, at least, this part through.

A flash of super dark smoke rises from the shell, and a

gasp slips past my lips as I lean forward, trying to figure out what the hell is going on. The beasts have joined hands, and they chant a strange humming sound punctuated by a grunt. More smoke rises and I can't look away, not even when Fluffy hands me the shell. There's a liquid of some sort inside of it and he motions to my mouth and lifts the shell toward me.

"You want me to drink it?" I give a glance at the dark brew, then give it a sniff. The drink neither looks nor smells like something I want to drink. "No."

But he holds it out again, arms extended, nods, and pushes it toward me.

"No thanks," I say slowly, narrowing my eyes.

In response, Tiny and Daddy come up behind Fluffy and cross their arms, all leveling me with a look I easily recognize. This is the same look one of my dads would give me if they were one hundred percent certain I needed to do something, and my dads weren't going to bend. Like if I refused to go to school, or if I climbed up too high and they wanted me to come down.

For some reason, the look makes something inside of me calm. My stepdad never gave me this sort of look. One minute he'd be sitting on the couch flipping through TV channels, and the next he was breaking my ribs. People who gave looks like this wanted to give you a chance to do the right thing on your own.

But if I ignore this look? I have no idea what would happen next, because I always obeyed my dads when they were the only ones who pulled out this look. *So, do I really want to find out what the consequences are for disobeying? Here? With these three huge men?*

Nah.

"Fine." Not because I want to, but because I *have* to.

I stare down at the smoking liquid and swallow hard, willing myself to just get it over with. Reaching out, I take the shell. Instantly, a vibration moves through my hands, and I almost drop the shell. Somehow, I manage to cling to it, then lower my head and *really* stare at the liquid. My thoughts feel strange. My mind has locked onto the liquid, and it's like nothing outside of it exists.

A force, not part of myself, compels me to bring the shell to my lips. A force I'm powerless to say no to. And before I know what I'm doing, I'm drinking it.

It tastes acrid, like smoke smells, but I consume every drop of it and swallow even when I only want to spit it back out. My stomach rolls, my head swims. *Damn it, I'm probably going to die.* I need air, to breathe deep and fill my lungs with as much oxygen as I can manage to pull in. But the walls of the cave waver, like a flag in a breeze. They snap and distort, and fear and anguish burn through me.

My chest heaves as I stagger, then fall into the wall.

One of the beasts grabs my hand and pulls me through the cave to a tunnel that leads deep into the darkness. I try to pull away. The last thing I need to do is to get stuck in the dark with this big guy, but the blonde leads and the other two each grasp one of my arms in their cold hands. Or maybe they feel so cold because my skin is on fire. I can't tell because I'm no longer in my body but watching from above it.

"She's weak," a gruff voice says. The one beside me on the left tightens his grip, and it feels like my body tries to pull away. I'm rooting for it to be free, but I can't help myself from where I float above.

My body is no longer my own. I should be terrified, but I'm not.

"She's fine. Keep moving," says a deep voice that rolls against my skin like velvet.

Wait. I can understand them! Except that their voices are far away, further down the tunnel than I am, and I want to catch up to where they're tugging my body along.

Are they even really talking, or am I imagining it?

Probably I'm hallucinating. My conscious mind knows that, like it knows that none of this is real. It can't be. But the pain in my head, the throb of my pulse inside my brain, says otherwise. Panic burns in my veins and my body begins to struggle, but they continue to move me forward, unhindered through the tunnel that smells like earth and my own fear.

"It's okay." I don't know which one is speaking, but the slow cadence, the gentle tone, comforts me. A moment later, or a year, I can't tell, we emerge into the forest and the light of morning hurts me, so I shield my eyes with my hand.

We've gone only a few steps, maybe more, I don't know, when I see a black cloud, ominous, just a few yards ahead. It moves like black smoke, only it's made out of something thicker than smoke. Oil maybe. It spreads out as far as I can see in that direction, and even up so high that I can't tell where it ends.

I don't want to go near it, but it summons me much the same as these beasts draw me toward them. The slow-moving, twisting, black cloud holds answers. It holds something dark and dangerous that wants to consume me, I'm sure of it.

But if the beasts see it, they don't react. They continue forward on a path I can't see.

I want to ask them about it because it feels significant, but my mouth doesn't seem to work. We move away from it until it's hidden by the trees. And for some reason, I can no longer see it in the sky. Not at all.

Which is impossible.

I'm definitely hallucinating.

The forest moves around me like I'm speeding through a cave, and the early morning sun is rising and climbing across the sky in the blink of an eye. The second cave they bring me to is much smaller, almost too small for the four of us, or even just for the three of them. The walls are closer, the ceiling shorter, and even though they don't duck, the sheer size of one of them overpowers the space.

The green-eyed beast looks at me, and I must be hallucinating because I think he smiles, almost as if to say, "Welcome home."

THREE

Ann

My eyes flash open, and I half expect to see the ceiling of my room in the dorm at Royal Fae Academy. I roll to my side, looking around me, but I don't see my huge bed or white-washed walls, I just see...a cave. And three shadow beasts around a fire, eating.

Slowly, I sit up, and all eyes go to me. I'm lying on some kind of bedroll near them. My throat feels dry and sore, and my head spins a little before the spinning stops.

What now?

"Do you...know me?" My voice is tentative, softer than I've ever heard myself, and I don't know that I intended to talk, or if this is real, or if I understand what's happening, but I have to try to figure out who they are, why I'm here, if I'm in danger of some sort. *If I can only get around to why I'm here, I'll be able to figure out how to get away.*

Or if I want to get away. Which is a strange thought. Of course I want to get away! Yes, it's true I don't have my mate any longer, and that Esmeray is my only true friend. But I miss my dads... That's enough reason to go home. *Right?*

But what if you only imagined the shadow beasts talking? What if--?

"Yes, we know you." The green-eyed shadow beast's voice is soft, deep, not gruff like I would have expected from someone so big.

Okay, alright. Be calm. They can talk. You can understand them. This is progress.

"Why can I understand you now?" There's some sorcery going on here. Maybe even some wickedness, although I don't really get that sense. Despite their size, the overall menace between them, my senses tell me they aren't dangerous. But this isn't a typical enchantment or magic. This is more and, while I'm not frightened, I'm going to be careful.

"We made it so." While the one I'd nicknamed Daddy continues to speak to me, the blue-eyed one communicates by hand with Tiny, the massive blond.

"How?"

For a second, I don't think he's going to answer me, and then he sighs. "We could speak some basic words of your kind after being kept prisoner, but we speak another language that doesn't exist in this world. The brew we gave you allows you to speak our language and to understand it, without any effort."

I'm speaking another language? I don't know if I find that cool or terrifying.

"What's he doing?" I nod to the blond, who is now answering the other one with his hands.

I've probably spent too long around the humans. I've mimicked an unflattering tone, a demand that is common among their kind, and I want to take it back, but the green-eyed beast looks at the other two.

"He was injured." There's a story there, and it would be

impossible to miss the flash of guilt that's so vivid it changes the green-eyed man's entire face for a moment. This one feels bad about whatever happened to the quiet one. But as quickly as it appeared, it fades and he's back to himself. I don't know for certain if it was real or if my imagination is running away with me.

There's so much I need to know, so many details my mind can't fill in without their help, but I don't know if I can trust my own mind, or the men in front of me.

"I am Phantom," the first one I'd nicknamed Daddy says. He lifts his head a little, and his dark tangled hair falls back from his face. My breath catches, and I realize this man is more than just a pair of green eyes and a commanding presence. I feel kind of silly for even nick-naming him Daddy, because the name doesn't fit him at all. He looks like some kind of muscular model, but with a strange, regal quality.

"This is Dusk." My gaze moves to the man next to him. Hesitantly, I reach out, while he watches me, and I brush the hair back from his face with shaking hands. My breath catches, and I stare and stare. There's no doubt that Dusk is Phantom's twin, even though he has pale blue eyes instead of green, and a narrower face and body.

"And that is Onyx," Phantom continues, gesturing to the giant. I turn to Onyx, and he lifts his own hands, pushing his blonde hair back from his face, as if he knows that that's exactly what I want to do. Onyx is different from the other two. Not only is he huge, but with his hair pushed back, I can see the jagged scar that runs from beside one ear down to the side of his throat. He also has a slightly broader nose, deep, dark eyes that seem to stare into my soul, and lips that are fuller, and strangely fascinating.

"I'm Ann." My voice comes out a whisper. "Technically, Mary Ann Hart, but I hate the name Mary so much that I wish I could burn it and stomp it into the ground."

Phantom lifts a brow, and a small smile curls his lips.

Okay, so they don't mind my nervous babbling. That's something! Now, time to get into the tough stuff...

"Why am I here?" It's probably the most pertinent of my questions, and I've adapted my tone, added a note of caution, but managed to keep the fear at bay. For now.

Somehow, I expect it when both Onyx and Dusk turn to Phantom. I had named the guy Daddy for a reason. It always seems that when something needs to be decided, both heads turn to him. Onyx begins to sign rapidly with his hands, and Phantom shakes his head. Onyx's expression shifts into an unreadable one.

"Phantom..." Dusk begins.

The other man cuts him off. "Outside."

He walks out of the cave with the others quickly following behind him, without answering. My chest heaves, maybe with relief or more likely, just because they're too massive, too powerful, and it's intimidating to be in such a closed space with them.

And yet, I don't like being ignored. I don't like that the shadow beasts simply left when I asked such an important question. It's not just rude; it feels like I'm being treated like a child.

So, I stand and creep to the edge of the cave, flatten myself against the wall, and hold my breath.

"She's our mate." They're just outside the cave, and I can hear them distinctly, as if they're close and speaking to me, but Phantom's words hold an unexpected edge.

Mate? Hell. Who could possibly be a mate to these three massive men?

I hear a sigh, and then Onyx speaks. "The creatures

from the Void will come for her. It was foolish to bring her here." There's a note of reproach in his voice, an I-told-you-so inflection that means he might've spent a bit of time observing humans also.

But I'm busy dissecting the words for meaning. *Creatures from the Void?* I don't know about any creatures, or what the hell a Void is. Not sure I want to, either.

"Yes. They will come." Their cadence is the same. It's as if when Phantom is speaking he's almost answering himself. There's little difference, other than the fact that Onyx has a slightly gruffer note to his voice. "But leaving her would not have protected her. They would have found a way to reach her, and we wouldn't be around to keep her safe."

I peek around the opening to see them, to watch their body language. I'm also too far away to be able to tell the dark-haired ones apart, but the blonde is speaking without the benefit of sound, and I can only tell because of the attention the others are paying him and the slight movements of his arms against his body.

A gentle rain falls through the trees, and every once in a while, a droplet glistens on the blond's back, the bigger dark-haired beast's shoulder, the smaller one's chest. I can't see much more without giving myself away.

"I don't want her in danger, either, Onyx, but we can protect her." He nods at the blond, at *Onyx.* "We *will* protect her."

The emphasis is comforting, but I don't understand what's going on. I'm about to move away when Phantom looks to where I'm standing, his gaze hot, assessing, his tone vibrant when he speaks. "We know what she is, but now it's time we find out *who* she is." My body flushes with heat.

He nods to me and the others turn, and now three gazes land on me. Another burst of heat blooms through me.

Instead of inviting me out, they stalk toward me, hulking, muscles bulging, eyes dark.

"The creatures will come for you." Phantom looks me up and down, closer, and I think maybe they already are.

And then another thought hits me. *Were they talking about me the whole time? Hell, do these guys think* I'm *their mate?*

Oh, fuck. Of course they were talking about me! I smack myself in the forehead, then lean back against the cave wall, trying to catch my breath. *Their mate!*

FOUR

Phantom

SHE EMERGES from the cave like a vision of beauty, and my heart is taken by the prospect of touching her. Of throwing her over my shoulder and bringing her to safety. Ann is without a doubt a vision with her long blonde hair tied in a braid that moves down her back, and the leather clothes that hug her every curve. She is not at all who I thought our mate would be. I never even imagined we'd find a mate after all we've lost.

But as much as she complicates this, as much as I fear for her, the mate pull can't be ignored. The instant I smelled her, I knew she was ours and ours alone. The only thing we could do was take her, for her own sake, and for our own sanity.

Still, we need to tread lightly with her. In our time as prisoners with the light fae, we saw a dark and terrible side to who they are and what they can do. They claimed the dark fae were the evil ones, but we could see the truth.

Good people don't trap and enslave others. They don't put collars on them and force them to kill.

The thought of the many innocents we were forced to kill because of those collars that gave us no choice makes my blood boil with rage. There are many things I've done in my life that I regret, but the helplessness I felt as a prisoner, the disgust I felt with myself when I killed like a dog with a master, it was not something I'd soon ignore.

And with Ann, we had to have her. There was no choice. But we *did* have a choice in how we approached her. Our mate would not be treated like a prisoner, any more than we could help it. We would always treat her with kindness and respect, even if we don't know yet who she is as a person, nor what to expect from her.

Dusk looks at me then her, while Onyx focuses on nothing but the woman, and I can't blame them. There's something about her, a glow, an aura that shines like a beacon. If she were one of our women, we would have already bedded her. She would be in our arms night and day.

But no matter how she calls to us, we have to accept she is not of our kind, and that her mate rituals might be different.

"What is the Void?" Her voice is like a melody, a song that hits my guts and makes me want, makes me long to crush her against me.

Yet I can see it in her face. She is frightened of me. Of all of us.

So, we would start slower.

"Something bad." I smile like by that motion alone I can dispel her fears, or at least make them subside, but it's a fool's notion. Her fear is as visible as it is potent and I want to touch her, but Dusk is there with one hand on her shoulder. He's gentler, less fierce, smaller in stature, and less threatening. It's better to let him comfort her.

But it isn't him she to looks for answers. It's to me. "And I'm in danger?"

Fuck. That's not what I want her to know. Not yet. Our tiny mate is already afraid of us. I don't need her to fear the Void yet, or the monsters that lurk within it.

"We will protect you." I leave no question in my tone, no reason for her to doubt, but her gaze falters and her eyes darken. Her fear is real.

"Why?"

The question takes me off guard. "Why are you in danger or why would we protect you?" One of those answers is infinitely easier to explain than the other.

"Yes." She nods and half-smiles, hiding her fear behind curiosity. But I can still feel it vibrating inside her.

"We have much to discuss." I sound like one of the elders, and Dusk chuckles beside me. He knows we can't tell her everything. He also knows I'm fluttering, rippling, and the woman's is not the only body vibrating. We're tuned in that way.

"Yes." I draw her to the fire outside and we all sit. I'm beside her, Dusk on the other side, and Onyx across from her. Dusk signs to him, telling Onyx to offer her food and drink.

"Are you deaf?" She's looking at Onyx. It's one of the easy questions for everyone but me. For me, it's a bad memory laced with so many bad memories that just thinking about any of it makes me want to punch myself in the face, or race through the woods, destroying everything in my path.

Onyx stares at her, unwilling to show himself as he is. He's an enigma. A man of few words even before he lost his hearing. Once he told me that losing his hearing wasn't as bad as I imagined. That at least it gave him an excuse not to talk to the others. I'm truly not sure if he said that to make me feel better, or because he wanted to ease my guilt.

Probably the latter.

Dusk answers for him, something he often does, even from the time we were boys. "He is."

She watches us, fear still glowing. Eyes still bright.

"You're our mate." I've seen what happens when this information isn't communicated with strength of tone, with decisive command. It isn't pretty. Compliance is requisite in this situation.

But she scoffs. "I've had a mate and lost him."

That does surprise me. She's young to have lost her first mate. "Perhaps, but it doesn't change that we're your mates. The mate bond is too powerful to be anything else."

Her expression says she doesn't believe me. "I just want to go home now."

She's brave. Her voice is strong, eyes piercing as she glances from me to Onyx to Dusk. There's a confidence in that gaze, as if she can use her beautiful blue eyes to entice or enchant, to convince us of something we know can never happen.

"No." The answer doesn't require expansion. She can't go home. Period. It isn't an option.

"Yes. I want to go *home*." She speaks with force now, a panic inside of her erupting through her tone. The inflection comes with strength.

"No."

Softer, Dusk adds, "You aren't safe there." Onyx nods as Dusk speaks again. "You're safe here. You're our mate and we will protect you."

Her nostrils flare. She's angry and it's beautiful. The

glow around her changes colors, darker now. "Who's going to protect me from you? You're kidnappers."

"You're our mate. We didn't have a choice." And that's all she needs to know. Dusk and Onyx watch her intently. I think they're hoping for any sign that she realizes this mate bond between us can't be ignored.

But I can already read her feelings well. Whether it's from the trauma of losing the man she believed was her mate or something else, she's blocked her awareness of this tie between us. It can't last forever, but her disbelief of the truth will certainly make things harder.

Dusk puts an arm around her and hauls her into his side. Her eyes go wide, and she shoves against him, glaring. Then, she crosses her arms in front of her chest and glares at all of us as if her eyes alone could make us all disappear in a puff of smoke.

A look of hurt comes and goes in a flash across my little brother's face, and my chest aches. After all he's been through, he deserves to have this one thing go smoothly. When he's ready and willing to give all his love and affection to one person, it only seems fair the woman should want him back. But nothing in our lives has gone the way it was supposed to, so it's no surprise to me this hasn't either.

Unfortunately, my brother has always been a bit of an optimist.

I slide my gaze back to her and see the defiance in her eyes. It hits me that this stubborn woman still doesn't understand. Even after we've explained that she'd be in danger without us, she thinks that going home is what's best for her. And a thought like that could just get her killed. "You can *never* go home. Do you understand me?"

She frowns, then stares into the fire. "I'm going home."

"No."

The fire crackles, spits embers into the air, and she watches them while I watch her. The light shines off her hair, giving it an even more golden glow, mimicking the flames themselves. She's holding her body rigid now, head straight, shoulders back. Defensive, ready to run. And as much as the desire to get away radiates off her, her resignation is only visible in the thin line of her lips.

Her attitude is an insult. It's hurtful even, but I ignore it because she's here and she hasn't yet decided to leave. Although, she will, and then our game changes to something else. One where if she wins, she dies. And if we win, she might just die anyway.

She glances at me. It's then, in that short look at her face, that I know. She's planning something. An escape.

And it's going to be up to me to stop her.

FIVE

Onyx

It was never my idea to have a mate. I hate the concept. To need someone, to want someone so much every decision and action is about them, their safety, their happiness. I don't want my life to be tied so closely to anyone other than Phantom and Dusk.

I couldn't stand the thought, and I *still* can't stand the thought.

It's why I wanted to leave her behind, why I wanted nothing to do with her... I hate fae. But even if I could get over my hatred of the people who kidnapped us and forced us to break every code of honor until we were no better than our captives, it's more than that. No matter what she is, bringing her along brings her closer to the danger, and that's on us.

I watch her though because she's stunning. Fair, crystal-eyed, curved. She entices me to watch her with every tilt of her chin, every parting of her lips. I'm enthralled.

It's the mate bond. I know it. But it doesn't make me stop wanting her.

As a captive of the fae, I learned about them, their ways, the darkness they hide behind their light. I shudder as I think of it, and the woman turns to me. Her name is Ann, Mary Ann, to be exact, and she's hiding behind her anger, hiding the real emotion she doesn't want us to see.

"We should take her back." I sign the words to Dusk and he shakes his head.

"No!" Phantom mouths the word as he signs. "She belongs here with us."

"She doesn't want to be here." This isn't a mystery. Her posture, the flare of hope in her eyes, the scent of her desperation all say that she's looking for a way out, a gap where she can flee.

"She's our mate," Phantom signs to me, fast, furious, determined, but her safety can't be assured, can't be guaranteed.

"She's a complication. The fae will be hunting us." I can't make them listen to reason.

"They always hunt us."

"The creatures of the Void will sense her too. As soon as the mate bond was formed, it was like we put a spotlight on her," I sign back, feeling even more frustrated.

Phantom gives me that princely look of his and uses his hands to basically tell me it's already done, so I should get over myself.

I sigh. I don't want to bring it up, but it's the only way to make them understand the danger. I turn all my attention to Phantom because he carries most of the guilt from our downfall, although we'd all made the same mistake. We'd underestimated an opponent. "Do you remember what happened the last time you didn't listen to me?"

I haven't heard a word in years, not a sound, not the chirp of a bird, or a siren's song, or a voice, a gasp, a bird's whistle. Not so much as a peep. That's what happened. That was the consequence of not listening to me. And I'm sorry to throw it in his face, but it's true. When I warned him that something was off, Phantom didn't listen to me. Any smart person would have walked away then, but I could never walk away from the two men I saw as brothers.

Instead, I stayed close to keep them safe, and when trouble came, I took the blow meant for Phantom, because my death would mean nothing, and his death would destroy everything. And in all this time, I've never once used that moment against him.

Until now. Until I'm staring at a beautiful woman who has no idea the hell we've brought her into.

"That's fucking low."

"I'll bring her back myself," I sign in anger. And I will. Because then maybe the gnawing and longing inside of me will stop. *I hope.* It won't matter either way anymore because she won't be here to remind me. We can all move on. In time maybe we'll even forget her and our mate bond.

Although, I've also heard it can go the other way. But only for the weak, which none of us are.

Except if the Void creatures manage to reach her wherever she goes and we have to live knowing we abandoned her. I push the thought away. Yes, they can find her now anywhere she goes, but with her so near danger we've certainly made it easier for our enemies.

Phantom glares at me because I've brought his guilt to the surface and he doesn't like to look it in the face. It makes him feel less than he is. We're warriors and tragedy happens to warriors.

"She's a light fae." Although she shows no sign of an ability to hunt. The fact that she's fae isn't something we should discount. She's in danger, and by definition or circumstance, her existence poses a danger to us.

"And we're shadow beasts. Warriors." Dusk slashes the air with one arm, as he would if he was holding a saber or a lance. "We can protect her."

"It isn't only about her." I nod in her direction as I finish.

Phantom blows out a sigh. I remember the sound used to be accompanied by something more guttural, something that sounded like it came from his soul. It's times like these I miss sound.

Also, when I look at Ann and wonder what her voice sounds like. If it's soft and breathy, raspy with a huskiness that drops men to their knees, or if it's sharper, shriller with notes of tin and vibrance.

The yearning in my gut strengthens my resolve. She should go. They should be able to see the reason behind my argument. It should be stronger than their need to mate with her, to make her ours. But they're blinded by desire. It's a weakness, and we can't afford it. "She needs to go back."

Dusk shakes his head. "No. She's ours now. Our mate."

Phantom rises and kneels down in front of me. "And I forbid it."

I shove Phantom because he's in my face, almost nose to nose with me. He stumbles backward.

"Who the fuck are you to forbid me anything?" Fire burns in my gut and I jerk my thumb toward the cave. "She's a hindrance."

"A hindrance to what?"

Hands are flying as they both sign the words at the same time. I chuckle, still angry. "Your twin brain, or lack of, is showing."

"Hey, fuck you, Onyx." Phantom is first. But Dusk will follow. I've pissed them off and telling me so isn't just a pleasure for them, it's an obligation.

Dusk glares but doesn't speak.

I shrug. There's isn't much I wouldn't do for them. Not much I wouldn't say to appease them. But this time, I'm right. They would see it if they weren't blinded. "Okay fine. But if you're thinking at all, it's with your dicks because she's beautiful and because you're tired of being alone."

"She's your mate as much as she's ours." He punctuates every word with a snarl of his lip and over-exaggerated motions of his hands.

"You keep her and it's going to be the death of all of us." I shake my head. "Mark my words." Then because I can't look at them anymore, I walk away. I'll be back, of course, but I need a minute.

For so long, all we've had is this war. This drive to keep the world safe.

How can I be the only one still focused on that? Mate or not, the world will fall without us. *Isn't that more important than one woman?*

I hate that my thoughts whisper, *No.*

SIX

Ann

They're fighting. I can't hear anything because they're signing, but the looks on their faces, the motions and speed with which they sign, say more than words ever could. Not only that, but they motion at me. More than once. With their heads or their hands, and one even kicked his leg out in my direction. Which is okay. I'm not any happier about being here, about "never" being able to go home again than they are about whatever it is that has to do with me.

I stare outside the cave as Onyx storms off. He's the biggest of the three, and a brooder. He's solemn and quiet, although I would bet my left eye he has a lot to say that he doesn't. I would bet aside from his posture--straight as a board--he's the rule-follower. Phantom is all command and order. I don't know about Dusk.

The two brothers work together to get some kind of soup brewing over the fire. They give me time to use the bathroom, well, the woods, and show me a river close by that I can clean up a bit at. Then, I'm led back to the fire, where Dusk quietly stirs the fire, and Phantom sits nearby sharpening a huge pile of swords and daggers, before carefully reattaching them to a wall with leather cords.

I eye the weapons. If push comes to shove, I can use them to escape. Every student at the Royal Fae Academy was forced to take various fighting classes, including with swords and daggers. I didn't exactly excel in the classes, but they might be enough to give me a distraction long enough to get away from them.

Again, if needed. As of right now, I don't know where I am, but I do know that these guys don't seem to want to hurt me. And, apparently, there are creatures in these woods that do. I'm not exactly a whiz at logic, yet I think it's smart to stay here.

For now.

When Onyx comes back, he's calm, his face almost serene as he signs some words to the others. I know a few words. "Fight," for example. And the circular motion made to say "ready."

Then Dusk and Phantom speak and I catch a few words. "Into the woods." And, "For her safety."

Okay, some of my classes are coming back to me!

Onyx settles near the fire, ignoring me, as Dusk hands out bowls of the soup, me first, followed by the others. It's steaming as I hold it, but I almost dig in anyway. How long has it been since I ate last? I have no idea, but I'm not exactly the kind of girl that misses a lot of meals. Some of the bitches at school regularly made comments about my looks and my weight. But when Rayne, from one of the most powerful fae house, claimed me as his mate, every mean comment I'd ever heard seemed to fade away.

I felt like the most beautiful woman in the world. And, somehow, that feeling still hadn't changed. It lingers inside of me, almost like Rayne is still with me, building me up, and making me feel loved. Even from the afterlife.

As a light fae, I can't see the dead. But sometimes I wonder if he comes to visit me in his ghostly form.

I smile at the thought, lift a spoonful of the soup to my lips, and blow softly. There's no way Rayne is visiting me. After saving his sister and the other dark fae, his soul has to be at rest. And I'm glad for it, even if my heart still longs for him.

"What are you thinking about?" Dusk asks, and I realize they're all studying me.

My smile fades away. "Nothing."

They have their secrets, why can't I have mine?

All three of them focus back on their food, eating slowly, and I eat too. For some reason, it bothers me a little that the mood changed after my words. I'm their prisoner. It shouldn't upset me if I hurt their feelings, or they realize that I'm keeping things close to my heart too.

So why does it bother me? I ponder the question while I eat one bowl, and then another.

The sun makes its final descent, and the colors of night blend with the last rays of day across the sky. Bits of color filter through the leaves and branches. A bird flaps and squirrels run and trees rustle. The sounds are all magnified in my mind by the silence of the men I wish I could hear speaking.

Phantom offers me a leather waterskin, which I eagerly drink, and then Onyx takes the pile of bowls and washes them in a little basket of water tucked into one little area of the cave that almost looks like a shelf carved out of the stone. Randomly, the men sign to each other, and I try to pick out any words I can, before I realize that I'm just getting frustrated and give up.

I stand up and look out at the night. Why do I like this place so much? I was never a huge outdoor person. The outdoors were pretty, but there were always more important things to do. But out here it feels like I've stepped into another world, and it's a world I enjoy in an unexpected way.

Dusk moves to stand in front of me at the edge of the cave where I'm leaning against the wall, going between trying to eavesdrop on the almost silence of their ASL, and looking back out at the woods.

After a second, he moves past me to one corner of our cave and kneels down briefly, before standing back up. He turns around and comes back with weapons--a broad sword, a dagger in a sheath he attaches to his belt, and the more modern handgun combo in some sort of utility belt that gives him a Rambo look Stallone would appreciate. They'd been hidden under a shroud that blends in with the dirt floor and walls.

Phantom gets another stone and is grinding a dagger's blade over the whetstone's smooth surface. He also has a gun--a *go ahead and make my day* kind of revolver--and what I think must be a harpoon gun.

Onyx moves back a boulder and pulls out a quiver and bow. He strings the bow--not the Robin Hood type he would've made from a tree branch and some sort of string. Definitely not from the woods, but one from Cabellas or Bass Pro. It's fancy. Black. A composite. He has a mechanical pull and a hand trigger along with his black glove. Certainly, it isn't what I expected.

"You use human weapons?"

Phantom's mouth draws into a thin line. "Some of our men have ventured further into the human world to seek help in our war."

"War with who?"

But they aren't listening to me. They're preparing for battle. That's what the signing must have meant.

I imagine any minute one of them will be accompanying me "into the woods." And by *accompanying*, I mean drag me out there for my own safety. Probably Dusk. Actually, I hope it's Dusk. Onyx seems to dislike me, and Phantom, well, he's a bit more intimidating compared to his brother.

And like I'm sending telepathic messages to him, Dusk, the man not the time of day, locked and loaded with weaponry, turns to me and moves as if he's going to come to collect me. But I don't give him the chance. I walk out of the cave past him, then turn. "Well, let's get on with it, shall we?"

If I have to go out somewhere with him, it should be on my terms, even though we both know it isn't. Nothing has been on my terms for a while now, not from the moment I met them anyway. So, this feels like a small way I can take back some of my power and remind these three that I'm not going to just lay down and accept this whole "mate" thing, nor the idea that I can never go home.

They all give me a look of surprise, but Phantom's gaze turns to one of pleasure. Onyx, on the other hand, somehow seems even more pissed off. *What is it with this guy?*

Dusk just grins. "I'll show you the way."

He guides me deeper into the woods and away from the cave. I don't know where the others are or why I'm being led away, but the air is thick with tension. Whatever bravery I felt a minute ago starts to fade, and my heart races. I've felt this way before. During the little bit of time before the light fae attacked the dark fae.

A battle is coming.

When we've gone a few hundred yards, he pulls me into a crouch beside him. He leans away from me, and I can almost feel his heart pounding as fast as mine is. I want to ask him what he's doing, but I don't want to bring any more trouble down on my head.

I turn to look into the woods where he's looking. I narrow my eyes, and my stomach suddenly flips. I stand, feeling strange, almost like I'm walking in a dream, because there's an incredible light, and I'm drawn to it. It's a glow. A beacon, calling out to me, drawing me in. I edge closer, and now Dusk follows me, his hand on my shoulder.

He glances at me. "Holy shit."

And I know exactly what he's saying. The closer I get to it, the brighter the light gets, the sharper the glow. I've never seen anything like it. It's beautiful and mesmerizing.

Dusk stands staring, mouth agape, eyes wide.

"What is it?"

He doesn't speak. Maybe he doesn't know either.

And neither of us have time to figure it out, because behind us we hear the sounds of battle: men grunting and the clashing of swords. Dusk picks up the glowing piece--a stone maybe--and we race back to the cave, or near it, where the battle has begun without us.

I follow him because I'm drawn to that glow like a life-force. I don't know what it is, but it's incredible, and I'm not letting it out of my sight.

Nor do I want to be left alone at night, in the woods, with enemies around me.

SEVEN

Dusk

Grave trolls. Rot monkeys. All the bastards have arrived with the darkness, just as we expected, just as they *always* do, only there's more in our area than usual. For a minute I wonder if they're starting to narrow in on where we live, but I push the thought aside. *We're always careful.*

And I don't have to guess what they're doing out of the Void. Or what comes along with their arrival. The monkeys--and there are three of them--run when I come near.

Typical. The trolls are sent here to fight us. But the monkeys? Those little assholes are here for trouble, and only trouble. I just wish they weren't so damn fast, or I'd kill more of the bastards.

"This way," I whisper to Ann, switching directions.

She stumbles, and I grasp her arm, pulling her along. But as beautiful as she is, as brave as she is, she's much slower than my kind. Dragging her along with me is definitely harder than just leaving her behind, not that I would. I'm tasked with keeping her safe, but that doesn't mean I can't try to stop the monkeys.

Especially after what I just saw with the moon shard...

"What are we chasing?" she says between pants.

"Demons," I hiss. Okay, so they aren't demons, but they may as well be.

They're so quick that if I wasn't so experienced with dealing with them, I wouldn't even know for sure that that's what they were. Unfortunately, I would know them anywhere. But as fast as they are, I only get a good glimpse of red eyes in the dark night. They stick to the shadows, because in this world, everything is too bright for them. It's only their king's power that keeps them from turning to ash beneath the light of the moon, even in the shadows.

Yet, I can't seem to catch up with them. It's irritating as hell. But with my much slower mate at my side, I guess that's to be expected. There are three heading deep into the woods, deeper than I took Ann, racing through the under-growth of the woods like the nightmarish little tricksters they are.

Luckily for me, the moon shard still glows brightly, lighting the forest around us better than any torch. I've honestly never seen anything like it before. Moon shards always glow a tiny bit in the night, but not like this, *never* like this. But for right now, I can't focus on why it's doing such an incredible thing, or how it's connected to Ann.

I race along, still holding the shard of moonstone in one hand, and chasing a rot monkey holding another shard. Because now that I'm gaining on them, I know for sure he's holding a shard. They always glow with the same light, not quite like the crystals in the Elder's cave, but with a pale blue light that I've never seen anywhere else in this world, or ours.

But as beautiful as the shards are, as much as a small part of my soul longs to touch them, to be close to them, I fight the desire to do anything but collect them. They're dangerous. And as we've learned the hard way, their power has a way of corrupting. No matter how much time I spent focused on the moonstone as a boy, no matter how much I missed it, I'm not happy to see the shards here. Because they can only mean trouble now, and trouble we have more than enough of already.

If they're planting a perimeter of shards, the Shadow King is up to his usual shit.

Bastard.

I've chased my share of these little fuckers, but these guys must be training hard. There's only one moment when I think I'm gaining on them before they take off again, and I'm left in the dust faster than ever before. But even if they are getting quicker, I have a job to do. We're getting too far away, and I can't let them get away.

If the Shadow King succeeds, it's game over. No more humans. No more supernaturals. No more world as we know it. *And this world can't be destroyed like our own.*

Phantom and Onyx can deal with the pair of grave trolls they're fighting--they've never lost to a troll--but I wish it was one of them chasing these monkeys. The monkeys don't have the fighting skills of a troll, but they fight dirty--biting, clawing, spitting in the eyes. Last time I hunted a pair, one threw the other at me then they both attacked. I'd had eleven separate bites.

But I guess it makes sense. Phantom is clever enough to handle the trolls, and Onyx is...well, the best warrior I've ever seen in my life. He isn't just big, he's smart, calculating, and well-trained. While I'm not exactly bear shit, they both handle trolls better than I do.

Even though I hate that fact, it doesn't change the fact that it's true.

Plus, I have Ann with me, and I'd much rather have her around these fools than the trolls, who could easily kill her with one well-placed blow. Yes, it's easy for me to slip into my duties in this world, but I have to remember that keeping Ann safe is now my most important responsibility.

When the monkeys are about thirty yards ahead, they stop and turn. I have enough time to think, *"Oh shit"* and tuck the moon shard into my belt, before two of the trio roll themselves into balls and the third launches them one at a time like bowling balls. I push Ann out of the way and side-step one, then the other changes course and takes me down.

"Fuck!" I manage as I go flying back.

From my position on the ground, I fend off one attack, holding the rot monkey over my head while another climbs up my body and goes right for my ears. He has a hand on each, legs around my throat, which puts his dick danger-ously close to my nose and this thing stinks. I drop the one in my hands and grab this nasty bastard by the scruff, then fling him so he smashes into a tree.

He yelps and goes down, head wobbling back and forth before he slumps forward, out cold. One down, two to go. The one I dropped sinks his teeth into my ankle, which sends a shot of pain through my leg, and I yank him off by the tail and hurl him. He goes up then down and lands at an odd angle on a mossy patch. But he recovers quickly and comes running at me, arms curled outward, teeth bared, eyes wide.

One big boot later and it's down to me and the last little rot monkey. His eyes are red and he's pounding the ground like he's a three-hundred-pound gorilla. It would be comical if not for the eyes. The angrier these things get, the brighter they glow. And judging by that fact, this guy is super pissed.

He circles me and I turn. Maybe I should grab him first,

but I want to see what he has planned. These things are fast, but hand to hand combat isn't their forte. This guy, though, facing someone ten times his size, has balls of steel. He's hissing and snorting, nostrils flared. He's dropped the shard, and before he moves, Ann touches him and a light shines out of her. No, it *bursts* from her, like a laser, or electricity, rather than an actual light.

My jaw drops, and I just stare and stare. *What the hell is that light? And did it actually come from her?* I know she's a light fae, but as far as I know, her kind can't *literally* make light.

Whatever it is, it's powerful, and monkey-man flies back from her, smashing into a tree and crumbling to the ground. Without any direction from me, she walks toward the other monkey at the base of the tree with a confident stride and her lips in a tight line. He's starting to stir when she kneels down over him. But when she touches him, the glow in his eyes dies, like a candle being snuffed out, and I have no doubt that the monkey himself is dead. D-E-A-D.

She turns on her heel and starts toward the last living money, but she stops halfway to him. I wait for her to keep going toward the third, but it's like she's waking up from a dream and finds herself sleepwalking. The confidence is gone from her face, and her expression is confused and maybe even afraid. She looks at her hand, open-mouthed, twisting it, palm over then knuckle up.

"Wh-what was that?"

"You don't know?" I ask, surprised.

She shakes her head. "I don't know how that was possible..."

Yeah. I feel the same way. Whatever just happened was like nothing I've seen before, or even imagined, and we've been fighting these assholes for longer than I can remember.

I know for sure Phantom and Onyx aren't going to believe any of this.

When she glances at me, she asks, "Should I touch the third one?"

Honestly, I can't think of a reason not to.

I shrug. "Go ahead." Partly because I want to see it again. Seriously. It's better than any parlor trick to see creatures that have been torturing us for so long get snuffed out from the touch of a tiny fae woman. But partly because I want to confirm that everything I thought just happened actually did.

She draws her shoulders back and gives a nod, before marching the rest of the way to the monkey. Again, she looks between it and her hand, as if she's not sure which thing is scarier, but then kneels down beside it. I see her take several deep breaths as the monkey begins to stir. Some unexpected instinct makes me hold my breath. If it tries to hurt her, I'll be there in an instant, and I'll make it wish it had never touched my mate.

But I need to give her a chance to try out that light thing again...

Before the monkey can fully sit up, she lays her hand on him and the red light in his eyes fades away just as fast as with the first one. But instead of pulling away, her hand remains on him, and her brows draw together.

Within a few seconds, the fucker actually bursts into flames.

"Holy shit." Her whisper in the now-silent forest mirrors my thoughts exactly. I don't know if she knows what this means, but we need to figure out what to do about it.

I nod to her, and gesture for her to join me so we can get back to the others. But as we pass the last body of the monkeys, it turns to ash, just as all rot monkeys from the shadow world do. The trolls are worth enough to the king that if left alone here, they'll come back to life, just like they do in the shadow realm, but not the rot monkeys. They simply turn to ash. *Every* time.

"Is that...normal?" she asks.

"With the monkeys, yes. The grave trolls are...more complicated to get rid of." She doesn't need to know about the beasts coming back to life if we don't burn them. She seems scared enough.

We go to where the other moon shard was left by the monkeys. And just like the one in my belt, it glows brighter and brighter the closer Ann gets to them.

"Those are beautiful," she whispers.

"Beautiful and terrible." I lean down, pick it up, and tuck it next to the other moonstone.

The shards we collect are hidden by Phantom. We're the only shadow beasts that know where they're concealed, because the power within them could tempt any man, even men with good hearts. And not all our shadow beasts are as bound by honor as they once were. So, these will go with the others, in a place the Shadow King can never find.

As we walk, she continues looking at her hands. I don't know if it's for my benefit and she already knows what she is, or if she's legitimately confused by what she saw and what she did.

Neither of us speak, though, until we get back to the cave. Onyx has one of the trolls thrown over his shoulder, and his broad sword back in his belt. We'll burn and bury him in the pit at the edge of the forest before morning comes. I'm not looking forward to it, though. Trolls smell like a sewer when they're alive. Burning them doesn't help the stench, but we don't have a choice. The trolls can't be allowed to regenerate.

At the beginning of this war, we didn't realize just how durable they are. We knew that in the Shadow World the trolls were formed by the bodies of various dead creatures and could die over and over again. I guess we shouldn't have been surprised that they could find a way to come back here too.

Even if getting rid of them for good is irritating.

But any day we can send a troll back to The Wasteland, the better. Onyx drops his troll with a thud that echoes through the trees and cocks his head at me. I sign the story then repeat it again for Phantom out loud, who's already taken his troll to the pit.

I don't bother keeping my voice low. Ann was there. She knows what she did.

He looks her up and down and doesn't speak. Onyx purses his lips and signs at me, "We should get rid of her now. Before she kills one of us and before the king hears about her."

He's probably right. He usually is. Ann's power to kill the rot monkeys so easily, along with her ability to make the moon shards glow, could turn the tide on this war, which will make her even more of a target to the king. But a part of me can't stand the thought of sending her away, not just because of our mate bond, but because the king might find her at home just as easily as he could find her here.

"We can't just get rid of her." Before I've finished the sentence, she lifts her head and stares at me like I'm the one who made the suggestion.

Watching her handle those rot monkeys was actually one of the sexiest things I've ever seen. All she did was touch them. It's like this tiny, beautiful woman has a strength that doesn't come in muscles and tactical moves, but is just as important. If not more. And that's sexy as hell, and also a little scary.

"Ann..." I begin, trying to find the right words.

But instead of talking to us, explaining what she knows or doesn't know, she stalks into the cave, head high, back straight. She turns to stare for a second and there's no doubt that if there was a door, she would've slammed it.

EIGHT

Ann

WHEN I WALK into the cave, Onyx follows, glaring at a wound on his shoulder. The others can talk outside all they want, but I don't care. I'd heard all I'd needed to hear. *Get rid of her.* He'd said it. I didn't catch the rest, but he'd suggested it... I would scream if I thought it would do any good.

Jerk.

Were these three actually acting like I'd come here of my own accord? Did they not remember the whole kidnapping thing? Hadn't I already asked to go home?

But instead of listening to me, or even explaining things to me, they'd insisted I was stuck here. It was annoying, but I was working on my plan. Then I went and used some weird power that's got me really freaked out, and suddenly they're ready to kick me to the curb?

Nice, real nice.

Onyx sits across from me on a pallet of blankets near the small fire in their cave. He's quite good-looking except for the scowl he's wearing when he looks up at me. I get the feeling--those scowls say a lot--that he doesn't like me. I don't know much sign language, just enough to ask a couple questions, but I move closer to him and touch his shoulder.

When he looks at me, I sit for a second, dumb-founded because he's beautiful. Blonde and built for battle. His hair is gathered on top of his head in a ponytail. And he's bare-chested, so there are acres and acres of muscle and skin in my eyeline.

"Are they your brothers?" I mouth the words as I sign them because I'm not sure if I'm signing the right words.

He doesn't answer, and I don't know if it's because he's a rude asshat or if I'm mangled the question so badly he has no idea what I'm trying to ask.

I drop the ASL and use generic signals that make sense in my head. "Is this where you live?" I point to our cave then air-draw a house.

He shoots me another glare then winces. The cut on his shoulder is seeping blood down his left arm and he pulls it around to look. The laceration is deep but something inside me is drawn closer. Like the moment I first saw the light in the forest. Somehow, I can feel power vibrating inside me. It's like an angry bee, buzzing to be released, but I don't know why or what it'll do if it gets out.

I sit beside him and like my hands have a mind of their own, they glow and he pulls away, flinches, shakes his head. This is different than the glow when I...killed those disgusting creatures in the woods with Dusk. Still powerful, but soothing. There's no part of me that thinks the power will hurt anyone, but I honestly don't know what it'll do.

I slide my thumb against my fingertips. The light doesn't even flicker. And then I have a strange sense that makes a shiver roll through my body. I've never seen a light fae's hands glow, but I have spoken to fae with the ability to heal. It's a rare gift, but when they described how it worked, they described it like this. Like a power in their hands. Like a buzzing through their body. Just not with the weird glow.

All fae want to try to utilize the rarest of our kind's gifts, but those that have it, simply have it. They can use it, even from a young age. Still, there were times through the years where I concentrated and willed myself to be able to do something special. I wanted so badly to be *someone* special.

I never was.

But right now...right now I have the strangest feeling that I can heal him, if I just try.

Instead of reaching to touch him right away, I continue trying to touch the light until a loud breath whistles out of his nose followed by a huff like I'm annoying him. It's enough to snap me out of my amusement with my glowing hands.

"Hold still." Either he understands or my touch repulses him enough the he holds still in the hopes I'll think he died and leave him alone. But as I lay my palm on the wound, the power flows between us, more from me to him, and his head tilts to the side, exposing a long length of neck I have the sudden and powerful urge to taste, especially when my gaze runs along the scar on his beautiful neck. The need arises inside of me, and then I'm imagining more. More than just touching him.

I jerk away because no way should I be thinking about licking the guy who is clearly repulsed by me. It just shows that I'm even more screwed up than I thought.

But I am.

Thinking about it.

Still.

And my mouth waters. I let my tongue slide along my lower lip and his eyes follow the trail. And just when I think he's going to get up and walk away from me because I'm too close and making too much out of all this, he lifts a hand and brushes the back of his finger along a trail from my jaw to my chin then lets his fingertip tease the skin just below my lip.

The touch might not glow like my hands, but his touch is electric and it tingles through me all the way to my toes. "Wow."

He smiles, or as close to it as he probably ever gets, and I swallow hard. When I said he was beautiful, I lied. He's whatever is better than beautiful. His dark eyes smolder with what I hope is desire because that's what's purring through me.

And it's as scary as being stuck here with these guys. I don't know everything. I don't really know anything, if I'm honest, but I can't stay here. I can't be attracted to a guy who thinks he's "claimed" me as his mate. *What the fuck does that even mean?*

Honestly. There are three of them and they *all* claimed me. Truth be told, it's flattering, especially since these guys are built like gods and look like GQ models. And the thought of three of them claiming me, wanting me, is hot. For a second, my mind spins with fantasies--erotic and blissful--and I lose the reasons I want to leave. But just for a second.

Then, I remember Rayne. My mate. He'd walked onto campus with all the strength and power of a royal fae. Every woman had wanted him. Every guy wanted to be part of his crew. But when he'd spotted me, he had eyes only for me. The connection between us was like nothing I'd ever felt in my life. It was a calling. A deep need to be with each other or cease to exist.

My gaze moves to the Blood Stone necklace that's been around my neck every day since he gave it to me. It's dark red, a deep scarlet color like nothing else on earth, save maybe blood itself. And the colors swirl together in a mesmerizing way.

It's priceless. Quite literally. If someone tried to sell it, they'd be offered any number under the sun and have to take the highest offer, even knowing it was worth more. The stones are rare, and only found around Rayne's lands. And he'd given this to me.

Because we were always going to be together. We were mates. For life.

Tears sting my eyes. These men claim I'm their mate. I feel a connection to them, but not the same way I did with Rayne. With him, there was no question. With these men, all I have are questions, and one of them seems to be whether they plan to get rid of me or not.

Now, I really want to go home.

I pull my hand away from the giant man. His hand has already dropped back to his side. On his shoulder, blood has stained his skin. But underneath that, his wound is gone.

Any other time, I'd be dancing around hooting and hollering that I was actually able to heal someone. But I don't feel any joy at the realization, just a mind-numbing sadness for all I lost, and all I can never forget.

I move back to my own side of the cave and sit. *There has to be a way out of here. I have to get back to my real life. Away from these men...*

He stands and moves to the cave entrance and walks out. I frown. *He's not going to guard me? Are the others staying close to ensure I don't run?*

Or is now my chance?

I creep to the doorway and look both ways. None of the guys are there. In fact, everything is almost painfully silent.

If I'm going to go, it's now or never.

I scan the woods one more time, take a deep breath, and run like I'm the anchor in the last leg of the Olympic relay. The air whips around me, and I run and run until I'm sure I can't see the cave any longer, then keep going as fast as I can.

The forest around me feels dark and creepy. This far away from the cave, there's no light from the fire. There's only the moonlight and stars. My mind keeps flashing back to the shadow beasts and the creatures they fought. None of it makes sense. And as much as I want to believe the beasts are the good guys, I'm not really sure.

I don't even know how long I would have been safe with them. Or if when they said to get rid of me, they meant to let me go back home, or if I was going to end up on the end of one of their swords. It's true fae would never kill their mates, but I don't even know if I believe these guys about the mate bond. For all I know, it's all just a lie.

So why does it feel like I'm running from safety into danger?

Out of breath, and with my legs burning, I stop to lean against a tree. I have a cramp in my side, a rock in my shoe, and not enough breath to pant, but I'm not going back. I'm going home. *Period.*

But as I catch my breath, the birds and night creatures go silent around me. Every hair on my body stands on end, and I slowly look around, even though I already know I'm not alone. My gaze connects with two silver eyes in a hulking shadowy creature. And then, I spot another pair of silver eyes near the first.

Fuck.

Okay, so I'm going home. No matter what... As soon as I figure out a way around the hideous and terrifying trolls who've come to stare at me.

I inch away from the scary creatures and glance at my escape. A second later, Onyx is there, breathing so hard his entire chest rises and falls like he's run a marathon. And the look in his eyes? Even beneath the moonlight it's scary as hell.

Even if I'm not sure whether his anger is directed at me or the creatures in front of me.

So, I guess I'm going home. After I escape the trolls, *and* the ponytailed-blonde man who is still bare-chested and behind me now.

I might not have thought this through...

I fake left, dodge right, and try to weave around the pair of ugly trolls blocking my path, but not only are they the most unfortunate-looking creatures, they're sturdy *and* wide. My fades and dodges are no match for the bulk of these critters. No matter which way I go, they seem to be in front of me again.

One grabs for me and I duck under his arms and around him. He doesn't come after me though, even though I hear growls of rage and anger. Which means I should keep going, right?

So why do my steps slow and I feel like I have to go back?

When I turn to glance behind me, the trolls are both attacking the shadow beast, and Onyx is fighting from the ground. *Probably not because he finds it easier.* His sword gets knocked from his hands and goes flying out of his reach, but he's quick to recover, grabbing a dagger from his belt. He thrusts it into one of the trolls and wraps both hands around the handle then twists, and the squishing sound makes my stomach turn.

Okay, he's got this. So just go.

I blow out a few quick breaths, trying to convince myself to see this as an opportunity to escape. But one of the trolls takes a log that I never even saw him pick up, and swings at the shadow beast. Onyx drops his dagger and catches the log, but it still crashes down on him.

And then, the troll races forward, disappearing into the night.

I should run. I should escape while I have the chance. But for some reason, I stay rooted in place. A little voice whispers in the back of my thoughts that I can't just leave Onyx like this.

The log is suddenly shoved off of him. He manages to get it onto the ground beside him, but he barely moves. He just lies in place, and all I can hear is the sound of his uneven breathing.

Help him, my conscience whispers again, and I want to obey.

Which is stupid. But even still, I rush back to him.

I kneel beside him, and see that his eyes are squeezed shut, and he's most definitely breathing unevenly. There's no blood, except for the black troll blood that covers him. Nothing immediately off. But I don't believe for a second he'd be lying here if something isn't terribly wrong.

Just the thought of his internal injuries from that log has my stomach turning. *Try to heal him. You did it once, you can do it again.* I bit my lip, and hope that when I hold my hands out, they glow.

For a second, I'm just a fool holding out her hands while

a man dies in front of me. But then, they surprise me by slowly glowing until they're as bright as they were last time.

Swallowing hard, I lay my hands on Onyx...and hope.

NINE

Phantom

THERE IS something to be said for a woman who can shoot lights out of her hands like some kind of goddess. But this is different. *Bad* different. Goddesses probably know how to turn their powers off and go to their safe little castles. This woman clearly doesn't. And she chatters.

A lot.

Since she and Onyx returned to us, her half carrying him, that's all she's done. Even when we were still outside, guarding the cave and waiting for morning, she'd been asking questions. Usually, I'd enjoy the break from the silence that often descends between my brother and our best friend. Usually, the perfect cadence of her voice would be just the sound I'd want to fall asleep listening to all night.

But after she tried to run from us, escape from us like we're monsters, and then nearly faced down two grave trolls on her own, I'm too wound up to just enjoy her talking. I mean, technically she hadn't confessed to trying to escape from us, but there was no other reason for her to be that far in the woods on her own.

"I mean, the troll was..." She spreads her arms out like she's planning to take flight. "And then, he picked up a log--half a tree really--and swung it like he's Mark freaking McGuire trying to break a record." I don't know the reference, but she hasn't wound down enough for me to ask and I don't really care anyway.

Yeah, Onyx was good. Really good. But even he can't take down two grave trolls, especially if he tried to lure them to him and away from Ann.

Most of us wouldn't have walked away from that fight alive. But most of us don't have a tiny, talkative woman who has our backs in a battle.

"Then Onyx went down and I mean, he *really* went down. And then I knew I had to get him back to the cave, so I started screaming, trying to get your attention."

"Yelling for help in the woods with trolls running around wasn't the best idea." Dusk stares dubiously, like he honestly can't believe anyone would just sit in the woods and scream, without realizing they were just as likely to attract their enemies as they would to attract allies.

He's almost as shocked and amused as I am as he tends to Onyx, pressing a cold cloth to his head. When our eyes lock, he shakes his head with a slight smile and makes a bomb explosion motion at the side of his head behind her back.

I would laugh, but I have too many questions. "What were you doing running around in the woods?" It doesn't matter but I have a point to make.

Her enthusiasm over the fight drains from her face, and she gives me a clearly defiant look. "You're the ones who stole me. Who decided we're," she air quotes, "mates. I didn't get a choice, or a say, or even a pick."

Even glaring at me like I kicked her pet, she's lovely. And I've never seen eyes so like the sky.

Focus. Your questions. The problem.

I glance at Dusk. "If the trolls got away, then the Shadow King knows about her. Not just that one of us found a mate in this world, but that she's here, with us." The words taste bitter as I speak them.

Maybe even that she's the mate of the three of us...

Honestly, that's the only reason I can come up with why the trolls left when they did. They saw her. Felt that she was our mate. And they raced off to tell the king, so that he can make our lives even more miserable.

Yes, it was going to happen eventually, but I would have felt better if things were more established with our connection before he learned of her. Still, she's our mate, and if the king comes for her, we will each die to protect her.

Unfortunately, he knows this too.

"Yes." Dusk nods. He glances at her and holds her gaze for a second.

I know what he wants to say. That we've discussed letting her go. That Onyx wants us to do so. But that because of our connection to her, the shadow world is aware of her now, and she'll never be safe again. It's something she needs to know. But, somehow, I fear it'll make her hate us, make her afraid, and lead to her trying to escape even more.

So, it's smarter not to tell her, even if it feels a little wrong.

"What does that mean?" she asks with a frown.

Onyx lifts his hands and signs, and my little brother interprets for him. "That things are going to get a lot more dangerous."

Her face goes pale. "More dangerous than creepy creatures attacking us?"

"They're called rot monkeys and grave trolls," I explain, suddenly feeling weary.

"And they'll tell this...Shadow King about me? Which is a problem?"

"Exactly," Dusk says, but the tone of his voice says he doesn't want to keep talking about the man who ruined all our lives. The man I should have seen the truth in, and who Dusk should have killed when we had the chance.

Neither of us like to talk about him. Any time his name gets brought up, Onyx grows quiet. Dusk trains harder, wanting to become a better warrior, even though we both know he'll never train hard enough to *feel* good enough. Not unless training harder can somehow turn back time. And I just hate myself a little more.

"Are you guys ever going to explain anything to me?" Ann asks, her brows drawing together in frustration.

"What my little brother means--"

"Little brother?" She perks up. "I thought you were twins."

Ah, this. "Technically, we are. But in our world, the child who enters the world first is the oldest, and that is a very important difference."

For me it means the responsibility of our world falls on my shoulders. It means never having the luxury to be softer like my brother, to enjoy poetry or reading the same way he could. He could explore his friendships and his life in a way I never could. For him, apparently, it means always living in my shadow.

Both of us envy the other in ways that are hard to explain.

"And is Onyx your brother too?"

"Yes," I say. "Not by blood, but by our bond."

Onyx signs. "You need to stop saying that. Your blood matters more than any bond."

I mouth back, "*Not to me.*"

Since Onyx spent most of his life able to hear, he's very good with reading lips. He can often speak without hearing himself, but has chosen not to. Partially, I believe, because he knows his voice box was also injured in the attack, so he fears what he sounds like now. He's only spoken since his injury when it was a life-or-death situation. But luckily for all of us, signing is something most shadow beasts know how to do, because there are many creatures in our world that only communicate with their hands.

"So, things are going to get harder," Dusk says, and the exhaustion in his voice is evident.

I was worried about my brother and my best friend before Ann came along. And when we were taken and imprisoned, each day was horrible. Not just the torture. Not just the terrible things that we did, things I'll never forgive myself for. But because we knew we were leaving the other shadow beasts to fight a war they couldn't possibly win.

With our help, they were surviving.

While we were gone, we lost three men. Technically, Adrik isn't dead yet, but he might as well be. And all the death of our kind, every day, it was all my fault. My blindness that led us to this life of misery.

My mistake.

"Tomorrow, we're going to have to tell the others that the Shadow King knows of her existence so close to the Void." The increase in troll activity alone will be a tip-off to the others that something is going on, and there *will* be an increase. There's no getting around it. As soon as the king finds out about Ann, he's going to throw everything he has in his arsenal into finding her. We're going to be overrun with rot monkeys, trolls, maybe even smoke dragons, if he can muster the strength to send one to this world.

The shit show is about to begin.

"They won't be happy," Onyx signs.

Dusk signs back, looking grim. "Or will they? If we found a mate in this world, maybe they can too."

The implication of his words is more than I can handle. Ann's existence would bring hope to our kind in any other world. But in this one, her presence brings trouble, and we have enough of that already. And yet, will her existence finally be the thing that makes them give up this fight and go out into this bright world looking for something else, even knowing what that decision would bring?

No...they can't be that short-sighted. Can they?

"I'll keep first watch," Dusk says, even though he knows no one needs to keep watch during the day.

He stands and walks outside the cave, and I don't know what to tell him. He's angry. Angry that Onyx was hurt. Angry that the woman is the cause. Angry that because she's our mate, we're going to be hunted by every troll and rot monkey the king can send our way. Probably angry that we have to tell the others the coming assault is our doing.

I can't blame him for not wanting to be inside the cave with us.

Onyx is lying on his fluff of blankets and pillows. He had recovered enough to walk back here, but he'd been left with a blinding headache, and an exhaustion that's weakened him. I can't even imagine the state he'd be in if Ann hadn't used her strange ability on him.

That was another thing we hadn't discussed. Ann could kill the rot monkeys. She could heal us. And the moon shards glow when she's close to them, like the Moon Goddess herself. *What else can she do?*

I rub my face. I can't keep worrying about her strange abilities or what it all means. The second morning arrived, it was time for us to rest and recover. If I waste my time thinking about things I can't control, I won't be at my best when the night comes once more.

Sighing, I grab my blankets and pillows from where we keep them tucked away during the day and lay them out near the fire. Then, I check on Onyx.

I sign, "Are you okay?"

He nods and signs back, "Just tired." And his eyes flutter shut.

I remove the wet cloth from his forehead, dip it in the bucket of cold water from the river, squeeze the excess water out, and lay it on his forehead once more. He makes a content noise and his breathing steadies.

Okay, that's done.

When I turn around, Ann is lying on my blanket near the fire. I smile. *Well, at least that's a good sign. She might not like us, she might not trust us, but she was willing to share my blankets.*

That's something.

I climb onto the blankets behind her and feel something in my heart ease. Her body is soft beside me, and I lay my arm over her and pull her back against my chest in a way that feels strangely natural. More than natural. It's like we've been doing this all our lives.

That feeling within my heart seems to grow. Touching her feels *right*. Being near her feels *right*.

I never told Onyx or Dusk this, but my only interactions with the people who lost their mates were not good ones. It wasn't as if they just lost a part of themselves. It was as if they lost the part of themselves that made them happy...that gave them any peace.

And we've already lost most of that.

As much as they others thought they could leave Ann behind, I knew better.

"What are you doing?" Her voice is soft, breathless almost.

What am I doing? She chose to lay on my blankets. Was I wrong about why? Maybe she never wanted to be close to me. She just sought my protection.

I feel like a fool. *Okay, this can just be about keeping her safe.*

"Protecting you." The answer is stern. Definitely stern. Not husky. Not passionate. Not needy.

"Am I in danger right now? Even in the early morning?"

It wouldn't take much to turn her so her chest is against mine. "Not as long as you don't try to leave again." I concentrate on keeping her safety and her compliance as front and center as I can so I don't think about the scent of sunshine on her skin, the gentle brush of her hair against my skin every time she shifts or breathes, the pressure of her ass against my cock.

Oh shit. New thought.

"Just go to sleep." This is gruff because I'm trying to get my cock under control, and I need to not hear the melodic sound of her voice. "Tomorrow is a big day."

When I look over at Onyx, he's watching, eyes narrowed, mouth in a thin line. *Damn it. How long has the asshole been awake?*

He's made no secret that he never wanted her here. That he knew this kind of thing would happen... us wanting her, and it distracting us from our responsibilities. That he wants us to send her away. Yet none of that explains why he went after her, except that she escaped on his watch, while Dusk and I were torching the trolls.

Onyx is always so damned good at hiding his gentler emotions. Did he pursue her because he didn't want to lose her either? I have no idea, but the look in his eyes definitely isn't one of happiness.

She shifts again and her ass rubs my cock so that I moan. I hear myself do it, then angle my body away from her.

It's going to be a long night.

TEN

Ann

THE MORNING TRUDGE through the woods is long and tedious because every few yards, every time a bird flaps its wings or a breeze blows through a branch, one of these super-careful guardians of mine yanks me down while the other two assume warrior poses until the "danger" has passed.

The danger of a little bird. Real *scary*.

It's been a day and a night since the battle with the trolls. After we'd slept for most of the day, the guys had taken me around the woods, and four more shards had started glowing when I got near them. None of them said anything about it, but I got the sense that the shards' reaction to me was really important. They'd simply collected the glowing pieces, refusing to let me look at them more closely or touch them before we retired to the cave to sleep more during the day.

Dusk, at least, had explained that they always slept

during the day, because the creatures couldn't come here when it was light out. No matter what. He said that even on nights when the moon was full and bright, there were far fewer attacks because it was harder for the Shadow King to keep his creatures together in the light. So, at night the shadow beasts stayed awake and ready for attacks, while combing the forest for the gently glowing moon shards, because until me they couldn't see them at all during the day, and during the day they rested and prepared for the next night.

They were also even more careful with me that night after collecting the shards too. We stayed in the cave, and all three of them stood like guards at the door all night, while I tried to ask more questions. Questions that none of them answered.

These guys are a frustrating lot...

Now, it's the crack of dawn, right before the world wakes up, so there are noises that don't belong to trolls, even though they seem to think they do. They see danger lurking under every blade of grass and every tree trunk. It's a little frustrating. Not just their overprotectiveness. No, it's not just all of that. It's also that I barely slept all the day before, and that right now I wish we were sleeping instead of hiking through the woods.

I'm exhausted enough to sleep right here and now. But I don't get to sleep under a random tree in the woods. Nope, that would be too easy. My only semi-comfortable place to sleep is on a bedroll with one of the guys. And, so far, I've slept next to Phantom each night, which is frustrating for entirely different reasons. When we are first falling asleep, Phantom always tries to keep a few inches between our bodies. But when he eventually falls asleep, he always pulls me closer and cuddles into me.

And, fucking hell, sleeping next to a half-naked hunk of a man is like being tortured. I can feel his very hard cock against my ass all night long, and any time I shift, he groans and rubs against me a little.

I should have pulled away from him. I should have kept to my side of the blanket, or woken him up and told him to get his dick under control.

Instead, I held myself still. I maybe even rubbed my ass against him every so often to see what he would do. Part of me wanted to see if I could make him come in his sleep from something so small. I wanted to feel him begin to thrust against me until my own control slipped.

Which is insane.

Just the thought of it makes me ache to touch myself. Several times while we were laying together, I ran my hands along my stomach, debating about whether anyone would catch me. It became such a terrible need that I was undoing the button on my pants when Dusk stirred from his sleep and turned to look at me. I stopped myself before he saw anything, I think, but then he'd woken Phantom up and switched places with him.

And, hell, it must have been as long for them as it had been for me since they had sex, because Dusk was equally hard. It was even more difficult to pretend to be asleep as he adjusted, sighed, and moved around, his hard dick pressed against my ass the whole time. But eventually he too fell asleep, and I was left wondering if I was still adjusting to their sleep schedule, or if I just needed to get laid.

The tightness in my body since then said the latter, and the urge to sneak away and get myself off was building. When it was fully light out, I'd have to seriously consider whether relieving this pressure was worth the possibility of these three hunting me down and catching me in the act.

Probably not, but damn it I'm horny!

"Ann," Dusk whispers, pulling me down behind another bush.

I sigh and shrug him off, feeling frustrated for way too many reasons.

"It's just another fucking animal," I mutter under my breath.

My gaze connects with Onyx's, and there's no doubt the bastard read my lips, because he looks irritated.

So, I mouth back at him, "You are annoying."

His brows rise, and then I give him the universal sign of annoyance and flip him off.

The big man's dark eyes darken further, and I swallow, a little too hard. But he just turns away and focuses back on the forest around us. Which is probably a good thing. As irritating as I find him, I don't think I want to find out what he'll do if I push him too far.

"It's nothing," Phantom says, and we all rise to our feet and start back up.

"What are you doing out here exactly?" I repeat the question, figuring I'd get the same standard answer as before: walking.

But Dusk shakes his head, a smirk on his lips. "You really like to know everything that's going on, don't you?"

"Uh, yeah, who likes to be kept in the dark?"

Onyx shakes his head and turns away from us.

Dusk laughs. "Okay, I guess it won't hurt anything. We're checking the perimeter."

"The perimeter of what?"

Phantom and Dusk exchange a look.

I glare at them. "Come on!"

Dusk pushes some branches out of the way and indicates for me to keep going.

I cross my arms in front of my chest.

"Just walk," Phantom says.

"I think I'm done walking without any information at all."

Phantom glances over me as if he's considering just picking me up again, and I hold my breath, hoping it won't come to that. "We're checking the perimeter of our area for any enemies."

Okay, I guess that's *something*. Dusk parts the branches for me, and we keep walking. It honestly seems like a waste of time. We'd spent most of the night at our camp. We'd eaten, and then they'd checked over their weapons and supplies before we'd started walking around. The guys, apparently, had some kind of freaking night vision, so they seemed to know where we were going and what we were doing, but it wasn't until the sun's early rays started streaking the sky that I had a clue where we were.

Not that seeing a bunch of trees helped me determine my position *at all*.

So, a walk that should probably only take about an hour takes until the sun is up, beating down through the trees, because they're treating me like I'm made of glass. A sheen of sweat coats my skin and I wipe my brow with my forearm while Onyx and Dusk walk silently beside me and Phantom leads like he's the one in charge.

It's another twenty minutes before we make it to the large cave they'd shown me before full of shadow beasts. We go through the moss as before and circle deeper and deeper into the earth until we reach the massive cavern. There are men sleeping in various states of undress around the fire. None are completely naked, but none are completely dressed either. And the amount of muscle in this cave makes it look like the Gold's Gym models have all decided to commune together in this one cave.

A woman in a leather top with straps, torn to reveal her stomach covered in scars, comes down the stairs on the side of the cave. A strange eagerness fills me. Another woman, an actual woman! Yeah, she's a shadow beast, but us both being female is something, right? But I don't speak up because as she passes, the look she gives me--half grimace, half scowl--isn't one of friendship.

Damn it. I guess I'll be as good at making friends with the shadow beasts as I was with the fae...

We take the tunnel that we'd taken before, and it brings up unsettling memories of the strange drink, suddenly understanding my men, and a strange black cloud. We pass the unconscious guy, and I hesitate at the doorway. In a strange way, he reminds me of Rayne. They both have more delicate features than the shadow beasts, and the shade of almost-blonde hair. But it's more than that.

I take a step to go inside, and Phantom catches my arm.

"We're not here for that this time."

Well, that's good at least. "Who is he?" I ask, wanting to move closer to him.

"Adrik," he answers, and there's sadness in his voice. "Come on."

"What's wrong with him?"

I feel the tension instantly hit all of them, and hold my breath, but none of them answer. Glancing between the man and them, I decide this might be one thing best left alone.

For now.

I force myself to turn away from him, and then we move deeper into the cave. The tunnel is lit by candles, which give a definite old-world feel to the place. There are also the same glowing crystals as before, but there are fewer here.

"Where are we going?" I ask Dusk, who's walking beside me, but it's Phantom who turns around and answers.

"We're going to see a tribe elder. He's the oldest living member. He'll know what to do."

That's ominous since I don't know which part we'll be asking him about.

But I follow. And follow. And follow, because this is the cave that just doesn't end. We have to be halfway across the state by the time we come to a shoot of the tunnel that ends in a small room lit by rustic-looking lanterns. There's a man sitting in a small cocoon chair hanging from the ceiling, a cocoon chair that reminds me of a hammock. His feet rest on the ground though, and he seems content. He's just reading a dog-eared copy of a leather-bound book and has a pair of glasses perched halfway down his nose, turned a little to catch the light of the flames from a fire in one corner.

Phantom approaches him slowly and gives a little bow. I don't know why that surprises me, but I expected a secret handshake or something similar. Anything but this formal bow that feels more like the actions of a prince than the shadow beasts I've met so far.

"Hello, *Solemus*," he says to both Phantom and Dusk with a bow of his own, before giving a nod to Onyx.

"Hello, Elder Auero," Phantom says, and his expression is grim.

Dusk and Onyx make their way forward to greet the old man, who looks a little like Sam Elliot but sounds a lot like Sean Connery. He has shorter hair than the others, but still touching his neck. It's pure white in color, and his eyes are a light brown. He has a thick white mustache and no beard, but he does have an easy smile.

He's not at all what I expected one of their elders to look like, in all honesty. Yes, it's true that the fae have a lot of old traditions, and that those traditions often merge with newer, more modern technology, but I thought this elder would be sitting in a corner over a fire, chanting to himself, for some reason.

He moves from his seat to another arrangement by the far wall, one closer to the fire. There are a bunch of fur cushions gather together on the floor, facing each other. I sit beside Phantom while Dusk sits across from us and Onyx remains standing against the wall. The old man walks toward us and sits in one spot that I suspect is his typical seat between us all.

Onyx watches Dusk, who seems ready to translate anything that Onyx might need. Or, maybe, there's another reason Onyx is watching Dusk. One that I have no clue about.

More secrets and mysteries...who would have thought?

"The shadows are whispering." The old man glances at me. "I guess you're the reason." His smile is serene and if not for the tension among us, I might smile back. But I don't. I sit with my hands folded in my lap and my body curled in so I don't accidentally rub shoulders with Phantom, who spent a very long night with his body pressed against mine. And I could feel everything from his shoulder to his knees.

Every. Single. Thing.

"Whispering?" Dusk asks, and I lean forward, eager for his answer.

Do the shadows really whisper to these people? And if

they do, what do they say? And what's so special about it this time?

"Fortunately, or unfortunately, yes." I like the elder's voice. It's smooth and rich and the accent is one of the most decadent sounds I've ever heard.

"It's been foretold that the end of this chaos will be brought when a light fae," his pointed look is directed at me, "and the shadow beasts are mated." He looks at Phantom who nods, then at Dusk and Onyx. They all turn to look at me. "The bond must be made if there is any hope of defeating the Shadow King and saving this planet from his creatures."

Mated. Bonded. These aren't words I'm particularly overjoyed to hear, even though I'm hearing them a hell of a lot right now.

I shake my head. "No. No. Not me. I'm not...mating or bonding. No." I hold up a hand and stand. "Whatever world saving you guys are doing, it seems you were fine before me, and likely will be fine without me. So, the answer is no." Four pairs of eyes are pointed at me and not a single person in this cave is smiling. Me included.

But I don't care. Let them stare. I already had a mate once and I lost him. It tore out my heart and destroyed something inside of me that can never be repaired. So even if by some miracle I could have another mate, I wouldn't.

I will never hurt like that again.

Onyx begins to sign from his spot by the wall, and Dusk speaks for him. "Are you sure? There's no other way?"

The Elder shrugs. "I am not the Moon Goddess. I do not know everything. But I have listened closely to the shadows, and they are excited. They see this as a chance to win, not just a battle, but the war." He hesitates, his gaze moving to me. "But you should mate her soon, or it could open us up to more dangers."

"Moon Goddess? War? Danger?" I give a humorless laugh. "You guys get that I'm just a normal light fae, right? That if you hadn't kidnapped me, I'd probably be taking classes right now and worrying about finals. Not...saving the world from whatever imaginary thing you're afraid of."

Not that the trolls and monkeys are imaginary...

Dusk moves to stand in front of me. "Ann, there is a dark cloud waiting to take over this world." He tilts his head as if that is the thing that's going to change my mind or make him look more sincere. "The Shadow King isn't going to stop sending rot monkeys armed with moon stone shards. And once they're in place and the cloud spreads, he will block out the sun, and people will die. The earth won't be inhabitable."

Wait. What? I stare at them in shock and confusion.

Phantom stands on the other side of me. "And you can save them."

My gut churns. *No, I can't save everyone from some magical cloud. There's no way.*

"By mating with you I'll save the world?" I look at Dusk. "But not just you, you too." Then at Onyx. "And you."

And what girl wouldn't consider having these hotties as anything but good luck? But there's too much pressure. This isn't like when Esmeray fell for Rayne's best friends. No, she had never had a mate before. She'd never really loved before or lost before. We were different people. And I am not someone who is ready for *any* of this. I'm not someone who can handle any of this.

Besides, I'd had my mate. "Isn't it possible that you guys have this wrong? That I'm not even your mate?"

This time, they all look at me like I'm a fool, but

Phantom is the one to answer. "No. The mate bond is as real as this cave. It's not something that can be questioned. We feel it with each breath we take. We feel it down to the deepest parts of our souls."

"Then why don't I feel it?"

A hurt expression comes over Phantom's face. He opens his mouth, then closes it.

"Are you sure you don't?" Dusk asks softly. "Because I think you do, you're just trying to ignore it."

I don't want to hurt them, but I want to be clear. "I've felt a mate bond before. With Rayne. My kind usually only ever have one mate... Well, they can have more than one at a time, but typically they feel the connection all at the same time. They don't have one mate, lose them, and then walk down the road and find another mate. That's just not how it works!"

"Our connection can't be wrong," Phantom says.

Onyx signs something with a frown.

Dusk glares back at him. "Even if it isn't convenient, it's not wrong."

I shake my head. "How is it that you guys aren't getting this?" I feel tears prick my eyes. "My mate died not so long ago. I still miss him each and every day. You guys aren't my mates."

"Be reasonable," Phantom says.

My spine stiffens, and I know I either need to get angry or cry. "You be reasonable. Because you might see me as your mate and some weird piece to some weird puzzle, but you're just the guys who kidnapped me to me!"

I walk out of the cave into the tunnel and make my way along to the main cave. At first, I'm just storming along, but my anger seems to fade with each step I take until I'm pretty sure I'm just going to start crying.

Was I mean to them? I can't imagine feeling like someone was my mate and them saying those things to me. But at the same time, I'm right. I don't feel the connection like I did with Rayne. Yes, I feel something, something I've never felt with any other men, but that doesn't make us mates.

I'm suddenly striding past a familiar cave. I pause in my steps and look inside. The unconscious guy is still there, like some kind of strange Sleeping Beauty. *Is he in a coma? Is it something else?* I don't know, but I feel compelled to go closer to him. And I can't help but be curious about these hands of mine. *Can they help whatever's wrong with him?*

Looking in both directions in the tunnel, I see no one. Biting my lip, I get the sinking sensation that this is a bad idea, but I enter the room anyway and cross the space to stand beside him.

When I crouch next to him, he doesn't move. Doesn't even shift. But the slow rise and fall of his chest isn't normal either, human or not. It's jerky and uneven. Like someone fighting for breath.

That's not good.

Reaching out, I push back the hair from his forehead and stare down at his handsome face. He really does remind me of Rayne in a way I don't quite understand. Rayne rarely ever slept. He was so focused on solving the problems of our world and uncovering the secrets of our kind.

But even though I don't understand why they feel similar to me, I have a yearning to try to save him. If only for the fact that he's a young man who seems to be slowly dying.

I try to summon the power to my hands, to focus on the energy inside of me. At first, I just stare at my hands. Then, I glare at them. When nothing happens, I try to remember how I was feeling when I healed Onyx. I wasn't really thinking about my hands, I was thinking about my desire to save him.

My hands suddenly glow. They're brighter in this cave, somehow. They're a bluish light stronger than the moon. And as I picture the moon, their glow seems to brighten, and I feel a strange tingle move through my body. It makes a strange warmth spread over me like lying in the sun. *What did the healers call this? Life force?*

Yes, that's what they called it. Life force. A power you take from deep inside yourself and push into another person. Even though I don't understand why this ability would awaken within me so late in life, I don't care. I'm strangely glad it's here. And, right now, all I want is to push this energy into this man and see if it can help him.

So, I touch him, lightly pressing my hands on his head.

To my shock, he moans as if in pain.

I'm trembling. *What if what I'm doing is wrong? What if I hurt him worse than he already is?* In some strange way it feels like I'm both trying to save Rayne, and may watch him die all over again.

It's scary, but for some reason, I don't stop.

After a second, I move my hands down to his shoulders, over his heart, down to his ribcage. I don't know exactly what I'm doing, but it feels right. Like falling asleep or waking up. Something that's so normal that I don't even have to think to do it.

A breath fills his lungs, a bigger breath than before, and then his breathing evens out.

I leave my hands there for a long minute, but the glow from them fades away. Whatever this new magic had done, it was finished. And based on his breathing, it must have helped something.

But what? And will it be enough?

"Something is better than nothing." I whisper to myself.

But this absolutely doesn't mean I've developed any kind of interest in saving the world. I just couldn't watch this one man die without trying to help.

I have no desire whatsoever.

ELEVEN

Onyx

I'M USUALLY NOT one to complain. As a man not born to a life of privilege, I understand hard work. I understand having to do distasteful tasks for the good of all of us. But this, *this* I don't like.

Why do I have to take Ann home?

Probably because I won't be able to hear her excuses, her complaints, and what has been described by Dusk and Phantom as whining. Plus, I lost the Rock, Paper, Scissors game, a strange game that we learned from the fae that the others like.

But I'm the only one who doesn't want *to get stuck with her, so how is this fair?*

Throughout the night, my headache had woken me up a few times. And each time I'd looked over, either Phantom or Dusk was snuggling with the woman as if they'd already mated her. I knew they hadn't. But I also expected it had more to do with the fact they'd given her their hearts than anything else.

"Hey, we both know you don't like me, so why not just let me go?" She had stopped walking and turned so that I could read the question on her lips.

It's strange. Most of the shadow beasts took time to figure out that they could communicate with me, both with their hands and by letting me read their lips. They would turn away from me while talking, and then realize I hadn't "heard" most of what they'd said. But this Ann had picked up on the fact too quickly.

Which makes it harder to ignore her.

I point to the path back to our smaller cave with my free hand, then tuck the small package I'm carrying beneath my arm.

She glares, and I don't need to read her lips to know what she's thinking. But still, the delightful woman slowly mouths the word, "Ass."

I smirk at her, trying not to admire her attitude. "Walk," I mouth right back.

Flipping that ponytail over her slender shoulders, she lets it fall back along her spine and continues marching in front of me. Yeah, march. Be mad. Because I *really* want to be babysitting you right now. Even while the angry thoughts enter my mind, my treacherous gaze goes to her ass. Ann is not as lean as our women, but I find her shapely rear end surprisingly pleasant.

If she wasn't her, and I wasn't trying to save the world...

But no, those kinds of thoughts would get me nowhere. From a young age I had discovered that few people could be trusted. Most would slit your throat in your sleep for something you'd willingly give them. My own mother sold me at just a few years old.

I still remember her smile as she shoved me toward the captain and said goodbye over her shoulder. She tossed that bag of coins up and down as she walked away, whistling. There wasn't even a hug, not even in our final moment together. Just a sense that I would never see her again.

Most kids would have followed her, but I knew that wouldn't matter. My mom had wanted to be rid of me, and she had. And this Ann? She wants to be rid of me too. Eventually, I'm sure she'll be successful.

My gaze returns to her. She's still walking with purpose--fast with strides as long as her legs allow--but it's not quite enough to keep up with me.

Sighing, I move around her and see her lips form the word, "Ass," again.

Fine, at least the feeling is mutual.

I try to remain three steps ahead of her now. It seems to quicken our pace through the woods, although every time I look back, I see that she's struggling to keep up with me. I try to not feel bad about it. If she wants to survive out here, she'll need to get faster and stronger.

But deep down I know I'm not walking ahead of her just to get her in fighting shape. It's as much to find danger before it finds her as it is so I don't have to pretend to care that she's huffing and puffing. Every once in a while, I see a tear that trails down her cheeks. Each one rips my heart out, until I force myself to stop looking behind me.

Feeling sorry for her, growing attached to her, accomplishes nothing.

I stiffen when I sense something behind me and freeze when I see that she's hurried up to me. Her hand is outstretched, as if she planned to touch me. "I need to rest," she mouths.

I shake my head. No, we can't rest. But I could carry

her. I sign that back to her, then realizing she's not under-standing me, sign more slowly, pointing from her to my shoulder.

"Not a chance!" she mouths, and I can tell by her face that she's mad. "I don't want you touching me."

Oh, really? She doesn't want me touching her? Fine, then she can enjoy the rest of our walk.

Spinning on my heel, I keep marching, only briefly glancing back to see her dragging herself along behind me.

The truth is, as much as I hate it, all she has to do to make this thing right is agree to mate with us, to form a bond. It's not like we're going to sacrifice her in some reli-gious virgin ceremony. I mean, I don't know the exact cere-monial procedure, if there even is one, but I highly doubt we're sacrificing our light fae to save the world. At least, that doesn't really make sense in the grand scheme.

Because even though I don't want her as my mate and I don't want to focus on this sulky woman, if what the elder had said was true, that accepting the mate bond could end this war with us as the victors, I would accept the mate bond and move on.

I'd decided it in the cave. But now, I'm rethinking my decision. *Is winning the war really worth dealing with her?* I don't really mean it, any price is worth defeating the Shadow King, but I am frustrated as hell.

I glance back at her. Even in her anger and frustration, she's lovely. And her spirit isn't exactly lacking. *We could certainly do worse in a partner.*

Mating, in my opinion, doesn't sound *all* bad. As a matter of fact, it's been a while since I "mated" with anyone. So, to me, *mating* sounds damned nice. Even with the irri-tating light fae.

But I try to keep my back to her and stay silent.

She lays her hand on my shoulder, and I stop and look at her. My breath hitches but I cover it with a cough I can't hear. Damn. She's beautiful.

Her mouth says, "Can we *please* take a break for a few minutes?" but her hands say "Buy me a seat." A few of the other words she's trying to sign are wrong, but I'm barely paying attention to them. I'm reading her mouth.

I do, however, appreciate that she's trying.

Sighing, I stop. I guess we've made *okay* time. Not how quickly I could go on my own, but we're getting close. So, we stop, and I lean against a tree, shuffling the leather-wrapped package under my arm, and watch her.

"What?" she asks.

I just lift a brow. What does she think? Does she think it's easy to babysit her and go so slowly that a quick trip cuts through far too much of our daylight hours?

She shoots me a glare, and I shake my head and roll my eyes. Women hate that. As a matter of fact, everyone universally hates the go-to-hell eyeroll. It's why I use it with a degree of undeniable success.

When she walks in front of me, she pops her hands onto her hips. "I know, okay? I know you think I'm selfish, and that I don't care, but I can't bond or mate or whatever this stupid idea of that old guy's is."

Stupid old guy? This woman is arrogant. And I'll just say it. She's high maintenance. Not that she's asked for anything much over the last couple days besides food and warmth, but she *has* whined a lot. Even when I showed her the clothes that Imara, the only female shadow beast in this world, had lent her, Ann had simply wrinkled her nose at them. I'd still brought them, tucked under one arm, but I wanted to toss them back to Imara and tell her the female didn't appreciate them, so didn't deserve them.

With my hands, I tell her she's selfish and that because of her children will die. This planet will die. I add the appropriate grimaces and scowls as I sign. It's chicken shit to say these things to her this way because she can't understand them but she understands the anger, maybe even the disappointment.

Not because she won't mate with us, but because...just because.

She hasn't said a word, probably hasn't deciphered the signs I've used to insult her. But she turns and stomps off like she has a fucking clue where she's going. At least she's going in the right direction, so I follow. But this time I stay a couple of steps behind her.

It's daytime and shadow creatures will all be fast asleep right now since they can only wreak their havoc in the dark of night. And knowing what she can do, I'm not a hundred percent certain she would need me or that I could even be more effective than she could. Still, it isn't in my nature to leave her to flounder on her own, even if I'm only backup.

We come to the river by our cave. She stops at the edge of it, then looks back at me.

I lift a brow. It's a river, so what?

She mouths, "I want to wash up."

Wash up? An image of her naked makes my mouth run dry. My gaze sweeps from her toes all the way up, and I feel my cock hardening with every inch of her body I imagine. When I come to her face, she's staring at me, one brow lifted.

I straighten, then toss the bag containing the spare clothes at her.

She takes it, nibbles her bottom lip, then looks back at me. "How about some privacy?"

Privacy? Our women prefer safety to privacy. Even in

the large cave, our shadow beast female bathes in the center of the cavern. The men do their best to be respectful, and the female is not left out in the open for any attacks.

I start to shake my head, but her entire frame goes rigid.

"I am not letting you see me naked," her mouth says, as she draws out each word.

Damn it. The stubborn woman does need to bathe.

I give a curt nod, then turn around and walk a few steps to a tree at the edge of the woods. A sudden instinct has me turning back, just to be sure she isn't running for it. But she's still standing in the same position, glaring at me.

When our eyes meet, she points to my eyes, then at the forest behind me.

Okay, yes, I'll look away. She asked for privacy, so I will give it to her.

She reaches for the hem of her shirt, and I forget to breathe. She snaps her fingers in front of her, and I remember that I'm supposed to be turned around, and do so. I only subtly glance back once to see her toss her shirt on the ground, to be sure this isn't all some ploy of hers.

After that, I keep my gaze on the woods, missing my hearing. If I could hear, I'd know if she was splashing around. I'd hear her if she was in trouble, or if she was screaming for me. With my back turned to her, I feel like I have to let my instincts stretch out around me, to warm me if trouble has come.

Still, the seconds turn to minutes, and the minutes seem to stretch on forever.

I'm about to turn back, the hell with what I told her, when I feel someone behind me. I wait, trying to decide if I'm about to be attacked, or if it's her, when I feel a light tapping on my shoulder.

Turning around slowly, I see Ann. Her hair is wet, and braided once more down her back. She's carrying her old clothes, wet and freshly washed, in her arms. And she's wearing one of Imara's outfits. It's cut to show her belly, and seems to stretch a little more over Ann's fuller breasts. I'm a bit surprised, as I stare at her, how pale the skin of her stomach is. And how much I like the way the brown leather hugs her shorter legs. The ends have been rolled up above her boots, probably because Imara is so much taller, but somehow it suits the little fae woman.

I find myself smiling.

"Better?" She mouths the word, playing with a loose hair.

I lift my hand, almost touching her face, then draw my hand back. She doesn't want a mate. She doesn't want me or the others. I can't imagine she'd want me to touch her either.

And yet, as I drop my hand, I get the sense that she's disappointed.

Instead, I nod in the direction we must go.

She nods back, and then starts walking again. We're almost home, so when she seems to hurry to avoid me, I let her get a little space between us. Or, maybe I need the space away from her too. Not just because my dick is straining in my pants, but because I need to remember that I don't want a mate.

A fact that keeps getting harder to believe.

Right about now, I wish the others were with me, especially because I feel their reason for remaining behind was stupid. Phantom and Dusk wanted to speak with the elder to learn more of the details about the whispers he'd heard from the shadows about Ann. But whatever he'd heard, it probably didn't matter, because she refused to be our mate.

They also wanted to ask about her powers. Which, again, don't seem worth discussing, even though I'm curious too. Because there aren't any other light fae around. None that we've come across anyway. So even if we realize the fae have some kind of awesome power, we don't exactly have an army of them to fight the coming battle with.

Ann veers a little out of sight as I keep my pace slow, she disappears behind a tree or bush, then reappears as I catch up with her a second later. It doesn't really matter, this close to the cave, in the daylight, with just a few extra feet between us. I'm near enough to mitigate any danger.

The thought makes me complacent. Lazy, even. I look away for a couple seconds--literally two--and it's a mistake.

Fucking hell.

Somehow my troublesome thoughts got me a little turned around, and I didn't realize she'd veered a little from the path to our cave. She's found the Void. *Or maybe it's found her.* Knowing what I know about her now, that's even possible. *How hadn't I realized she overshot the cave? She's not ready to see so much so soon, nor should she be this close to it.*

I haven't used my voice in so long that when I try to shout at her, to make a sound to warn her away from it, nothing comes. Not even a vibration from my throat.

My feet are moving faster before I know what I'm doing. Her eyes are wide, and she reaches one hand out as if to touch it. Her fingers don't come close to it, but it doesn't matter. The Void drags her in.

Her arms flail and her mouth is open in a scream.

Normally, I'd be slowing down right now. Staying far enough away from the Void to be sure I couldn't be pulled in also. But none of that matters now. I have no choice, no other way to save her than to go in after her.

And so, I leap in before I even have the chance to look, knowing that I won't live long enough to tell the others how our lives ended.

TWELVE

Ann

BY THE TIME my eyes adjust to the darkness of this place, I've been clawed and scratched by those same kinds of monkeys Dusk fought in the woods as they drag me I don't even know where. Sounds--cries, squeals, screams, and screeches--assault me so that I want to cover my ears, but I don't want to show fear because this is the kind of place that probably feeds off of fear.

A place of nightmares...

The monkeys move away from me a little bit, but I'm still in a circle of them. A sea of glowing red eyes in a world that shouldn't be able to exist. When I look up at the sky in terror, I see nothing. No sun. No moon. No clouds. It's as if a blanket has been cast over this world. A blanket of grey, as if some small light source exists, somewhere in the sky. Enough to make out the things around me.

But not enough to allow any kind of life to survive.

I wrap my arms around my knees, pulling them closer to

my chest as some of the monkeys race around me. Some small part of me wants to understand where I am, and if there's any way out. But the little bit of the world I can see outside of the monkeys doesn't give me hope.

In fact, it terrifies me.

It's a replica of the world I live in, but without any sort of nurturing or life. It's like a twisted version of the forest I've been yanked from, but where my world has trees, lush moss, and waving grasses, this is a wasteland of death, brown and burned. Everything here is dead. And it looks as though, as I'm propelled forward, that I am about to join those ranks.

What the hell have I gotten myself into?

I try to stand, and a monkey knocks me onto my back on the ground. Their screeching grows louder, and they slash at me as I try to curl back around myself. It seems they aren't ready to attack yet, unless I try to stand or escape.

Noted.

But then, how in the hell am I going to get free? *I can use my touch on them. But will it work here? On this many of them?* My gaze darts around me as movement stirs behind the blackened, charred forest of leafless trees and the huge boulders that seem to litter the ground. The ground itself begins to vibrate beneath me, and "What the hell?" explodes from my lips.

My arrival seems to have summoned all the creatures in the area to come to this place. On one side, there's a tribe of monkeys with glowing red eyes and fur the color of coal lined as far as I can see in the small clearing in the woods around me, and a half a dozen trolls, large and ugly, leering and drooling, on the other side. Where the two groups meet, there is a slim void and through there I see him--the Shadow King.

Because that's the only person it could be. I feel it to my *core*.

As if he knows I'm looking at him, he drops his chin, turns his head, and smiles. *Smirks* might be a more accurate description, but I'm willing to wait until he speaks to decide. Unlike the shadow beasts, his dark hair is trimmed, and his green eyes are small and sunken deep into a thin face. He wears black leather that encases him like a king, rather than a warrior, but whispers he can still kick ass if needed. His gaze clings to mine, and he holds up his hand and slides it to the left before he turns to look at me, then drops his hand in a quick motion.

Suddenly, the sound stops. *All* sound stops. And had birds been able to survive here, I could've heard one shedding a feather.

This isn't good. None of this is good.

I try to recall everything I've learned up until this point from the shadow beasts, and all I seem to remember is that this man is bad. That he's their enemy. And somehow, he's tied to this plan to destroy my world.

So, definitely not a good guy. Not at all.

But what does he want with me?

"You are as luscious as my watcher said." He slaps one of the trolls on the back, gives him a shoulder squeeze, and makes it look like one smooth move as he makes his way toward me. "I think I'm going to enjoy being married to you almost as much as I'm going to enjoy us taking over your world."

Married. Mated. Bonded. There's a disturbing trend happening in my day.

"Married?" The word slips from my lips, but it's barely louder than a whisper.

The Shadow King wants me to marry him. Maybe I

should be flattered. He's a king. Who doesn't want to be queen? But the answer comes easily. Me. Especially a queen to a Shadow King whose minions look like something out of a twisted version of a child's cartoon.

Oh yeah, and a psycho who wants to destroy my world.

And like he can read my mind, the king lifts an eyebrow. There's something about him... He's almost handsome in a wicked sort of way. Familiar, too, but I can't place why. Maybe it's because dark hair and green eyes is a rare combination, but it feels like more than that.

Another question without an answer.

When he gets about ten feet from me, the monkeys part in his wake, and he stops walking. He eyes me up and down as he purses his lips like he's about to blow me a kiss. "Oh, yes. I do so look forward to the wedding night." There's something about his cadence too. It's like he's jovial and dangerous all at once. The combination is both strange and unsettling. But like someone has tapped his shoulder, he turns to his side. There's no one there, but he frowns, tilts his head for a second, then smiles at me. "So, what do you say, my future queen? What do you say to the man who is going to give you everything?" His gaze appraises me, and his tongue slides along his lip. "And give you a wedding night to remember."

What is this guy? Some kind of gross villain from a cheesy play? Wedding night? No, sir.

I look behind me and eye the direction I'd come in this place from. It looks like a wall of black oil, except it moves and slides, twisting in the air like smoke. Technically, there are only a few of the monkeys between me and that wall, but I can't imagine a way in which I can reach it before they, or this king, can catch me. Still, if the right opportunity presents itself, I'll try.

Until then, I need to buy myself some time.

"Well, as lovely as your proposal is, and as enchanting as I'm sure the wedding night would be, I'm afraid I have to decline." I'm babbling out a ridiculous number of words, words that make me sick to even say.

But as hard as I'd tried not to tell him the idea made me want to vomit, his eyes flash with rage, as if I had actually said the harsher words I'd wanted to say. I rise slowly to my feet, eyeing both him and the monkeys, and I back up a step because this guy's cool appraisal has turned murderous.

"Respectfully, of course." I back up two more paces, and he moves faster than I can see and takes my face in his hand. His touch is harsh, painful, as he squeezes my jaw until a small cry of pain escapes my lips. But he doesn't seem to care. He jerks my chin up so that I'm forced to look directly into his cold, cruel eyes.

I shiver. *This man wants to hurt me. Not just me, but everyone.*

But instead of smiting me, or whatever the king of the shadows can do, he cocks his head then throws it back and laughs. The sound is not what I expect. "Of course, you'll marry me." He grins and lets go of my face. It burns where he grabbed me, but I breathe out a slow breath. "I'm charming. And handsome."

If you have to say it, it's probably not true...

But I nod because there's no advantage to telling him he isn't my type. Probably because if I was the evil form of myself, this guy--a little old maybe--would be right in my wheelhouse. But it's sort of like seeing a hot picture of a murderer on TV. The first time you see him, you might think, "Oh, nice!" But the second you hear his list of crimes, your vagina feels like it closes like a steel trap.

And I'm a steel trap right now, in every way. No, I definitely don't want this guy. He scares the hell out of me, and I'm pretty sure whatever the guys were trying to warn me about, this man is a lot worse.

A cold shiver passes through me. *I need to escape. But how?*

There's a small sound behind me. Like I've dreamed him into being, Onyx comes exploding from the dark cloud, splits through the crowd of monkeys, running like he's taking the ball into the end zone, and throws his arms around me. I barely have a moment to gasp, when he drags me backward and away from the king.

I see the king's shocked expression as we're bolting to our escape. The monkeys go wild, but Onyx punts the ones that cross our path away. A roar sound behind us that seems to echo through the entire world, and I see a giant dragon made of smoke rising into the air like a demon of vengeance.

"Onyx!" the king roars.

The trolls advance, and one has a staff. It's long and curved, like a cane but with a bladed end. He launches it, and I see it coming straight at me and twist in Onyx's arms. He reacts in an instant, shielding me with his big body before I can stop him.

The cane is a blur of motion above us, and then Onyx stumbles like he's drunk and about to hit the ground. I can see the blade sticking out of him from behind, but the man just keeps stepping forward in an unnatural way. I look in front of us to see how close we are to our escape and see that we're nearly at the wall of smoky tar.

I can almost see outside of the cloud to our own world. And I might be imagining it, but I think I can hear the whistle of wind. *We're so damned close to getting free of this nightmare!* I need to get Onyx out of this place. *Now!*

His face is pale. His feet seem to be moving more and

more slowly, and he's leaning on me so hard I think we might fall over. He's heavy, but I wrap both hands around his waist and drag him. The screeching of the monkeys' grows louder. The ground shakes as the trolls approach us, and I hear the shadow king scream something although I'm not sure what. And then, suddenly, we're through the wall of black tarry smoke.

"We made it," I whisper, but my voice shakes.

I keep dragging Onyx as far as I can, even though he seems to be getting heavier and heavier, but I don't want to stop. Not until I can't see the cloud of black any longer. But when we're almost out of view of it, Onyx crumbles to his knees.

His eyes keep fluttering closed. I kneel in front of him, trying to catch his eye. Trying to get him in a position so he can read my lips. "I'm going to heal you, okay? You freaking brave man! I'm not going to let you die because you tried to save me."

While I'm speaking, his eyes close, and my heart races.

"I got this. I got this. I can do this." I know he can't hear me, but I need to say the words, even just to myself.

Awkwardly, I try to reach around him to work on the staff. Normally, I know it'd be better to leave the staff where it is until we could get to a hospital. But since there's no hospital anywhere around, and we only have me, I know we need to get the staff out before I can try to help him. Pulling it out slowly, an inch at a time, I grit my teeth together. Onyx moans and makes a few sounds of pain that make my gut clench. But as much as I want to stop, I know I can't.

So, I just keep working, inching it out, but the damn thing is in deep. But finally, it works free, and as I toss it aside, he falls, then coughs, and blood spatters the ground beside his head.

It doesn't take a PhD in internal medicine to know this is bad. My heart hammers.

"You're going to be okay. Remember my glowy hands. They can fix anything."

I try not to notice the blood that spreads beneath him onto the ground, or the way it seems to be expanding faster than it should. Because no matter how bad things are, I can't let him die. Not after he risked his life to come in after me.

After he saved my life.

I'm going to do whatever I can to save him. But I have to do it quickly.

Trying not to look at his pale face, or the way his chest rises and falls erratically, I breathe in slowly. I try to center my thoughts the way I had before. I try to focus on healing him.

As I concentrate, I feel the power inside of me vibrate. It feels natural, almost the way I imagine it feels when someone is an amazing athlete and catches a ball, without even knowing it was coming. My hands begin to glow and I close my eyes, then lay my hands on his wound and let the healing force surge from me to him.

It's working!

Almost before I've finished, Onyx is moving on his own to sit up. I try to gently push him back down, but he sits up fully, and my hands drop away. He looks at me, then down at the blood that stains the ground.

"Thank you," he signs.

I sign right back at him, "Thank you." Then, because I don't know the other words, I say, "For saving my life. For going into that place after me."

Even though he still looks pale and exhausted, he nods his head, a small smile curling his lips. I'm surprised when he takes my hand covered in his blood and squeezes it. As I gaze into his eyes, such a dark brown they're almost black, warmth flows through me followed by butterflies in my stomach. This man is so damned handsome. And when he smiles, he's absolutely breathtaking.

"You should smile more," I say.

"Ann! Ann!"

It's Phantom, and he sounds scared.

"We're over here! But Onyx was hurt!"

A second later, Phantom and Dusk come exploding out of the trees. They both have their swords out, but when they see us, they look around as if expecting trouble, then their swords slowly drop to their sides.

And then, Dusk seems to spot the staff. "How the hell is that here?"

I don't know what to say. "We...had some trouble."

Their faces fall, and they both resheath their swords, then join us. Phantom kneels down and begins frantically signing to Onyx. He responds, more slowly. All three of the men's gazes keep snapping to me, then back to Onyx's signing.

Oh boy, if they didn't think I was useless before, I'm sure they do now.

Finally, the signing stops, and Dusk picks up the staff I tossed aside and looks at Phantom. "Shit."

And I don't know what he means by it and certainly we aren't at a place in our...friendship...where he would tell me, but I agree completely.

THIRTEEN

Dusk

"WHAT DO WE DO NOW?" Ann asks, and there's a quiet worry in her voice.

Onyx and I exchange a look, and then I speak. "Getting close to the Void is never a good idea, but normally, the creatures within cannot reach us during the daylight. The fact that they were able to drag you in says they're getting stronger."

"What does that mean?"

I try to phrase my answer in the least scary way possible. "You know those shiny shards you found?"

She nods.

"They are pieces from a moonstone." Just mentioning the name of the precious item makes my stomach turn. Dark memories boil up, and I have to push them away. "The Shadow King has tasked his rot monkeys with planting the shards at night. It takes a great deal of his power to keep his creatures from...shattering in this bright world, even beneath the moonlight, so he is limited by how many he can send and how often he can send them. But if he leaves enough of the moon shards here to create a ring around the Void, he'll be able to use his powers to expand his world. And once it expands, everything trapped inside the Void will be consumed by the darkness. He'll use that power to spread the Void further and further until this entire world is gone."

She stares, and I'm not quite sure if she's having trouble picturing what I'm describing or if she doesn't want to understand the implications of what I'm saying.

"So why don't you just remove all the shards?"

Onyx signs, "Is she fucking serious?"

I glare at him, and Phantom answers her. "The shards are nearly invisible. They cast a small light on their own, but during the day, we can't see it at all. And at night, we search for the shards, but miss many of them. We really have no idea how many the king already has here, nor how much time we have left before he has enough to destroy us all."

"But the way I saw them glow...was really bright and really obvious."

"Exactly. For you," Phantom says, letting the words hang between us.

Her eyes brighten. "So that might be part of why the elder thought I could help? Because they light up for me, so I can actually find them?"

"Yes," he says.

Onyx signs, "She's conveniently forgetting that she's supposed to accept our mate bond to really be able to help us win this war."

I sign back, "One thing at a time. Now, lay back, you

idiot. Rest. We don't know exactly how her healing works, but it's best to be careful."

He glares at me from his bedroll and takes a sip of his soup like he's a child I'm punishing.

"I want to go back home," Ann says. I open my mouth to argue with her, but she continues. "But after being inside that place... I can see why you don't want it spreading. I could stay, for a while, and help find the shards."

"Progress," Onyx signs to us.

Yeah, it really is. "That would be wonderful."

Phantom refills all our bowls of soup, and I go with Onyx to watch over him while he bathes, bathing myself at the same time. Then, we swap with Phantom and Ann, giving them a chance to bathe in the river, although neither Onyx nor I can help looking after them in longing.

When we're all done and the camp is clean and ready for the next night, we fall asleep. Ann, surprisingly, lays by me, but she doesn't touch me. She just gives a little moan, turns her back on me, and is asleep within minutes.

Good. We'll let her sleep now, because in a few hours, there will be work to do. Namely, work to see if all the shards will react to Ann the way the other ones had. And then, to see how many of them we can collect before the night falls. And we have to be ready for an all-out war.

With enough shards collected, hopefully the king will be weakened enough that things won't get too bad.

Hours later, I blink awake as Phantom shakes me. "It's time."

He shakes Ann too, although far gentler, and she mutters, "Wake me up, and I'll put a fork in your eye."

We both laugh, and Phantom goes to wake Onyx. Hopefully, he's feeling a little better. Because as much as

142 LACEY CARTER ANDERSEN

we'd love for him to spend the rest of the day resting, we just ticked off the Shadow King.

And that *always* has consequences. Consequences I remember far too well.

Onyx signs to us, "What do you think about the Shadow King wanting Ann as his bride?"

Phantom and I both stiffen.

Ann says, "I need you guys to teach me more signs and start telling me what he's saying. I feel left out."

Oh, right. We're so used to working like this I think we all kind of forgot. "He asked our thoughts about the king wanting you as his bride." Then, I start signing back while saying the words aloud, knowing this is one of the best ways for her to learn. "That means it's even more important to form our mate bond so he can't make her his bride without killing all of us."

Ann tenses. "I don't want him to try to kill all of us."

I sign as I talk. "He's already trying to kill all of us. The only difference is that right now, if he gets to you, things will get a lot more dangerous for you...for us...and for this world."

The elder had explained things to us very clearly. The shadows said whoever should marry the light fae will win this war. We asked if that could mean the Shadow King himself, and the elder winced and said it could. He made it very clear to us that although he would never ask us to force Ann to do anything, if the king got her, we'd all be in trouble.

Onyx signs, "The woman needs to accept the mate bond. This is stupid and dangerous," and I translate for him.

Ann's mouth pulls into a tense line. "I'm not willing to discuss that right now."

All three of us nod, but the frustration in the room is

palpable. Who would have thought when we finally found our mate, she'd reject us? Even when faced with a very dangerous possibility, like the king taking her for her own.

Which leads me down a dark path. Why does he want her in the first place? It would be enough for him to know it would destroy us to lose our mate, but I'm sure it's more than that. Does he know what the shadows are whispering? Does he know if our mate bond is solidified that we can win this war?

I hope not.

We ready ourselves, then step outside. As we knew it would happen, two warriors have come from the larger cave. Having a light fae in our circle is not only a novelty, but as it turns out, a necessity if we're to put an end to the chaos. And that starts by collecting the moonstone shards, as these warriors seem to have realized.

Our elder would have told them. Unfortunately.

"Hello," Slade calls. The big warrior has reddish brown hair, a large smile, and more scars than most of us. Whenever there was fighting afoot, Slade was always sure to be in the middle of it.

"Hello," Phantom greets, in a voice that is barely welcoming.

Flame looks at Ann. "We are Slade and Flame, shadow beasts and warriors, and we have come to help you in any way we can." Flame is almost the same height as Ann, but he has braids weaved throughout his hair, and there's no one better with a staff.

Both men stare at Ann as if she's a miracle. And I don't like it one bit. My only solace is the fact that Ann is regarding them like two very annoying children that she doesn't want to deal with.

When everyone continues staring at her, she does this

weird, awkward thing with her mouth and then says, "Uh, okay."

Both Flame and Slade seem a bit defeated. No doubt they hoped that, after only seeing one female for so long, Ann would be a bit more welcoming to two good-looking men. *Sorry, assholes, if Phantom and Onyx don't do it for her, you sure as hell won't.*

"We are glad to have you back, brothers," Slade says, and there's a solemn note to his voice.

"We're glad to be back," Phantom says with a little bob of his head.

"It wasn't easy these last few months without you, but Elder Auero explained your disappearance, and your capture by the fae." There's a note to Slade's voice I don't like. I can't decide if he's suggesting we got captured on purpose, or he's hinting it's an embarrassment that we allowed ourselves to be made prisoner by such weak creatures.

Either way, I don't like his tone.

"Since it led us to our mate, it must have been part of Fate's plan," I say, a warning in my voice.

Slade seems to have remembered just who he's talking to and gives a little bow to us all. "Of course. We only came to offer our help in collecting the moon shards."

I want to refuse him, but we can't be prideful in war. "We would appreciate that."

My brother lifts a brow, and I almost apologize before I remember that our roles aren't quite the same as what they once were, and that I can make decisions too now. In this world, my voice matters just as much as Phantom's.

When I remain silent, clearly not willing to bend to him, Phantom clears his throat. "We shouldn't waste any more time."

Despite the fact that darkness is looming near, we set out into the woods. The warriors, Slade and Flame, walk on each side of Ann and I follow closely behind, because no way do I trust these fuckers with her. Even if I trust them with my life, my mate is worth more to me than that.

They need to understand that she belongs to *us*. And any designs they have on claiming her for themselves, to be the heroes in a story that doesn't involve them, will be notions I disabuse them of.

At first, we're just kind of wandering around, but at one point, she just stops and switches directions. None of us say anything; we just watch her. When a stone shard suddenly lights up from a nearby bush, we all freeze. The light is so damn bright that even in daytime, it's obvious. She hurries to it, then hands it to Slade. He takes it with a shocked expression on his face before handing it to Phantom.

"Is this good?"

"Very good," is all I can manage.

She does it again. It's like we're all just walking together, and she freezes, and switches directions. I swear we're all in some kind of shocked stupor. After spending years combing the woods, hoping like hell to find a shard, digging through bushes, looking in the branches of trees, we've never seen anything like this. And yet, when the next shard starts glowing like mad, none of us are surprised, just overwhelmed.

I swear Slade is holding back tears when she gives him the next one, and Flame murmurs a thank you that's choked. Yes, we're big warriors. Yes, we've been through hell and back. But it's like we're all watching a miracle.

Even Phantom and Onyx look a little choked up.

She leads us to four or five shards within an hour or two, but there are more and she's like a bloodhound, her steps quick and decisive after she realizes she should follow her gut. I don't know that she knows how incredible what she's doing is, but either way, the joyous surprise on her face isn't the kind of thing she can fake. So, whether she knows how important this is or not, it's a good thing that she's happy about it. Not that I can think of a reason why she would want to fake it.

Our mate likes helping. And she has a skill that I've never seen before. She should be proud.

The shards glow brighter as she gets closer each and every time. And with every shard we collect, we take back some strength from the Void and the Shadow King himself. That we're only able to do this because of her strengthens my need to mate with her.

To make her mine.

I've never been so compelled...not even before our lives were destroyed. This desire to make things formal between us is more than a want, it's a *need*. The deep connection between us means that there is no one else for us but her, and that without her, we'll feel like we've lost a part of ourselves. But in the grand scheme of this war, making her our mate will be the thing that turns the tide. I know it! Not just because of the shadows' whispers, but because of her unique ability.

The desire to pull her into my arms, to tell her every-thing I'm thinking and more, is overwhelming. It builds inside of me until I'm panting. Does she understand? Can she even realize what all of this means?

I would marry someone I didn't love to save my people. But to have a woman who is destined to be our perfect mate? To have a woman who makes my heart race at just the sight of her be the person to save our people?

It's almost more than I can handle.

She looks at me. "Are you okay?" And there's a little worry in her eyes.

Smiling, I nod, not wanting to scare her off by telling her how I feel. "I'm fine. Just keep doing what you're doing. It's wonderful."

I push back the overwhelming feelings and stare at her as she picks up another shard and hands it to Flame. He's a bastard who's ogling her like she's lunch, and he has about three seconds to stop before I take his head off. She turns away from him, and his gaze goes to her ass. I feel my teeth clench together so hard I'm worried they'll break.

Flame hands the shard to Phantom, still staring at Ann. Phantom and I are the only two shadow beasts who have the ability to resist the call of the shards, but him more than me. Over the years, we've had to execute a couple of our kind who kept their shards, and let darkness into their hearts. But since then, luckily for all of us, the others have been quick to return any shards to us.

They avoid them, knowing that their pull is too strong to resist.

Even though Ann doesn't seem to have the same... connection to them.

She sets off walking again and Flame drops back. "She's something, isn't she?"

I give him a non-committal grunt and watch her. Ten steps after she's taken off left, she stops like she's listening. And even if it's just some inner voice, she makes a quick U-turn and goes back.

Slade shakes his head. "This is so fucking easy with her."

I nod. I search for shards all the time. Never have I found so many in such a drawn-out area. We've probably walked five miles already. This will quite literally change the way we work.

With every shard she hands off to Flame or Slade, their smiles spread. But by ability alone, she has a target on her back. After a while of suffering the fawning and flirting of Flame and Slade, she drops back to walk beside me. "What do you know about the Shadow King?"

Oh, that's a dangerous question. Not as dangerous as the answer, though. "Why do you ask?"

She shrugs one elegant shoulder. I stop walking. *Elegant shoulder?* Oh God. This mating bond situation has me spinning. I don't look at her again while I wait for her to answer. "He wants to marry me, so I figured I deserve to know more about him."

"He's a man who likes power more than anything," I say, choosing my words carefully.

"But...he's trapped there, right? He can't come to get me?"

"No, he can't. The king can't leave the shadow realm or it will cease to exist." It's true, we *think*, but it's a hell of a lot more complicated than that.

"So, he'll have to get me back there if he wants me?"

"Yes."

I sigh. None of this is good news. He not only knows about her, but he's decided he wants her for himself. He'll have every troll and monkey in his army hunting her like a Christmas goose. Probably using his powers to a level he never has before. The only way to save her is to convince her to mate with us, to perform the bonding ritual, not that she seems to understand the practicalities of that point.

Or that we don't like trying to push her toward the mate bond because it's a smart move. That's not what being together should be all about.

"And how did you guys become the official army to stop this guy?"

My gut clenches. "That's...complicated." And painful.

She seems to realize that I'm done talking. And, for once, she drops the topic. She goes back to hunting moon shards. As we come across more, we see more warriors hunting for them too. Yet every time another glows near her, the warriors stop their own searches and begin to trail her with awe in their eyes.

Before night has even fallen, the forest is crowded with warriors who are all watching her. She's the new toy for a bunch of warriors who haven't had anything to play with but themselves for a mighty long time. And they all want her.

But it's more than that. In the years that we've been protecting this world, all we've experienced is loss. Our numbers are a fourth of what they once were, and we carry every death in our hearts. At times it feels as if we're protecting a world that doesn't even know or appreciate all we had sacrificed for it. So, to watch this woman ease some of the burden from our shoulders...it's like watching hope take flight within all our men.

I overhear someone say, "She hasn't accepted the mate bond yet."

Another responds, "Why not?"

"No idea, but it means she hasn't been claimed. No one could blame us if..."

I turn around and punch the asshole square in the face. He hits the ground and looks at me with wide eyes, wiping the blood from his nose. The man he was speaking to stares at me like I've grown another head, and a growl slips from my lips.

Multiple warriors move away from me.

Onyx signs, "What's wrong?"

I sign back, while Phantom watches me, "They think that since the mate bond hasn't been completed, she can be claimed by anyone."

Onyx and Phantom's eyes narrow.

Flame holds up his hands as if in surrender. "We would never."

"Oh?" I say, and there's a threat in my voice.

Ann is suddenly in front of me. "What's wrong? What happened?"

"Nothing," Phantom snarls, his hands in fists.

But it doesn't matter how much we intimidate the other males. If Ann decides for some reason to pursue something with them, we can't stop her. Even the thought of it makes me sick, and something inside of me twists like a knife. I feel a desperate need rise inside of me.

"Everyone go ahead, we'll be there in a moment," I snap.

The other warriors look from Phantom to me. I know Ann is changing something inside of me. Normally, I don't give orders. My brother does. But when it comes to Ann, I can't seem to just wait and see if Phantom will do what I feel is best.

"Go," Phantom says, and the men quickly obey, not going far, but giving us just enough space to talk.

"Ann, you have to listen to me." I take her by the shoulders and turn her toward me so she can see how important this is. "You can never venture out without me, Phantom, or Onyx."

She shimmies her shoulders as if she's either dancing or she's trying to break free from my hold. The scowl says she isn't dancing. I let go and cross my arms.

"For my safety?"

I nod and she rolls her eyes. I hate that. "Yes. For your safety."

"Like mating is for my safety and not because you guys have some sort of group sex fetish?" Her words say she isn't about it, but a flare of desire darkens her eyes.

"Mating with you is for the good of us all." But she huffs away before I can explain.

She walks to the center of the group and looks at Flame. "We're done here. Take me back."

I warn him off with a look and get a glare in return, but he backs off and follows behind as I walk beside her while she stomps away. She's angry. I don't blame her for her confusion, but I do blame her for her unwillingness to do what has to be done for the good of all.

Onyx seems frustrated and signs that he'll get dinner. Phantom agrees to go with him. I look after them in longing. Ann has to be protected. She has to be watched. But I feel like I desperately need space from her. Every dirty look, every refusal, cuts me so deep inside that I feel like I'll never recover.

By the time we reach the cave, Phantom and Onyx have hunted dinner and it's on a spit over the fire in the center of the huge cavern. And while the warriors are enamored with Ann, they love food even more. And since they caught enough for us all, we invite them to join us. Yes, we're protective of our Ann, but we're not assholes.

Besides, while they're eating, she'll have a reprieve for a few minutes before they start trying to find ways to get close to her. To claim her for their own.

I brush past Phantom, feeling my anger rise.

"What's the matter with you?" he asks me, but we both know that what's the matter with me is the same thing that's the matter with him.

"Hungry," is all I manage.

He catches my arm and speaks in a whisper. "Do you think she'll come around before it's too late?"

His question is one without a clear answer. The truth is that if Ann doesn't want to step up and do her duty, if she doesn't agree to bond with us, the Shadow King will find a way--by either manipulation or force--to marry her, and then nothing else will matter. Now that he knows she's here, there's no way to keep her safe without guarding her every minute. And she's never going to allow that.

I nod to Ann, who's taken a flask of water from Flame and tips it back. Her neck lengthens as she drinks and I can't stop staring at her. "The Shadow King wants to marry her, and I don't know if we can stop him."

Phantom nods. "I don't know either." He blows out a harsh breath, eyes dark with anger. "But never again are we going to let a woman we love near the Shadow King." He speaks with quiet force. And I agree.

The loss is too much for my memory to bear.

FOURTEEN

Ann

WHILE THE OTHERS stay around the firepit in the center of the massive cavern, Dusk leads me away from them, up the steps along the walls of the cave, where he says I'll be safer from the Void and the creatures that took me. I don't argue because, even though it isn't fully dark yet and I suspect he isn't as worried about the Void as he is about the other men, he looks exhausted. And for some reason, I don't want to be the reason he looks so tired and worried.

Besides, if he really wants me inside the cave, he can put me there and likely make sure I never leave. As cool as all my new powers seem to be, they wouldn't exactly stop a giant like him from forcing me to stay somewhere. Although I doubt he would actually do that. Not so long as he thinks there's a chance we'll all be mating soon. *And also, because I actually think he seems to be a nice person.*

So, for now, I guess I'll take their protection, whether I really need it or not.

We stop outside a cave with a curtain across the front for privacy. "Onyx is inside," Dusk says, then casts a glance back the way he came. "Do you need anything else?"

I shake my head, push back the curtain, and walk in.

As my eyes adjust to the lack of light inside the cave, a blanket rustles and a man moans. *Onyx.* He had eaten a little with the others, then came back inside, a pained expression on his face.

He's still healing, even though he'd acted like he was all better. He'd had a deep and round wound. My touch might have removed the evidence of his injury, but I'm sure there was damage I couldn't see.

Even some of the most powerful fae healers don't have the power to heal an injury like that all at once, so I doubt I could either.

But in small bursts, so long as he doesn't get wild and reinjure himself, and my abilities don't wither and I don't end up married to the Shadow King, I should hopefully just keep getting stronger and better at all of this.

Going to the smaller fire inside the cave, I stir the embers, brightening the cave, and put more logs on it, along with kindling. Within a few seconds, it's definitely brighter. At least bright enough to see each other.

"Are you hurting?" I mouth to Onyx.

He lifts a brow, but doesn't even try to communicate back.

"Do you always have to be a stubborn ass?"

His expression is one of surprise for a few seconds before it's blank once more.

"You know, for a guy who keeps trying to get me to mate him, or whatever, you're not exactly being very nice. I mean, I don't know how dating and courting works where you're from, but where I'm from, guys try to be nice at the very least. But also romantic too."

He doesn't react, but he shifts, and then I see the pained look that shoots across his face.

Guilt eases some of my frustration. "You know, it's okay to hurt. You can tell me."

I go to sit beside him on his pile of blankets. It's much softer than it looks, and the blankets are plush beneath Onyx. He stares up at me, and I reach out to put my hand on his chest. The wound on his back is closed. Whatever injury is left is inside now.

"I'm going to try to heal you a little more."

He catches my hand, his expression unreadable.

"Trust me, okay?"

After a second, he releases me.

So, I look down at his expansion of perfect skin. I concentrate on the big man. His breathing is low and slow. Almost calm. But I didn't imagine the look of pain on his face, nor do I think he'd be laying down right now if he was feeling one hundred percent back to his old self before the injury.

His skin is surprisingly warm. And kind of nice. Hard and defined and really sexy, if I'm being honest with myself. For a second, I'm distracted, and sorely tempted to run my hand over those big muscles of his. He's made it clear that he thinks becoming his mate is essential, so I'm kind of tempted to see how he reacts to me touching him. But he's also made it clear that he doesn't really want me as his mate.

With Phantom and Dusk, I can tell they find me attractive and like the idea of me being with them. With Onyx, I almost feel like he sees this situation as something he can't escape from, and so has accepted that we have to be together. Like an arranged marriage to someone he finds irritating.

It makes me push away the thought of touching him romantically. The last thing I want to do is cross some line with him and have him no longer trust me to heal him.

"Okay, time to work," I whisper to myself.

Then, I focus on my hand and my desire to heal. The desire flows through me, and my light begins to glow brighter and brighter. I let out a slow breath, glad the ability is still there and working. I'm surprised when he actually covers my hand with his own. The glow spreads light over his face, and it's like I'm staring at an angel. He looks up at me and smiles.

It's the first time he's smiled *at* me. He's breathtaking. More so in the golden glow of my hands.

I am mesmerized. Maybe hypnotized. I'm captivated in a way I barely remember anymore. I've only felt this way once before, and it feels as if it was a thousand years ago.

Unable to help myself, I lean closer to press my mouth to his. Even if I wanted to stop myself, there's no way I could resist him. It's like the pool of the moon and the waves.

Unstoppable.

As we kiss, I feel the fullness of his lips, the gentle caress of his thumb on my cheek, the murmur of his breath on my skin. I'm as intoxicated as if I spent a night shooting tequila. Desire flows through me, making my inner muscles clench and heat pool at my core.

He sits up and angles his body so the only thing holding me up is his arm. He doesn't make a sound as he lowers me onto the blanket, but somehow, we've turned and his body is stretched beside mine. Or I'm stretched beside him, but he's leaning over me, hand splayed on my belly.

I've never been kissed with such utter possession of my body and soul. This guy uses every square inch of himself to brand me, to claim me, to make me want to be claimed.

When I kiss him back, I surrender. There's no point in fighting what I feel. No point in denying what I want from him. From *them*. Because now I have to accept that whatever this is, it *does* feel like a mate bond. It *does* feel like something more than love or lust.

And I like it.

Because it feels right. Because it feels like I can't possibly be making the wrong choice. Being with a mate isn't a choice, it's a need. An impossible connection that can't be ignored.

My fingers curl into his hair, massage his scalp as the kiss goes on and on. It's a melding of our mouths that burns through my body.

Because my body is now acting independently of what my brain would tell it to do, my leg hikes over his hip and the hard length of him hits me just right. I suck in a sharp breath, my head spinning. I hold myself against him and pull back just a little when heat flows through my body. I bite my lip, absorbing the feel of this gorgeous man against me, reveling in every sensation, every touch and breath.

A whimper slips from my lips, because I want more than this. I *need* more.

I pull him down for another kiss and align our hips once more as his hand glides up and under the hem of my shirt, warm against my stomach, and I want him the way I haven't wanted anyone since Rayne.

At the thought of him, I can't breathe. I can't think. I tear my mouth away and the tears come, unbidden, unchecked, unwanted but painful. Rayne. *My* Rayne. And here I am kissing another man, holding him, being held by him.

A sob warbles out, followed by another and another until I'm crying into his shoulder, blubbering, and it has nothing to do with him, but my sign language isn't good enough to convey that to him.

Onyx pulls back and tilts my chin toward him then uses his thumb to dry my eyes.

"I'm sorry." Of all the things I could've said, I go for the lamest, most pathetic. I don't know why I'm crying or if I should be sorry or how to make him understand my reaction has nothing to do with him, only my broken heart.

"I didn't mean to...do this." I motion between us, and he smiles softly. "It's just...I miss Rayne." He cocks his eyebrow, and I know what he wants. "Rayne was my mate. I loved him, but he was...killed. And now, I'm here."

He nods like he understands and whether he does or not, I'm staring into the eyes of a man who cares enough to pretend he does, and that means something to me.

When he bends and kisses the spot on my chest over my heart then pulls back and smiles softly as he strokes my face, my heart lightens. He *does* understand, and for as long as it lasts, I'm going to lay my head on his chest while his arms encircle my shoulders, and I'm going to enjoy it. Because when I lost my Rayne, I had no one. No one to heal my broken heart. And in a strange way, it makes sense that this big, sulking man might be the one to help me.

Even if I still can't accept him as my mate. Not yet.

FIFTEEN

Phantom

THE OTHERS KNOW what Ann is and what she can do, and there isn't a warrior among us who doesn't know that with her by his side, he could be more than he is. It makes it dangerous for her to be anywhere with anyone but Onyx, Dusk, or me. Even though we are a group of shadow beasts, loyal to one another, there are men in our ranks who would think to usurp the power of the Shadow King. The current or the future. And every man here is armed. Knives, bows, guns. We are warriors, and to be without weapons would be the same as being naked.

For those reasons as much as to be close to her, Onyx, Dusk, and I surround her on our way back to the large cave. After much discussion, we decided there is safety in numbers. We've also decided that she shouldn't be left alone until the bond is complete.

Her step is light but sure. There's power in her and I don't know if she has any idea how alluring she is. Her beauty is obvious, but the intensity of her strength is another layer in the complexities of who and what she is. It's a pretty package, and she wears it well. She will make a good companion and a good mate.

At the thought of what that means, my body warms, responding to her nearness. Because we can't risk her safety, I followed her from the cave to the river this morning where she bathed. I didn't look on purpose, but as I was watching, she came out of the water. She's as exquisite as any woman-- human or fae--I've ever seen, with full breasts, wide hips, and the kind of curves every man dreams of.

I shake my head and look at the forest. It's ripe with color and scent, but she's probably used to far better with the fae. The only thing we had to offer her this morning was yesterday's venison and some berries Onyx found. This is less than she's used to, less than she deserves, but we'll make that up to her when the Shadow King is defeated and the world is safe again.

Ann stumbles a little, and Onyx is catching her in an instant.

Her cheeks heat. "Thanks," she mumbles.

Onyx smiles in return, holds her a second too long, then releases her.

Dusk casts him a look, and Onyx just shrugs and turns back to focus on the woods.

I don't know what happened in the cave with Ann and Onyx, but something has changed. She's softer now. The way she walks, talks, looks at him, at us. I have to remind myself more than once that she has her own mind and that she's resistant to the bond we need to form, even if she's subconsciously feeling the connection between us.

Later, I'll have to explain to her that even with the other shadow beasts, she isn't safe. They know the prophecy, too.

But I don't want to worry her right now. I'd prefer she believe our actions come from jealousy rather than fear.

"Are you going to tell her?" Beside me, Dusk leans in and speaks low, referring to the secret I've been so hesitant to reveal to her. Around the fire, Dusk had begun to push the issue, fearing that if she learned the truth from someone else, it would shatter the trust we've been building with her. She's walking in front with Onyx, and thank goodness, because even speaking low for Dusk isn't nearly as soft as it should be if we want this to be private.

But she stops and turns to me. "Tell her what?"

Well, I guess her hearing is better than we thought too...

I shake my head because this isn't how I planned to break the news. I planned to sit with her tonight, lay it all out there for her and let her know how things would unfold if she agrees to bond with us. And I would find the words now, but my mouth is dry, and her wide-eyed beauty robs me of every sensibility I have.

"I'm going to be king." I blurt the words, shrill and high-pitched, like a teenager whose balls haven't dropped yet.

She nods. *"Really?"* But the light in her eyes dies, probably because she thinks I'm either a liar or a bragger. And I'm neither. If she took a minute to get to know me, she would discover that herself and I wouldn't have to tell her. "And what happens then?"

I consider the question. I've always known I would be the next king. I'm older than Dusk by thirty minutes, and Onyx is a friend, not related, but I've not really considered more than that.

"What happens then depends on you." Onyx has come to stand beside her, signing the words, and I speak them aloud for him. "With you by our side, the prophecy will come true and we might be able to defeat the enemy."

"Who is the enemy? I mean, I get that he's this Shadow King and everything, but I don't know anything beyond that."

Her question is a fair one. And an important one. Dusk takes over the signing because my hands are useless now. If I can't use them to pull her to me, I don't want to use them at all.

"The enemy is anyone who threatens the safety of all we see, our place in the world, *our* safety, anyone who threatens you." I don't know that I meant to add the last part, or that I meant to say it in the same tone I would use to tell her I love her, but that's how it comes out.

She nods and her lips twist to one side. "And who exactly is this king now? And why, if you're supposed to be the king, is he?"

I glance at Dusk then at Onyx. "He's a man who's lost his way. A man who isn't interested in what's best for the world, but what's best for himself, what makes him powerful."

When we start to walk again, Dusk and Onyx fall in behind us. I've understated the danger of this king, of his strength and the lengths those loyal to him may go to end the humans and expand their world into this one. I will make those things clear later, when I need to, sooner if I need to use them to convince her to fulfill the bond.

Because Dusk's question right now is for a reason. We can't keep waiting for her to accept this mate bond. Even waiting this one night scares me. She's unbelievably vulnerable, and the fact that the king's people will come for her makes us all vulnerable.

But, for now, I'm happy to have this time to walk with her, to hear her voice when she talks to me, to notice the way it changes--deeper, softer, sweeter--with each question.

Hell, with Ann here, the forest is fuller, greener, more robust. With her beside me, I'm stronger, more determined.

These are the notions of a romantic fool, and it's only bound to get worse the longer it takes her to bond with us.

So, we'll discuss this all later. When she's ready.

"So, I'm the key to saving the world?" When I nod, she scoffs, rolls her eyes, and shakes her head. There's nothing soft or sweet about her voice now. "But no pressure, right?" She runs her hands through her hair and flips it to one side so the loose long blonde strands brush against her shoulder and the lighter curls at the ends fall forward, shielding the side of her face closest to me.

I wish she could be happy. She's going to be a queen. Revered. Maybe even loved.

You know, if we can take down a mad king, his army, and return peace to both worlds.

I'm sure that if we could do that first, before the mate bound, she'd come around, but we don't have that luxury. She'll have to decide if she can accept us, if she can be with us, without the crowns. Without the luxury. She'll have to see within three exhausted men the possibility of a good life.

Maybe I don't blame her that it's hard.

"It's getting too late," Dusk murmurs.

I look up, frowning at the sky. He's right. The sun is setting. Normally, we can get back from the main cave to ours in no time at all. But with Ann being so much slower, we should have timed things better. If we don't hurry, we'll be caught out in the open when darkness hits.

And that would be stupid.

I realize that the forest is quiet. Maybe *too* quiet. Not like when the king's creatures come, but still more quiet than I like. *The Shadow King knows she's here. Wants her for himself because he can use her to make the prophecy come true. Or just to hurt us. And he isn't above it. He's a prick who cares about his power, his minions, and having a world under his complete control.* I thought we knew the extent of his powers, that we were safe until every last ray was gone from the sky, but what if I'm wrong?

I turn to Ann. "When we get to the cave, you must stay inside. We can protect you anywhere, but it'd be better to have a defensible location." My thoughts are spinning. "And he'll strike when he thinks we are at our weakest, our most vulnerable." That's anytime she's with us, for now anyway. While she has the power to make us strong, until she agrees to bond, we're weak. Until then, she's the chink in our armor that can be pierced.

I shift my pack to the opposite side because without holding it, our arms brush when we walk, and even that small touch is electric to me.

Because she hasn't answered my request, and only because, I slide the back of my hand against hers and when she looks at me, we're still touching, my finger now curled around one of hers. "I need you to be safe."

"Because you want this bond so you can be king?" It isn't an accusation in tone, but the implication is there.

I draw my hand away. "No, because I want you." The words are out, honest, truer than any I've spoken. "King or not."

She nods and we walk on. But I'm pretty sure she doesn't believe me.

SIXTEEN

Ann

AS SOON AS I'm settled in the cave, Dusk, Onyx, and
Phantom go outside and start setting up for the trouble they
believe is coming our way. There isn't a lot here to amuse
myself with, and I wish I had a book at least to read. Instead,
I sit and stare around the cave. This room is large enough,
larger than I first thought. There are three bedrolls around
the little fire that the guys had built up a bit before heading
outside, and shelves formed into the walls that they keep
things on. There are also weapons on the wall.

But nothing at all that I can see to do.

I guess spending all their time fighting a dangerous
enemy doesn't leave a lot of time for hobbies. It makes me a
little sad to think about. Their lives have been entirely
devoted to protecting the humans and supernaturals of my
world, but at what cost to themselves? I understand that
they'd go down with all of us if the Shadow King won, but
not everyone would do this to save the world.

I'm not even willing to become their mate to save the world. The thought bothers me more than I like.

Sucking in a deep breath, a scent hits me. Right now, someone is cooking and the smell of meat and smoke permeates the cave. I figure it's one of the guys outside, but I kind of wish they'd come in and make it here. I could use the company, and they'd be able to protect me even better if they stayed close. Right?

It's kind of pathetic. I definitely wish Onyx was here, or Dusk or even Phantom.

Suddenly, there's a ruckus outside the cave. I stand, looking at the wall of weapons and wondering if I could actually do anything with the huge swords. *Maybe a dagger?*

A shadow beast enters, followed by several others.

The first man nods to me. "I'm sorry, but a few of our men stumbled into a trap and were injured. We were closer to your cave than to our own." He's older than the others, with white in his long hair and braids woven in with the loose strands. His face is wrinkled, and he looks dirty and tired.

My fear fades away. "Of course! Come in!"

Two men carry one of the men over to a bedroll and lay him down. Another man limps over to a spot by the fire and sits down with a wince. And a third is over a man's shoulder. He's gently placed on another bedroll while the man who spoke to me opens his pack and starts to pull out first aid supplies.

"Do you want me to help?" I hold up my hands to indicate my powers, even though I'm not sure they know what I can do.

The older warrior shakes his head. "No, it shouldn't take us long to patch them up. Night has fallen, so we have to be ready for anything." But he sounds tired.

If I knew him better, I'd push to help. But instead, I just try not to get in their way.

The uninjured warriors choose various places around the cave and sit down, drinking water, taking snacks from their belts, and resting. They have the same energy as nurses after they've worked a long shift in the emergency room. It hurts my heart to see them looking so broken.

"What kind of trap was it?"

The older shadow beast sighs. "The same shit as always. Usually, it's placed near our main cave. The Shadow King doesn't know where we sleep, but they seem to realize the general area of the cave. But this time, we were trying to get closer to your cave before night fell. We went a different path than usual. And, well, surprise, the bastards expected it."

Damn it. I get the feeling this is the last thing these guys needed.

"Are my guys outside?"

The warrior is unrolling a bandage. "They're bringing fresh water and a nearby herb that helps with injuries. I gave them my word that every one of us will die to keep you safe." His gaze catches mine, and he gives a weary smile. "But they were still running for the supplies."

Because they want to keep me safe. The thought makes my heart ache.

One of the warriors is staring at me from where he's sitting with one leg stretched in front of him across from me. He's not smiling, not particularly fearsome, but staring. It's unnerving. I'm unnerved. But instead of holding out my hand so I can see how badly it's shaking--and it is--I slide it under my leg and look everywhere else but at him. Although, when I glance back, he's still staring.

Uh, okay. This is the first time I'm actually a little

worried about these guys. Maybe my men are right to be worried about me.

I don't know if he's actually supposed to be my protection, but I don't feel safe here with him. And I might've promised Phantom to stay inside, but I would bet my future that this guy means to do me harm. Fear of reprisals or Phantom's wrath isn't enough.

I stand and breathe out, but as soon as I'm on my feet, he's on his. When I move toward the entrance of the cave, he's there too, arms out like he's playing basketball defense.

"Excuse me."

His grin is more of a leer. "No, my lady. Excuse me." Still, he doesn't move.

"Please, get out of the way." I don't know if I can hurt him, but if I can heal Onyx, I might be able to put this guy down, at least take him out of the game long enough that I can get past him. But if it doesn't work, I've put myself close enough for him to grab me and do...whatever it is he has planned. I don't want to think about what that might be or the fear might drain the focus I need to get out of here.

"Move."

The older shadow beast says, "Move, Wraith."

To my surprise, he lowers his head and steps out of my way.

The man speaks from near the fire. "But your mates did want you to stay inside."

"I'll be right outside the cave. Close enough that if there's an issue, you'll know it. I just need a minute alone and a breath of air."

"She'll be fine," the creepy man named Wraith says.

The older shadow beast sighs. "Okay, the Moon Goddess knows that my own daughters wouldn't have been able to tolerate a cave full of men for too long. But, stay close."

Nodding, I rush out of the cave. One side of the sky is grey, which I think is still light enough to keep the Shadow King's men away, but still, I stay close. Just far enough away to avoid the creepy guy, but not so far as to get into trouble.

"I'm surprised you didn't want them."

I stiffen and whirl around to see Wraith way too close to me.

"Few women would refuse the king."

It's hard to form a response when my instincts are screaming to run. I glance between the cave entrance and him. If things go wrong, I can definitely scream, and maybe get around him. "A king or not, a woman likes to have a little time to think."

He moves closer to me, and I lift a hand to tell him to stop. His gaze goes to my hand, and he smirks, still coming closer.

I dodge left then quick-fade right, but his gorilla arms wrap around me, and he lifts me off my feet. When I open my mouth to scream, one of his hands goes over my mouth. He takes a few steps and pins me between his body and a tree. As he uses his body to hold me there, his hand is still covering my mouth. I scream against his hand and struggle, but I barely make a sound, and there's no way to get leverage or to move. He pulls a knife from the sheath on his belt.

"You should've gone with your mates."

I know that now. And I won't be making this mistake ever again. Assuming I get out of this alive and have that kind of choice.

"You're coming with me." His voice is hard but a rasp, like he's hoarse, and there's nothing sexy or husky about it.

It's pure gravel and if I never hear it again, it will be too soon.

His hand slowly lowers from my mouth, and I feel the coolness of his blade against my throat.

My heart hammers, and I realize that I might not be able to take this guy out by fighting, but I can out smart him. Deep down I already know that he'll have to kill me before I go anywhere with him. And he won't.

So, that's something.

"I won't go anywhere with you." Okay, there, I said it. Carefully, I crane my neck back to look at him, and kind of wish I hadn't.

He holds the knife closer to my throat and laughs. "Allow me to introduce myself. My name is Wraith and I don't kill." After a few seconds, a slow grin that is mostly snarl slides across his face. "I'm the torturer." Pride blooms in his eyes. He's cocky and overconfident. Weak because of it.

But even so, it doesn't stop the fear that races through me. He's right. He might not be able to kill me, but I'm not exactly experienced at resisting torture.

My mind is racing, moving so fast that I'm not sure any of my thoughts are logical. It's like they're just screaming at me to run or fight, and I don't know which idea is better. *Maybe fighting* and *running?* If I can just get one leg free, I can use that and go for the family jewels, maybe put him down long enough that I can get out and find Phantom or Dusk or Onyx.

"Why do you even want me?" I don't see desire or interest in his eyes. So, is it just his hunger to lay claim to my power?

He whispers into my ear, "Years ago, when I followed Phantom to this world and decided to follow at his side instead of the king, I felt I made the right choice. Now, if I could turn back time, I wouldn't waste my life fighting a battle we'll never win. I would have stayed with my king. So, when I learned of your existence, I made a deal with the king. You...in exchange for his pardon and a comfortable life. More than worth it, if you ask me."

"And you think that man will keep his word?" I laugh. He can't be that naïve.

His grip on me tightens. "Come on now. We're going to walk out of here nice and quiet. And you're going to do exactly what I say." There's enough menace in his tone for me to know he means business. But I'm trained. And I'm powerful in more ways than this dolt probably knows.

"And if I don't?"

"Then I'll go and come back during the day, when everyone is asleep, and I'll gut Phantom first, then the other, then the dumb one. And I'll take you anyway." He's a shadow beast, and I don't doubt that he thinks he can do this. I only doubt whether he could ever be successful. "And don't try anything. You're the outsider here. You're the one they all fear."

Okay, so is he going to torture me now if I don't go with him? Or is he going to come back for me later and kill my men? I don't know, but the guy definitely seems to be unstable, and I don't think he's bluffing either way. All I know for sure is that I need my hand free to touch him with my energy, maybe kill him if I can the way I did with the rot monkeys. Then I need my leg free to put him down if I'm able to catch him off-guard with my magic in any way.

Okay, that's the plan then. Catch him off-guard, get him on the ground, then run for my guys.

I don't know how far away my guys are, or why I've suddenly taken to thinking of them as *my guys*, but I breathe out slowly because I'm determined to see them again. And I'm going to use that determination to get free.

"Remember, peaceful. Quiet." He brings his knife hand to his mouth. "Shh." I nod, and he spins me toward the forest and presses his knife into my back, while he holds me by my shoulder with the other hand. "Walk."

As we walk, a plan forms in my head. It isn't much. It's nothing really, just a self-defense tactic I saw in a movie once. I'm going to drive my foot into his instep, jab my elbow into his gut and run like hell screaming like a fool every step of the way.

It isn't until I stop walking and lift my foot to stomp that I lose confidence in the self-defense plan. I summon the power to my hands. It's darker and angrier than the healing energy I used on Onyx, and I savor it for a second before I turn it on him. I twist, jab my hand against his heart, and nothing.

Now, I don't have a choice. I try to stomp his foot, miss, and he picks me up again, both arms around my waist because I'm writhing and wiggling, twisting and using my body weight to fling myself around.

Finally, I remember I need to scream. "Help me! Phantom, Onyx, Du--!" When this bastard tries to clamp his hand over my mouth, I bite his finger as hard as I can until I taste blood and he jerks it out of my mouth.

Footsteps pound toward us, or maybe that's my heartbeat in my ears, but he drops me and I crumble to the ground as Phantom, Dusk, and Onyx race through the brush to where we are.

"Ann!" Phantom comes in and passes me with a flying kick that levels the prick.

Dusk helps me stand and Onyx sits in a crouch in front of us, a dagger in his hand, in case Phantom needs help. But

Phantom has the other guy on the ground and is busy pounding his fists into my attacker's face. Dusk pulls against his side and holds me there, safe against him as the adrenaline takes over, and I start trembling.

Eventually, Onyx pulls Phantom off, and the other guy lies groaning on the ground. Onyx, Phantom, and Dusk all check on me. Then, Wraith moans again and says, "The king will get her...it's only matter of time."

A look of cold fury comes over Phantom's face, and he rises from beside me and goes back to the man on the ground. I don't realize what's happening until Phantom's knife is stuck in Wraith's heart.

I gasp as the shadow beast's head flops to the side. "Oh, shit."

But none of my men seem surprised. Sullen maybe, but not surprised.

"Take her back to the cave." Phantom motions with his head. "And stay with her."

Dusk hides my face in his chest, and I breathe in the earthy scent of him as he walks me away. His hand is warm at the center of my back, and eventually, my heart rate slows and my breaths come evenly.

"It's okay, now. I've got you."

I nod against him, safe.

At least for now.

SEVENTEEN

Onyx

FUCKING WRAITH. We need every man we can get, but even so, Phantom had to kill him. Right now, we don't know if he took her for himself or the king, but either way, he's too dangerous to allow to remain alive. I only wish I was the one to end his miserable life, but Phantom got there first.

I'm still wired. Dusk is holding Ann in a corner of the cave, away from where Phantom and I are by the fire. After we told the others what happened, they apologized profusely for not watching her more closely and left, taking their wounded with them.

Yes, I felt a small bit of guilt watching them leave, but they knew enough that it was safer for them to leave than to stay. With our current state of mind, we could end up hurting them. They knew that, understood the strength of the mate bond, and left without argument, also promising to destroy the bastard's body when they came across it.

She looks up and I nod at her because while I'm ready

to go out and slay the world for her, I also want to be the one holding her against me.

"One of us should stay with her at all times. We can trust no one," Phantom says, while signing.

I agree. The prophecy says a light fae will mate with shadow beasts and end this war, so every beast thinks he can gain power or advantage by being with her. I don't know what Wraith's plan was, but she's safe for now. And we're going to keep her that way, no matter what it takes.

"She needs the protection of the mate bond," I sign back. He knows this already, but I am giving him an opening to share his plan. Phantom always has plans and they almost always work.

He turns to look at her and the want is plain on his face, the desire dark in his eyes. I recognize it because I feel those same things deep in my gut. I want her too.

"She's been through some...turmoil." I haven't shared anything she told me about her boyfriend, Rayne. That she confided in me isn't something I take lightly. But she had told all of us about him and suggested he was part of the reason she didn't want other mates or feel like this thing between us could be real.

He nods. "Yeah." He doesn't ask me what I know, and I'm grateful. I'm not sure if I would be able to tell him.

"We have to find a way to persuade her. This...stubbornness," I know it isn't wholly obstinance standing in her way, "could get us all killed."

He nods, signing back to me, "The king won't take her and she'll be safe if she mates with us. It will happen. She can't fight the mate bond forever." I wish for the kind of confidence he has. Until he frowns, anyway. "I'll also tell her that we can't make her." Because Phantom is nothing if not honest on a level I've never seen matched.

I follow him to where she's sitting huddled with Dusk. That lucky fuck. He has his arm around her shoulders, her head tucked against him. As far as protectors go, she could do worse. And I smile. I won't be telling him that.

She looks up and gives me a soft almost smile, then gives one to Phantom. Or maybe it's him first, but it doesn't matter. She's not fallen apart despite what she's been through and what she's seen. That alone marks her strength.

"Are you all right?" I read the words off Phantom's lips, then turn to her for the answer.

She nods. "Yes."

"Wraith won't be bothering you anymore."

"He made a deal with the king," she tells us. "He was tired of fighting."

My gut churns. Phantom and Dusk didn't think the others would betray us to the king, just that they would try to steal her heart. I reminded them that the last time they underestimated someone, we paid dearly.

They said nothing else, but I don't think they believed it could actually happen until this moment. Now, I see it in their faces. Their people aren't just exhausted and miserable. They're looking for an easy way out, and that's never a good thing.

Dusk looks at me and winces.

I nod back at him and sign, "It's okay. Not all of us can be as jaded as I am."

Their mother died, but she loved them every second of her life. My own mother sold me to a man she probably thought wanted to use me for unspeakable things. It was pure luck that the captain of the guard felt I reminded him of the son he lost, and so, took me in to keep me safe. Even as a small boy, I trusted no one, until Dusk and Phantom.

And I still didn't.

Although Ann is growing on me.

I move to sit facing her, though I wish I could sit beside her. And I could. Neither Dusk nor Phantom would deny me, but I wouldn't be able to talk to her if I did.

For a moment, I miss hearing. I'm angry that I can't. It's been so long since I've heard the sound of a woman's voice. Since I've heard *any* sound. And I again wonder whether hers is sweet and soft or if she has a huskiness, a depth to her tone. I would love it either way.

It bothers me that this seems to matter to me. The knowledge that I can't hear her seems to circle in my mind any time I'm alone with my thoughts. Since my injury, I've mostly kept any frustration at my circumstances shoved deep in a dark box inside me. I don't understand why I can't seem to do that now too.

I sign, "Are you really okay?"

Dusk speaks my words to her.

She smiles, and I watch her lips as they move. "It was a little scary, but you guys got there in time."

We watch each other, her eyes piercing, as though she's trying to see inside my mind just as I am hers. When she looks away, I smile. There are things I want to say, things I want her to hear, but I don't dare because I'm not sure that I remember how to. And I can't hear myself to know how I sound.

What if I embarrass myself? What if I horrify her?

She looks at me and holds out one hand. She offers the other to Phantom while Dusk continues to hold her. "Thank you for rescuing me."

It seems like a year ago rather than only a few days since I wanted the others to leave her behind. Now, I've risked my life twice to protect her. And I would do it again. As many times as she needs. And as scared as some deep part of myself feels about that, there's another part of me that feels excited.

Maybe I'm not as broken as I thought I was.

I nod, even though I want to tell her that I'll always save her, and she gives my fingers a squeeze and tugs me closer. I scoot, but it isn't what she wants. She pulls until I'm leaned in far enough to kiss her. She's as delicious as she was when I was injured. When she healed me with her touch, saved me with a kiss like this one.

Her mouth is soft, lips full, and I savor the touch for a second after it's over before I pull back and she kisses Phantom with the same fervor, the same desperation. He tangles his fingers in her hair and holds on, tilts her head, opens his mouth.

When she finishes with Phantom, she kisses Dusk, and I'm lost to everything I feel, everything I want. The three of us have shared women before, a lifetime ago, but it was always just sex for me. I never thought I was capable of feeling close to anyone other than Dusk and Phantom. Not even a woman. But now, I like watching her kiss my best friends. Not just because it's strangely hot, but because it feels like it deepens our bonds, with her, and with each other.

She's ours whether she knows it or not. And no way in hell are we letting her go.

After she's kissed the three of us, she nestles with Dusk on one side of her and Phantom on the other, but she stares at me. I want to know everything about her. I want everything she has to offer and so much more.

"How did you come to be with Phantom and Dusk?" Her gaze holds mine as I sign the story and Phantom translates.

I struggle to find the right words. "My mother sold me

as a child to the captain of their guard. Their mother had just died, and the captain, in his wisdom, thought we would be good for each other. He trained me as a guard, but when he was busy, I spent my time with Phantom and Dusk. As time passed, we formed an unbreakable bond."

There was more, so much more. Even now, I remember the three broken-hearted boys coming together. We were less playmates, and more a strange support group. We spoke about our losses with ease, and for a time it felt as if no one in the world existed outside of us.

When we got older, things became more complicated. Phantom would be the future king. His brother, a prince of our world. And me, their ever-loyal guard. In public, we were formal. In private, we were family.

Until the event.

I'm not going to tell her about my hearing, or how I lost it, but Phantom fills in the gaping hole in my story. "He almost died saving my life when...the Shadow King tried to kill me."

"I'm a warrior." I smile as I sign the words. "I could no more let the shadow prince die, than I could let my friend die." The words translate well enough and Phantom shoots me a rueful smile. There are days his guilt is bigger than he knows what to do with. He's never quite gotten over the fact that I lost my hearing to save him.

"Why did the Shadow King want you dead?" Now she's on to Phantom.

"He's a bad man." Phantom doesn't say more, and I don't blame him. I would cut the story off there, too. No need to get maudlin or haul the family skeletons out of his closet.

"His arrogance makes him a bad king." Dusk looks down at his lap.

"And his greed. And his unwillingness to change." I smile at her as I finish and Phantom, again, translates.

"I wish I could hurt him with my powers, but I tried with Wraith, and nothing happened."

"Some things can't be solved with magic," Dusk says.

We'd all learned that lesson well.

"I tried to save that sleeping warrior, Adrik."

That surprises me. *When had she done that?*

"Why?" Dusk asks the question we're all wondering.

She shrugs, and there's hurt in her eyes. "First, I just wanted to see if I could do it. But also, in a strange way, he reminded me of Rayne. Of my first mate."

First. The word holds a special meaning, but I try not to focus on it.

It was noble of her to try, but we could have told her it was pointless. He's dying slowly, but it's only his body that's still alive. His mind and spirit went to the Moon Goddess long ago, to walk the Ever Fertile Fields. It is the same way with all warriors in his condition.

Phantom squeezes her hand. "Adrik was dragged into the shadow world and fought, but a smoke dragon consumed his soul. Now, his body is dying." There's so much more to the story and I wonder exactly how much she knows. "He's already gone. Only his body remains."

To my surprise, she nods. "It's like the opposite of ghosts."

"Ghosts?" Dusk asks with a frown.

"Yes, the dark fae have the power to see ghosts. They're actually all around us. People who died with unresolved issues."

That surprises me.

"So, their spirits are here, but not their bodies?" Phantom asks, and I see some disbelief in his eyes.

I don't blame him. The idea that all unhappy spirits could be walking around us without us able to see them is creepy and unsettling. In our beliefs, those who were good in life go to the Ever Fertile Fields. A place of peace and prosperity. And the people who were bad in life go to the Wastelands. The smoke dragon is one of the few creatures that's capable of devouring the soul of a person and leaving their body behind.

But ghosts? That's too strange a notion for me. These fae have very different beliefs from our own.

"Yes, that's exactly it!" Ann exclaims. "Dark fae have had to stay hidden for a long time, so no one sees their powers, but I read a lot of the lore about them with Rayne. They don't just see ghosts; they speak to them and often help them to find peace."

Dusk looks around the cave and his mouth says, "Do you think there are any of them here?"

A coldness rolls through me, and I shiver. Glancing around me, I feel a strange sense of unease. *Was the chill from a spirit or ghost? Or had I just imagined it?*

My imagination. Definitely my imagination.

"Let's eat again," Phantom suggests. "Then take turns resting. The others are patrolling the outside of our cave. If something tries to attack us, we'll know before anything can get in."

And that's what we do, passing the night by eating, resting, and talking to Ann. She nods off to sleep many times, but when she's awake, it seems, she always has something to say. Dusk and Phantom ask her about her life. I see hurt in her eyes, but I don't press her for the things she doesn't want to share. She simply tells us about her mom, who got pregnant by a human. In order to cover up the fact that she's not a full fae, another man claimed her child as his own.

The man, apparently, loved another man. Something that is common even among shadow beasts. Mates, after all, can be of the same sex, or different, it didn't really matter. And because this father of hers could never have a biological child of his own, he was more than happy to take on the role of her father.

She describes a good life, if a lonely life. Until she comes to her mother marrying another man. Then, she seems to struggle with her words before she says she's tired and pretends to sleep.

I decide that one day I will ask her about this man her mother married. And if he was unkind to her, I'd find him and kill him.

Not that I'll tell her that.

Outside the cave, day is about to break and she yawns, this time for real. Her eyes open, but they're pooled with tears of fatigue. My mind spins with memories of happier days, of times when I could hear, and I can imagine Ann there with me, putting her in the vivid scenes in my mind. Making her laugh. Showing her our world before it all fell apart. And I smile to myself because it isn't a surprise that she fits with us. Into our lives. Now, yes. But when things are better, yes too.

I yawn and my eyelids close so I can drift off to sleep. I'm strangely filled with hope that after tonight, after getting to know us better, she'll be willing to mate and form our bond.

Then, hopefully, we would have more good days than bad before us.

EIGHTEEN

Ann

I'M in the massive cave the shadow beasts all stay in, walking through the dark halls until I come to the place I knew I was heading towards. Inside, I spot Adrik, the sleeping warrior. Only, he's no longer asleep. He's half-sitting, half-lying against the wall. He turns his head and looks at me, eyes bright with awareness, a slow smile on his face. It's familiar, but I can't think about that because something is wrong.

The earth above us shakes.

"There's trouble coming." The man's voice is deep, but familiar. "You need to wake up, Ann." Adrik says my name like he's said it a thousand times before.

"You're here?" My words come out breathless. "Awake?"

"I never left your side," he tells me. "But we'll have time for that later. For now, you're in trouble."

The earth shakes above us again, and dirt and dust fall

around us. *What the hell is that? It can't be thunder or a storm making that rumbling. And why is this warrior telling me to wake up?*

I'm not asleep. *Am I?*

"Darling, please!"

Darling? Rayne was the only one who called me darling.

When I jerk awake, my strange dream fades away in the light of the afternoon. It takes a moment for the fog of sleep to clear as I blink and try to clear my head. I'm not a "morning" person. And I was up late talking with Phantom and Onyx and Dusk. I'm still wrapped in Dusk's arms, my back against his chest while Onyx sits against the wall, eyes closed, a peaceful smile on his face, and Phantom lies facing me.

With a clarity so vivid I can almost taste each one, I remember the kisses. The way Phantom twisted my hair around his hand when I kissed him. The way Dusk cupped the side of my face. The way Onyx stroked my cheekbone.

Thunder rumbles through the roof of the cave and bits of earth fall onto my face as the light of day filters in through the door. But it can't be a storm. I can see sunlight. So, what is it?

The chaos of the moment finally comes through. I look around us and see about a dozen warriors asleep all over the floor. As thunder roars above us, and the light of day grows duller. *Clouds? A storm? How strange.* The next time the thunder comes, it shakes the entire cave. The shadow beasts inside the cave awaken in a rush. Metal clanks. Armor buckles. Knives are unsheathed in preparation for a battle, and the men beside me tense, awake, aware of something I'm not.

My stomach churns. I don't have to know exactly what is happening to know it's bad.

"What's happening?" I ask, grasping Dusk's shirt.

He freezes. "A storm."

I frown. "Why does that require all of this…?" I ask, pointing to all the warriors rushing to prepare.

His eyes narrow. "Because a storm creates an unnatural night, which allows the creatures from the shadow realm to come. And because we've only experienced a storm like this once before, and that was a magical storm, and a planned attack."

Oh, shit. This isn't good! I thought at least we were safe during the day. I guess I was wrong.

Phantom is on his feet while everyone is still preparing. "It's a fucking army. Get her out of here!"

Dusk hauls me to my feet and takes me by the arm, pulling me along to the back of the cave.

I frown, but he rolls a boulder in the corner away and shows me a dark tunnel underneath it. A creepy, dark tunnel that I absolutely don't want to climb down into.

Dusk stops and looks down at me, worry etching lines in his face. "Here." He hands me a compass. It's old and heavy, plated with gold, the needle pointing northeast. "Take the tunnel. It will lead to the main cave, and then beyond. Stay to the north until you get to the river. Then follow it west. Use the trees for cover and hurry. You have to get to safety until we handle this." There's a note of desperation as he takes my hands in his and squeezes.

"I want to stay and fight with you." My skill could be of use. And right now, by the weight of the footfalls, it sounds like there is an army of a thousand men coming for the forty or so shadow beasts getting ready to fight.

To survive, the shadow beasts will need every available hand, every available weapon. I'm both.

"No!" His voice is sharp and loud. "If the king finds you, he *will* take you, and we might not get you back this time. Listen to me. Say what I say. North to the river."

I can't fight him. He's right. I'll be a better weapon when we have a plan for how to best make use of my talents. "North to the river."

"West to the two towers."

"West to the two towers." I repeat his words like a good little parrot. "Stay in the trees."

"Yes. Once you're at the two towers, wait for us. We'll come for you."

I nod because even though I would rather die than leave them, they won't be safe if I'm there. And they won't concentrate on their fight because they will be worried about me. It would put them in more danger.

He pulls me close for a quick hug and places a peck against the top of my head, then pushes me forward. "Go."

"I... be careful," I say to them, because all three of my shadow beasts are staring at me.

They nod at me, and my heart aches. I want to say more, but I can't seem to form the words.

Dusk hands me a piece of wood from the fire. It's burning on the top, but not on the bottom, like a torch. He helps lower me down into the tunnel, gives me one last intense look, then rolls the boulder back over the opening, sealing me inside.

I've only walked for a minute or two when I hear the fighting. It's loud, and the stomps of the men above the tunnel force more dirt to rain down on me, but I keep going. My entire body shakes as I try not to think about the danger my men are facing.

For some reason, I find myself crying. Phantom, Dusk, and Onyx had kidnapped me. They had been bossy and over protective at times. And...and I think I've fallen in love with them.

Love.

The notion makes me stop. I brush more tears away. But the deep sense that I love them remains. I don't know when it happened. Visions of their grumpy faces and harsh words come to me, but they seem fuzzy, not at all clear like the memory of their smiles, their laughs, and their soft touches.

They're mine. I don't just love them; I like them too.

I almost turn around, then force myself to stop. They would struggle to concentrate on keeping themselves safe if I went back to the battle. I'd already seen that they'd give their lives for me. It would be selfish to go back and make things harder for them just because I want to keep them safe.

But, I swear, when we're back together, I'll no longer fight the mate bond. I'll do whatever needs to be done to show them that I love them. That I care for them. And that I will remain by their sides through this war, whatever it takes.

When the thoughts come to me, it's like a tension I didn't know I was carrying fades away. This feels right. Being with them is not about replacing Rayne. No one would ever replace him. But just because I lost one mate doesn't mean I need to be alone for the rest of my life.

"I love them," I say to myself, followed by a small laugh.

And then, I rush faster through the tunnel as if moving faster will make this battle end more quickly and get my men back to me sooner. The numbers might not be in their favor, but I'd never seen warriors like them before. They would succeed, and the Shadow King's army could go fuck themselves.

My torch is burning low by the time I know I've hit the main cave. The crystals blossom on the walls, lighting the darkness more than my torch ever could. I stop and realize where I am. If I take the right path, it'll bring me to the unconscious man. Aldrik.

Suddenly, my strange dream comes back to me, and I leave the tunnel I'm in. In the back of my mind, I know I'm disobeying Dusk. But for some reason, I have to see the man. I have to know...I don't know what.

I reach it faster than I thought possible. The crystals on the walls give enough light that I set my torch down and inch closer to the sleeping warrior. Gazing down at him, I see that his chest is still rising and falling evenly. Even if I couldn't heal his mind, it seemed I'd healed his body.

"This was foolish," I tell myself. "I need to go back. To stay to the north, like Dusk said. I don't even know why I'm here."

And the warrior's eyes pop open, the same shade of blue as Rayne's. My breath catches in my throat, and I feel like I'm in a dream or a nightmare; I'm not sure which.

"I thought you were dying," I whisper. Because this isn't Rayne. Because this is someone else, no matter how much the dream shook me.

"New life has been breathed into me."

The ground above us shakes, and my head jerks up. The army. It's here too.

"We need to go or we'll end up dead. Can you stand?"

His brows draw together, and he tries, but stumbles several times before he manages to remain standing. I wrap an arm around him and lead him back the way we came, snagging the torch as I do so. Every time I glance at him though, he simply looks determined. Not scared. Not confused.

Just determined.

Whoever this warrior is, he's bouncing back into the fray of things faster than I would have. I only hope he can be trusted. If he ends up like that bastard Wraith, I don't care if I saved his life or not, I'll end it.

We run through the tunnel, him leaning on me less and less, and don't stop running until we're at the river, following the bank. With every step, we're trying desperately to ignore the grey clouds overhead and the spikes of lighting in the sky, followed by roars of thunder that sound like a battle in itself. Only then do I feel some small sense that we might be okay. We're doing what Dusk told us to, and I trust him. With my life.

With my heart.

We've slowed now and I can't shake the feeling of familiarity every time I look at the man beside me, the sense that I know him, though we've only just met. Officially anyway. He's been unconscious the rest of the time, and the feeling is unsettling.

"Should...should you be back fighting with the others?"

"The others?"

I frown. "The other shadow beasts. Or are you still too weak?"

Or is this guy some asshole working for the Shadow King, and the only reason he seems familiar to me is that he's in on all of this too? Maybe even leading me into danger? My stomach turns.

He stares at me for a moment, then laughs and the sound is so similar to Rayne's that tears sting my eyes. "I'm not a shadow beast."

What the hell does that mean? What does any of this mean?

My steps slow and my heart races. "Then, what are you?"

He stops and holds my gaze. "Do you really not recognize me?"

"What? You're the injured shadow beast..."

But his only answer is another laugh. One that there's no denying.

He has Rayne's laugh. And Rayne's eyes. "*Rayne?*"

NINETEEN

Ann

I CAN'T BELIEVE I'm even thinking this. "Is it you?"

He nods, watching me. "Of course, it's me." His chuckle is like music to me, a symphony, rich and wondrous, and my heart is in my throat.

"This can't be possible. It can't be you." The words come out strangely hurt.

Or maybe it isn't strange. Having someone claiming to be my dead mate doesn't happen every damn day.

"But it is," he says with a little shrug of his shoulders.

"No," I say, shaking my head, fighting my panic and confusion.

He frowns, but it's quickly replaced by a smile. "So, were you as surprised as I was that it was Professor Windrawl behind my death and the attack on the dark fae?"

My jaw drops open.

"I mean, that guy seemed like a bumbling idiot. Sweet and totally harmless. I thought I was so clever, discovering all the secrets beneath the tunnels. But apparently, it was the one truth I couldn't figure out until it was too late." And then, he rolls his eyes. "And then telling everyone my death was an accident because I played with that sword... How insulting."

I realize my mouth is hanging open, and I close it.

"How?" I don't need all the details, just enough to make sense of what I'm seeing, what I know is true.

"I...don't really know. I was a ghost, watching you, following." His words are punctuated by breaths and half-smiles. "I couldn't leave the earth until I knew you were safe. But I don't know, it was more than that. When they murdered me, I didn't feel like I was dead. I felt...like I was waiting. I know that doesn't make sense, but I just had this deep sense that I wasn't done yet. Especially since I didn't awaken until just before the shadow beasts took you. Before that, I was just...nowhere."

"So," my mind is trying to untangle this unbelievable turn of events, "when I healed the warrior, it might have created some kind of...opening for a mind." That sounds dumb.

He shrugs.

The truth is that I'm only guessing. How he ended up in Adrik's body might just be one of life's many mysteries. But there's no way this warrior would know everything he just said if he wasn't Rayne.

I stare. "So, you're really him?"

He smiles. "Even though this body feels a little weird. Definitely bigger than my last one."

Rayne is right about that. He was never a huge guy. Being half light fae and half dark, he had the nimble body of most fae. His buddies always towered over him, but he was still more than tall enough for me.

Perfect, I had thought.

Now, he's like my giant shadow beasts. He looks like a warrior, every inch of him. But despite the slight difference, I don't know how I didn't see it. Or maybe because he was unconscious, I didn't recognize him. None of it really made sense to me yet.

I can't believe it's him, but on the other hand, I can't believe I didn't know it immediately when he followed me out of the tunnel, the second his hand touched mine. My mate is like my soul. I shouldn't have just had an instinct that he felt familiar. I should have known.

Shouldn't I have?

A strange thought comes to me. *Maybe since I met my shadow beasts I'm not as connected to Rayne.* My chest aches. Part of me had said goodbye to him. Part of me had accepted that he was gone. And maybe, just maybe, I'd given that part of myself to Dusk, Onyx, and Phantom.

What does this mean? For them? For us?

Suddenly, the sounds of the battle are loud--metal clanking against metal, grunting, a random burst of gunfire every once in a while. It surprises me how close it is. It's as if the entire forest is under attack.

How big is the Shadow King's army?

A chill rolls down my spine. *Too big.* I can't bear to think of Phantom, Dusk, and Onyx in danger, and I shiver. They're good men. Men who were prisoners of my people. Men who have been fighting, in secret, to save a world that doesn't know they exist.

And now, they're fighting for me too. Because there's no doubt in my mind. This army wouldn't have come if not for me. If the Shadow King didn't want me for his own.

"We should go, Ann. It's not safe for you."

And something strange occurs to me.

"Were you with me in the shadow world?" There was a distinct time I can remember when the king acted as if someone was tapping his shoulder.

He nods. "I've been with you since you met the shadow beasts."

This is information I don't know what to do with.

"But, Ann, we do need to go. We can talk about all of this later, okay?" He pulls me into a hug, but I don't relax against him. Even knowing that it's Rayne doesn't take away from the feeling that I shouldn't be touching another man like this.

My shadow beasts have stolen my heart.

He releases his hold on me, and our eyes catch. "I know things have changed, but we're going to figure it out. We just need to get to safety first."

He's right, even though running feels like the last thing we should be doing right now.

We move down the bank of the river to the west, and I would think *two towers* as a name would mean *towers*, something man-made. But when I see them, I know I've found where I'm supposed to wait.

There are two giant oaks at the edge of the river, shading a cave that seems to run underneath the water. "That's where we're supposed to go." I point to the opening and Rayne nods.

"Okay."

"Another damp cave. Figures, huh?"

He chuckles and pulls me into another hug. "I've missed you, Ann."

When he lowers his head, pressing his lips against mine, I'm surprised, but I don't pull away. His kiss is tentative at first, like he expects that I might punch him. And maybe I will. But then, he plunges his fingers into my hair and holds my head as he slides his tongue into my mouth, teases, coaxes, tempts me. It's so strangely familiar that I close my eyes, and I'm taken back to a simpler time. A time before I lost my one and only mate.

Tears spring to my eyes. It's Rayne and he's here with me. I don't need more than that. Not right now anyway. Later, I will figure out how to tell him he's not my only mate, not anymore, and see if we can all find a way to be together. Even if some small thought whispers in the back of my mind that before Rayne touches me again, I'll need to talk to my other men. I might have never imagined that Rayne could come back, but he has. We will have to deal with it.

And I hope my men can accept Rayne. Because I don't think I can lose any of them without losing my heart.

TWENTY

Phantom

THE BATTLE IS INTENSE. I watch men fall, both my men and his. In the past, it's been rare that the king has sent other shadow beasts into this world. I suspect it required more power than he was willing to spend. But today there are many of them. Shadow beasts the king has turned to his side, fighting us beside trolls who have no choice but to show their loyalty in battle.

There are forty of us left of the fifty or so we started with. Men who were spread all around the Void, but had come to offer their support when news of Ann and the whispers of the shadows were spread. We're facing more than twice as many enemies. The only benefit from them having brought the fight to the forest is that the terrain favors us, giving us the home field advantage.

A troll who is proficient with his sword steps forward. He comes at me, broadsword raised above his head to swipe in a downward motion, an ark that's designed to sever limbs and end lives. But the movement leaves his center open, and I plunge my dagger into his chest, then wait for him to fall. The resilience of the trolls makes them easy to kill, harder to keep down once they're dead.

While he's down, I douse him with flammable fluid and light him up. His leathery skin crackles as it melts from his body and makes a molten pool in the grass.

A few yards away, Onyx is battling two trolls with another shadow beast beside him, while Dusk is hand-to-hand fighting a shadow beast only slightly smaller than he is.

A rot monkey grabs onto my leg. I kick it away as hard as I can, working to get closer to my brother and best friend. Dusk is solely focused on his opponent. A punch grazes the shadow beast he faces, by then I spot a troll creeping up behind him.

I shout, "Dusk!" But it's too late. He shoves the shadow beast in front of him away, then spins around. The glint of a blade at least as long as my arm catches the light a split second before it slices him open from nipple to belly button.

He falls to his knees, and I cut off the head of the troll who steps between us, racing to my brother's side. When the troll that attacked him so cowardly goes in for the kill, I use my sword to chop off the bastard's hand first. His blood-
-it's black and gooey--sprays, and I try to get out of the way, but it splatters my clothes, my armor, my face.

I wipe it out away from my eyes, then take up a braced stance to fight anyone who comes near Dusk as Onyx protects the other side. We're gaining ground, and there are fires lit across the forest where trolls have been put down. They comprise the bulk of the Shadow King's army.

Suddenly, we see the Void surge in the distance. It

crackles, like it's filled with lightning, and a massive shape explodes out of it. *A smoke dragon. Fuck.*

The creatures are beyond dangerous. And as far as we knew, couldn't exist outside of the Void.

I have no idea how the Shadow King managed this. The dragon would need an incredible power source, and I can't think of any that could bring him here. But what I do know, the king has thrown everything he has at us. If we survive this battle, he will be left weak. It will give us an opportunity.

But first we have to survive.

"Dragon!" I shout at the others.

There's a chorus of shouts as the other men scream the word, warning everyone in our army of the coming danger. At any other time, this would be the moment we retreated, but we don't have that luxury now. Even though these creatures and the dragon can't get far from the Void, with enemies all around us, neither can we.

Besides the fact that if we run, they'll simply plant the shards, and we'll have lost.

As the dragon draws closer, Onyx is behind me. He's trying his best to wrap up Dusk, to stop the bleeding, but I can see the fear in his face. My brother is in trouble.

"We need to get him to cover, where the dragon can't reach him," I mouth, unable to sign with my sword in one hand.

Onyx nods and puts his arm around my brother's back.

"You're going to be okay," I tell Dusk.

He doesn't respond and the pain in his face says he can't.

The shadow dragon is already too close. I hold out my sword, taking deep breaths, knowing that my sword will do next to no damage against a creature that powerful. When...

when I see something that makes my blood run cold. Someone is on the dragon's back.

The Shadow King himself.

Someone shouts, "The Shadow King!"

If there was fear before, it's a thousand times worse now. I half expect to see my men running in the face of the king and his dragon, but to my amazement, they don't. If anything, my men close in closer to me, still fighting, trying to offer their would-be king support.

The smoke dragon lowers to the ground not far from us, on the other end of the clearing. The king climbs off his back, hitting the ground. His clothes are all black, as they've always been, but his cape moves about him in a way that's both creepy and frightening. It reminds me that once upon a time this man was a shadow beast like us, but now he's something else, something terrifying.

The smoke dragon shields the king with its wings, taking arrows and bullets that mean nothing to him. His wings temporarily hide the king from us until the attack stops. And then, the massive creature lifts its wings and lets out a roar that shakes the air around us.

The king raises his hand and the shadow beasts fighting for him stop, moving away from their opponents, then bow their heads. My own men seem to struggle against the need to bow themselves, but I'm proud of them when they don't. They simply stop fighting, staring, waiting.

He walks toward me, toward Onyx and Dusk. And he smiles. "Your brother is injured." He cocks a brow, glancing from me to him. "It looks bad."

"It is," I say.

For some reason, my treacherous heart wants to see any sign of concern in his face. Anything to signal that the man I loved, the man I admired once upon a time, is still somewhere in there.

But I see nothing.

"It doesn't have to be like this," I tell him, again some small part of me hoping to see a soul somewhere inside this terrible man.

He tilts his head, still smiling. "I thought you loved battle."

Battle, yes, but nothing like this. Not my brother gravely injured behind me and shadow beasts fighting shadow beasts. He knows this. He knows everything about me.

Or at least he did, once upon a time.

"You like it too," I challenge right back.

"I do." He wags his eyebrows. "But I don't love battling my sons."

Sons. Does he even still see us as his sons? Because no father could hurt their children the way he'd hurt us. No father could watch his son in pain and smile.

"Then stop." The words leave my lips before I can contain them.

If my father wanted to stop, he'd had a million times before this to do so. And he hadn't.

The moments before we left our world flash in my mind over and over again. I trusted my father. I never saw his desire for power above all else. There was cruelty, yes, but I never thought *he* was cruel. Even when Onyx warned me. I never thought any of it could be true.

Until he stole the life from our world to feed his own power. Until the moment my brother had a chance to kill him and didn't, and only seconds later we realized he should have. That was the first time I knew he had to die. Knew that he could no longer be king.

"Rule with me. We'll end this ridiculous human occupation and the earth will be ours. You, me, your brother, even the little deaf boy. There's a place for all of you." Onyx breathes in deep but doesn't move. Not because he's afraid, but because I haven't given a signal.

And because he doesn't believe him either. My father is gone. Only the Shadow King remains. And given the chance, this man would kill us all.

The Shadow King doesn't know the meaning of the word *mercy*.

I smile and clench my sword more tightly. "I would rather die than rule with you." I pause, hoping Ann is safe, praying for Dusk to get away, knowing this could be my very last battle. "Father."

And my father, the Shadow King, smiles. "You've grown. Because, no matter how you answered, you were all going to die today. And you actually knew it, didn't you?"

The dragon behind him roars, and it shakes the very earth beneath us.

I turn enough so that Onyx can read my lips "Get Dusk to safety. There's nothing else you can do here."

"Phantom," my brother says my name weakly.

"I need to do what neither of us was strong enough to do before."

Not looking back to see if he understands, I clench my sword tighter and start running, blade held out before me.

My father smiles, not even reaching for his sword, and I know. I know this is the moment one of us will die, either way, and this will all be over.

At last.

I picture Ann's face. *This time I can't hesitate. I won't hesitate.*

My mate needs me to be strong.

SHIFTERS' SECRET SIN

STOLEN BY SHADOW BEASTS:
BOOK TWO

ONE

Ann

MY SHADOW BEASTS are battling an enemy they can't possibly defeat. I know it in my heart. There was no other reason for them to send me away, except that they wanted to protect me and no longer felt they could. They've gone into this fight believing that they won't survive it, and I can't let that happen.

No matter what it costs me.

I stare at my mate, my heart aching. Even though he's in Adrik's body, there's no denying that it's him. Not just because only Rayne could kiss me like that, not just because I see Rayne in this man's eyes, but because I would know the man who stole my heart anywhere.

My mate. Dead and now somehow back with me.

It hurts me more than I ever imagined that I have to turn away from him now. That in one direction is freedom, the two of us escaping back to our fae brethren and leaving behind all the danger that comes with the Void and the shadow king, and yet I can't go in that direction with him. Instead, I have to go toward the battle. Toward almost certain death.

"They're not going to survive," I tell Rayne, hoping he sees it in my face, sees what I want to do.

He frowns at me, his brows drawing together. "Maybe not, but this isn't our battle."

Maybe it wasn't... once upon a time. It wasn't when the shadow beasts first took me from the Royal Fae Academy, but things have changed. If the shadow beasts fail, the world will fall. What's more, Phantom, Onyx, and Dusk aren't just random beasts to me any longer... I care for them. And I'll never forgive myself if I walk away now and leave them to their fate.

"I have to go back."

A stubborn kind of anger falls over Rayne's face. "No."

I almost laugh. "You can't tell me *no*."

"Ann, this isn't our fight. What's more, there's nothing you can do against enemies like that." I know he doesn't mean to sound like he finds me weak and useless, but that's exactly how it comes across.

Irritation blossoms inside of me. "I saved your sister. I protected her from the light fae who wanted her dead. I risked my life for others. Just because you... weren't around, that doesn't mean it didn't happen." He's about to interrupt, but I hear the roar of a creature so large I can only imagine what it could be in the distance. Where the battle is taking place. My pulse picks up, and I try to push aside the images of what my shadow beasts might be facing right now while I'm wasting time arguing. "I'm going back. Because whether you believe it or not, I can help."

"I'm alive," he tells me, his voice tense. "You and I can finally have the life we always imagined."

His words are like a knife shoved straight into my chest, because if it was only just him and I, he'd be right, but now something has changed. *I've* changed. "I need to go."

Rayne puts his arms out like the barricade of his arms is enough to discourage me. It isn't. Nothing is going to stop me from getting to the men who need me. And yet, Rayne only remembers me as the young light fae who followed him around, curious about the world. He doesn't know who I've become now.

But he's about to find out.

"Move."

"No," he says, his tone leaving no room for argument.

The sounds of evening — chirps of crickets, leaves fluttering, the whistle of dragonflies moving around us — aren't enough to overpower the sounds of battle, to suppress my urgency. Fires rage in the forest, somewhere far up ahead, but I can see the light, even from here. The shadow beasts are burning grave trolls, or maybe some new creature that burns has escaped the Void. I don't know which, and I don't care.

I have a purpose, a need, a force driving me, even if I don't understand it or how I know it.

I darting one way, but Rayne is suddenly there, his huge frame dwarfing my own. "Stop this nonsense. These men took you. All you have to do is use this distraction to leave with me. To return to the Royal Fae Academy and our lives. We'll finish our classes. We'll get married. It'll be like none of this ever happened."

That's not how the world works. "Okay."

His hands drop, and he gives me a tentative smile. "One day you'll see this was the right choice."

Yes, it is.

I race around Rayne, only seeing the shock in his eyes

for a moment before I'm leaving him far behind. The battle, the click and clack punctuated by the grunting of men fighting and the groans of men in pain, calls to me. I swear the forest flies by me, almost like when the shadow beasts had carried me on their backs and stolen me. It's like in just a short time I changed from the girl at the academy to a woman of the woods, and I like the change.

Behind me, I hear Rayne shouting my name, but I just keep going, closer and closer to the battle, the flames, the sounds of pain. My heart is racing. Sweat is running down my back. When I reach the battle, I know things are going to be bad. I know there are better people than me to be running into battle, but I will do whatever is in my power to protect the three men who have taken root in my heart.

My mind moves, not to saving the world, not to the battle, but to *them*. Dusk and Phantom, tall and dark with long tangled hair, and Onyx, sweet, silent Onyx, with his blonde hair and huge body. All three of them are big, strong, and powerful. And all three of them have a softness inside of them that is so unexpected, and so perfect. My heart aches at just the thought of them. The thought of them getting hurt.

And then, I hear a voice and slow, slipping behind a tree. Hugging it, I peer out at the battle. In front of me... a massive dragon made of smoke and ash rises up behind a king. *The Shadow King.* The man wears a black cloak and stands tall and proud, but not regal. No, he holds himself like a man who doesn't deserve the title of king. A man who cares for power more than his people. A man who oozes a darkness that drips deep into his soul. And yet, the sight is terrifying. Some of his beasts, shadowy wolves with red eyes, fight against our men, who stand as humans, fighting with swords and shields. And yet, my gaze slides across them all and to where the king stares.

At *my* men.

Phantom is injured. Blood rolls down one of his arms, but he stands tall in front of his brothers, as if his body alone can protect them from this twisted king. Dusk lies on the ground behind him, covered in blood, with Onyx cradling him on the ground. I have no idea how bad Dusk's injury is, but I know if he isn't standing, he can't stand. Which is worrying.

My breathing comes in and out faster and faster as the king's deep voice rolls over the crowd. "Rule with me. We'll end this ridiculous human occupation, and the earth will be ours. You, me, your brother, even the little deaf boy." The shadow king's voice is as clear in my head as if I am standing behind him. "There's a place for all of you. "

Destroy the earth? Insult and hurt my men? Not on my watch.

"No," Phantom says, his voice louder and stronger than the shadow king's. "Leave this world. Release your hold on our people and allow me to take my place as king."

Silence stretches for a painful moment before the king speaks again. "You can't possibly think I'd agree to that," he says, and I can hear the mockery in his voice.

"I didn't, but I wanted to give you one last chance." And, somehow, even with the odds against him, I almost believe Phantom. Almost believe that he thinks he's about to win this battle and is giving the king a chance to bow out.

But then, the king laughs and gestures to the smoke dragon. The nightmarish creature rises up onto its back legs and roars into the air, shaking the ground with the sound. Flames grow in its belly, bigger and brighter. The scent of smoke fills the clearing, so strong I'm almost choking on it.

And I know that if that dragon releases its flame, my men will die.

But you can stop it.

Rayne showed you that you can do more than what they said the light fae can do. That you have the power of the dark fae too, within you, so what else can you do if you try?

The words are foreign in my mind, spoken as if by someone else, and yet, I believe them.

So I do the only thing I can; I run into the heart of the battlefield, frantic, because this is where my men are. *Where I need to be.* I don't know when I started thinking of them as *my men,* but it's a truth I can't deny. I hear a gasp from Phantom as I sprint in front of him, and then I channel every drop of anger, every drop of frustration, and the deep desire to protect the people I love into my hands, into my heart, like I do when I'm healing. Only this time, I need my powers to do something different.

If they can.

Please, I beg.

To my shock, light blossoms in my palms, growing brighter and brighter. My gaze locks with that of the shadow king, and there's amusement in his face. But as the light in my hands continues to grow, I see his amusement fade away. I also know it's too late for him to stop this. I *feel* it. *Know* it. This power is ready.

Ready to save us all.

I concentrate on launching the light out, forward, toward the danger, toward the dragon and the shadow king himself. It explodes from me in a wave of bright yellow light that blinds me for a moment. I'm sure it blinds *everyone* for a moment.

My eyes squeeze into slits, but I don't stop. I just keep pouring this strange light out and toward our enemies.

It feels natural, this magic. Like it isn't a part of me, or like it's from some deep part of my soul that I never knew existed, and yet, somehow, also like it was always there, just waiting for me. Like the first time Rayne taught me to use the dark fae's abilities. He said that our abilities were limitless, we only needed to learn.

My eyes adjust and I see that the light hit the dragon first, over the shadow king's head. The creature makes a strange sound, almost a wailing. Cracks of light form over the dragon like lava awakening in the earth, and then the creature shatters, sending ash everywhere.

There's shouting. Panic. But I ignore it and turn my light onto the king. Before my eyes, the glowing cracks form in him too, and pieces of him begin to turn into ash and fall. The scent of burned flesh fills the air, nauseatingly powerful, mixing with the coppery undertones of the blood that's splattered everywhere. But then, the shadow king makes a sound, one I don't understand, and suddenly waves of the dark shadow wolves with red eyes leap in front of him. My light hits them as the king runs for the Void, and a dozen or so of the beasts die before my eyes, crumbling to ash, while the others chase after their leader.

I try to turn the light onto the king, but the glow from my hands fades, not strong enough to reach him any longer. And then the king is inside the Void. He's half a man, half a crumbling pile of lava and ash. But still, he's alive. His remaining beasts follow him into the Void as my light completely vanishes, and then it's silent all around me.

The battle is over.

I'm shaking. *How the hell did I do that? What the hell was that?*

Rayne is behind me. I didn't realize it until he spins me around by the shoulder. I blink at him, feeling strangely confused, my head light, my legs shaking, but I will myself to remain standing. To focus. "Ann, we need to run!" He sounds desperate, but I feel far away.

I pull free of him and look toward my shadow beasts. Phantom, standing, injured, but okay. His bright green eyes looking at me with awe. Onyx, sitting on the ground holding Dusk, his gaze sliding from me to Dusk, his expression frantic.

And then, Dusk. Fallen. Bleeding, but breathing. Yet he's dying in front of my eyes. That feeling deep inside of me, the one that I didn't know was there until I first healed these men, roars to life within me, screaming that he needs help. That with each second that passes, he moves closer to death.

My body wants to collapse. I know it. But my heart firmly tells my body to toughen the hell up.

It feels like someone else who walks toward him, even though I can sense the eyes of all the men on me. Phantom casts me an uncertain look, then hurries to his brother's side, with me right behind him. Crouching down, I brush the long hair back from Dusk's face. Even in the dark I know the pallor of his skin is too pale. And his gaze seems far away, like he's not aware that I'm even in front of him.

Men come with torches. They stand just close enough to bathe my men in light, but not so close as to make me feel crowded. The harsh light makes a strange pounding form in the back of my head. Nausea rolls through me, but I take deep breaths, willing my body to obey me when it feels like it wants to fail me.

Looking down at Dusk, I freeze. My hands reach out, then pull back. So much fucking blood. I pray that it isn't all his, but as I push aside the shredded remains of his shirt, my heart is in my throat. Some bastard tried to cut him in half.

Slashed from one shoulder down to his hip on the opposite side of his body. And the wound is more than flesh deep; it's struck organs. Vital organs. There can't be much blood left in him.

He's hurt. Gravely injured, even. If I can't heal him, I don't know how he'll live.

He won't, a soft voice whispers in my mind. It's the same strange but soothing voice I'd heard in my mind when I'd fought the shadow king.

"I'm so sorry," Phantom whispers to his brother, bowing his head over Dusk, and his voice is filled with hopelessness. Almost like instead of saying sorry, he means to say goodbye.

Onyx signs something, his hands covered in blood, but I only pick up the words, "not yet."

"No, not yet," I whisper back.

Not if I can help.

"I-it's okay," Dusk murmurs, his eyes filled with pain.

"It's not," I say, swallowing around the lump in my throat. "I can fix this."

He starts to shake his head, winces, and his eyes close like even the movement was too much for him. "You can't."

Yes, I can. I will!

I feel tears rolling down my cheeks as I press my hands to Dusk's chest. He winces, and I hate that I have to touch him. Hate that I have to cause him more pain. But I will, if I can save him.

In my mind, I picture every moment we've shared. The times he's made me smile. The times he's made me laugh. This man is special, important. There is no one like him in the world, and I can't lose him. I *won't* lose him. I have the power to heal, even if I don't know entirely how to use it. I beg my powers to help me now, when I need them the most.

But nothing happens.

I try to focus. I try demanding that my powers work. But still, nothing.

Reaching for the strength inside me, the source of my power, I sense... emptiness. Panic unfolds inside of me. I have to save Dusk. If I can't save him, nothing else matters. Not myself. Not this fight. Nothing!

Heal, damn it! I scream into my mind.

And then I feel it, a power that wasn't there a moment ago flaring to life, filling me. My body shudders in protest, almost like it's too much for me to handle. But I ignore all the warning bells and reach for it, knowing it's Dusk's only chance.

My hands begin to glow. My breathing grows harsher as I try to focus on how much I care for this man, and how important it is that he heals, that he survives this. Every healer said this was essential to their magic, this focus on the task at hand, on the person who needs healing. I'd never more than causally listened to healers discuss their magic, but now I channel that idea with every thought in my head focused on Dusk and my desire to save him.

My hands glow brighter and brighter against his ragged flesh. Maybe I press, I don't know, but he makes a miserable sound, almost a scream that he's trying to swallow down, and it takes everything in me not to stop and check in with him. Instead, I stay focused. He begins to fight beneath me, and I see Onyx and Phantom take hold of him.

Dusk's entire body begins to glow. I feel a little like someone who can suddenly control electricity but doesn't know how the hell to do it. There's so much power at my fingertips, power that I hope I'm funneling into him as I picture the parts of his body that need this magic. I don't know if that's exactly what I should do, but it feels right. So I keep going, watching, hoping.

Before my eyes, I see the bleeding slow and change. I don't understand what's happening inside his body, but *something* is happening, something I hope is good. And then the sides of his flesh begin to pull together, closing the massive wound in his chest. Time passes, and I'm not sure when to stop, when it's enough. I feel sweat dampening my body, and now I'm shaking so hard my teeth are chattering, but I don't stop.

And then the glow radiating from my hands begins to dim. My gaze clings to Dusk, trying to notice any small detail about him. *Is he better? Will he be okay?* After a tense moment, his breath comes easier, his pale skin floods with color, and he opens his eyes, a smile on his beautiful lips.

I touch his cheek, returning his smile. But then I hear men screaming, moaning, and I jerk. It's like I'd tuned out every sound and sense around me, just focusing entirely on Dusk, and now that I'm not, the world has opened itself back up to me.

It's overwhelming. The smell of coppery blood and smoke in the air. The trees in the clearing splattered with blood. The bodies everywhere. My gaze sweeps over the battlefield, and I realize that most of the men are injured in some way, although their friends are already helping them, already scooping them up and carrying them from the battlefield. But it's like a nightmare as the various torches and burning piles of grave trolls light the dark night, sending shadows dancing like more enemies come to destroy us.

I shiver again. *War. This is war.*

A man passes Phantom. "We're taking them to the home cave. We'll save everyone we can."

Phantom looks grim. "The shadow king and his men

won't be back, at least for a little while, so just focus on our injured. Take whatever you need of our supplies to save them."

The man nods and disappears into the woods.

I try to stand, to help, but my legs give out from underneath me. I try again, falling once more.

"Ann, rest," Phantom tells me, and I see it in his eyes: he knows what I want to do.

"I can help."

"You already have."

My eyes sting. "Not enough."

A man screams when two people lift him from the ground. His scream carries above the others, and he struggles in their arms. His screaming turns to begging, and then they set him back down. There's a flash of a sword.

Then silence.

I try to stand again. This time when I fall, I start to crawl. Phantom is there in an instant, scooping me up and placing me right back beside Dusk.

"Rest," he says again, and there's a warning in his voice.

If I was stronger, I could save them all. But I'm not. I never have been. At the academy, I was average at best. The most interesting thing about me was that someone as powerful as Rayne was my mate. Here, strange and unexpected powers are awakening that someone like me shouldn't have. But despite all logic, I do. And yet, they're not enough. Even if my men could carry me to the injured, I can feel it inside of me. I only have so much left. There's not enough for even a fraction of the damage I see around me.

But I can do *something*.

Turning my hands to Phantom, I reach out for him.

He catches my wrists. "How did you do that?"

What? The healing? They ray of light? Regardless, the answer is the same.

I shake my head, feeling the gazes of Rayne, Onyx, and Dusk on us. "I don't know."

"Well, it was amazing," Dusk whispers, and he sounds tired, but not in pain.

I can't focus on any of this now. That little bit of power is still pulsing inside of me, looking for direction, looking for a release. It's not much, but it is something. And before I collapse in exhaustion, I want to use it.

Phantom has a gash on his arm. Blood darker than a human's but still pungent with heavy metals slides down his arm and chest. I pull free of his touch, then reach tentative fingers toward him.

"I'll survive," he tells me.

"Please," I whisper, and he doesn't stop me as I place my fingers on his wound.

He seethes a sharp breath in then out as I focus on his injury, on healing it. But I have to push the sound away. I have to forget that I'm even a person. All I am is a tool for the magic, for these brave men.

I let the energy flow between us. My hands feel warm. My body is exhausted. But strangely, as my hands glow and the light spreads down his arm, it all feels natural, like this is what I've always meant to do. It only takes seconds, the sides of his flesh pulling together as the gash fades away, and then I'm done.

My power is done.

The light fades from my hands, and I shiver, pulling away from Phantom. "Better?"

"Better," he says, then signs to Onyx.

The big man signs back something I don't know, then a sign I did know, "okay."

"Do you need me to try healing you?" I ask, letting my gaze run over him, even though I don't think I have anything left.

He shakes his head, then stands, poised to fight. As if he can feel all of our exhaustion, and he's not yet ready to believe we're safe. Like he alone can protect us all. And somehow, as I look up at him, I believe he really could keep us safe from anything and everything. He's just so beautiful, towering and hulking over us like a guard. His long blond hair tied at the back of his head in a warrior's tail, his dark eyes scanning the trees with narrowed eyes. He's like... a god. A prince. A man more legend than reality.

I want to touch him, but I curl my fingers into my palms and try to push aside the feeling. There will be time for that later. For now, we need to get our men to the cave and check to make sure I've healed them enough.

"Help me." I glance at Phantom, who, for such a big guy, moves with the grace of a gazelle. He lifts Dusk to an upright position. But as we get him to his feet, Phantom staggers, then shakes his head. He tries to take a step forward, then falls to his knees.

Onyx is there in an instant, saving Phantom from a face plant, letting his best friend lean on him as he half-carries him. Then, taking one of the torches and starting forward, he begins leading us through the dark woods, one arm wrapped around Phantom as he hauls him along.

"Come." I motion for Rayne to help me with Dusk, but Dusk shoots Rayne a cautionary look and Rayne holds up both hands, stepping back as if worried about the guy who can barely stand.

Rolling my eyes, I shove myself under Dusk's arm and wrap mine around his waist. His body is firm, warm, solid, but I treat him gently as I remind myself of his injury.

We make our way back to the tunnel that will take us to our smaller cave. Dusk is obviously trying to help, to not put all his weight on me, but the walk back to our little cave seems to take forever. I'm definitely sweating, focusing on putting one foot in front of the other, and trying not to think about the battle... about my strange powers... about what refusing to leave with Rayne means.

"Thank you, Ann, for coming back." Dusk's voice is husky and deep, and I can't help but look into his eyes. They're pale and glowing with need, with desire so potent it's like a caress against my skin. Which is just crazy. This guy was at death's door a moment ago, and now he's looking at me like he wants to jump my bones.

Oh yeah, and then my "dead" fated mate is alive in another man's body. So if I need things to be more complicated, well, they are. And I have the feeling this is just the tip of the iceberg of the problems heading our way.

"We thought we didn't need you," he continues. "We were wrong."

"Yeah, you were," I say, trying to make light of this whole strange situation. But the truth is, it isn't like I ever had a choice. I'm drawn to them, all of them, the same way I'm drawn to Rayne. "And I'll always come back." It isn't just pointless words. It's a sentiment. One that is no more my choice than who I am is.

One that means I'm accepting that they're right... that we're something important to each other, even if I'm afraid to admit what that something is.

As we walk toward the cave, Phantom is leaning on Onyx in front of us, with Rayne following Dusk and I. "You brought a... friend." Dusk stumbles and I catch him. I can't deny what I know in my heart. The moment is upon us. I have to be honest, to tell them.

I nod, almost stumbling on a tree root before I right myself. "Yeah." Never has a glare felt so powerful. "But it isn't what you think." They won't guess. If I give them a hundred years, there's no way they're getting this one. And it isn't like they're going to like this story any better. "Adrik is Rayne." That isn't enough. "Rayne is Adrik." Although God knows how I'm going to make this make sense. Even to me, a fae, it's not usual. "Rayne's ghost took Adrik's body. I don't know how, but I'm thinking because Adrik's soul, mind, whatever, was already gone, it made it easy for Rayne to step into him. To use his body."

"*Rayne?*" Phantom glances from me to Adrik's body and back. "Wait. *Your* Rayne? Your *mate?*" He jabs a finger behind him at Rayne, who's hanging back as we walk toward the tunnel.

"Yeah."

Phantom's eyes flash, his jaw ticks, and Dusk glances down at me.

"I'll explain when we get back to the cave." I don't wait for him to agree. I can't. I need these few minutes to organize my thoughts, to make sense of everything I haven't had time to digest. I just have to figure out a way to explain this that makes sense to all of us.

TWO

Phantom

MY THOUGHTS ARE A MESS, even more so than my aching body. Battle is never easy, not on the mind or the body, but especially when I'm fighting my brethren. It's somehow much worse than fighting my father. For a short time, I tried not to hurt the shadow beasts controlled by my father, knowing that if they were free, they would never fight us. But that notion was dashed away pretty quickly when I realized fighting one of my own, while trying not to hurt them, was a good way to end up dead.

Still, every time I look into their faces, I wonder who they are. The baker who snuck me treats as a boy? A maid who cared for our home? Friends? Boys who grew into men right alongside me?

It's a cruel thing to wonder these things, so I try not to, as impossible a thing as that is. Instead, I try to see them as just an extension of my father, because it's the only way to not lose my mind as I end them. They are *not* my people, trapped in their beast-form, unable to escape. They are enemies.

And if we can win this war, maybe I'll be able to free them.

At least what's left of them.

With time I've accepted that the man I once loved, once placed on a pedestal, is not a good man. He's enslaved my fellow shadow beasts, all but the small pack that stands with us on earth. And no good person has ever enslaved others. That means that all the pleasant memories I have of my father when I was a boy no longer matter. That man is dead and gone. All that remains is a dangerous enemy.

But still, seeing him is only a touch easier.

Not that war is ever easy.

The tunnel we've entered is silent as our haggard group makes its way back to our little cave, past the section that connects to the main cave. Sometimes it's strange to me that we chose this cave away from the rest of our people. At first it was mostly out of shame. Had we been smarter, had we seen the truth in our father sooner, none of this would have happened. But it was more than shame that kept us away after that. It was knowing that our people weren't as comfortable around us royals. It created a tension in the main cave that was palpable, and our people already have enough to deal with without being uncomfortable in their would-be home. And then, finally, it was because with our father's anger mostly directed at us, we hoped to keep him from finding their home.

Which has worked. Even if it has the price of keeping some distance between us and our people.

When we reach the hidden cave entrance, Adrick—no, Adrick's soul was consumed by the smoke dragon—*Rayne*,

Ranye in his body, says, "Allow me," like he's welcoming us into a castle rather than approaching our cave.

It irritates me, but I keep my mouth shut, watching the man as he moves forward. Adrik is a big man, not nearly as big as the three of us, but large like all shadow beasts. His hair is light brown, cut short, which is uncommon for our people. His weeks spent lying in a cave, his body wasting away, had weakened his muscles... but apparently, not as much as I would have thought.

Rayne, because that's who this is now, moves the boulder protecting the hidden tunnel's entrance with only a little difficulty. When he's done, he turns to us with a grin. A grin that doesn't make sense after our battle, after the loss of my men, after seeing my father again. It's as if this man has no concept of war and of life and death, even though he himself was dead.

Dead. It's still hard for me to wrap my mind around.

"After you," he says, his grin now falling away, as he waves us forward.

Still feeling irritated, I allow Ann and Dusk to stagger in, followed by Onyx, and then I come through at the rear, eyeing this Rayne critically as I do. When the boulder rumbles back into place, leaving only a small amount of space for Rayne's hands, I try not to feel irritated that he seems to know how things are done around here. Because that probably means this ghost has been haunting our Ann and watching us.

Kneeling down, I stoke the embers of our fire higher, carefully, then add fuel to the flames until it's crackling once more. My body still aches, but not like it did right after I'd been healed, which I'm grateful for. At least I don't have to appear weak in front of this man.

Ann has helped Dusk to lay down on his blankets. She

pulls off his bloody, torn shirt, then goes to a bucket of water we keep in one corner and begins to slowly clean the blood off of him, staring at his chest as if to check for more damage. Dusk's eyes close, and he lies back on the blankets, his face tense.

My mind goes back to him during the battle. He was marked for death. He should have died. And now, because of our Ann, he's lying down being touched by the woman he loves. It's good, but it's confusing.

"Onyx? Phantom? How are your injuries?" She doesn't look up from where I sit, watching her.

Onyx signs, *What does she want me to say? There's always pain after battles.*

I sign back to him, *She wants to help us.*

So that she won't feel guilty when she leaves with her real *mate?* Onyx's words are harsh, filled with an anger I understand.

He stares at me, waiting for my answer, maybe my reassurance, but I don't have it right now. My mind is still on the battle, almost as if it can't handle what this man means to our already chaotic world.

"Is there anything to eat?" Rayne asks.

Onyx's glare slides to the man in our cave, and I feel my own annoyance rising as I rub at my sore arm. Rayne doesn't *belong* here. And the more I think about it, the more I realize that I hate that he's here. I hate that he's the master of her heart. Her *supposed* mate. Because he's *not* any more, shouldn't be any more. *We're* her mates—Onyx, Dusk, and I.

This is the fucking last thing we need after a battle.

Rayne's pale brown eyes move to me, and his casual demeanor changes a bit. "Anything at all? I'm starving. At this point I'd eat some berries if I had to."

If he had *to? Is this how all fae royals are?* Ann was never this way.

Still, I rise and go to one corner. I unwrap some of our jerkied meat and throw a piece. It hits him in the chest, and he barely manages to catch it before it hits the ground.

"Uh, thanks."

I grunt in response, but I really want to tell him to just leave. That he isn't needed here.

"So, what happened to the rest of those guys?" Rayne asks, biting into the jerky, wincing, and chewing slowly.

The other shadow beasts in the battle against our father are back at the main cave, healing, recuperating, benefiting from tried and true medicine that had been passed from age to age, administered by the elders. Those who weren't injured are patrolling, watching for trolls who escaped the battle, who weren't killed by the blinding golden light Ann used to kill anything in her path. But Rayne should know this if he's been haunting us, shouldn't he?

When none of us answer, Ann finally looks up and seems to realize there's tension in the air. Her mouth pulls into a thin line, and she says, "They'll be at the main cave, healing."

Rayen nods. "Wouldn't it be smarter if we were with them? You know, strength in numbers."

Onyx huffs and goes to his belongings. He grabs another rag, removes his shirt, and uses some water to begin to wipe himself down, ignoring the man in the room. A man I wish I could ignore too.

"This is the way we've set things up." There, I answered him.

Rayne lifts a brow but seems to realize we aren't in the mood for his chit chat. Instead, he positions himself against a wall, then slides to the ground, resting as if he were the one to take on our enemies. A small voice in the back of my head reminds me that he's using the body of someone who is probably feeling frail and weak without eating for so long and only drinking the little bit of water that our healer could get into him, but a louder part of me just feels annoyed by everything the man does.

"Well, Dusk will be okay, but he could use some more healing," Ann says, and she sounds relieved. "I'll try to use my powers again when I can. Right now, I still feel a bit weak."

In response, Onyx silently brings her a water skin and some jerky. She thanks him with a smile, but shares it with Dusk before she has any herself. He drinks the water eagerly, then begins to gnaw on the half of the jerky she handed him. It's almost enough to make me smile. We tend to care for our women first, but Dusk would never have been able to turn down something Ann offered him.

She begins to eat and drink slowly, and the firelight illuminates her face in a way that reminds me of when she used her powers. Her remarkable, unexpected powers. Her ability that saved us all and might be the key to winning this war, if we can figure out a way to harness it without putting her in danger.

"What was that light?" I don't mean to blurt out the words. But now they're out there, waiting for clarification so she doesn't step around them. "The one you used to obliterate the trolls, the one you used to heal us."

"I don't know. I just knew it was there and I used it." Her big blue eyes blink as if she doesn't believe it herself. And that's at least one small measure of relief. Ann wasn't hiding this great power from us. She wasn't holding back. It came as unexpectedly to her as it did to us.

But my relief is short-lived when Rayne stands up, his

jerky finished, and sits down beside Ann, his hand running along her back. "It was incredible. What you did tonight... just incredible."

She gives him a little smile, but there's something in her eyes I can't read. "Thanks."

He returns her smile, and the look of contentment is gone from Dusk's face, replaced by concern. And Onyx isn't fooling anyone, chewing his jerky like he wishes he was tearing Rayne's head off instead.

Normally, this is the time when I'd step in. When I'd cool things down. When I'd remind my brothers about the logical aspect of this. Rayne being back doesn't mean we'll lose Ann. It doesn't mean she'll choose him.

But she could. And that small chance makes something inside of me unravel.

I can't be here in this space right now. My head is too muddled with the things I know and those I don't. And her presence blocks any sense I might be able to make of it. All I want to focus on is her and our relationship, on how Rayne complicates it, but there's so much more outside of that. I should be the leader of my people, even though I don't feel like one. I should be thinking about our next step. Our next plan.

And I can't do that around her.

She sighs. Not in sadness, maybe not even in frustration. But the sound shoots through me.

"I'm going out to get supplies." Not because we need anything pressing, but because I need to clear my head. I don't wait for an answer but walk out. Past the shelves where we keep our supplies, away from the bedrolls near the always burning fire where she helps Dusk recline, away from her, from Rayne.

From a problem I can't seem to find the answer to.

The sunrise burns on the horizon. It's normally a time I would bask in the dim light, but I hurry through the woods, almost running, like I'm trying to escape things that aren't even chasing me. But my mind moves in circles, entrapping me, refusing to let me pretend, even for a moment, that things are like they were before Ann.

I should be plotting a way to take down my father and end him in a way that leaves no doubt the next shadow king is me. But instead, I'm thinking of Rayne. And Ann. Always Ann. But Rayne is a new twist in our story. A bad twist I never saw coming.

I stomp toward a clearing. There are healing herbs here I can gather, even though I don't care about them. I can't see past my own anger. Rayne is back. After all the work we've done, now that Ann is so close to accepting us as her mates, he's back to take her from us. This fucker has come home in Adrik's body, no less. It's true he and I weren't close, but I knew him, and he was a good man.

Rayne is her true mate. She's said it before. And the way she pulled that light, she must have drawn it from his energy. That kind of power can't be hers singularly. *Can it?*

I think of all the things I know about Rayne. Conversations we've had about him. Things she said. Ever since Adrik was drawn to the shadow world and his soul consumed by a smoke dragon, his body had been dying. I suppose this fixes that, but Adrik isn't Adrik now. He's Rayne. Her mate.

No matter what I do, I can't forget that. He is her *true* mate, at least in her eyes.

But aren't we too? The mate bond can't be ignored, can't be falsified. What my brothers and I feel is just as real as what he feels for her, what she feels for him, but does she feel that way for us too? I think she does, but I'm not sure any more.

I sigh and walk on. The herbs grow wild at the edge where the forest overtakes the grass. When I bend to pick a stalk of hilder root, I hear the footsteps behind me. Nudging my dagger from its sheath, I'm prepared for someone stupid to be behind me. It isn't often anyone tries to sneak up on me. Never does anyone succeed.

I twist and hold my blade to his throat. Adrick. Rayne. *Shit. Of course it had to be him.*

"You're following me." It's obvious by his presence, but I needed an opening that doesn't make me want to kill him.

He touches the point of my blade, with a brow raised. "Sharp." And there's mockery in his voice, almost like it's beyond the possible that I would actually kill him, which speaks of an arrogant man.

You've already died once, you fool.

"Phantom?" The fact that I haven't lowered the blade makes the mockery fade from his voice.

I don't have to tell him I'm going to kill him. He's the kind of warrior who knows it. "You're here for her?" Also likely obvious.

He stares at me, and I lower the dagger. I might kill him, but it won't be today. No, because I'm not that kind of man, and I wouldn't deserve Ann if I was.

"I saw you take care of her, be kind to her. I saw everything you did for her." His face... there's sincerity in it. Sincerity I don't want to see right now. "And I appreciate it."

But...

I wait for it, knowing there will be more. If he's followed me to tell me he can take it from here, I'll hurt him. I won't want to, but the primal need that drives me to put my mate above all else will make any other reaction impossible. If he speaks those terrible words, he'll taste my fist.

"And?" I cock a brow because I've seen Onyx do it, and it never fails to get his point across without words.

He releases a slow breath. "Thank you for taking care of her. And thank you for keeping her safe."

I shouldn't have to tell him that she's done as much for us as we have for her. He should know that, if he knows her at all. I shouldn't have to tell him that protecting her isn't a choice for us. It's who we are, who she makes us . And I want to kill him because he doesn't know, because he's reduced her importance to us to nothing more than a duty rather than an honor, rather than a desire, rather than passionate obsession.

"She's my mate," I tell him, choosing each word with care. "That's my job."

His gaze sharpens. "I know you three think she's your mate and that she's important to this battle of yours..."

"There's no *think* about it, on both accounts."

"I guess she's the one who will decide that though," he says, running his fingers through that short hair of his. Not nervously, but almost like he feels sorry for me, like he knows her choice, and it won't be to stay with us.

"Are you going to take her away from us?" The question might make me weak, but the answer has the power to crush me. To destroy all of us. And I get the sense that so far in this conversation, he's dodged whatever he truly thinks. Whatever he's planning.

He sizes me up with a glance, with a gaze so stark it's clear what he wants. But instead of honestly telling me that, he shakes his head and shrugs. If he had pockets, he would shove his hands in them. "I don't know. Like I said, it's up to

Ann and what she wants. That's all that's ever mattered to me. All that ever will."

And fuck if I know what she wants.

"If you try to take her, I'll kill you."

Some men have whimpered when I've spoken similar words. Others have cowered. But this Rayne? He gets that look of pity on his face once more. Probably because he knows that as much as I'd want to kill him for taking our Ann, I wouldn't. Because she's not just some prize, some possession, some tool to win this war. She's a woman, a person, and if she decides to leave with this man... we'll let her.

Because what else can we do?

I turn away from him, heart in my throat. Tonight, we won a battle, but we may very well have lost the war.

THREE

Ann

The cave is quiet and awkward. Rayne had kissed me before saying he needed to step out for some air. I wasn't sure if it was because I was exhausted, but the second he left I picked up on just about every emotion in the cave... and the emotions weren't good. Onyx and Dusk seemed to be more angry and jealous than upset after the battle. Part of me wanted to shout at them, to ask them if this is really the time and the place for this kind of nonsense. But another part of me wonders how I would feel if some old mate from their past life came back.

The thought alone makes my teeth clench together. As wrong as it might be, I would never want another woman touching them, being near them in any sort of romantic capacity. At the Royal Fae Academy, Rayne was constantly hit on by other women. They knew I was his fated mate and there would be no one else for him, but they didn't care. They saw me as so far beneath him logically that it might be the one time a mate-bond could be broken. At least, I'm assuming that's what they thought. The thing is, it didn't bother me that much. I knew I wasn't the prettiest, the smartest, or the most powerful. But I also knew that Rayne barely noticed the women, so this rise of jealousy inside of me over a non-existent woman is new to me, and a bit of a hard pill to swallow.

Rubbing the back of my neck, looking between the two men who seem upset, I drink more water from the waterskin I'd been given and eat more of the jerky. My muscles feel tight. My head aches, and my body has that sore feeling that comes after a hard workout. The thought of laying down right now and falling fast asleep sounds amazing, but I close the waterskin and finish the jerky, knowing that no matter how much I might want to rest, there's still more work to be done.

Dusk's wound might be healed, but his chest still has a massive black and blue bruise on it, and I can see him wincing and holding back a groan every time he moves. If I can help him, if I can ease even a little of his pain, I need to. Regardless of the tension in the room.

If I can.

My magic isn't without limitations. I know it. They know it. And I'm wondering if I can even do more tonight after all I'd already done.

I move closer to Dusk, and he puts one hand up. "No."

No? Since when doesn't Dusk want me to touch him? Since when does Dusk tell me *no?*

"Dusk." I try to keep my voice gentle. "I want to help." I want to ease his suffering. But when he glances at me, there's a fire blazing in his eyes, mistrust where it used to be only trust.

"Are you leaving with him?"

Oh. I thought the men were just upset about Rayne appearing back in my life; I hadn't considered anything after that. But now it's suddenly making a lot more sense. They're afraid I'm going to leave them.

"Just let me try to heal you." I reach for him again, but he jerks back from me, hissing in pain.

Which makes me feel about an inch tall.

He would rather suffer than have me touch him. Rather just lie there in pain if there's any chance that I might be walking away from him and his brothers. But I don't want his healing to be connected to whatever decision I might make in the future. These things aren't connected. Not in any way. And yet, it seems clear he won't let me help until I give him an answer.

Whatever that answer might be.

I'm not dishonest. I can't be with them. Any of them. So I just speak without thinking. "I don't know."

Damn it. Okay, that is definitely an honest answer, but not at all what I meant to say.

I shake my head not as a negative answer, but because I'm confused. I love Rayne. He's my mate in every sense of the word, but there's no discounting what I feel for Dusk and Phantom and Onyx.

"That's your answer? You don't know?" Dusk repeats, his expression furious.

Onyx begins signing, and I glance toward him, only picking out a few words, but his movements say it all. He's pissed. More than pissed. And then, he pushes to his feet and stalks out of the cave.

Dusk watches his best friend leave, then his narrowed eyes return to me. "Do you care about us at all?" The question and his tone as he asks it are loaded with emotion, with demand and anger and frustration.

I nod. Of course I care about them! I care so much. And I would die to keep from hurting them, but I can't give him the answer he wants about our future. Not one hundred percent. What if Rayne needs to go back to stay in this body? What if these shadow beasts can't provide him with the care he needs? I could never let him die again, nor would I want to ever just walk away from this fight or these men.

Dusk stares down at his hands and I know he's building to saying more. I try to prepare myself for his words, but I know I can't, because these men can hurt me in a way I never imagined possible. And heal me in a way I never imagined possible too. With a word. With a touch. It's like they're the ones with magic within them.

"You know Rayne coming back doesn't have to be a terrible thing..." I don't know if that's what I should have said, but it feels like it needs to be said.

"Bullshit. The minute he came back something changed." His voice is edged, sharp, damning.

Anger boils inside of me. It's like these shadow beasts want Rayne to stay dead... a concept I can't imagine them being okay with. What's more, it's like they want me to see my mate returning as a bad thing, which will never happen. "Well, it isn't me. It's not how I feel that's changed."

"You aren't glad he's back?" The accusation is implied. He thinks I've used them to pass the time, to make myself happy, to squander their feelings.

Which... just pisses me off more. *Is that how they see me? Is that who they think I am?*

"Glad he's back? Damned right I am."

A low growl rises from his chest, and he stands, even though it's obvious the movement pains him. He paces for a moment, then presses his hands against the wall of the cave like he doesn't know what to do with himself.

His distress makes me stand, even though I'm still angry. But it's like I can't just stay sitting when I know he's hurting. When I feel his pain like it's my own.

I move closer to him, wanting to touch him, but I stop myself. "I *am* glad that he's here because losing my mate was consuming and painful. It was devastating, like a piece has been missing from me every day since I lost him." And now comes the biggest truth. "Much the same as Onyx is a piece and Phantom is a piece." He turns a little toward me, his hands dropping, and this time I can't stop myself, I reach for him, and curl my hands into his hair. "You're a piece of me, too, but... I'm confused."

"This should be easy. You said... you made us think..." His arms come around my waist, pulling me against him, holding me in an embrace that is neither short nor sweet. It's powerful and persuasive and now I'm intoxicated by him. My head swims a little, and I stare into his eyes. Wanting him to touch me. Wanting him to kiss me. It feels like the whole world is holding its breath, waiting for this moment, for a reminder that Rayne's appearance really hasn't changed anything between us.

But then he pulls away, moves to the side, and I'm denied contact, the warmth of his body.

It's more than I can stand. I reach for him and he shakes me off. "Don't try to seduce me."

I've never seen him like this. Never heard him like this. He's trying to sound angry, but the hurt in his voice comes through stronger.

"I'm not." And now my voice isn't more than a whisper. "I'm not." I plunge my fingers into his hair and pull him down for a kiss that is meant to brand him into my mind, to let him know that the force of what I feel for him is not tempered by what I feel for Rayne. But instead, his kiss conquers me. His lips are hard and possessive against mine, claiming me as his woman in a way no one can ignore.

He holds me against him, *hard*. Then he turns us so I'm trapped between him and the wall. His body keeps me in place, so I can feel every inch, muscle, and plane. And I do. I *feel* him, this big man, this creature of muscle and strength. So big compared to my tiny size. So large that it feels like I'm surrounded by him, not that it's enough. As he kisses me, I just want more. *Need* more.

His kiss slides down my throat, greedy and hungry, while I grasp his shoulder with my free hand, while I moan and whimper and throw my head back into the cave wall. When he reaches for my shirt, he pulls it down to expose my bra, then unclasps it, letting the cool kiss of the chilly air touch my bare skin. I almost tell him we have to stop, that he was just hurt, that there are a thousand reasons for us not to do this, but the words die before they leave my mouth. Instead, I just hold myself still as he cups my breast, kneads it, then uses his palm to tease my nipple.

My breath sucks in, and I pull him into another kiss. His tongue duels with mine and there's power in what he is, who he is, and in that kiss I feel the rawness of it, the untamed, unknown. I'm captured in the moment. Wanting more, but not sure what. Just knowing I need it. Need *him*.

He jerks away from my mouth and takes my nipple between his teeth, sucks, flicks it with his tongue so I am writhing, moaning. I love the way this man kisses me, touches me, knows just what I want even when I don't. It's like we're one. Like we've done this a thousand times before, and at the same time, that it's new and perfect in every way.

I let my hand drift lower, between us, to squeeze his

cock. He's hot and hard and long. Despite all logic, I want him inside me. And the second that thought enters my mind, I can't think about anything else. That's exactly what I need, what we both need.

When I hike my leg over his hip, he growls down at me, "Tell me you're my mate."

"What?" I'm beyond words. Beyond thoughts. I'm cloaked in confusion. Dizziness. And I want him. I'm so hot for him I can't even think. "What?" I don't even know if I spoke aloud the first time, or just thought I had, so I say it again.

"Say it, Ann. Say I'm your mate."

I grind my hips against his. "Please."

"Say it, Ann." His voice is desperate, filled with a husky desire that only increases my desire.

And I know... I know I can just say the words. I can speak them, and he will fuck me, and it will be glorious. Divine, even. A memory that will keep us both warm even on the coldest nights.

But I can't say the words. I just don't know.

"Just... forget about that right now," I say, panting each word, stroking his cock through his pants, reminding him of what we could have.

"Rayne can be your mate." His voice is laced with a desperation that mirrors the one in my soul. "But is it possible that we are, too?"

I want to say yes. I want it so bad. But it's wrong. I can't because I just don't know. "Dusk, don't. Please, don't ask me this right now."

To my shock, he pulls back, hard. Turning away from me so fast that my shaky legs almost give out from under me.

I don't know when my shirt went askew or how. I know

nothing except that I'm bereft without his touch. Every breath is hard and shallow, every beat of my heart labored.

"I'm sorry." These are the only words I can speak.

And I don't have time to speak another. I barely have time to straighten my clothes before the elder Auero is standing at the entrance to the cave.

He's old, although I can't say how many years he has under his belt. His hair and mustache are equally white and he stands with a hunched back and eyes pointed at me. He's the kind of character who would be equally welcomed in Mordor or Hogwarts.

His voice is gravel. "Ann of the light fae."

"Yes?" I don't know what to say. My gaze goes to Dusk, but he has his back turned to me. And I don't care about Auero or what he has to say, I just want to speak to Dusk. I want to know that he's okay and that whatever just fell apart between us can still be fixed.

"Tell me about the light you summoned. Tell me how you did it." These aren't gentle commands. He wants to know, and I should be fearful of whatever consequence comes when I don't have an answer, but I can't. Because that kind of power, it's feral. I can't control it, I know that, and I'm afraid that one day it's going to control me.

I don't even know if it was me controlling it. Not really. Because if it was me, why didn't I have this ability before? Why didn't I use it when the academy was under attack?

I shake my head. "I don't know. I just wanted to protect my men... and the light came."

He sighs, disappointed. Disillusioned. Unhappy. *Sorry, big fella. The truth is the truth.*

He looks at me, from my hair to my toes, and when his eyes find my face again, they aren't happier or kinder. "If the shadow king attacks again, if he brings another army, we won't make it unless the prophecy is fulfilled."

Oh, the prophecy. I sigh. This is an old argument. Everyone here seems to believe that a mating bond between me and my men is needed to secure the lives of the shadow beasts outside the shadow realm, to win this war. It's a lot of responsibility to hand to me. My sigh is my only response.

"Ann, we have some time before the shadow king regroups and builds his forces, but the next time he comes, it will be the end. The last time." He eyes me again, one brow up this time. It's a look Onyx has mastered, and now I don't wonder where he learned it. "Are you ready to create the mate bond with Dusk, Phantom, and Onyx? To be the savior of the shadow Solemus?"

I'm not. I can't. The slightest shake of my head is enough to make Dusk huff and puff like he wants to blow the cave down.

"Her true mate is back from the dead. He's in Adrik's body." Dusk is quite the news anchor and the words ring in my ears. I can't imagine how it sounds to the elder, but his face blanches, so I don't really have to ask.

"Does this mean you aren't going to fight with us against the shadow king?"

I don't have an answer. I don't want to answer him about this or the prophecy because the future, mine specifically, is uncertain.

Auero turns, shaking his head as he walks out.

His frustration is a fine commentary, fitting to my very existence.

But when I look at Dusk, he simply goes to his bedroll, lies down, and turns his back to me. The urge to lay with him, to touch him, is there, but I push the feeling down.

Instead, I wrap my arms around myself and sit against the wall, feeling lost.

Figuring out who I love, who I care for, who I feel a mate bond with is more than enough pressure. But doing it while being told that my decision might impact the fate of these people and the world itself? Well, I'm going to need some sleep if I have any hope of untangling this mess.

FOUR

Rayne

I FEEL LIKE A GIANT ASSHOLE, and it makes absolutely no sense. And yet, I can't seem to forget the expression on Phantom's face when he threatened to kill me. He looked like a man desperate to keep the woman he loved. A desperation I'd felt myself many times since my death.

And I hate that I can relate to this strange man. Well, to all three of the men, with their eyes filled with love every time they look at my mate. It's like seeing my own emotions, which should make me feel connected with them, and it does, but it also gives me the sense that we're in competition with each other.

But there's no competing with fated mates... at least, that's how I'd always understood it. Ann is mine. I am hers. Yes, fae can have multiple fated mates, but the men usually have a bond that makes them a unit, and then they together fall in love with a woman. It's true these men have a unit themselves, but I'm on the outside of that.

In my experience, I've never seen anything like this.

But then, there's a lot that hasn't made sense since I died.

Finding a stream in the quiet woods, a stream I'd seen Ann and the men bathe in before, I take off the warrior's clothes I'm wearing and step into the water. A shiver rolls up my spine. The morning sun has just barely made its way over the horizon, and the water still holds the chill of the night. But I don't care. I just want to feel clean.

No, I want to feel like *me*. Like I did before.

Naked, I wade deeper into the water and go under the surface. I scrub at my hair and body, trying to wash away the scents on this body. The general feeling of misuse. When I'd first awoke in it, I'd just felt... like myself. Like I finally had a way for Ann to see me and speak to me once more. But the more I use this body, the more I feel like it isn't my own. It's massive compared to my other body in all ways, taller, more muscular, and somehow less... regal, as dumb as that sounds.

And now that some of the shock of "coming back to life," has worn off... I feel strange. I keep thinking back to my time as a ghost. Before Ann was taken by the shadow beasts, I remember very little. That I was murdered in the dark tunnels beneath the academy, yes, but not much beyond that. And then, Ann was taken. It was like the dim world I was in, where time seemed to have no meaning, was gone, and I was just left to shadow her.

But that's all I was. A shadow. A part of me always knew that eventually I'd go to wherever a ghost went when they were done with whatever was anchoring them to this earth. My heart broke watching Ann get taken. It broke me even more that I couldn't do anything to ease her fear of the shadow beasts. But even while she feared them, even while something inside of me raged at not being able to protect my mate, I recognized myself in those men. I saw the way they looked at her and knew they could no more hurt her than I could.

I, well, I watched her falling in love with them. And in my ghostly form, I felt confusion. This war, this danger, was not part of our world. Ann should have been safe, with her family or at the academy, not dragged into the woods with a dark shadow waiting to consume us all. It felt unfair after all she'd been through, and a part of me blamed these men for putting her in this situation.

Scrubbing my body in the water, I notice goosebumps forming all over my skin, but the chill is good. It's clearing my head, making my time as a ghost feel further and further away. I try to focus on what was important in that dark time. But all I remember is having a deep sense that Ann was in danger, and that she was falling in love with the shadow beasts.

I could do nothing about the situation. I couldn't help anyone, or change the path my love was on. But now I can, and yet, it still feels like I'm a ghost. Ann ignored me when I tried to keep her away from the battle, then proved me wrong in every way by ending the battle with power I never knew she had inside of her.

My shy fae... has changed.

Still, after she saved them, I naturally assumed we'd be gone, away from this war, and away from these shadow beasts, these creatures of legends. Instead, my mate seems to have no idea who she wishes to be with, nor what path she wants to be on, and that's frustrating as hell. What's more, the shadow beasts don't seem to like me in any way. It's like they blame me for being in Adrik's body, for coming to her, for being alive. I never thought it was possible and I sure as fuck don't understand the magic that made it happen, but I'm here. With Ann. Where I belong.

I don't know how long the magic will last or if it's going to fade before I get the chance to see this through. All I know is that I have this chance and I'm going to take it. Being with her is all I want. To make sure she's safe. Happy. Protected.

But I can feel that she loves the others. If not loves, has feelings for the others.

I can't tell her it's wrong. I can't beg her to be with me because I don't know what the future will hold. And because, well, I don't beg.

Even if this whole situation is making me miserable.

When I feel clean enough, I get out of the river and dry under the rising sun. Then, I put the clothes back on, which isn't what I'd prefer. Clean clothes would be far better, but at least these seem to be fresh. And since I'm no longer at my manor, or at the school, I don't have servants to lay out nice clothes or serve delicious meals. This outfit seems like only the first of many adjustments I'll have to make until I can convince Ann that we don't belong here.

Not that I need all the luxuries my life as a powerful royal fae brought me. They're just nice.

I walk through the woods back to their little cave. It's quiet, time to think about all the things being back means. If only I could figure out what those things are. I have no idea. Maybe a greater purpose? Maybe because I wanted so badly to be with her? Maybe she wished me back? I don't know. I just want to figure it out.

"Rayne?" An old man steps out from behind a tree to stop in front of me. I'm so startled by this random man in the woods that it takes me a minute to realize that he didn't call me Adrik. *So he knows who I am.*

But I know who he is too. Elder Auero. The man my Ann and her men had gone to for advice. Not quite the leader of the shadow beasts here on earth, but someone that has a wealth of knowledge within him. And someone who, apparently, has the ability to listen to the whispers of shadows, whatever that means.

I straighten my back and square my shoulders. "Yes?"

"A word?" He says it like I have a choice. He's an old man—really old—blocking my way.

I nod. "Okay."

He takes a moment, purses his lips, chooses his words. "She's vulnerable. And you make her more so."

I don't know that I like where this thing is going. "I make her vulnerable?"

He nods. "Yes. She has a prophecy to fulfill." *Yeah. I've heard about the prophecy. It's shit.*

I release a slow breath. Fae are typically respectful to their elders, but most people, even the elders, knew better than to challenge a Bloodmore. Having a dark fae as a father and a light fae as a mother, most people believed I took after my mother... that I was simply a powerful light fae. But it didn't stop the small look of fear that I sometimes saw in their eyes. Yet, this man doesn't have an ounce of fear in his eyes, which is oddly unsettling.

"The prophecy that she has to accept those three as her mates to save us all?" I scoff. "I'm sorry, but no. This Void, or whatever it is, doesn't have the power to destroy our world. Not for a second. If it did, my people would know about it. This little battle between your own people doesn't really involve Ann and I. So once she accepts that, we'll be out of here, back to our old lives."

There. I wasn't quite respectful, but I'd tried not to be an ass.

"Let's pretend I agree with you. How long do you think occupying that body is going to last?" He looks me up and down with eyes glazed by disappointment.

"I--" The truth is I don't want to think about it. I am above all else an expert at researching. And through my research I've read many things about ghosts. In the past, ghosts have been able to occupy bodies for a limited time, a day or two at most, but the host is always battling for control. The ghost always eventually loses to the host, and then they're back to just being a ghost. But with me, there is no Adrik left in this body. No one battling me for control. It doesn't feel like I took a body that I can't keep, it feels like my spirit found a new home.

Still, that doesn't mean I can occupy it forever. But every time the thought blossoms in my mind, I push it aside. Live each day like it's your last has always been my philosophy, so the fact that any day actually could be, even more realistically now, is not something I'm going to waste my time thinking about. At least, if I can help it.

"Do you want her to be alone?" He's studying me, waiting for his words to sink in, and I hate that they do.

Ann alone. It's a sobering thought and one I'd selfishly not considered. "I don't—I don't..." I'm stammering like a child. Shaking my head. Fidgeting from one foot to the other. And in this body, the body of a warrior, I probably look ridiculous. And I can't control it.

"She lost you once, and her heartache might be the reason she's rejecting the others. Her heartache might be the reason she won't fulfill the prophecy." He gives me the look again—blame and disappointment mingling in his eyes, his mouth a tight line, his brow creased. It's the guilt and the blame that I look away from. "If you don't set her free, let her do this, you've made the choice for her. You've taken it out of her hands. You've..."

I hold up my hand to stop him. "Okay. I get it."

"I don't think you do." He shakes his head and his long white beard sways. "I think you're selfish. You're hanging on to a woman who needs to move on."

"I'm not hanging on. She didn't even know I was still... in this world, until today." I don't know that it matters.

"Without you, her heartache will fade eventually." At least he gives me that. *Eventually.* Not that tomorrow she'll replace me with those three big men, which I'm sure he wants to say. "But if the boys all die, she won't stop grieving. Whether it's the prophecy or the emotion, she won't recover. And she'll never forgive herself. Or you." He cocks a brow and I'm measured by the look.

"This isn't her fight. Or mine. And we've put ourselves in danger, almost died." I *did* fucking die. I don't know that reminding him is purposeful, but I cock my head and breathe out. It's done. He's reminded.

"Rayne, in all your vast years of life and death..." Oh, this man knows the power of words, "have you ever known a ghost to take a body permanently?" He stares with one eyebrow cocked, lips parted, breath in one sturdy huff. Every move of his body, every turn of his head and blink of his eyes judges me, makes me the inferior party here.

I sigh. The weight of all this is crushing to my soul—the only part of me not up for discussion with Auero. "This is different. And you know it just like I do." The accusation is heavy in my voice. "I took the shell of a body. There was no soul in here fighting me for space."

Auero stares. "Are you sure?"

"What am I supposed to do if I'm not sure?" It's my turn to shake my head. "Leave her now?"

"No. By all means, wait until the body rejects you and thrusts your soul away. Leave her alone so she has to face your death a second time." The old man knows sarcasm.

So that is what he wants? For me to turn around and leave now because... because it'll be easier for all of them? Does he not understand fated mates? Does he not realize that would hurt Ann just as much as seeing me actually leave this body?

No, it's too late. I'm not leaving Ann. Not until I have to. Not ever again.

And yet, is he wrong about everything else?

"What then?" I'm shouting because I'm frustrated. And I'm frustrated because he's right and I don't know what to do. Maybe I need his advice. He's an elder. Made it to the ripe age of... who fucking knows. But he made it. And that means he's seen a lot. Heard a lot. And if he's never seen a soul take an empty body and survive it, then maybe listening to him is in my best interest. But he's actually suggesting that I leave her. And he knows I came back for her. "What do you want from me?"

"If you die again, Ann will be alone whether you like it or not. Unless she has them. The men she's destined to be with, just as much as she was destined to be with you. Only, your time with her was cut short. Theirs doesn't have to be." His voice is low, quiet, the punctuation to end a conversation. If his statement hadn't ended it, walking away would've.

No matter how much I hate it, he's right. My situation isn't guaranteed. There is no promise I'll live ten minutes, much less be able to guarantee a lifetime. And she would be alone. There's no way I can leave her to that fate.

"Fuck." There isn't much more I can say.

"And what about that light of hers? The one that destroyed a creature as powerful as a smoke dragon? The first thing to hurt the king?"

My thoughts sharpen. My sister had always been more of the adventurer, running with the monsters on our lands, talking with the ghosts in the graveyard. I'd always been the one to like books, reading, researching, and, well, making observations based on my research. Through my investigation at the Royal Fae Academy I'd learned that light fae weren't just what we thought we were. Yes, we fed on good emotions. Yes, we could create glamours and grow plants. But there was more to us, so much more. I focused my research mainly on the difference between light and dark fae, and our powers, but there were other things. Legends about why the light fae were called light fae.

But now, I can't quite remember what the books had said. It hadn't seemed important at the time. Yet after seeing what Ann had done, I wonder if I'd read something about that particular power... the ability to control light. If it was a common power we no longer knew how to access, a rare one, or just a legend.

I don't know.

All I know is that her powers surprised me. Maybe even scared me a little. If she could do that, maybe she could defeat this king of shadows. But if she was the only one who could stand against him, that also meant she was in the most danger of anyone here. And I couldn't stomach the thought of her in danger.

"You know something," the elder says, and I realize I've been lost in my head for too long. My sister always said I was in my head more than I was ever in this world. Something that would make me smile, but I'm not smiling now.

"I'm not sure."

His gaze narrows. "Can you control the light too?"

My stomach flips, and despite myself, I reach for my magic. Only, it's not there.

Every muscle in my body stiffens. I try again. Turning away from the elder, I reach my hand out and point it at a flower. As a child of powerful fae, my ability to control nature was always easy, like breathing, not at all the struggle it was for Ann. But still, nothing happens.

"I-I don't think I have magic in this body." I speak the words aloud before I even process them myself.

No magic? That's impossible. Magic has always come easily to me. It's like part of my soul. *Without it, who the hell am I?*

When I turn back to the elder, he's frowning. "Perhaps because you're no longer technically a fae."

Is he right? Am I... am I a shadow beast now? If I return home, will I even be recognized by my kind as one of them? Will my parents accept me as their son? My sister... my sister would love me in the body of a duck, but everyone else... even if I return home, I may not be able to convince them. And that means no longer being able to provide Ann with the life she deserves.

"Fuck," I mutter.

"Fuck indeed," the elder says.

Things just got even more complicated.

FIVE

Ann

TIME HAS PASSED, but the tension in the cave is still at an all-time high. Onyx allowed me to check over his injuries, which were thankfully not so bad, but he treated me like a random healer rather than someone he's kissed. Someone he's touched. Skimming my hands along his arms, back, and chest only made the torturous feeling between my thighs increase. Every so often, I'd steal a glance at Dusk. But he didn't look back at me. He just laid beside the fire, with a clear erection that made my mouth feel dry.

"You're looking much better," I tell Onyx.

His gaze falls on me, but all I can read in his eyes is disappointment before he pulls away from me and struggles back into his shirt. Then, he goes to clean his weapons, seemingly ignoring me, and yet, I know he isn't. I know neither of them have forgotten I'm here, even if they might wish they had.

We're all exhausted. Battles aren't easy, but we haven't had much of a break lately either, so it makes the feeling of pure exhaustion take on a whole new meaning. The sun has risen, which is usually time to sleep for us, so I feel like everyone is just holding their breath, trying to decide what Rayne and I will do.

The thing is, I don't know. But I do know I'm not going anywhere, at least any time soon. Unless Rayne needs me to, *truly* needs me to in order to stay in this body. But not unless it's a life or death situation. Deep down I realize that Rayne coming back should have changed everything for me, and maybe it would have a few weeks ago, but now, now it feels like the most bitter-sweet gift I've ever received. My love, my fated mate is back.

But my shadow beasts, they're important to me too. Too important to walk away from, no matter how much Rayne might want me to.

When Rayne strides back into the cave, my gaze snaps to him. He stands in the doorway, radiating that regal energy he always seems to radiate, even in a different body. But then, Rayne has never had anyone look down on him. Not anywhere. Being the only son from a powerful family, he was treated like a prince among our people. Meeting him at the academy was like meeting a celebrity in real life. Realizing he was my mate was like winning the lottery.

Yet, it surprises me a bit that even here, far from our home and people, he still enters every room, or in this case, cave, like he owns it. It's sexy in a way, but also stressful, because there's no way the shadow beasts are going to appreciate his confidence.

And when Dusk's eyes open and he sees Rayne at the entrance to the cave, I know I'm right. Dusk's eyes narrow and he huffs out a breath, winces for his trouble, and then huffs another. It's like the man can assert his alpha presence with a huff alone, which is oddly impressive. Each movement he makes, even the way he glares at Rayne, screams that *no one is tougher than Dusk*. That's the message he's trying to convey anyway.

After a moment, Rayne shoots him a glare right back. He crosses his big arms in front of his chest, stretching the brown leather clothes he wears. My gaze moves over him, and then up, realizing for the first time that his light brown hair is wet. *He must have taken a bath in the river.* Somehow, it's hard to imagine Rayne bathing in a river.

"So, where do *we* sleep?" he asks, and I know his question is directed at me, but his words are meant to be a blow to the shadow beasts.

And they are.

Dusk scoffs. They don't exchange any more words. Mostly it's posturing—a series of grunts and angry stares.

Finally, I break the awkward silence. "There are bed rolls over there if you want to grab one and put it by the fire."

He tears his gaze from the other man and gives me a hesitant smile. "Any place in particular you want us to lay?"

Us. We. These are all things he's saying to make a point that I'll be sleeping with him today, and I want to scream at him. To tell him this is not the place to piss all over me and claim me as his own. We have enough shit to deal with.

"Just lay it anywhere."

He notices the edge to my voice and lifts a brow, but I don't explain. I don't need to. He knows exactly what I'm doing and exactly why I'm doing it.

"Ann," Dusk says, rolling a bit to look at me, then patting his bedroll. "Should we get some sleep? It was a long night."

"She's not sleeping with you," Rayne says, venom in his voice.

"She's not sleeping with you," Dusk throws right back at him.

"And who is going to stop her from sleeping with me? *You*?" Rayne looks at Dusk like he's looking at a spider he could kill with a flick of his hands. I almost remind him that killing someone with his mind doesn't work against shadow beasts, but I'm sure he remembers. Maybe he's already tried his abilities since he came back.

Dusk slowly climbs to his feet, and I match his movements as the big shadow beast crosses the cave to stand in front of Rayne. "Try me."

Rayne steps a little closer, chest puffed out, eyes dark and flashing with anger. "But you're injured. It wouldn't be a fair fight."

"And you're a dead man in a borrowed body. I think I'll do just fine." Dusk's light blue eyes scream insults his mouth never forms.

"Guys." I'm not quite between them, but I'm moving closer, trying to decide just how to handle all of this. I've never had men fighting over me before. I've never had anyone outside of Rayne even give me a second glance. "Let's just cool down." The words sound lame, even to my own ears, but I can't help it. "We're all just tired and overwhelmed."

"This isn't about any of that," Rayne says, still glaring down at the other man. "It's about this prick having a chip on his shoulder."

Onyx rises from where he was sitting, and I swear the tension in the room grows tenfold. While Dusk I can trust enough to not start an all-out fight, I don't have the same faith in Onyx. If he gets involved in this, they're all going to end up hurt. And that's the last thing we need right now.

Lifting my chin and putting out my hands, I say, "Stop this right now! I'm not kidding!"

Onyx moves to stand near me, eyeing Rayne.

Dusk looks back at him, and Onyx signs something that I'm sure isn't good.

"You're right," Dusk says. "Maybe the dead man should go back to the main cave so we can all relax."

"No." Everyone looks at me. "You are not kicking him out of this cave. Because if he goes, I go too, and I don't want that. And I don't think you guys want that either."

Dusk shakes his head, his expression one of disbelief. Like my words are a betrayal. "Let's get out of here. I need some fucking air."

They walk out of the cave without a backwards glance at either of us, and I have the miserable feeling that they think I was taking Rayne's side. I wasn't. I just don't want there to *be* a side. I don't want it to be me and Rayne versus them. We're on the same team. They just need to realize that, and Rayne's behavior isn't helping.

"Fuck, Rayne." I'm torn between the man I know as my truest mate and the men who say I'm theirs.

He shrugs. "It's not my fault the beasts are so unreasonable."

I glare at him. "They're not beasts. They're men. Men who have saved my ass more times than I can count. Men who care about me."

His cocky demeanor falls away. "This is hard."

"I know." My gaze holds his. "But has anything ever been easy between us?"

"Between us? Yes." He gives a small smile. "It's the rest of the world that hasn't made our romance easy."

I wrap my arms around myself. "Rayne, you know I love you, and that I've missed you. Missed you more than words can say. But things are already hard enough. Can't you just make them easier?"

His face says it all. He knows he's fucked up. "Come here." He holds out his hand and there's nothing I can deny him, not after I lost him. Not after the hole he left in my heart.

I take his hand. He grabs some new blankets and lays them down by the fire. Then he sits down and pats the space next to him, all the tension gone from his body, from his expression.

I sit beside him, and he wraps an arm around my back as we stare into the crackling fire.

"I missed you so much," I admit.

He kisses the top of my head. "I missed you too."

I relax, closing my eyes, taking a moment to pretend we're not in the middle of the woods. Or in the middle of a war. Or that Rayne's existence has complicated things with Onyx, Dusk, and Phantom. I just lose myself, imagining that everything is back the way it once was.

He's in Adrik's body, but he's Rayne. He smells like Rayne. Sounds like him. I've missed him with all the parts of myself that are responding to him right now, to the devastation of my loss, to the possibilities of his return.

Opening my eyes, I look at him, and he looks down at me, that familiar mischievous glint in his eyes. The one that always made me laugh. The one I imagined never seeing again. I kiss him and it's perfection, soft and sweet and filled with happiness, just the way it always was, until he pulls back and puts his hands on my shoulders.

His sigh is loud in the silence of the cave. "Ann, I don't know how long I'm going to be able to stay here."

"What?" I was gone for a minute, lost in my fantasy, and his words are like a bucket of cold water.

"I'm a ghost. Ghosts don't stay around forever."

The fact that he's back at all is a miracle I've only just begun to digest and he's talking about leaving or not being around, which is the same in my head. *Why? Why do we need to talk about that? Why do we need to think about it? Can't he just pretend along with me?*

"One day, there's a good chance I'll be gone again."

"Don't say that." It feels like he's twisting a knife straight through my heart.

"Ann…" He shakes his head and whispers again, "Ann."

"Don't say it." I lost him once. He has to know I can't lose him again.

His expression becomes unreadable. "Ann, could you walk away from them, from your… shadow beasts for me?"

How can I answer that two seconds after he's told me he doesn't know how long he'll be able to be with me? "Rayne, you're here." It's that simple and I don't want to think past this moment. But it doesn't answer his question. "I don't know." What I have with Rayne is one side of a coin, but Onyx and Phantom and Dusk are on the other and I don't want to think about losing any of them. There's been too much loss already.

He swears softly. "You really care about them, don't you?"

I don't answer him, but he reads the answer on my face.

"Maybe you'd even love them… maybe even feel the mate bond with them, if I was really gone?"

I feel tears burn my eyes. "It doesn't matter because you're here."

"It does, because if I can't be around forever, and they're your mates too…" He seems to be struggling to form the words. "Then you can't leave them behind. You have to make sure they win this battle, so you'll be safe. So you'll have a future with them."

My head is spinning. "What are you trying to say?"

He growls low in his throat, and I hear his teeth clench together. "You should make room in your heart to claim them as your mates"

My eyes widen because those words are the last ones I expected to hear from him. I don't know if it's a test or not, but it sure as hell isn't permission. They're only words. They have to be. This isn't the Rayne I know. "What?"

"You'll regret it if you don't. I know it. You know it. If you don't... the consequences..." This can't be him either. Or he's not just changed bodies.

Either way, it sounds like he's trying to let me go. Again.

"It's a prophecy. Do you know how many of those don't come true?" My words sound far away, even to my own ears. And not at all logical. I feel like I need to pick a team, pick a path, and stick with it, but I can't seem to. I don't know why.

"And I know how many do." He doesn't, but he speaks with an undeniable force. "Are you willing to risk losing them because you're afraid?"

What the fuck? "Afraid? Holy fuck, Rayne. Are you saying goodbye to me? Giving me your permission so I don't get lost in my grief again?" It's like he's already out the door. "Fuck you, Rayne."

He curls his fingers into my shoulders. "Listen to me, Ann. I've only ever done what's best for you. Ever."

I scoff because he honestly believes his own bullshit. It's in his eyes. His tone. "You go ahead and lie to yourself all you want, but don't you dare sit here and spew that idiocy at me." I know too much and the pain of his lie rockets through me. Spurs me on. "You left me alone because you had some ridiculous quest for the truth for your sister and the dark fae. You left me alone. How was that what's best for me?"

The heat in my body radiates from a place deep in my chest. It burns along every one of my cells.

He stares at me, the kind of gaze that's meant to wither my resolve. It's a Rayne tactic and I'm immune.

"Do you care how fucking hard that was for me?" The tears come from the same place as the heat.

"It was necessary."

"It wasn't. It was ego. Your over-inflated ego." That isn't true. Probably isn't even fair. But he left me and he's laying the groundwork to do it again. I'm trying so hard to make it not matter, but it does in my heart where it's always mattered, where *he* matters.

"Ann." His voice is gentle, almost gentler than I've ever heard it. "You grew up with a stepfather who beat you. Who hurt you. Who made you feel ugly and unloved." My heart stops. My fingers are trembling when they come to my lips, but he just keeps talking. "I think if I hadn't been your fated mate, you never would have been able to let your guard down with me. You were... scared of men. Of all men. I'd see you flinch when one would try to touch you. I'd see you... Ann, is it possible some of that fear is triggering you now? Making you wonder if these men will hurt you like he did, intentionally or unintentionally?"

My tears become sobs and he pulls me to his chest, crushes me against him, and it's like coming home. "M-maybe."

And that's all I can say, because I don't know. My stepfather is someone I try never to think about. I've placed that man in a dark place in my soul and walled him off from the rest of me. No matter how many times he hit me, no matter how many times he broke a bone or made me bleed, I told myself that he wasn't hurting me, he was just hurting my body. When he called me ugly and told me no one would ever love me, I told myself that everything he said was true, and because it was true, it couldn't hurt me. He was just stating facts. So the idea that any of that pain, any of those words could hurt me now is something I can't accept. Can't think about.

Because that man is behind a wall. If what he did to me is making me push the shadow beasts away, then my stepfather is still hurting me. Still has control over me. And I won't let that be real.

Even if some voice in the back of my head whispers that it could be.

"Don't let him take anything more from you," Rayne whispers, brushing away my tears.

"But if I lose you, it won't be because of him or anything in my control," I sob the words. "You could just be... gone, just as quickly as you came back."

He doesn't deny it, just strokes my arms.

"I can't lose you again," I tell him, then kiss him, tasting my own tears.

He pulls me into his lap and kisses me just a little harder, just a little more eagerly. It's like he wants to see how I feel, what I need, but I know what I need. I want to feel safe and unafraid, if only for a minute, the way I used to feel in his arms. My Rayne, he's safety and desire and passion all rolled into one. It's his skin under my hand. His hair in my fist. Mine in his. His body lying on mine, touching me in all the ways I want to be touched. All the ways I want to be brought back to life.

He rolls so that I'm beneath him on the blankets, and his hands skim my rib cage and slide beneath my shirt to cup my breast. He holds himself up, but I want to be crushed under his weight. I want the decadence of his touch. He squeezes my breast, teases my nipple until I'm writhing beneath him, until my eyelids flutter closed and I'm lost in the sensations.

His tongue probes mine, duels with it until I plunge my hands into his hair and hang on because I'm free falling. I'm losing myself for the first time in so long in pleasure, not the pain of my past, not the pain and complication in my present. I'm just all nerves, nothing more.

When he grinds his hips I suck in a ragged breath, a plea for more. "Rayne."

"Take your pants off, Ann."

I need this now. I need him inside me. Real. Touching me, fucking me until I can't breathe, until my eyes roll back, until I'm nothing but a quivering mass of woman surrendering to the passion and need.

I shed my clothes and lie on the blanket, waiting for his body to cover mine, to use this moment to reconnect with me. And he does. His weight presses down on me, a blanket of warmth and muscles. The weight of a man I love, who I've missed more than I can say. It's perfect beneath him. Safe. A fantasy brought to life that I want to drown in.

He kisses me again, harder and longer, while stroking my arm until goosebumps rise on my flesh. I'm caught between panting and holding my breath, savoring each small touch, each small sound he makes. My thighs spread for him as he sinks down further, and he positions himself at my opening, his mouth still crushing mine, claiming mine.

At first, he just slides up and down in my wet folds with his long, hard erection. It's almost painful. My nerves scream to life, screaming for more. But I force myself not to beg him to fuck me, because I know he will. When he's ready.

When *I'm* ready.

But then he does, surprising me, entering me with just his tip as my insides turn to jello. My nails dig into his back and I shift and wiggle, wanting him deeper, feeling impatient. But he senses what I need, and he slowly presses into me, one inch at a time, until he comes to his hilt. And, oh God, it feels amazing! His cock is hard, long, and thick, filling me in every way, and I moan at the delicious intrusion.

He rocks us while I gasp his name, then turns so I'm on top of him, letting me take control.

And I do, grinding my hips, riding his cock, letting every nerve inside of us scream in pleasure.

I throw my head back in ecstasy, my hands gripping his shoulders hard as I thrust myself on him over and over again. His body is powerful beneath me, his muscles corded, his thighs tight. My body trembles and shakes, shifts to go deeper until pleasure spirals through me, until my stomach clenches and cries erupt from my throat. "Rayne!"

I keep saying his name, keep riding the waves of my desire until I feel him coming too. And it's perfection. A moment in time I'll never forget. A moment I never thought I could have again.

I collapse on top of him and he strokes my hair, breathing hard. I feel like everything that matters is finally clear. I'm going to enjoy having Rayne back as long as I can. I'm going to pretend that I'll never lose him again. And I'll make it clear to Onyx, Phantom, and Dusk that I care for them too, and they won't be second to Rayne. They just need to give me a little more time.

It feels as if things might actually turn out well.

I turn my head, adjusting, and spot Phantom at the entrance to the cave. A cold chill rolls over me, and every muscle in my body stiffens. The look on his face, it's like I used my hands to rip his heart out of his chest. *How stupid was I to think I could have this time with Rayne without... this?*

Phantom staggers back and away from us, his face pale. The pain in his eyes is a blow to my very soul, and then he turns and leaves. Just walks away, like I hadn't just hurt him.

Shit. "Phantom!" I push away from Rayne in a panic. I have to fix this! It isn't a desire; I'm compelled by a force greater than most.

I start to stand and Rayne grabs my wrist. "Leave it alone, Ann."

I jerk away, hard. "No." *Doesn't he understand? Can't he imagine what Phantom is thinking right now?* "He's going to think... he's going to be hurt..."

He shakes his head and lowers his hand. "Ann, if I was the only true mate you have, him seeing us wouldn't matter to you." Like I need him to clarify he adds, "You wouldn't care that he caught us."

It isn't an accusation, but a statement.

"Fuck." He doesn't get it. I'm not sure I do either. "Fuck." I dress in a hurry and walk out of the cave because I have to repair all the things I've made wrong, before it's too late.

I've hurt them by refusing to be their mate. By bringing Rayne back with me. And the last thing these men need is more hurt and more pain.

By the time I get to the river where Onyx, Phantom and Dusk are sitting, they're fully dressed, clean from a dip in the water, their long hair left loose. But as much of a rush as

I was to reach them, I have no clue what to do now. I'm more confused than when this all started.

What do I even tell them? Yes, I slept with Rayne. Yes, I've refused to mate with them. It seems like a clear message that I've chosen him over them, but it's not. It doesn't mean that. It's just... confusing.

"H-Hi," I stutter out lamely.

Dusk and Phantom stare at me, but Onyx won't even look in my direction. The anger and hurt coming off of them is palpable. Phantom told them. Of course he did. And my betrayal is what I see in their faces.

"I'm sorry about... that." *Damn it. Do I really lack all social skills? Is that really the best I can come up with?*

Phantom crosses his arms in front of his chest, but his face has the same hard, cold look it gets when he talks to the other shadow beasts. "You are free to go, Ann. Whenever you're ready."

"Free to go?" *What the hell does that mean?*

"We won't stop you." Phantom won't meet my gaze now. He's angry. They all are. And it radiates off them like another presence.

"But what about the shadow king and the war? The prophecy?"

Phantom looks toward the river, his mouth in a thin line. "That's none of your concern. Just forget you were ever here."

Forget? "You don't mean that..." My voice comes out high and hurt.

Dusk shoots me a glare and I almost shrink back. "We *want* you to go." There is such venom in his tone I can't be sure I heard all the words correctly.

"What?"

When I don't move, they stand, leaving me looking after

them, taking my heart and all the little shattered pieces of it with them so that all I can do is crumble and cry. This is what I deserve for what I've done. Of course it is. So why does it feel so wrong?

Maybe because I love them.

I cry harder.

SIX

Dusk

SHE'S STILL THERE, sobbing at the bank of the river. The scene is familiar except that in my memory, I was the one broken-hearted, devastated at my loss. Once upon a time, there was a woman the three of us loved, and she turned away from us for another man. She was never our mate, but we loved her. Cared for her in all the ways men could. And it still wasn't enough.

Maybe *we're* just not enough. Maybe the three of us are so broken that no one, not even our fated mate, wants us.

My eyes burn. A smart man would walk away right now, would leave her crying alone on the river. But I'm not a smart man. I care about her, about her safety, more than I care about my heartbreak. I'll do what my kind are good at. I'll slip into the shadows and watch her until she reaches the cave, and her true love, once more.

Knowing we've lost her is indescribable. It's painful in a way that is worse than any injury. Right now, my skin is the only thing holding my heart in place. I want to shift into my shadow beast form, even knowing that doing so would make me vulnerable to the shadow king, vulnerable to the sun in this bright world. I want to race through the woods, as far and as fast as I can, until I leave her behind.

Yet, I'll never escape her memory.

And I can't risk her safety, no matter how angry, how hurt I am. I've sent Phantom and Onyx ahead of me so I can make sure she gets back to Rayne. As much as I hate him, she doesn't. As much as it hurts me to know, hurts all of us to know, I can't let her be hurt. I won't.

After a little while, she strips and goes into the river. She hasn't stopped crying though, and I try to keep my gaze on the ground. Try because this is not how I want to see her naked. But even so, her pale skin glows beneath the sun's rays, and her blonde hair makes her look like a mermaid of fantasy when it's wet and hanging down her back and shoulders.

When she climbs out of the water, dries, and dresses, she's still crying. Her sobs never slow. It's as if she thought by being clean, she'd feel good again.

Or maybe she thought washing off the scent of another man would calm us.

It doesn't. Whether she smells of Rayne or not, she's made it clear that he's her choice, and there's no way to accept that. To move on from that. To simply be okay with losing our one and only mate.

And yet, I keep watching her. Waiting for what she'll do next. Not knowing what to do when she remains there, crying her heart out, on her knees, looking so damn lost.

Her eyes look even larger when they're filled with tears. The shades of blue within them are the colors of the ocean, the colors of a pure waterfall. The liquid that slides down her pale cheeks draws attention to the scattering of tiny marks, freckles, across her cheekbones. And her blonde hair, pulled back once more in a warrior's tail, is messy, with little tendrils flowing around her face. A hairstyle that I find oddly suits her. Even the clothes the shadow beast female lent to her suits Ann. They're big on her, but they draw attention to her curves in a way her other clothes didn't, at least not as well. As I stare at her, I swear my heart aches even more. This tiny, perfect woman is mine in my heart, but that's the only place she belongs to me.

She lifts her head as though she can sense me or hear my thoughts. When her gaze falls on me, her eyes widen, and she wipes the tears from her eyes and her cheeks, as if doing so will hide the fact that I was watching her cry. She's trembling a little when she stands from where she's fallen to her knees, and she makes her way toward me.

I should've hidden better. I wanted to keep her safe, but I'm too raw to speak to her, to be close to her in any way.

Yet, I stay rooted in place, watching the swing of her hips as she comes toward me. My heart is in my throat. My mind is spinning through all the possible things she might say when she reaches me. It clearly isn't that she regrets fucking that fae and refusing to be our mate, so what is it?

"Dusk." Her voice is soft, a touch, a reminder of a memory that she wasn't even in. My mind flashes back to a woman with long white hair and a smile she rarely gave. Then on the body dragged from the moat, the one I couldn't bear to look at closely. One of my clearest memories is of her long white hair flowing around her in the water. Of her still, dead corpse.

We lost our woman then, just like we're doing now. But the outcome this time will be different, although the heartache will be the same. The wreckage. The utter destruction. But even worse because this is our mate. Even worse because losing one's mate is something that is impossible to move past.

"Listen..." she begins again, but she doesn't sound like she knows what she plans to say.

And I realize that I can't hear her words because I'll break. I have to stop her.

Whether she leaves now or later, it's going to destroy us. "Stop talking." I sound angry, which is better, infinitely so, than the sadness burning through me. "If you're going to go, do it."

Her eyes flicker. She's so fucking upset, so hurt it pains me to look at her. It pains me to see what this is doing to her on our behalf. She's not doing this on purpose and my heart knows it. Hell, even my fucking head knows it. But the rage inside of me, the part of our father that always exists in Phantom and I needs an outlet.

"I don't want to leave you when you guys need me."

I scoff. I laugh because I know it's going to hurt her and none of us are going to be okay. "We don't fucking need you."

"What about the prophecy?"

"Were you thinking about the prophecy when you were with him?" Jealousy isn't an emotion I'm good at. "When you were on top of him with his dick inside you, were you thinking about the prophecy?"

She shakes her head and looks down. "No."

"So why do you give a fuck now?" I hate talking to her this way. Hate feeling any of this shit.

She doesn't answer with more than a loud exhale through her nose.

"That's right. We got along before you came here and we're going to get along after."

The surprising shove against my chest is enough to make me stumble. The grunt from in her throat is half scream, half anguished bellow. She's angry. It's in her eyes, her voice, her stance. The way she stomps away.

I sit at the edge of the river and watch her go. It's probably going to be the last time I see her, the last time I get a whiff of her natural scent in all its flowery goodness. I touch the scar on my chest where she healed me. It's red. Puckered. Not painful, though. She took that away for me.

Once upon a time I thought my father's betrayal was the worst thing we would ever have to survive. I thought nothing could hurt inside me worse than that. But I was wrong. This is way worse than that. Partly because a king betrays to keep his throne. It's historical in the human world, in every world. The dark things they do to keep their power are the things no one ever talks about, the things that haunt dreams, what nightmares are made of.

But Ann leaving us... this will annihilate Phantom. He won't bounce back this time. For all I know, I'll be lighting the pyre for him. And Onyx just learned to trust again. He took a leap for her. He worked so hard to overcome his fears of love, of caring.

And even if they somehow survive what she's done, her betrayal, we're toast. Dead. Because of the prophecy. Because we couldn't fulfill our part and she refused to fulfill hers. She goes, we die. It's over. And there isn't a fucking thing we can do to stop it.

I wish I could find solace knowing she might leave and find happiness with her fae, but I must be a selfish bastard because the thought only makes the pain in my chest worse.

SEVEN

Ann

WHEN I LEFT Dusk at the river, I walked. I cried. I cursed and stomped my feet like a child. It was all pretty pointless, I knew that. I knew that if I wasn't me, I'd slap myself for being such a mess. But since I am me, I had to just work through my feelings until I got to a strangely numb point, then head back home.

Now, I'm standing at the mouth of the cave looking in. Only Rayne is inside, sitting facing a fire that crackles and sends embers rising into the air. He doesn't notice me at first, just stares into the fire like it'll give him the answer to the things in life he doesn't understand, probably me. But it's strange to me; as I look at him, it's not at all like looking at someone else. It's like this is Rayne and has always been Rayne, which is an unexpected sentiment.

Not that anything has been normal since he died.

I want to walk in and let him hold me, let him absorb the pain of my chat with Dusk. Let his heart speak to mine.

But I can't. Instead, I go to the fire and sit on Phantom's bedroll, gazing into the fire and letting the heat lull me into a fake kind of peace, one that calms my visceral reactions but does nothing for the aches in my emotional heart.

There won't be true peace until I figure out how I'm supposed to feel and what I'm supposed to do. There's nothing in the handbook about what to do when a soulmate inhabits a new body and comes back after the situation has changed, after acceptance has been achieved, after the moving on has progressed.

And what progress it is. But I can't think about them now, either. It'll drive me mad.

I look at Rayne from little slits that are my eyes. I know him like I know myself. But my feelings are all over the place. One part of me wishes my shadow beasts would come back right now, but another part needs a minute to get my head together. And the one thing I don't do when Onyx, Phantom, and Dusk are around is think clearly.

"Rayne?" I hold out my hand because as confused as I am, Rayne's presence is a balm to my soul. He comes to lie beside me, and as much as I want to fall into him, I fall asleep instead. It isn't until a voice wakes me that I realize how tired I was, how hung over all these emotions make me.

Flame, one of the other shadow beasts who was involved in the battle and is still healing—slowly—from his injuries, is standing over me. "Ann, the men will be taking turns guarding you throughout the night. The shadow king won't be strong enough to attack again right away, but it's a valuable thing to have you here and now he knows it." He gazes at me for a long moment, something unreadable in his eyes, then steps back out of the cave.

"A valuable thing," Rayne mimics after he's gone, and I can feel tension singing through every inch of his body. This is hard for him, which I'm well aware of, but there are things I can't control. Like the shadow beasts' response to me. "You're valuable to everyone here, I guess," he adds, and he sounds angry.

I sigh, not feeling ready for a verbal battle already, but I can't help but ask, "What's that mean?"

"It means you seem to be really popular here." He's taking that tone. It's accusation and jealousy and anger all rolled into one.

"You died. I mourned. I cried. I had to get through it." Our voices are raised, and I stare at him like his leaving was a choice.

"Every one of them just seems to look at you like you're theirs," he says, his words edged with frustration.

"They're desperate. They're lost. Can you really blame them for being excited when some random woman comes, kills a smoke dragon, and helps them win a battle?" He has to see that this is more than just that a bunch of lonely men who want a piece of me. It's about survival. It's about these people needing *something* good in their lives.

After a minute, his anger dies away. "I know. Sorry. I didn't mean it like that." He shakes his head. "I'm being such an ass, about everything. I know I am. I'm trying. There's just no way a man can prepare to die, come back, and have to share the woman he loves. It's... a lot."

My heart melts a little at the lost look on his face. "I can't imagine this is easy for you either."

"Ann..." He stares back, his eyes soft with hurt and disappointment. "It's hard to be here, to see how you are with them." He sighs and shakes his head. He's building up to whatever he wants to say. "I can share you with them. It's going to be hard, but I can." The sincerity in his tone, in his eyes, in his everything... He means it as much as he can and he will try because that's who he is.

Share me? Rayne? "Are you sure?" My voice is filled with disbelief.

He can't be. This man... he's never been the type to share *anything*. What's more, he doesn't seem to like my shadow beasts, or believe in their war. *What's compelled him to go from running from here with me to giving me his permission to link myself to them forever?*

"Yes. I can't lose you to them, but I also can't destroy what's between you. Because I can see you have feelings for them just as much as you love me." His voice is so earnest, so honest my stomach aches and all the love I feel for him vibrates through me.

Blinking away tears, I say, "Do you think this is where we were meant to end up?"

When my men took me, it felt like my life had been completely derailed. But since our connection has grown and Rayne has returned, it kind of feels like I'm on the path I was always supposed to be on. Which is weird. I just wonder if he feels the same way.

His gaze grows distant. "I don't know. But I do think we're here for a reason. And as hard as it is for me to believe that that... Void could swallow all of earth, that there's a danger the fae aren't aware of, I don't think these men are lying. And, certainly, seeing that king and his dragon means trouble. I can't imagine what would happen if they could walk the earth freely."

"So you believe the prophecy?" I ask him, really needing to know the answer. Because hearing that I could save the world seems more than a little unbelievable to me.

He shrugs. "I don't know. But *they* believe it, and some-times belief is more important than reality. Men and women can do incredible things when their faith in an ideal is strong enough."

So, he's like me. He doesn't know if it's true, but he knows it's important. Which is a vast improvement to when he first came here in Adrik's body.

He gives me another small smile. "So, I guess I'll be sharing you with those three assholes. But they better treat you well, or they're going to have me to deal with."

I tangle my finger into his hair and force him to look at me. "Rayne." I don't have more to say. Only that.

His eyes, his, not Adrik's, are kind, loving.

He smiles. "You know all I've ever wanted is to make you happy."

"Well, having all of you working together and not competing with each other is definitely the right step if you want me to be happy."

He kisses me lightly. "Better tell them before I have an *accident* and end up at the bottom of a cliff."

Laughing, I shove him a little. "They're not going to murder you."

"You sure?" He flashes me that familiar grin of his.

I want to throw myself against him, thank him because a weight has lifted off me. Because I've realized that this is what I needed. I needed the mate from my past to say it's okay to love my shadow beasts and that by doing so I'm not betraying him. Even though I didn't realize it until now.

Every uncertainty within me falls away. I care for my shadow beasts. I know this fight is important and that I'm not walking away from it. As long as Rayne is on board, as long as he can accept this, I can finally take the three big men as my mates.

Four mates. It's a lot. But it's better than one mate and four broken hearts. Mine included.

And like my mind has summoned them, or my heart, or even the unknown force in my body that connects me to them, Onyx and Phantom walk in with Dusk trailing a few feet behind. They all look exhausted, their shoulders slumped, and their faces pale. But maybe some good news will be the thing to cheer them up, if only a little.

I squeeze Rayne's hand and smile, then mouth, "Thank you."

But when I look up, nothing is the way I expect. The second their gazes fall on me and Rayne together, they only seem more tired, more angry. And it hits me! They don't know about the fabulous revelation that's just happened.

I look up at Onyx and smile. He turns his head as if looking at me isn't the way he wants to start this day, which hurts more than I can say. But I won't be discouraged. I untangle myself from Rayne and sit up.

"You guys get any rest? Did you stop at the main cave?"

Onyx and Dusk avoid my gaze, going to the shelves where they keep their supplies.

I glance at Phantom, who stands by the entrance to the cave, arms crossed over his chest. For a long minute he seems to be trying to avoid my gaze too, but then he shoots me a scowl. "We're only here to get stuff to patrol tonight."

He's angry. They all are. I get it, but I hope my revelation will ease some of that.

"I'm staying here tonight." My words come out firm and proud. *That's right, guys, I'm not leaving. I don't have to be torn between Rayne and them. We can all stay at this cave, together.*

He nods. And I realize my words came out all wrong. I meant that I want *them* to stay with me. That we can be here together, share this space. Share *me*. But instead, maybe they think I just meant Rayne and I would be taking over their cave for the night.

No, no, that's not it. I'm not saying anything right. "I'm not going back to the academy."

But they don't speak to me. They just... leave.

"Hey!" I call after them. I have to say something. I have to explain the amazing thing that just happened.

But a group glare points at me from outside the cave, and the other things I wanted to say die on my lips. By the time I have a plan of what to say and how to say it, they're long gone. I sigh, scolding myself. Yes, I've always been a bit awkward and not at all good with challenging situations, but I thought my time with the shadow beasts had changed me, at least a little.

Apparently, not so much.

It's going to be another long night.

EIGHT

Onyx

THE NIGHT IS dark with an edge of chill. The moon is
waning overhead, slowly stealing the light from the night,
one day at a time. Looking up at it, I'm reminded of home.
Our world was always like a bright night. Brighter than it is
now, the sky streaked with grey, forever and always. And
beneath the pale light of the moon that forever hung in the
sky, we flourished. Shifting into our other form, we'd race
through our lands, enjoying the different plants, chasing the
different animals, and living in a world that was as much a
part of our soul as our own hearts.

That world is gone now. After the king stole the moon
from the sky and blanketed it all in darkness, the plants
died, most of the animals died, and those that remained
were dark creatures with dark souls. Except our fellow
shadow beasts, the poor bastards, who were simply forced to
remain in their other form, under their father's control.

Working with the very creatures they once hated, once hunted for the protection of our people.

But I don't want to think about them now. I can't think about my friends, lost to an enemy I can't control.

Nights like tonight just make me miss our home. Make me miss the moon goddess in the sky. Even the smells are different here. Richer and fuller in many ways, but less herbal. In our world, flowers bloomed in the darkness, radiating with light. They also released a scent similar to caramel, only a touch less sweet. Any time I was walking around the palace back home, I would stop and breathe in that familiar scent.

It feels like we came to earth with nothing from our world, but at least, I have my brothers. And they're better than any light, or smell, or sound.

Dusk and Phantom walk beside me in silence, their backs curved, their strides slow. We're all still sore from the battle. And heartbroken from Ann. As easy as it would be to do, I don't blame her for all of this. Being homesick isn't her fault. Feeling lost and alone isn't her fault. But still, I can't push away the pain I feel every time I think of her. It's as if we were barely holding our heads above water before, and now someone has given us a stone to carry too.

It's too much. For all of us.

Not that I can let my brothers see how much this is hurting me. They need someone to be strong, so it might as well be me.

Even though we're all suffering together.

A patrol to protect Ann while she's with *him* seems a fitting punishment for whatever horrors we've inflicted on the world. Because, truly, this is a punishment. Maybe Rayne is having sex with Ann right now. It's a thought that makes me want to punch my fist through every tree in this fucking forest. Maybe he's just holding her close. But it doesn't matter: we're out in the cold, and our mate is with another man. It's painful, to say the least, and easily one of the most miserable experiences of my life, and I've had a lot of miserable experiences.

My brothers aren't any happier than I am and instead of making our way through the forest silently, they're almost stomping, I can see it in the way their feet fall. We're looking for anything out of place. Looking for shards of the moonstone that will make it easier for their father to expand the Void into this world and claim it as his own domain, killing everything inside except the dark beasts he controls. It's something we've done more times than I can count, minus the stomping, minus the silence and the tension in the air. Mostly, we've done this patrol like soldiers in a battle that will never end.

Now, we're like soldiers in a battle that will never end *after* knowing our mate fucked another man.

Awful doesn't begin to explain the way we feel right now.

Dusk nudges my shoulder and points ahead at a shard in the grass a few feet beyond the path we're walking. Beneath the light of the moon, it just barely glints, and could've been easily missed. It's good that Dusk saw it. Moon shards have always been difficult to find... well, until Ann showed up and made it all seem simple.

Ann. I sigh and slowly move toward the shard.

Logically, she should be here with us. Finding the shards is easier when she's with us—her light is drawn to them. Or their light is sharper for her. I don't know the science of it, only the fact that she's a beacon. But with our relationship in shambles, it seems easier to only spot what we can rather than walk next to a woman who has rejected us, who has decided that she isn't our mate, no matter how much this connection between us says her belief is a lie.

I kneel down and pick up the shard, placing it in the pouch at my belt. I'm about to stand back up when I notice that the turned ground is fresh. Which means that one of their father's minions was here recently. I motion for Dusk to have a look and he kneels too, then touches the dirt.

"Fresh." When I nod, he continues. That they learned to sign for me is not something I take for granted. "Apparently, even after everything, he's still on his mission."

"Father could be half-dead and still send someone to hide a shard, just to make a point that we'll never defeat him," Phantom signs, his mouth moving with each word, which tells me he's speaking aloud too.

I sign, "Did you see her destroy that dragon? Did you see the shadow king falling to ash? Your father would have to have a hell of an ego to still be so confident." I mean, that moment was incredible, one for the history books. With everything that's happened, it took away from that moment a bit, but now it's on my mind.

"I knew when all of this started that we were going to lose," Phantom signs with a tight smile. "I don't know that anymore."

Dusk nods, his hands moving quickly. "He's not as strong as we thought."

And it's a comfort. For so long, the shadow king has been alive and unstoppable in my nightmares. I'd see him standing, his cloak billowing behind him, his sword out and ready to strike. I'd feel that tip slicing into my throat. The scene would play over and over again, and I'd wake, a scream on my lips, then touch my face and the scar by my ear and know that it wasn't so much a nightmare as a memory.

Too many mornings I'd lie awake after, heart pounding, replaying the events of that day, the day when everything fell apart. I didn't know at the time what had happened to me. For one second there was just an explosion of pain, then a ringing in my ears that wouldn't go away... and finally, nothing. Every sound from the world was simply gone.

I was afraid. Confused. When I stepped in the way to save Phantom, I'd expected to die. I'd known that I couldn't let my friend, or the future king of our world, fall because he didn't see the truth in time. Didn't realize just how dark his father's soul was. Death I was ready for. This? Not so much. Continuing to live, feeling broken, it's not something a warrior is ever prepared for.

The only thing that kept me going were my brothers, and the idea that there was no other choice. It wasn't that I thought we would win. I never thought that. The king was just too powerful. It was that I had no other place to be than at the side of Dusk and Phantom.

Being taken by the fae, kept as prisoners, tortured and forced to do unspeakable things... that was just another delay. Another chapter in this fight between father and sons. We were always going to come back here. But with Ann, maybe, just maybe, we could win.

Not that we get any say in the matter.

"The light from her hands...strong enough to take him?" Dusk mouths the words as he signs.

I nod. There was something blinding and beautiful about her light, like it came from the heart of her. I've never seen anything like it, never been so drawn to anything as I am to her. But as beautiful as it was, it was also dangerous. Capable of taking down a smoke dragon and possibly their father too. If she could learn to harness that light, if we could have her use it at the right moment, this war could be over and done with no more bloodshed.

Not that I think that will happen.

"Yes," I sign. "If she's willing to."

We keep walking. The darkness seeming to stretch on forever. Phantom picks up another shard and puts it in his pack with the others then turns and leans back against a tree. I don't even have to wonder what he's thinking about. I know that look. He never thought it would turn out this way with their father.

"Until our mother died, he was different," he signs slowly, his face an expression of disbelief.

I watched them interact. I might have been there for the part of their lives when they lost their mother, but it was never the same for me. She was their everything. Their light in the world. She made them smile and laugh. She simply had the kind of presence that filled a room. But to me, she was never anything more than a kind queen. Someone I was glad allowed me around.

But for them, she was their mother, and her passing was the end of their childhood.

Dusk moves closer to Phantom and his brows draw together. "Fucking grave trolls." He shakes his head and drops a hand on Phantom's shoulder.

I've heard the story before. Grave trolls and rot monkeys are much the same as predatory animals in this world. Sometimes, humans fall to them. But more often than not, they live almost in separate places. Grave trolls and rot monkeys stick to dark corners of the woods, places where no reasonable person would go. Their mother was nowhere near a dangerous place. Off for a stroll, I believe, yet somehow they got her.

After the attack, the boys had found her. Dying. They

tried to save her. Tried to revive her. But it didn't work out. They'd returned home with faces puffy and red from crying and hands covered in her blood. I'd gathered most of what I knew from the guards who found them, still trying to save their mother, even though she was already gone.

At the time, I'd cried alone in my room, then hid my emotions to be there for my friends. Even as a boy I understood that her passing was sad, but that it was more important to help them than to deal with my own confusing feelings about loss, and my own mother.

"He changed after she died." Phantom says the words while signing them. "But I never thought he was evil until that day."

I nod. We all know the day. And it didn't happen until after their mother died. Years had passed, with me watching their father slowly creeping toward something dark and terrible. Years of the shadow beasts eying the king and wondering if he'd lost his marbles when he'd lost his mate. In the days leading up to their father's attack and theft of the moon from the sky, I'd been watching and listening, knowing something was wrong. But Phantom and Dusk had been so sure that this too would pass. That their father would find a way to come out the other side of her loss.

They were wrong. And yet, they'd more than paid for their mistake.

"You believed in him," I sign to them. "You believe in everyone you love. It's something I envy about you."

Phantom gives me a sad nod. He knows that I don't have the same faith in people. No matter how hard I've tried to see the good in the world, it's just not there, not the way it has always been for Dusk and him.

"I want to believe in *her* too," Phantom signs more slowly.

I can't help myself; I sign back. "Me too." Because I do want to believe in Ann and our connection, I just can't.

We spend a while longer looking for more shards without luck, then head back to the cave. Usually this is the point in our scouting that we get faster, that there's a little pep in our step. Some excitement for a warm bed, a warm meal, and a place to rest. But there's no pep in our step now; we're like men marching off to our deaths... or our mate who doesn't want us. It feels the same.

She's lying on my bedroll and *he's* across from her on the ground. They aren't touching and I don't know why that makes me happy. The three of us find stew cooking over the fire. It's not good, but we eat as much as we can in silence. Then, instead of waking her to put her on her own bedroll, I move to the wall and sit back against it. It isn't comfortable, but after all these years I can sleep just about anywhere. In fact, the cave wall is a vast improvement over a cage.

My brothers give me a look, then lie down on their own bedrolls. I know they probably want me to lay with her, to stake our claim in some way and make it clear to both Rayne and Ann that she's ours, but I can't be by her, and I don't want to wake her to face more sad looks. Away is better. If I touched her, smelled her, I would forget all about the fact that she doesn't want me, and then be heartbroken again in the morning.

I HAVE no idea how much time has passed when I startle awake. My gaze snaps to the entrance to the cave where the sun bathes the entrance in a soft morning light. Then, I look for Ann, but she's gone. I'm wide awake in an instant, searching for her. But not only is she gone, so are the others. I spring away from the cave wall, ignoring the stiffness in my back and neck, and rush toward the cave entrance, heart in my throat.

Outside Rayne is standing, holding court with Phantom and Dusk. And since none of them look panicked, I instantly calm. Taking a few deep breaths, I walk over, trying to hide the fact that a minute ago I was ready to go running through the woods like a crazy person, searching for a woman who doesn't want me. But seeing them all glaring at each other after just waking up isn't a massive improvement.

I guess I have to be ready for tonight's shit show.

"She's upset." Rayne's words are easy to read on his lips, punctuated by a gesture at the doorway. And he's directing his words and gestures at me.

Dusk signs to me, "She thought you would sleep beside her and when you didn't..." He shrugs and I fill in the blanks.

Rayne glares at me. "She's drawn to each of you and your anger hurts her."

Hurts her? To my surprise, Rayne seems entirely sincere. And I see it in his face: her pain is his pain. Like... a mate.

It feels as if a blade is twisting in my chest. This man seems like an enemy in every way. I don't want us to have anything in common. I don't want to see that he cares for my mate like I care for her. Part of me wants to turn with my trademark sulk and run from this problem, but I linger. Not interrupting, because he's not what I expected and I'm not quite sure what to do with that.

"We're dealing with our own hurt," Phantom says.

Rayne crosses his arms in front of his chest. "Understood, but we need to move past that."

Easy for him to say.

But Dusk's mouth pulls into a thin line, and he signs, while his lips are moving, "Agreed. There are other things to talk about since there doesn't seem to be an answer for our situation."

Phantom nods, and I can tell he doesn't want to linger on this conversation anymore. "Tell us about her light. About yours."

For a few long seconds, Rayne looks uncertain, like he really doesn't want to answer Phantom's question. But, finally, he speaks. "I don't feel the power of the fae anymore." He shakes his head. "I used to feel it here." He thumps his chest with his fingertips, probably for my benefit, but his lips are easy to read.

"What about her? Where did that beam of light come from?" Dusk asks the question we've all wanted to ask.

"I don't know, and I don't think she knows either," Rayne says, but he speaks slowly enough that I'm able to read each word.

I sign, "That didn't come out of nowhere."

Phantom repeats my words for Rayne, and I'm a little surprised to see Rayne watching the way his hands move while he speaks, as if he's trying to learn to sign as well.

Rayne faces me again, very clearly speaking his words so as to not leave me out of the conversation. Something that many of the shadow beasts here still don't do. "Her mother was a fae but her father was human, so Ann's never been particularly powerful." He shakes his head. "At all, actually. So that light that exploded from inside her is... more than unexpected. Probably even by her."

"She was raised by a human?" Dusk asks, looking as surprised as I feel. Ann never told us that. But then, we haven't asked her a lot about herself. Something we should correct if we want to grow closer to her.

You know, if she doesn't go running from us the first chance she gets.

He hesitates. "She was actually raised mostly by her mother and stepfather, both of whom are fae, and she doesn't tell people about her human heritage. It would be looked down upon." His face says he wants to tell us more, but maybe something he shouldn't say. After a moment though, he continues, "When she was young, her stepfather abused her. Broke her bones. Gave her scars. Made her feel like... garbage." Anger flashes over his face, but he doesn't elaborate any further. Not that he needs to.

Sharp points of rage stab through me. *Someone hurt our Ann?*

"She has problems trusting now." His pointed stare is directed at me. "She acts tough, but she doesn't feel worthy of love. She doesn't feel worthy of much."

And it's obvious by the way he's looking at me that he's trying to get me to understand why this situation is so difficult for her. Trying to justify why Ann can't seem to just accept that we're her mates... too.

It works. The anger fades. At her, anyway. But I would love to get my hands on that bastard stepfather who hurt her. I would kill him. And Dusk nods as if he can read my thoughts and agrees. Phantom's hands are clenched and his eyes are closed. I know him as well as I know myself. He's imagining tearing the son of a bitch apart, one chunk at a time.

"We understand. At least, a little. But she's not the only one who's been hurt. Who's lost someone." Dusk's expression is as solemn as he ever gets.

"We can keep her safe." I don't know if Phantom is trying to reassure Rayne or if he's asking permission. "All of us," he adds the words and Dusk and I nod. We can keep her safest.

Rayne smiles. "She'll appreciate that."

Sadness aches through me. I don't want her to want to be with us because we can keep her safe. I want her to want to be with us because... it's a desire deep inside of her, the way it is for me, for us.

Rayne hesitates, then continues. "And maybe you guys can talk to her soon. You know, get this all sorted out."

"I thought you and Ann were going to leave?" Phantom says, speaking my thoughts aloud.

He shakes his head. "No, Ann and I are here for as long as she wants to be here."

Wants to be here. And how long will that be? Never long enough for us, that's for sure.

"She wants to talk about this mate bond stuff too," Rayne continues, flashing a hesitant smile.

Talk about the mate bond? A spark of excitement and hope rises in my chest, no matter how much I don't want to react to his words. Yes, that's what we need to do. Talk about settling everything between us, because it's time we complete the mate bond, and maybe we can get her to see that.

But before we do that, I'm going to speak to the elder and find out everything I can about the mating bond and everything it entails. Maybe when Ann says yes, if she says yes, we'll then be able to proceed without any trouble.

I hope.

NINE

Ann

OKAY, so there's officially no reason not to create the mating bond with my men. Rayne has given me permission, and even though I wouldn't normally consider myself someone who needs permission for anything, I realize I did this time. A huge part of why I was refusing to let myself feel this connection to my shadow beasts is because I felt like I was betraying Rayne. And the other reason was because some part of me had already accepted that I'd never love again. Like most people who lose their mate, I'd closed that part of myself off.

I know deep down that Rayne might not be here forever. I don't want to think about him not being with me, but I also can't plan my life around what the world does with his ghost. Whether he finds a way to be with me for the rest of our lives or he disappears tonight, there's no reason to pretend I don't love Onyx, Dusk, and Phantom.

Now, I just need them to understand that. And to be okay with Rayne being with me too, as long as he can be.

And as crazy as it is, I'm nervous to speak the words. To officially agree to this connection between us. To navigate Rayne and them, and make sure I don't screw up with anyone.

Not that I'm accepting that I'm the answer to this whole war. Not even for a second. But I'm no fool. I did something on that battlefield. My light, my ability to find the shards, it's all useful. And if the prophecy suggested I could help win the war, well, it isn't wrong in that regard. Just not that I'll be some savior of us all. I don't think I'm that by any means.

But I can't avoid facing all these hard conversations any longer, so I'm not.

It's almost evening when I finish bathing in the river and return to the cave in clean clothes, apparently gifted to me by the only female shadow beast on earth, which I really appreciated. I'm refreshed, ready to face them, to make my position clear, to help them understand why things have happened as they did and what we do from here. My plan is to be clear about what I want, who I am, how important they all are to me. Most specifically, how much I want and need them. This is going to be an all-the-cards-on-the-table kind of night because if I can make sure they know how crucial they all are to me, maybe they can accept one another, accept Rayne.

The cave is alive when I walk inside, with light and the smell of food cooking over the fire, along with the sounds of voices that are low and not angry. My eyes adjust to what my brain is saying I see, and I smile. They're talking, sitting together, eating. I stand frozen for a second, so I can take it all in.

I don't have to fake my smile as Onyx brushes past me,

takes a plate, and serves himself a slice of the fresh bread with his scoop of stew. I move to sit between Dusk and Phantom, across from Rayne, who offers me a nod and a soft smile, while Dusk eats like this is his first meal, or maybe his last, I'm not sure. Then, Onyx surprises me by handing me his plate of food and goes to make himself another one. After a minute, I feel a little of the pressure ease from my chest, then begin eating like a woman who hasn't been fed in a lifetime.

"This actually isn't half-bad," Rayne says, giving them a teasing smile.

"One of us usually goes into town every month or two. There are some witches we trade supplies for, which allows us to get things like bread and spice," Dusk explains, and I can tell he's trying to be nice.

Rayne eats another spoonful. "I don't know anything about cooking. Our staff always took care of it at the mansion."

"We had a staff at our castle too," Phantom tells him. "But even so, we were expected to know how to do things like hunt and cook."

Rayne nods, and I follow their easy conversation with interest, wondering what the hell changed between them that they're talking so comfortably to each other now. "That wasn't so much our focus. My parents wanted me to learn politics, mostly. To know how to dance with young women, how to impress powerful men and women alike. I never enjoyed it much, but as the heir, it always felt like it was necessary."

"Being an heir is... difficult," Phantom says, and there's pain in his eyes once more.

"No matter what we do, we'll make mistakes." Rayne

seems to choose each word with care. "I mean, I went and got myself killed after all."

Dusk laughs. Onyx, who's been watching the exchange, gives a snort, and I'm still staring at all of them trying to figure out this new twist.

"You guys are getting along." I don't realize I've spoken aloud until all eyes are on me. Instantly, I feel my cheeks heat.

"Smooth, darling, real smooth," Rayne teases.

I feel like my face is on fire. "It's just that the last time you were all together I thought you were going to kick each other's asses."

"She's not wrong," Dusk mutters.

"But we came to an understanding of sorts," Rayne says, and he won't look me in the eye, so I don't know what to think, but my mind is spinning.

"What kind of understanding?"

Dusk gives me a small smile that makes my heart race. "Eat first, fae."

Fae. He says it like a term of endearment. But, hell, he could have called me *bitch* in that tone right now, and I'd be swooning. Damn that handsome shadow beast.

"Fine," I tell him, then eat even faster.

Rayne smothers a laugh behind his hand. The man *does* know me well enough to know that I'm not exactly the patient type.

After a few minutes, we finish eating and I look at everyone, taking a deep breath, but before I can say a word, Phantom says, "We need to talk."

I'm sure I look ridiculous. When I realize my mouth is hanging open, I close it, but it isn't enough. I feel like a train that was on a track, and now I'm in the middle of the woods, not sure how I got there.

I had a plan. A specific thing I wanted to say. But as I look at all the men, it seems, based on their expressions, that this is something they all want to be said. Something they want me to listen to. Considering everything that's happened, and how difficult my rejection of them has been, I finally nod. I can at least listen to them first, since they've been putting themselves in danger to protect me.

"We have to talk about the mating bond." Phantom's voice is deep, a half-growl that could be a purr.

"That's exactly what I wanted to talk about," I say, and I'm not sure whether I'm relieved or even more worried.

At least they're not fighting. *That's a good sign, right?*

Phantom squares his shoulders, and an air of a royalty instantly falls over him. "As you know, the shadow king pulled the moon stone from the sky and broke it into shards. These are the shards you are helping us find." Of course I know about the shards. *But what does this have to do with the mating bond?* "I don't know how he learned to steal our moon. I don't know how he learned that he could use the shards to create a connection to the earth, a way to expand the shadow world. But it's clear he wants to control the earth and put an end to humanity. Hell, he wants to put an end to all living creations here, just as he did to our world."

I nod, because what else am I supposed to say? The story isn't new, just varied by who tells it and what details they include.

"But you said this is about the mating bond. The thing is, I still don't understand how creating this bond will stop the king." It's an intricate ploy if it's only about having sex. That would be flattering if that is what it is, but I doubt it.

Dusk sighs, looks at the other two shadow beasts, then presses on as if he wishes they were discussing something else, anything else. "Once, we were in love with a woman."

Something strange and foreign twists in my gut. *They were?* They never mentioned this before. But then again, I'd be a fool to think I was the first woman they'd ever met or cared for. We're in our early twenties, at least, probably mid-twenties for them. By this point a lot of people have had a few heartbreaks under their belt, so why does the idea of another woman they were in love bother me so much?

"Okay," I manage, failing miserably to conceal my hurt feelings at the revelation.

Dusk nods at Phantom and it's like they're sharing a thought like only siblings can, but then Onyx nods, too, before Dusk continues. "She wasn't a mate, but a love. True and deep. We grew up together in our castle. We watched her grow from a girl into a woman, just as we grew from boys to men. We shared moments, stories, and it felt very natural. We had never felt a mate bond before, so part of us wondered if that was what we were feeling, even though we weren't sure at the time."

His expression falls and Phantom picks up the tale. "Our father thought she was the one from the prophecy. And he took her for himself."

"Took her? Since when can a man just take a woman? We're not luggage."

Rayne gives a little laugh, but Phantom is the one to answer. "You met our father."

I shiver. *Okay, fair enough.* "But then, did she put up a fight? I can't imagine many people would have been happy to see him dragging off a woman, you know, before your world went crazy."

Dusk answers. "That's not how it's done with royalty. We hadn't technically expressed our interest in Shenra, but we had an understanding between us. An understanding that we wanted to announce with an engagement at one of my father's big parties with the neighboring royalty."

"Okay... but then something went wrong?"

Dusk's brows draw together. "It was subtle, but it also wasn't... I don't know. One night at dinner, he took Shenra on his arm. He walked her about as if she were his partner for the night. She sat next to him at dinner, and the three of us didn't know what to say or do. We'd always assumed our father knew that we were interested in her, and that we felt a connection to her, but that night we all wondered if we'd been mistaken. If he hadn't known. We wanted to clear it up, but then, Shenra didn't seem... upset about the arrangement, just flustered."

Phantom rubs his face, like the memories are making him tired. "We had a decision to make. Did we address it with our father? Did we confront her and ask her how she felt? Whether she wanted him or us? But we were young and inexperienced. We'd never seen our father take an interest in a woman after our mother, nor had we seen Shenra blushing and flirting with another man. We knew if we spoke the words aloud, if we tried to lay claim to her and she rejected us, it would create a rift between our father and us, as well as a rift with her. We weren't sure what to do."

"And then one night became many nights, with her on our father's arm and us lost about what to do."

Onyx signs, and Dusk speaks for him, even though I pick up many of the correct signs. "I approached her one day, a brief moment without her ladies or her guards. It was uncomfortable. She seemed to want to tell me something, but she stopped herself. Instead, she said that she hoped that things were still good between us and that she planned to clear up a confusion with our father."

"We thought that was the end of it," Dusk said, sounding

defeated. "But then our father wed her in a private ceremony that night. The news was all over, as was the news
that they were spending their days and nights in his room,
enjoying their lives as a married couple."

"We were shocked," Phantom says, not that he needed
to. I would say hearing their father married the woman they
loved would shock anyone. "But it was also strange. For days
we didn't see her or our father. The maid who cleaned their
room seemed upset. The guards kept us from their floor. We
didn't want to make things worse. We assumed that perhaps
she had decided being a queen was better than being a
princess, even though we'd never suspected her of being
that type of woman."

"And then our father appeared once more, behaving as
if nothing had happened. We causally mentioned her, and
he avoided the topic before finally confessing that he felt
the marriage had been a mistake. That it wasn't what he had
thought it was, and that she had returned to her family's
lands." Dusk looks disturb. "We had no reason not to believe
him. He was our father. Cold, calculating, but our father.
He'd only ever been kind and gentle with our mother, so
why think otherwise?"

Onyx nods again and signs, "But we believe he killed
her."

"Why?" It isn't me who asks, but Rayne.

"Because the shadows whispered that our mate would
bring the person she's with great power, enough power to
rule a world, and he wanted it for himself." Dusk stares at
Onyx as Onyx finishes signing, then nods and continues.
"From a young age we knew we'd share a mate, and once our
connection was formed, the shadows began whispering.
The Elders are the only ones capable of hearing the shad-

ows, but they relayed the messages to the king and queen at the time, and their parents seemed excited. The idea that we could bring more power, more strength to our great nation, and that we were destined for a mate, it was all good things."

"Until Shenra," Dusk says in a sad voice. "Until our father took her as his own and nothing about our world made sense any longer."

"At the time, we didn't have any proof, you understand. We thought she chose him over us, then retreated in shame when she couldn't make him happy." Phantom nods to Onyx. "But Onyx didn't buy it."

He shrugs. "This was just before the destruction of our world." He speaks so quickly with his hands, I can't keep up. I look at Dusk, who translates. "The king was as charming as ever, so it was logical for us to think she chose him, loved him, wanted him. There was nothing in our father's behaviors that seemed strange. And he had never seemed interested in having more power than he already had, so we didn't think anything of the prophecy."

"But Onyx asked if we truly thought all Shenra cared about was a title and power. In truth, we'd never seen her that way. We argued that perhaps her parents pressured her to make him her husband, but again, Onyx didn't feel she could be pressured to do that. She was... soft spoken and often submissive, but she could be a lion when she needed to be. So her complete betrayal didn't sit right with him. He had faith in her feelings, in his own. Faith that we didn't have, perhaps because the man who had taken our love was our own father." Phantom stares down at the fire for a second before he looks at me. "Then Onyx found her body a couple of weeks later in the moat. At least, what we thought was her body. It was... difficult to tell by then, but she had white hair, and a cream gown similar to the type she slept in."

Dusk whispers, "But still, we couldn't believe our father could do that. I know that makes us sound like fools, but it seemed more likely that rather than return home in shame, she... well, she made a rash decision."

"We didn't know for certain that it was her at all though," Onyx emphasizes with his hand and looks at Phantom. "We'd sent word to her family, but we hadn't received word back yet if she'd made it to her home."

I'm trying to process all of this, but it's hard. All three of them have stopped though, and they're looking at me, so I try to sort my thoughts appropriately. "It makes sense. I mean, if you accused your father of something awful, then learned she'd just gone home, it'd be terrible. And you'd all already lost your mother; it's normal that you wouldn't want to lose your only other living family member." I clench my arms. "I did the same kind of thing with my mother. I-I, well, I sometimes forgave things that I shouldn't have, or pretended my mom was someone different, even though all logic said exactly who she was. A child's need to be loved by a parent is strong."

The men exchange a look, and then Dusk stares back at me, overwhelming emotion in his eyes. "We never saw it that way. Just felt like we were fools."

Onys signs, "And maybe I wasn't understanding enough because I'd never had that bond with a parent."

Unable to stop myself, I reach out and squeeze Onyx's hand. His eyes widen in surprise for a moment before I let go, and he turns away from me again.

"And killing your woman was what led to all of this?" Rayne asks, frowning.

"I wish," Dusk mutters, shaking his head.

"We didn't believe Onyx when he tried to show us his 'proof' that father had murdered her. We got into a fight, something we never do, and he went off alone to drink because we'd wounded him to his core. We chose our father over him, and I think it made him feel like... he wasn't part of our family, even though we're brothers in all ways except blood." Phantom's breath shudders out of him, and I appreciate the pain they're in to tell us this story.

"At the tavern, I overheard someone say that the king was engaging in some dangerous magic," Onyx signs as Dusk speaks his words aloud. "Surprised, I went around town, listening to every shred of gossip I could acquire. Everyone in town was afraid, and everyone had a different story. Some had seen the king in the forest, talking to trolls or rot monkeys. Others said the king was seen in graveyards, digging up bones. Some said he'd gone to the sacred cliff, the only connection to the moonstone, and a place that's forbidden, and they worried about why. All things that are the signs of a madman. A man up to no good. So, I again returned home and warned them."

Phantom's breaths become shallower. "We thought our father had lost his mind. Not that he was up to trouble, but that it was connected to our mother, and then there was the fact that his young bride was lost to him. Perhaps he realized that a man cannot fall in love again after losing his mate. Perhaps it was guilt for even trying. We weren't sure, but we thought he just needed our help."

Dusk's eyes are dark with guilt. Shame. Sadness. "We were wrong."

"Our foolishness cost us everything, cost our people everything," Phantom murmurs.

"I can't." Dusk suddenly pushes to his feet and walks to the entrance to the cave, standing silhouetted in the dim light of night outside. Even from where I sit, I can feel his emotion, feel how deeply he's trying to make it through this story, even though he's overwhelmed with the memories. And I want to go to him, to wrap my arms around him, but there's a sense that they aren't done, that there's more to say, so I stay seated, feeling on edge.

Phantom continues more slowly. "Our father *might* have lost his mind, but he *was* absolutely dangerous. He took the moon stone. He plunged our world into a darkness that spread across the land like a plague. We faced off with him. Dusk had... had a chance to kill him, but he didn't. Some part of us both thought he could still be saved, that deep down the man who still loved us as kids was inside of him." Phantom rubs his face again and Onyx reaches over, squeezing his shoulder for a long moment before Phantom presses on. "We made a mistake. My father tried to kill me and Onyx took the blow, losing his hearing in the incident. We barely got out alive with some of our men. We thought in coming to this world maybe we'd have a chance to figure out what was happening and then come back to save our people, but we quickly realized that we couldn't win this war. That all we could do was keep the earth alive as long as possible. There was... a brief time when we thought we could enlist the help of others here, but that was quickly proved to be foolish thinking."

Onyx begins signing after a quiet moment, and Phantom's voice carries his sad words. "And then we saw you, our mate, and we still weren't sure. We knew once we felt the connection with you that our father would feel it too. He might not understand it, but he'd track it down, find you, and either take you for himself or kill you. So, we had to take you with us. We were... defeated, to say the least. Not even really thinking about the prophecy. But, once we met you, then it was all we could think about."

The look in Onyx's eyes says something entirely different. Not that they were only thinking about the prophecy, but that they were thinking about me.

I feel my cheeks heat once more and try to pretend not to notice.

Phantom stares at his brother's back for a long minute then glances at me. "In our culture, the father can't have our mate once we've bonded with her, of course, which wasn't something we thought would be a problem. We naturally assumed our mate would... would want us too."

Ouch.

From the doorway, as if he's speaking to the night, Dusk continues, "It's the bond of mates that stops him, from what we understand. It's physical. He won't be able to take you or claim you. We don't know if it'll be enough to actually win this war and save our world, but it's the only hope we have." He sighs again. "That's why we need to do this. Not just because we love you and feel compelled by this connection, but because we want to keep you safe. And what's more, we feel we owe it to our people to see if this prophecy can save them. Not that you do. You owe us nothing."

So much pressure. Not from them specifically, but my heart is weighted with it.

"What is it exactly? The mate bond between shadow beasts?" Maybe if I know what has to happen, I can accept it, or at least understand it.

Dusk turns and shrugs. Phantom shakes his head. But across from me, Onyx begins to sign, "We each have to have sex with you."

"S-sex?" I stutter. *That's all?*

He continues signing, "It's more than just the physical act of making love."

Rayne stands and turns away because there's nowhere for him to go in the night that is safe for a fae in a shadow beast's body or certainly he would get out, but he's heard enough. I know deep down he knew this was coming. Eventually, sex would be on the table if he shared me with them. But I think knowing it and hearing it are two completely different things.

Onyx continues, his gaze locked onto mine. "You have to take us into your heart." *Whatever that means.*

Sex with each of them. Plus, the hard-to-pin-down 'take us into your heart.' All to save our world, their world, and fulfill a prophecy. Pressure is an understatement for what I'm feeling right now. But I had already decided to be their mate, to stay here for this fight and see it out to the end. So does it matter what they call this whole thing?

I'm not sure.

And like I don't know the time is falling away, Dusk clears his throat. "There isn't much time until nightfall. It's a lot, but you have to decide. Now, if you can. Because there are already signs of my father's men coming back, and if they can come back, father is getting strong enough to protect them here. Which means he's strong enough to come back. Which means... he's strong enough to come back for *you*."

For me. Great. Just great.

"We don't want you to say yes just because of all of this," Phantom says, giving an apologetic look. "We'll keep fighting, keep trying, even if you never agree to be ours."

Dusk clears his throat. "And Rayne has agreed to go along with whatever you want."

"So, what do you want to do?" Phantom levels me with a look that carries all the weight of this decision.

Oh yeah. I'll just maybe have a little sex, save the human race. All in a night's work.

Everyone stares, and I open my mouth, not knowing exactly what I'm going to say. Well, maybe knowing what I'm going to say, but not how to say it.

TEN

Phantom

I WATCH HER, waiting for her answer. Every change of her face enchants me, wraps me deeper in her spell, and for once, I don't care. That's part of the mating bond, this inability to resist her, but I can't find it in me to try to stop it. It's clear she's working through a thousand things in her mind. I find myself holding my breath.

What if she rejects us again? What if she concludes that she can never be with us? Or that all of this is more than she can handle? We're warriors. We're prepared to die from a sword or experience physical pain. We aren't prepared for the kind of heartache this woman seems to be able to wound us with.

Her lips part again, and my breath burns in my chest. "Okay."

Okay? Did she just accept us to be her mates with that one simple word? I'm shaking, pure joy exploding inside of me.

I glance at her and smile because I want this to be something she wants as much as we want and need it. "Okay."

What more can I say? I want to leap up and cheer. I want to thump my brothers on the back. I want to race around the woods and howl at the moon. But 'okay' is enough for now. It's not a word that scares her. It's simple, with no pressure.

"And we should probably do it soon," she continues, rubbing her palms on her pants as if nervous.

Rayne glares, and I actually hear his knuckles crack from clenching his hands so hard, but then his gaze catches mine. He gives a small nod, acceptance spilling over his face. I don't need his permission, only hers, but I'm grateful for it just the same.

"I don't think I can handle... all three of you at once." Ann looks like her cheeks might catch on fire. "Can I start with one of you?"

"Yes," Dusk and I say, while Onyx signs the word.

Then, we all stare.

She gives a nervous laugh. "So, who should I, uh, start with?"

"Whoever you want," I tell her, although my body doesn't seem to be able to accept that. Instead, my erection has already sprung up, demanding I give it attention. Demanding that this woman's acceptance of us, *finally*, should begin right now, this second. And that the only pause between now and being inside her should be tearing off her clothes.

Not that I'd listen to the horny bastard.

Her gaze moves over all of us while she nibbles her bottom lip, a movement that gets my treacherous cock even more excited, before her gaze lands on me. "I could start with you?"

Oh, boy. A shudder rolls through my body. "If you wish."

Onyx and Dusk cast me envious looks, then head out of the cave.

Rayne lingers, then looks at me. "If anyone should hurt her..."

"I'd kill them myself," I tell him, meeting his gaze. I hope he realizes that I'd rather cut my arm off than hurt my mate.

After a painfully long moment, he follows the others out, saying over his shoulder, "I guess I'll be learning about patrolling with shadow beasts tonight." He's trying to make it a joke, but his voice is a little too high.

I don't envy the man the experience of learning to share his mate while things aren't yet established in our own bond. But then, sometimes things go this way, even with my people. Not often, but sometimes. And the men still learn, even if there's a bit more fighting.

But I'm distracting myself. Perhaps I'm as nervous as Ann is herself.

Forcing myself to turn away from the cave entrance, I stare at her, unsure what to do. Ann is more fragile in so many ways than our own women. I don't know anything about their rules of courting. Yes, she's enjoyed my touch so far, but I don't want to cross any lines, nor break the trust that we've worked so hard to earn.

"Tell me if I do anything you don't like," I emphasize each word.

She gives a hesitant smile, like she's finding it hard to believe I'd do anything to her that she wouldn't like, which I'm glad for. "I will."

I almost ask her how she wants to do this. Does she want me to be slow and gentle, hard and fast? What does my Ann prefer? But I don't speak the words aloud. Instead, I remind myself that this isn't my first time. That I'll be able to tell more from the way she responds to me than from her words.

"Please, just kiss me or something. I'm nervous. You have to take charge." The words tumble out of her lips, surprising me.

Take charge? That is something I can do.

"Come here." I brush her hair from her cheek and thread my fingers into her hair to pull her in. The first kiss is a jolt, a shock, and I pull back because it's so potent. But then she moves in again, and I'm lost in every sensation of her mouth on mine. We kiss over and over again, like before, but not. Both of us know this time where we're going, will not be just more kisses, followed by guilt about Rayne. No, this time she will be my mate. This time, I won't just stop at kissing her. I'll make her mine, and then nothing will separate us.

She makes little sounds and moves in more closely.

I deepen our kiss, listening to her body's every reaction, sweeping my tongue inside her mouth to claim her as my own. Her hand strokes down my chest, tangles into my shirt, pulling me even closer. And for some reason, the more she reaches for me, the more she responds to me, the harder it is for me to control myself.

But I'll fucking control myself, no matter what it costs me.

Every tremble of her body awakens conflicting emotions: the need to mate her quickly, to claim her as my own, and the desire to move slowly, to make her pleasure above all else. The first need is a primal one, a desire that all shadow beasts feel. But the second is just as primal. A shadow beast would rather die than hurt their mate, and I'll be damned if my eagerness takes any pleasure from her.

I move one hand to her lower back, then slowly lie her

back, me on top of her. Not yet placing all my weight on her, just following the signs of her body, but still giving her a way out.

Even though I'm pretty sure my cock would explode if I had to stop right now.

She moans low in her throat, and I swallow the sound so that it's a part of me, a vibration in my belly that goes to my cock. I'm hard, but I need her to be ready. To want and need me, to accept me. Not just because of a prophecy. Not just because Rayne agreed. But because she wants *me*.

Her kisses burn me as she grows more and more feverish with desire, and I pull back, drag my lips down her throat, and yank her shirt away to expose her beautiful breasts, the tips hard and pink. She writhes as I take one pebbled peak between my lips, then I suck until her back arches and a moan slips from her lips. She holds my head in place, her breathing ragged. I move to her other breast, lavishing it with my tongue, then cup her breasts, touching, sucking, licking, and thinking about every time I wanted to touch her but couldn't.

It feels like too much. Like a dream come true. Something I don't deserve.

But I don't care.

When I pull away, she whimpers and my cock strains, searching for her. I adjust myself, even though I'm so hard it's painful. Yes, we shadow beasts take care of our *needs*, but I haven't since Ann came along, and my body is sure to remind me of that right now.

Down, you horny bastard! Focus!

Her nails rake across my back, and something snaps inside of me. I have to taste her. I have to be between this woman's thighs, hearing her scream my name. I glide my body down hers kissing and nibbling her skin. Her hands dig into my hair, and she makes sounds, half-frustrated, half-aroused, and for some reason, I love the combination.

I slowly pull her pants and underwear off, tossing them across the cave. Then I stare down at her, fully exposed to my greedy gaze. She's perfect, my fae woman. Wet, beautiful, and open for me. I realize that she's never been more lovely than she is right now, and that's a feat in itself.

"Phantom." My name is a plea and I spread her legs apart, settle in between so I can kiss the most sacred part of her body. With the first swipe of my tongue against her she cries out, and I take another, then wait for her to still and push a finger inside her.

There's nothing so delicious as the taste of her, nothing so exquisite as this woman and her passion. She plunges her fingers into my hair and holds me in place as she brings her hips up, and I use my tongue to tease her clit until she is writhing and crying out, moaning and thrusting against my hand, trying to take my fingers deeper. Her body convulses, throbs around my fingers, and my tongue is inside her now, too. "Phantom, please!" She pulls me away, sits up to unfasten the belt where my weapons are sheathed. I throw my shirt into the corner of the cave and just let myself feel every brush of her hand, every puff of her breath against my skin. It's only for a minute, but it's glorious. Divine. Fore-telling.

I would chuckle at how excited I'd been, how desperately I'd needed her that I forgot to remove it, but this moment is serious. It's important to me and I don't want to risk ruining it by laughing. When she's finally done getting my sword and dagger off, she tosses them aside and then begins unfastening my pants. It only takes her a moment before my pants are open, and then she wraps her hand around my cock.

Instantly, I lose my breath. I've known pleasure before, known the touch of a woman, but this is on another level. This is more than attraction. This is soul deep. Part of her is calling out to part of me. It's visceral. Necessary.

She pumps me over and over again, bringing a growl exploding from my lips. I sit up higher, giving her better access, and then I'm shocked when I feel her breath against the tip of my cock. But shock gives way to utter surprise as her tongue darts out and licks my tip.

"Fuck," I groan, rocking my hips, trying to get her to take my cock deeper.

A smile dances on her lips as she lets her tongue dart out over and over again as my erection jerks in her grip. And then she leans forward and sucks my tip so hard I almost explode right into her mouth. *Almost.* But then I'm pulling on the back of her head, trying to get her away before I embarrass myself.

To my relief, she stops, still grinning. Panting. Looking at my dick like she wants to taste it again.

But if she does, I'm gone. So, instead, I push her back and lay on top of her. Almost instinctively, her legs come around my hips even as her hand reaches between us and continues to stroke me, to squeeze with enough pressure to turn my dick to stone. I've never wanted or been wanted with such urgency. She needs to release me. She needs to let me bury myself in her before it's too late.

Pushing her hand away, I place it above her head and loosely grip both her wrists in mine. I press kisses down her throat, take another minute to suck on her exquisite breasts, then begin to rub her wet folds once more. And God damn, my mate is wet. I brush my thumb over every inch of her core, circling her clit then rubbing it, hard for a minute, enjoying the sound of her gasp, before I go back to circling it once more.

"Phantom, please, damn it, please!"

Oh, fuck. She doesn't need to beg me when we both want the same thing.

I pull my hand away from her and settle deeper between her thighs, while her legs wrap around me more tightly. For a minute I tease us both by letting the tip of my cock play in her wet folds, sliding it all around, making us both curse and cry out. But when a warning shudder moves through my body, I stop, knowing she's ready. Knowing I'm ready.

It's time.

My cock sits at her opening, and I ease into her, once inch at a time. My Ann is tight. But that's not a surprise. She's so tiny beneath me. My cock should be more than enough for her. And it is. The deeper I go, the more tightly she holds me. Every time it feels like there isn't enough room, I pause, letting her adjust to me until her legs tighten around me once more, urging me to keep going.

It seems to take a lifetime before I reach my hilt. Until we're both panting, ready, wanting more. And I have to grit my teeth when I pull back out, then plunge in again, because this is everything. Everything I've ever wanted and more. My cock feels like a fucking lightening rod, alive with every nerve, overwhelmed with desire. It's screaming to take this woman hard and fast, but I keep a handle on my control and ease into her over and over again, starting slow and building faster.

I groan with the perfection of how she meets every plunge of my cock, how she uses her legs like a vice to hold me and pull me in. She strains against the hand that holds her wrists, but not to get free, just to give herself more leverage. Not that she needs it.

Need and pleasure swirl, mingle, build inside me until I'm barely hanging onto whatever control she's left me. Then the spiral starts and my head throws back. I have no power to stop it. My entire body tenses and hers along with it. Our orgasms come at the same perfect moment, and stars explode before my vision as we cry out in one voice and ride the waves of the passion, clinging to one another until the tremors quit and our breaths come normally.

"Damn."

I roll away and lie beside her, gather her close to me. "Yes. Damn."

She smiles and brushes her hand over my chest, then presses a kiss against my nipple and I breathe in as pleasure skitters over me. I pull her up for another kiss and when we part, she smiles.

I've never been so happy.

"I, uh, am supposed to have sex with Onyx and Dusk now? After *that*?" She sounds incredulous.

I laugh. "You'll grow used to us and our appetite. Before too long, you'll be the one demanding we meet your needs. I swear it."

"And I believe it," she grumbles, but she does so with a satisfied smile.

ELEVEN

Ann

ONYX, Dusk, and Rayne have come back. I stretch languidly beside Phantom, wrapped in his blankets, feeling both comfortable and oddly vulnerable. At least until I see the look of raw desire on their faces when they stare at Phantom and I. Even Rayne's expression is one of need versus anger or jealousy, which is oddly reassuring. If he can handle seeing me like this in Phantom's arms, he can probably handle just about anything.

"Finished?" Dusk asks, and there's arousal in his voice.

My gaze runs over him, feeling oddly sexually alive. Dusk might be the younger brother to Phantom, he might be a little smaller, a little less muscular, but he has a different kind of attraction. It's like being asked to choose between donuts and ice cream. Sometimes you want one. Sometimes you want the other. But still, other times, well, you just might want to gorge yourself on both. And right now, freshly satisfied from Phantom, I would have never thought I could handle more, but apparently, my body has other ideas. Ideas about comparing Dusk and Phantom in ways I've never compared before.

If I was a cat, I'd be purring as I take the big shadow beast in. Dusk's hair isn't tied back the way it usually is. Instead, it's been left long, flowing about his face, flowing onto his shoulders. He looks beautiful in a way most men aren't. It softens the tough warrior a bit, in a way I absolutely love. And those pale blue eyes of his are burning with desire under his dark lashes.

I lick my lips, trying to find the words to tell him how I feel.

And then Onyx signs, "Regrets?" There's more to his signs, but that's what I manage to pick out with his fast-moving hands.

My gaze lingers on him as another wave of desire flows through me. It's clear Onyx isn't their brother in blood. Not just because of the fact that his hair is blond and his eyes are a brown so deep they almost look black. It's something in the lines of his face. They're somehow harsher. I think Phantom and Dusk could be models in the human world, or body-builders who model. But Phantom? I'm pretty sure no matter how he dressed or where he was, he'd be the kind of man people rushed away from. A man people feared. Almost like a god among humans. He just radiates a dangerous energy, one that I've realized is mostly a façade. But a part of me wants to see this powerful warrior in my fae world. Part of me can imagine taking these men back to my home and having them at my side while I rule my lands.

"Say something," Rayne says, followed by an uncomfortable laugh.

I realize they're all staring at me, and I try to find my words. "It was good."

"Good." Phantom runs his hand down my arm. "We can do better than good."

Rayne's gaze follows Phantom's touch, and again, my horny mind focuses on him. He's shorter and smaller than all three of the others, even in Adrik's big body. He still has that bodybuilder/warrior physique that seems reserved for the shadow beasts. But I still don't think he could go anywhere in the human world without getting more than a few looks and a lot of women checking him out. However, he appears more... human than the others. Less... too big for this world. The short hair helps though, drawing attention to his high cheekbones and giving him a less wild appearance.

The beauty of them is enough for my stomach to clench with need. But knowing they want me, knowing I'm with them and they belong to me, fills me with raw power. It's like I'm having my cake and eating it too. Well, cake, donuts, ice cream, and pie. Yum. Each of them looks more than a little appetizing, and it's almost overwhelming to know they're all mine.

But again, my treacherous mind pictures not just what it'd be like to taste all of them individually, but, well, what if I put all these delicacies together? I start to imagine it, and then it's the only thing I can think about.

I want all of them. Together. *Now.* "Can we...does the mating have to occur separately?"

Dusk looks at Onyx, who stares at Phantom, and I glance at Rayne. His eyebrows are raised like he doesn't expect to be a part of this, but I beckon to him, and Rayne slowly moves across the cave to stand in front of me. And I'm glad he's so willing to consider something that sounds a bit crazy when I say it out loud. But this is for all of us, not just my shadow beasts.

"Coming over?" I ask Onyx and Dusk, trying not to sound as excited by this as I am. But I fail miserably.

Onyx and Dusk cross the cave so fast that I check to see if anything is chasing them. Then, they grab a few more blankets and lay them around us, their movements fast and jerky, their breath coming in and out so fast I almost believe they were just running. Rayne throws another log on the fire, and then we're all close to each other, tension in the air.

Rayne falls to his knees beside me. We stare at each other for a long moment before he leans in and kisses me. It's gentle. Not possessive. Almost... happy. When he pulls back, his lips part and he inhales slow and deep. "Ann."

I stroke his cheek, kiss him again, and then pull back. His eyes hold mine, and he smiles. Actually smiles. And my heart skips a beat. He really is okay with this. I don't know how he is, but he is. I mouth the words, "thank you," then turn to my other men and kiss each of them too.

Our kiss feels strangely like a promise. An agreement. Like whatever happens from here on out, it's us together. And I couldn't have asked for more.

But when we're done, I'm left staring at them. Wondering what to do next. I hope to hell they don't think I'm going to be taking the lead, because I don't know what I'm doing.

"Phantom?" I whisper

He smiles, sits up, and looks at me. "I'll show you."

I've never choreographed anything like this, but thankfully, it doesn't seem like I'm going to have to. Dusk instantly begins to remove his clothes. My mouth drops open as his shirt hits the floor, and then his pants and boots follow suit. When he's done, he's sitting beside me, naked as hell, sporting an erection that makes my mouth feel dry. He kisses me again, and this time there's nothing sweet about it.

His tongue sweeps into my mouth, and I feel him untangling me from the blankets before he pulls me onto his lap and lies back, so that I'm on top of him.

I straddle his legs and let his cock slide against my folds while we kiss. He doesn't enter me, just teases me, making the combination of his lips and his cock cause sparks in my nerves. When his lips finally break from mine, I shudder. I glance at the other men, feeling overwhelmed

Onyx is standing. I don't even know how he got there, but now he's undressing too. Dusk's hands reach up, cupping my breasts, stroking my nipples while my muscles jerk with pleasure. But my gaze is glued to Onyx. He removes his shirt, displaying his wealth of rippling muscles. When he goes for his pants, I wish it were my hands undoing his belt, my hands yanking the cloth down to expose his long and thick cock. My eyes go to his face, and I realize he's watching me, and that I like what I see.

Phantom moves so that he's kneeling beside Dusk, and he pulls me into a kiss, reminding me he's there. Reminding me that even though we just made love, this next adventure will be for all of us. It will pull us together in a way nothing else can.

Dusk continues to slide me up and down the length of his cock, while Phantom lavishes my mouth. Dusk's hand falls from one of my breasts, but it's only for a moment before I feel someone sucking on it. Breaking my kiss with Phantom, I glance down to see Rayne taking my nipple into his mouth in a way only he could, teasing me with every flick and swirl of his tongue. As he does so, he's working on undoing his belt, but I can barely watch the delicious show in front of me. I'm overwhelmed by the three men already touching me.

I know where this is going. A shiver of desire rolls down

my spine at just the thought of it, but some voice whispers in the back of my mind that I sure as hell better be ready for this, because the four hard men already are.

Onyx moves toward us, and Rayne releases my breast just long enough to strip next to me, then return to my nipples. Sensations wash over me as Onyx sits behind me. I can sense him, sense the warmth of his body. But it's strangely erotic not to be able to see him. To not know what he's doing.

But I don't have to wonder for long. He lets his hand move from my shoulder to swipe down my spine and then to my ass.

Goosebumps erupt on my skin, and then, unexpectedly, Dusk slips the tip of his cock into my opening. I gasp, and Phantom covers the sound with his mouth. His tongue is sliding in and out of my mouth as Dusk pushes himself deeper inside my tight body, sending my nerves screaming in pleasure.

It's overwhelming. More than overwhelming. I feel like I've run a damn race by the time I reach his hilt, and I find myself moving gently on top of him, trying to get used to the sheer size of the big shadow beast's cock.

Rayne continues to cup my breasts, to tease my nipples, to play with them like this is all he's ever wanted to do. But every time I feel the muscles in Dusk's cock jump, I know he wants more, and I also know he's enjoying every second of what we're doing. As am I.

Onyx's hands continue to slide up and down my spine, then he gives my ass a little slap. Then another one, before he simply rests those big palms of his on my ass cheeks. It's strange. Like my brain has sharpened in on him, on the way he's touching me, waiting for more. Yet nothing else happens. But the moment I start to relax, he begins to knead one cheek for a second then spreads my ass wider.

I know what's coming. Kind of. Rayne and I had tried anal before, and it was pleasant, but I suddenly get a picture of the giant man's cock inside of me and tense a little. But instead of being met with a giant meat stick pounding into my ass, he simply spreads me even wider from behind. It's oddly vulnerable to know he's looking at me like that, but as strange as the moment is, it doesn't last long. After a couple of seconds, one of his hands releases me, and he reaches around my hip to slowly stroke my clit above Dusk's cock. I almost choke on a sound of shock as he continues to stroke me. Then he pulls back and I feel his one hand spread my ass wider before he slowly pushes one finger inside of me.

Gasping against Phantom's lips, I hold myself still. Shocked. The sensation of Onyx pushing that finger in deeper and deeper into my ass, alongside the sensation of Dusk's cock inside my pussy, is overwhelming. The fact that he's using my own juices to make my asshole wet, slides his finger in and out in rhythm with every thrust of Dusk's hips, isn't lost on me.

His lips press against my neck as he repeats the whole process, adding a second finger to my ass.

And now the two men are no longer as slow or as gentle as they plunge in and out of me. Their movements are still measured, still controlled, but it feels like they're testing me. Testing to see how much my nerves can take before I explode.

Phantom suddenly pulls one of my hands from Dusk's shoulder and guides my hand to his cock. His lips leave my mouth, and I turn to watch him slowly using my hand to pump his large erection. It's erotic, and I curl my hand around him, tightening my grip. It's almost humorous when his eyes go wide and his mouth drops open, but the sight's too hot to actually be funny.

On the other side of me, I feel Rayne stroke my cheek. When I turn, he kisses me again. Our mouths move in a rhythm that seems perfect, natural. It's a kiss I've missed for too long. But it isn't enough for me. I don't want to just kiss Rayne, I want to taste him. So I pull back from his kiss, trying to ignore the frown twisting his lips.

"I want to taste yo-" I whisper, but my words are cut off by my moan as the two men inside of me plunge in harder.

Rayne's eyes are wide, but he goes in to kiss me again.

I pull back. "Taste you," I repeat again.

It hits him. I see it. And he doesn't hesitate to sit up onto his knees, close enough that his big cock is bobbing in front of my mouth. I only have one hand to steady myself on Dusk as pleasure rolls through me, so I don't reach for my big man. Instead, I let my tongue dart out to lick his tip.

"Fuck, Ann," he groans.

I know just what he likes. I continue to let my tongue dart out, swallowing down curses as every nerve inside my body screams from all the many pleasure points where I'm being touched. At last, I take Rayne into my mouth, fully into my mouth, sinking down so far on him that I reach his hilt, the head of his cock touching the back of my throat.

He strokes my hair a few times, panting, then wraps a hand in my hair. Pulling me back, he slams his cock back into my mouth, and I swear I didn't think I could be more turned on. But I am. This man, he remembers what I like. He remembers how good it feels when he takes control. When he uses my mouth like he owns it. And damn it if he isn't doing that now.

"Shit," Dusk says beneath me, and the word comes out a

groan. I feel him jerk beneath me, and sense that Dusk might be at his limit.

And the way Phantom is slamming into my hand... I'm pretty sure he's damned close too. We all are.

Which is why when Onyx moans and his fingers slip out of my ass, I whimper around Rayne's cock. I want to demand Onyx keep going. To demand that he take me to the glorious place I'd felt myself going. But then, he pushes the tip of his cock slowly inside me, and I'm no longer frustrated, I'm losing my mind. My grip tightens on Phantom's cock, I feel my pussy tightening around Dusk's length, and I start to suck Rayne harder. I'm on the edge of losing all control.

This is easily the most erotic moment of my life.

Rayne curls his hand around the base of his shaft and jerks a couple times, matching his pumps to my mouth and tongue. I want to moan and scream and writhe and shimmy, but this is all so much pleasure my body is independent of me. I can only feel, only enjoy.

The passion in my belly spreads through my veins and I'm quivering, ready to split apart, muscles taut. Onyx and Dusk, sensing how close I am, pick up their pace. They slam in and out of me in rhythm, driving me wild. I'm right on the edge now. Climbing to a height I've never been. Feeling things I never thought were possible.

And then, I come, exploding over the edge, my orgasm hitting me like a train. It's indescribable. Every nerve in my body alive and crackling. Pleasure, hot and powerful, flows through my veins. Burning me. Leaving nothing but my pleasure behind.

I moan against Rayne's cock, continuing to ride the waves of my orgasm, until Rayne explodes in my mouth, silencing me. I swallow him as Dusk swells in my pussy, seeming to fill parts of me I didn't know still needed to be filled, and Onyx holds my hips and trembles behind me. A second later, both men come together, groans of pleasure filling the air as their hot seed fills my body. Quivers race through me, and I orgasm again, loving the sounds of their desire. Their desire brings mine to another level. A moment later, Phantom thrusts into my fist and grunts, falling over the edge himself, sending his warm seed onto my hand.

And then, it's silent except for our panting. Silent and perfect.

I give Rayne's cock one finally suck, then let it slip from my lips before collapsing onto Dusk. Behind me, Onyx covers me like a blanket. Rayne and Phantom lay down beside us, and it's like the world is finally right. Like everything is right.

There's never been anything like this before in my life and as they pull out and away, I savor every sensation, etch it all into my memory.

"Wow." I don't have another word. Probably it's going to be a while before I can think of any other.

The connection is a tether between us and I can see it, almost, like little wires from me to them and them to each other. "We're bonded now." I speak as certainly as I know my own name.

Rayne nods. He feels it too. "Yes."

I look at the others, all in various states of undress. "Can you feel it?"

"Yes," Dusk answers for them all, and I smile. This is the connection that's been missing my whole life.

TWELVE

Rayne

THAT WAS INDESCRIBABLE. So indescribable that I need a minute to wrap my head around the perfection of it. By morning, I've relived it over and over again in my dream. So much that until I open my eyes and look at her, I can't believe it's real.

My Ann is here with me. And yesterday I shared her with other men, and it was all okay. More than okay. I've never had a brother. Only Esmeray. She and I were best friends for most of our lives, until as the heir of our family, I had to leave home and go to the Royal Fae Academy. It was hard for her. It was hard for me. But I got to go there with a group of my best friends. Men who I was so connected to that I wondered why we never felt that bond, the one that said we would one day share a mate.

It wasn't until I died that I realized it was because they were in love with my sister. I never saw it. But then, Esmeray always joked that I could pick out any detail in a book but didn't have a clue about what was going on outside of my books.

And yet, I'd always liked the idea of sharing a mate with my friends. When I met Ann and they didn't feel a mate bond with her, I was a little disappointed. But they were the only men I could ever imagine sharing a woman with.

Until now.

It's true that my relationship with the shadow beasts has just barely moved from enemies to friends, but after I got over myself, I really had to sit with the idea that I didn't know what the future would hold. I had to ask myself what would happen if my ghost stopped existing in this body, and Ann was suddenly left alone again. And the final question... did I hate the idea of sharing my mate more than I loved my mate?

The answer came easily: no. I love Ann more than anything. More than the sun. More than the sky. More than any title, or any object, or any person. I would give her anything. So the least I could do was accept that she loved other people and that they loved her. *That's what anyone would want, right? More people to love the people they care about?*

And so, I'd accepted it.

What I didn't expect... was that I'd find the whole experience of sharing her to be so damned erotic.

I comb the hair back from her face and smile when her nose wrinkles up, and then she relaxes once more. Phantom, as if aware of her disturbance, tightens his arm around her. Behind me, Onyx makes a little sound in his sleep, as if the warrior is having the same kinds of dreams that plagued me all night long. Leaning up a little, I look for Dusk, then realize he isn't there. The fire beside us has been built up, and I smell cooking, but the man is nowhere to be seen.

So, I cautiously untangle myself from the blankets and step away from them. Onyx instantly rolls onto his side, so he has an arm over Ann too, and I grab a forgotten blanket and spread it over the three of them. My heart feels oddly full. One minute I was dead, the next I have the woman I love back and three men, who very well will become the brothers I always wanted. They're not a replacement for the friends I lost, but something different. Something good.

Dressing quickly, I walk outside and find that Dusk has built a larger fire just a short distance from the cave. Evening is almost upon us, blanketing the forest in golden light. He's standing staring out at the woods, a small smile on his lips. A smile that I can guess the source of. But what's stranger is that I don't think I've ever seen the man look this... relaxed and happy. It's surprising how glad I am to be some small part of his happiness.

As if he senses me, the shadow beast turns around. When our gazes meet, he smiles again. Another nicety that I'm happy to enjoy. These men, after all they've been through, need more friends rather than enemies. I hope they're starting to see me as one.

"Can I join you?" I ask him softly.

He nods. There are logs around the fire, and he chooses one to sit at, where it seems he's been fixing clothes beneath the light of the fire and the evening sky. He picks up right back where I assume he left off, stitching tiny threads into leather. I watch him silently for a bit, a little surprised by how much these men seem to understand. I don't know how their world works, but a royal like me has never had a reason to learn how to fix clothes. And yet this prince of his people knows how to. It's a curious thing.

"What?" he asks, no anger in his voice, just curiosity.

"I'm just continually surprised by how different your people seem to be from ours."

"Really?" His gaze is open as he looks at me. "How so?"

"I don't know." I rub the back of my neck, suddenly nervous. Things are going well between all of us for once. I don't want to say the wrong thing and destroy this hard-earned peace. And yet, I need to explain. "I feel like I don't have any life skills in comparison to you." I laugh, a little uncomfortable. "Growing up, my family were the most powerful of fae. We had property everywhere. We went to important functions. We had important guests to impress. I never had to learn things like cooking, cleaning, and sewing."

To my relief, Dusk doesn't seem insulted. "Our world is very different. Yours has a lot of strange things... technology, they call it. Things our people don't have. Whereas our world relies more on magic. We're just as likely to go out hunting with bows and arrows as we are to throw wild parties and invite the neighboring royalty."

I smile. "We're equally weird. We're just as likely to watch TV as we are to create strange spells under a full moon."

Dusk laughs.

I laugh too.

It's nice.

Dusk reaches forward and stirs the cooking stew for a minute before returning to his sewing. "Do you mind if I ask you a question?"

"Sure."

He hesitates, then seems to decide to go for it. "How did you meet Ann?"

It's an upfront question. Honest. Curious.

"At Royal Fae Academy."

He frowns. "The place they kept us in cages beneath the school." A harshness flows through his words. "Those fucking fae who lured us, who got those collars on us, who enslaved us."

I wince. "If it helps, most fae had no idea that was going on. We were as surprised as you were when we realized our own people were using you as a tool to kill the dark fae."

His lips curl a bit, but then he blows out a breath. "I don't blame you. I just hope your people don't blame us for killing all those dark fae. We didn't have a choice. We would never... never--" he shudders, "kill innocents."

"We know." I pause, then clarify, "I knew. I figured it out. But I'm sure by now my sister has explained it all to our people. If we ever get back though, I'll make it clear to everyone." I realize there's a bit of a threat in my words, and I realize I'm clenching my hands into fists so I slowly release them. I don't like what the fae were doing, and some small part of me feels strange that I didn't get to finish the mission I was so dedicated to, even though my sister and my friends finished it for me.

Then, I remember what he really wanted to learn about. Ann. "But as far as Ann, we saw each other at the Royal Fae Academy and just knew that we were each other's mates. It was... not what I wanted at the time. I was researching something dark and dangerous and never wanted to involve a mate in my trouble. But with love, we don't always have a choice."

He snorts. "Like when we saw Ann. We were completely under the control of that bastard fae. And we saw Ann and just knew. We managed to ask them to break our collars off. And the second we were free, we ran, with Ann. It was the only thing we could do at that moment, but it certainly wasn't the way we wanted to meet our mate."

"Somehow it suits Ann though," I say with a little laugh. "From the moment I met her, she was like no one else in this world. She seemed so quiet and shy. She seemed to honestly see herself as some kind of wallflower. But she never was. Not just because of our mate bond, but because there was a light inside her that no one could dim, no matter how hard they might try. She seemed to think she was so lucky to have a Bloodmore, to have me as her mate, but I was the lucky one. She was just unique, special in every way. I remember the first time I saw the scars on her hands." I hesitate, realizing that this isn't my story to tell, but then push on, knowing that this bond of ours means that soon we'll all know each other's secrets. "She said that her stepfather used to give her choices. If she made the wrong one, he broke one of her fingers."

Dusk gasps, and the look on his face, it's pure shock. "Is that... is that why she struggles so much with decisions? Why this is so hard for her?"

"Part of it," I say, nodding. "I have so few scars from my childhood. My father was a cold man, but never a cruel man, even with his dark fae heart. Ann, on the other hand, has so many emotional and physical scars. So many triggers. And yet, she seems to think they're nothing. She pretends they aren't there, I think, because it would be too much for her to see herself as a victim to that bastard."

"I'm surprised the man's still alive." Dusk's voice is low, almost a growl. "I would have killed him the moment I found out."

I smile at him, a smile that's all teeth. "There are other ways to break a man than murdering him, although the temptation was there." Again, I pause, trying to decide if telling him this secret I've kept from Ann is something I should tell him. "When I learned of what he did, I sent some of my men to... talk with him. He was out of her manor that day, and I am quite certain that if he ever steps foot on the continent my Ann is on, the man's body will never be found."

Dusk looks oddly impressed. "Good."

"Ann will never have to fear him again." Then, I add, "And what he did to her... I made certain he will have a scar in every place she has a scar. Every. Single. Fucking. Place. It would have been far more satisfying if I had been the one to do it, but I did what I could."

"And her mother?"

"Her mother is a woman I... lack respect for. When the stepfather left, she returned to live in an ancestral home far from the home Ann grew up in. I always thought that when Ann and I were done at the academy, we would remain at her manor, rule from her manor, until my parents were ready to step down. Now..." Now what? If I continue to live in this world, I would never expect to return home and take my sister's place as leader of our people. I would tell my family that I'm alive, because they deserve that, but I believe I would much rather rule over Ann's people than my own. Her lands are smaller, more comfortable, and somehow seem like a place I could grow to be something incredible rather than an empire that can't grow any more. "What will happen?" I manage to ask. "If we can take your father down, will you want to return to your lands and rule?"

Dusk shakes his head. "Honestly, I haven't thought past this war. Maybe once upon a time I did, but not in a very long time."

"Do you want to rule over your people?"

He frowns. "It's not about what we want, it's about what we have to do."

"So, that's a no."

He turns that frown onto me, and then it eases. "Right now, I want to find a way to save both our worlds. I think there's a good chance that if our father can be defeated, and his control over the shadow beasts destroyed, our remaining people will have to come to earth. Unless we can restore the light to our world. And if they come here, they will only be able to shift into their beast form at night, which will be difficult for them. Our other forms are like the other side of our souls. Without our world, things will have to change. A lot. But at least now we know enough about this world to help our people survive on it."

"And with the help of my sister, and Ann's position as lady of the Hart lands, it wouldn't be hard to establish a new life for your people. We can handle helping build them homes, a village. And between the two of us, we have more than enough lands to give them a solid start to a new life."

"Do you think your people could truly learn to tolerate us?" He looks sincerely curious.

I smile. "You don't know my sister, but you know Ann. Do you really think between two powerful women there's anything they can't accomplish?"

He nods and knots the thread he's working on, then cuts it with his dagger. He folds the clothes in a pile next to him and puts his thread and needles carefully back in a little case.

"If I'm still..." *Oh, what was the word?* "Alive when all this over, I'm going back to see my sister. It's one of the first things I want to do."

"And you'll take Ann? Even if we find a way to return to our world?" They've already built such a bond, an attachment with and to her, that I have no idea if I will ever be able to convince her to go with me.

"If she wants to go, but the choices she makes now

doesn't just affect her or me." I shrug, and he smiles because he damned well knows what I mean.

"I get what you're saying about your sister. I feel that way about my mom." He sighs, and I understand. "My mother was an incredible woman. When Shenra's mom sent her to live with us as a girl, my mom took her under her wing, as if she were her daughter. And I could almost believe she was. They both had the same white-blonde hair, so white that it was unique in our world. But it wasn't just their looks; my mom had that same quiet power. A way to get even our tough father to listen to her."

"But she died?" I ask.

"Grave trolls," he says tightly. "We found her body. Tried to save her. But... it was too late."

"I'm so sorry for your loss," I tell him, not knowing what else to say. I know what love costs, the fear and the need to protect. The devotion is extraordinary, at times untenable, but always there.

He stirs the stew again, his movements tighter, and I hate that I ruined his happy moment. I remember the way he looked when I stepped out of the cave, and I suddenly want to bring him back to that moment. My heart twists, and it's strange. Usually, I only feel this connected to Ann, my best friends, and my sister. Feeling this with a man I'm just starting to understand feels strange. But then, this must be part of the mate-bond. Now that we're all Ann's, it makes sense that we sort of become each other's too.

"I don't know much about the shadow world." I'm hoping the change in conversation might help. *Might*, because it seems like its own kind of problem to unravel.

He shrugs, poking the fire and sending embers up around the pan. "The legend is that we—shadow beasts— were shifters in another world. Hunted. Murdered one by one until our numbers were depleted." He shrugs. "The leader of the shadow beasts was a woman who was always searching for a new world."

"A new world?"

He nods. "Yeah. There are slivers between realms, little spaces connected through the power of the moon." He tells the story casually. "She was called the Moon Goddess. Every world she found was too bright for shadow beasts. The light would kill them, turn them to ash." He blew out a breath. "Then she found the shadow realm. It was too dark for anything to grow or survive there. So the shadow beasts would be safe, but they would die because they had no food, nothing. She created a light source from the power in her own heart, and she hung it from the sky. It meant that she lost her power, her life, but she did it for the love of us."

This was all old news to him. His history. Ancestry. He'd found a way to disconnect from all of it. But I found myths and legends intriguing. In fact, I'd read many of them that sounded similar to his story.

"From its light, an incredible world grew and the shadow beasts found a home." He looks around. "It's like here. The plants are different than they are here, but she breathed life into the dark realm. And when the plants grew, animals came too. Some good animals, and some like the grave trolls. It's always like earth's night there, but a bright one. Enough to flourish. Different magical creatures continued to be born there, under our goddess's heart, where the shadow beasts live. Wherever."

"It sounds like an amazing place." Boy would I love to take a journal there, to etch the plants and animals, to study their sky and figure out where their moon really came from and how they can exist without a true day and night.

"It was a wonderful place. But now the light source is

gone. Everything is dead in that world. The grave trolls and rot monkeys are all that's left. The shadow beasts that have stayed behind are mindless now, stuck in their beast form, trapped in the king's control." He's disgusted. "There's just... nothing left because he stole the light source from the sky. Until the light source is back in the sky, the shadow world will never thrive. The goddess's sacrifice will be for nothing."

Shadow world? Goddess's heart and sacrifice? I nod. I've heard it before. Not just myths similar to this one, but I believe I've actually read about their world, and old memories tickle the back of my mind. "I recall this story. Another legend, too." It's sketchy and in pieces. "Something about a light fae living in a world like that one."

"Light fae?" He frowns. "No, there had never been a light fae in our world."

Hum. "Well, perhaps I'm wrong." *But I didn't think so...*

Dusk doesn't say more. Doesn't say anything. He just looks behind me at the cave, which is when I realize there's a low murmur of conversation and movement. I'd been so caught up in our conversation that I hadn't noticed.

The others are awake now. Phantom joins us at the fire and eventually the others trickle out, all looking strangely well-rested and, not surprisingly, happy. There's no danger in the day. Not right now. And after our intimate time together, we all deserve a moment of peace to let the changes we've experienced sink in.

Dusk hands out the stew in wooden bowls, and we all eat in silence for a few minutes. Not a tense silence like before, but a comfortable one. Like we're a family enjoying breakfast, or dinner.

Phantom blows on his stew, then speaks, his words obviously carefully chosen. "We need to see the elder before night falls now that we're mated."

At his words, Ann looks up and smiles, each of us smiling with her. Mated. Bonded.

If the prophecy is right, we're all saved.

THIRTEEN

Ann

THE TRIP to the elder is short. Shorter than it was the last time we made this trip. Or, at least, that's the way it feels. In no time at all, we reach the entrance to the cave, nodding at each shadow beast that we pass guarding the area around the main cave. Making sure that the shadow king's minions can never take them by surprise, although it feels a bit pointless in the light of evening. But they've survived this long for a reason, so I don't question it.

Besides, I enjoyed the trip over. More than I would have thought. The men and I talked. Things felt... natural, calm between us for the first time. And as if to emphasize that we made the right choice, shards of the moonstone lit up along our path. My men picked them up and placed them in a pouch at Phantom's belt. Rayne made jokes, told the guys about things they could only find in our world, and the shadow beasts surprised me by expressing some interest in seeing these things for themselves.

It feels like... everyone is hopeful for the first time in a long time, and I like it. I like my men even more when I see an excitement for the future in their eyes. It also doesn't hurt that they keep touching me. A hand on my back, or on my ass. A kiss, a brush of my hair. It's like they keep coming back to me, reminding me that they're there and they love me.

A girl could certainly do worse than them.

And then, we're at the cave entrance, weaving down to the main part of the cave. I expect... I don't know what I expect, but certainly not the somber sight before us. The other men in the caves are still wounded, tired-looking men. It's as if only hours have passed since our battle with the shadow king rather than days. It makes guilt instantly awaken inside of me. While I healed my men with my touch, these men weren't as lucky. And it's not like they were in good shape before this. They seemed about to crack even before the recent battle.

Our good moods fade away. We stand together beneath the glow of the crystals that line all the walls of the cave, a short distance from a large fire in the middle. Some men are in the back of the cave in the little pool, standing beneath the waterfall, naked. These men look no happier than the ones lying on blankets near the fire. And all of their bodies show the obvious wounds they experienced in battle.

They shoot glares in our direction, and I suppose I understand it, even though I don't remember them being this angry in the past. As least not most of them. But I do get it. These are the sons of the shadow king, the man responsible for the war they're all fighting, for the deaths of their friends, for the shells of lives they're living as they fight his trolls and monkeys and beasts. As they bleed and ache and die.

I glance from Phantom to Dusk and Onyx, who stand together. Looks pass between them. Worry. Trepidation. Apprehension.

Phantom's brow is creased and his eyes are wide. These are his friends. His people. And his father is killing them for the sake of power. His guilt is visual. Even in the way he carries himself. His shoulders hunch. But then, he pulls himself together. He squares his body, lifts his head. "We're mated to this woman."

He levels a hard gaze at each man, friend and foe, then at his brothers and me. A couple of the injured shadow beasts perk up, looking interested, but the worry is still dark in Phantom's eyes.

One man approaches us. "Truly?"

Phantom gives a tight smile. "Truly. Just as the prophecy said, it has been done."

The shadow beasts murmur to each other, but no one else approaches. And, again, I'm surprised. I didn't exactly expect them to all leap up and cheer, but I expected some happiness. Some relief that at least one thing had gone in a good direction.

Do they not have as much faith in the prophecy as the elder did? My thoughts swirl together. And after a long moment, the shadow beast in front of us turns away and returns to the fire, whispering quietly to the others beside him.

Rayne and I exchange a look. *What the hell is going on?*

Dusk moves forward and takes me by the arm. "Come on. Let's go."

If the prophecy is true, if they know about it, the mating bond we've formed should've been cause for celebration. *Is there something I'm not understanding?* For the millionth time since I came here, I feel like I have a bunch of puzzle pieces that aren't going together, and I want to groan in frustration, hating that our special moment, our moment of happiness, seems to already have passed.

Dusk leads us to the tunnels. Torches line the walls. A couple shadow beasts walk down it, see us, nod, and continue onto the big room, but we continue forward through the dark, dank tunnels, past the room Adrik was in when I first saw him, to Elder Aeuro's room.

There, we pause in the entrance. It's the same as before. A simple room with pillows surrounding a big fire in the center. Aeuro sits on one of the tufted pillows, staring straight ahead at something I can't see. When Phantom clears his throat, his gaze sharpens and focuses on us for a minute before he seems to relax. My men give a little bow, and he nods at Phantom and Dusk, signs a greeting to Onyx, and ignores me. It's okay. I don't mind so much. I have a feeling right now he's a bit frustrated with me. But hopefully he won't be when he hears our news.

Phantom speaks first, his voice low and respectful. "The mating bond has been completed."

Aeuro's brows lift and he smiles, a relieved smile that eases some of the tension in my chest. "Good. Very good."

Dusk steps forward. "So now what?"

Phantom continues. "How do we win?"

It feels like we're all holding our breaths. Whatever this elder says, we've put a lot of faith into being the answer to all of this. He seems to have a power that none of the rest of us have, a power of prophecy, or perhaps just the power to hear these "shadows" whispering. Whatever it is, he has control over things that seem strange and magical to me.

Aeuro looks from one of my shadow beasts to the others. Then he glances at Rayne and me, shakes his head. "I don't know. I thought it would be obvious."

Obvious. Obvious in the human world is neon signs and flashing lights. I wonder what it is in the shadow realm.

"What's obvious?" Rayne asks, looking upset. "What usually happens when a prophecy is fulfilled?"

The elder seems to choose his words with care. "When the shadows whispered to our Goddess, they told her that there was another world. A world where the shadow beasts could be safe, could thrive. All she had to do was find it. And she did."

"But it cost her her life. Her heart." Phantom doesn't look happy. "It wasn't as simple as just finding the world."

"I never said it was simple," the elder says. "Just that it would take us down a path that will end in us successfully winning this war."

"*Great*," Rayne mutters.

"So it's just a legend? Creating the mate bond hasn't changed anything for the war." Disappointment deepens Dusk's tone and Phantom crosses his arms over his massive chest, widens his stance, and squares his hips as if he's preparing for battle.

Aeuro purses his lips. He isn't afraid to answer, but he is honestly considering. "I'll speak to the shadows and get back to you. I'm sure that now that we're on this path, they'll be able to lead us to the next correct step to winning this war."

But none of my shadow beasts look confident.

"Elder," I say, trying to make sure I'm being respectful. "Have the shadows said anything about my powers? If I could learn to use my light, maybe I could really help end this war."

Aeuro's brows draw together. "They have whispered about you. About your powers. That they're part of all of us. A key to turning the tide. But they have not... given me the manual for how to control your powers." He gives me a small smile. "Most of the time, powers like yours can only be influenced by the person controlling them. Perhaps you should spend more time trying to figure them out."

He's not wrong, but I do wish this *wonderful* source of information was more helpful. "I'll give that a shot."

"But I will speak to the shadows on this matter too." And then his shoulders curl a bit, and I feel a little bad. This man should be enjoying his twilight years, not trying to solve all the problems of the universe. "Before you go, please spend some time with the men. They haven't been coming to my cave recently and the shadows are whispering that trouble is brewing. Our men can't handle a lot more trouble. Not right now."

Judging by the disappointed nods, this isn't the best news. But my men each bow and thank the elder, then turn and leave. Onyx leads us out of the cave. No one speaks. His words seem to be hanging as heavily on them as they are on me. I keep staring at my hands, wondering about how exactly to explore my powers. They kind of just seem to be... gone when I don't need them. *So how do I convince my damn powers to let me practice with them?*

When we're through the tunnel and outside the main cave again, there are almost three times as many shadow beasts assembled as when we went in. They're standing together, talking in low voices, but when they realize we're there, all eyes turn to us. Rayne moves closer to me on one side, Dusk on the other. And the tension in the air... it feels like we're standing against enemies rather than allies. A feeling that makes me more than a little uneasy.

The shadow beasts close in, but the one I've learned is named Flame speaks. "How can we win?"

A murmur rushes through them. They're all waiting for

that one magical answer that will end the fighting and all the death. I just wonder how they'll respond when they realize we still don't have a clue.

For some reason, just the idea scares me. I look at my men. They're all wearing their confidence like a cloak, but I can see beneath it. They're worried too.

Damn it.

FOURTEEN

Dusk

I'LL ADMIT, I thought the mating bond legend was true. I also thought that as soon as we bonded with Ann that something magical would sweep over the land, that the shards would cease to light, and that the fighting would be over. Or something like that. But, basically, that we would win and all would be well in this world and in ours.

Prophecies are rare, even in the shadow world. When the shadows whisper one, people stand up and listen. They see a prophecy as something sacred and powerful, like fate. Something to believe in in the darkest times. And we're certainly in dark times. Times of war. Where brother is forced to fight brother. I wanted, no, needed, to believe that once we mated Ann, we would be free.

And apparently, I wasn't the only one who needed this to be true. They're staring at us. Waiting. Not quite hope in their eyes, but perhaps, desperation.

I hate that the prophecy doesn't seem to be that easy.

I've never feared our men before, but a streak of concern is flowing through me. Instincts are going off inside of me like alarm bells, and I actually wish I could speak to Phantom privately. Tell him to break the news gently, or with some hope still attached to it, since my brother tends to say things in a direct way. It's good for leading a war. Good for running people, most of the time. But not now.

Our men continue to close in around us, so we move more tightly around Ann. No, I don't think they would hurt her. But people are capable of surprising things when they're desperate.

Phantom looks at me, Onyx looks at him, and Rayne looks at Onyx. He's one of us now. And he isn't going to let anything happen to her. It's weirdly nice to know we have one more person who has our back right now. Who is here to protect our woman.

My brother stands up taller. "The shadows have whispered from the time we were children that our chosen mate would bring great power. And when this war came to pass, they whispered that she would be the one to end this war."

There's a low murmuring of agreement.

"We all saw Ann's power on the battlefield. Her ability to control the light."

More murmurs, these ones more excited than the last.

"Within her control is power enough to destroy a smoke dragon and to harm the shadow king."

"Get to it!" someone shouts.

Phantom glances in my direction. It's half a second, but I see the concern in his eyes before his expression is fully one of confidence. "The mate bond is complete. Now we need only wait for the shadows to show us the next step."

Silence. His words are met with complete and utter silence.

"So, you don't know what to do next?" Flame asks, pushing through the others and coming to stand right in front of us.

"Prophecies aren't simple. We must still be patient."

"We've been patient for a very long time," Flame says, and there's disappointment and frustration in his voice.

"I know," Phantom tells him, his voice gentling. "I know that when all of you followed us to this world, you had no idea what was in store. None of us did. But I'm proud of you. You're fighting, not just for yourselves, not just for us, but all the people still enslaved beneath the shadow king's hold. When we stop him--"

"*If* we can stop him," Flame says, his dark eyes locked onto Phantom's. "*If* we can stop him, then what? When we fight the other shadow beasts, we're fighting our friends, our family. If this keeps up, we'll be returning to a dark world we can't survive in, and all the people we once loved will be dead, casualties of this war."

"There are always sacrifices in war." Phantom's voice is grave. "But with the prophecy fulfilled, we just have to hold on a little longer. Not lose our faith."

More silence.

"We've run out of faith," Flame says, and his words sound like an apology, which I don't understand.

But I do sense the way the tension around us increases. I see the way our men's eyes narrow, and even a change that sweeps through them as they exchange glances.

This isn't good. Not good at all.

I breathe out slowly, my muscles tense, then slowly lay my hand on the hilt of the dagger on my belt. Maybe I won't need it, maybe I'm worrying about nothing, but it *feels* like a storm is brewing.

Phantom gives a slight nod, his gaze meeting mine, and

then sweeping over the others. If we have to fight, if there's no other choice than to go against the shadow beasts we've fought beside and would continue to fight beside, then we will fight them. But I hope that's not what's brewing. I hope this is just something that can be talked about.

Flame looks each of us up and down like he's sizing us up, like he's assessing the danger. And the rumbling in my gut turns to a roar. They're about to betray us. I can feel it. Then, he speaks to all of us, but looks at Phantom. "We're tired of the violence and all the death that comes from fighting the king."

"We're all tired of it," Phantom says, his voice patient. "But the alternative is to give into him, to let him destroy this world, and to let him control us all."

"This world?" Flame almost sighs the words. "It would be a shame for it to be destroyed the way our world was, but this was never about saving this world. It was about protecting ourselves, about fighting to free our people. But each day that passes, we have less people to save. Our men are dying. His men, our enslaved people, are dying."

"No one said war was easy." My voice is soft but it carries over the room.

"No one said we wanted a war," Flame counters, his expression still sad.

"There's no other choice," Phantom tells them, then raises his voice. "We have no other choice. We just need to keep our faith that the prophecy will be fulfilled and we'll save our people."

"There is another choice though," Flame says, and his hand moves to his sword.

My fingers curl around the hilt of my dagger. I don't want to fight today, but I will because I know what's coming. Desperation does not make for smart decisions, and these men think they've run out of options.

"I can use the light again. I can help us win this war." Ann's voices carries through the room, but no one seems to care.

"Can you control this power?" Flame asks, lifting a brow, but she doesn't answer. "We already know you can't. It's an incredible trick, but nothing more than a trick if you can't use it when we need you to."

"Be smart," Phantom warns, his voice almost a growl.

"I am." The circle around us tightens, and I watch Flame for any signal he might be giving. "We made a deal with the shadow king."

"A *deal*?" My words come out shocked, harsh. "For what? All the king wants is death and power."

"Not just that." And now, Flame won't meet my gaze.

And it hits me. *We're* their bargaining tool today. They've sold us out for their own safety. The sense of betrayal that flows through me is a shock. I didn't think they didn't owe us anything. But I've watched my brothers bleed, nearly die for our people. They deserve better. Hell, I deserve better. What's more, there's no world in which the shadow king will give these men anything. They have to be smart enough to know that.

I glance at Onyx. He's watching, reading the scene, body tense, eyes alert while Rayne moves to stand even closer to Ann, almost completely blocking her from the men, but she glances around him.

"Don't do this," Dusk says. "Only a fool would make a deal with a monster."

Flame nods at Phantom. "It's already done."

His men unsheath their swords and Phantom shakes his head. After last night, after we fulfilled the mating bond, we'd thought this whole thing was finished and the king would be nothing but a bad memory of a worse time. Now we don't even know if the prophecy is real. But either way, I don't think any of us expected this.

"What did he offer you?" Phantom's voice is strong and angry.

"He's pardoning us," Flame says, drawing his head up taller.

Phantom gives a humorless laugh, shaking his head. "He'll just enslave you in your beast form."

"But he won't be killing us." To Flame, enslavement beats death. Beats fighting to live. Beats suffering the torment of a mad king. To Flame, this is the best he could've done for the men who trust him to speak for them.

Phantom cocks his head, anger in his gaze. "I might just have to do it for him."

I've never had a gripe with Flame, but after today, he's top spot on the shit list. My hand curls around the dagger handle at my belt, and I imagine putting this blade through his skull. I won't enjoy it, but I also won't feel too bad about killing a traitor, a man foolish enough to be tricked by my father after all he's seen in these many months. Mistakes often have consequences, and it's sad that his death will be one, but I can't focus on that right now. Can't focus on the idea that soon I'll be killing my brothers in arms.

"We completed the mate bond. Don't you even want to see if it can be the thing to save us? After *everything*?" Phantom stares at Flame, but it's no use. They've decided already.

"The shadow king won't care."

"But he won't be able to claim her now, and getting to her before we mated her is probably why he made this deal. What do you think he'll do when he realizes he can't have her?" I have an edge of desperation in my voice that I don't like.

"The king said that mated or not, he'll have Ann." Flame winces as if he wishes he didn't have to speak the words.

My stomach bottoms out. *The king wants her still? He'll take her whether she want to or not, whether his sons have claimed her or not? I feel sick.*

"That's impossible." Phantom truly sounds shocked.

Onyx signs, and all eyes are on him. Finally, I reluctantly speak his words. "He believes father is so far gone that he'll take her to hurt us, not even because of the prophecy, but because he doesn't care about our most sacred of rules."

Flames sighs. "Just come with us. It doesn't have to be like this."

I draw my dagger in one hand and my sword in the other. "None of you will take her with me still alive."

There are easily thirty of them. Four of my us. And Ann. The odds aren't good, but then, the odds have never been good for us.

Phantom looks at Rayne. "Protect her."

He nods and the fight begins like an explosion. Like a storm that barely gave a warning before shaking the world.

Men surround us. Swords clank against swords. I see Onyx lop off a head as my own blade meets one enemy's then another's. They're trying so damned hard to reach us, but with us in a circle, we're making it fucking hard for them to catch us off-guard. There are screams of pain and growls of anger. But we encircle Ann, striving to keep her safe from danger. Even though it's obvious to us, to everyone, that we can only fight these numbers for so long.

One way or another, these men will get us today. And then... we'll be prisoners of the shadow king.

FIFTEEN

Ann

THE FIGHT ENDED with too much blood and too much death before all my men had their weapons stripped away and their hands bound. Phantom has a cut on his cheek that drips blood down his face, Onyx's mouth is swollen and bleeding, and Dusk's eye is swollen nearly shut. But I know those aren't the worst of their injuries. The worst ones are the ones I can't see, but distinctly remember. The backs of swords smashed into their stomachs, shoulders, and even the back of their heads. Punches. Kicks. Yes, it could have been worse. If these men wanted my shadow beasts dead, they'd be dead.

But it doesn't really matter. Even if they didn't kill us, there's no question they're marching us off to a fate worse than death.

We're out of the main cave. Other than the elder, it seems that every shadow beast on earth is around us. Most are in the front, leading our sad group. Apparently, they'd left before us to speak with the king and his minions, to let them know they were successful and that the deal would be completed soon. A group of about a dozen surround our group. Guilt radiates from them, but also exhaustion. I understand that, even if I don't believe they're doing the right thing. They're tired of this war. They're tired of the blood and death. But it doesn't justify making this horrible decision, and I'm pretty sure they know deep down that we're right.

It doesn't stop them from doing this though.

Half of them carry torches, but they're almost unneeded. Around us, shards light up in every direction in the woods. They're like a creepy path to our destruction. And it almost seems sad that they believe these pieces came from the heart of a goddess who saved them but are now being used to destroy a world. It's also creepy to see just how many there are in these woods.

"I thought we'd collected most of the shards," I say.

Dusk shakes his head. "There are almost enough for the king to expand the shadow realm."

Flame glances back at me, his mouth in a thin line. "We've been keeping a stash of them from the elder. Part of our agreement was to put them back."

"Are you fucking kidding me?" Phantom growls. "After all our hard work!"

Flame winces, but then shakes his head. "It doesn't matter anymore. This war has been lost."

"What would your goddess say?" Rayne asks, crossing his arms over his chest. Neither he nor I were bound. I'm thinking it's because they didn't see us as much of a challenge, which is more than a little insulting.

"Goddess help us," rises from a few of the men, but nothing else.

Rayne gets a familiar look on his face, one that says he's putting together pieces of a puzzle, and that he's close to making them work. I just hope whatever he's figuring out will help us when he does. Not that we have a lot of time left.

"The second they get us to the shadow realm we're done for." Phantom speaks in a low voice just beside Rayne, telling us something I'm pretty sure we all already know. But then he leans in and whispers something to Rayne. I can't see either of their faces, but I see Rayne tense, then give a subtle nod.

A second later, I watch Rayne slip Phantom something. I'm not sure what, but my mind is going a million miles a minute. There's a plan. A way to escape before we reach the shadow realm, I hope, but I don't know how it'd be possible. Not with a dozen shadow beasts around us, and dozens more a short distance in front of us. But I know we have to make a move soon... or never.

I don't know the plan, don't know my place in it, but I'm ready to fight. My muscles tense, and I watch my men, ready for the smallest sign.

And then, it's like an explosion. Phantom breaks free of his bindings, then uses his dagger to cut Onyx and Dusk free, the three of them have taken swords from our guards before our enemies know what's happened. I don't know what to do, but I clench my hands into fists, ready to help in any way I can.

But within seconds, a hand digs into my arm so hard it hurts, and then I'm being hauled away. Away from the fight and my men.

I look at the person taking me, feeling frantic. And... my gaze catches with Rayne's.

"Wh-what?"

"Just run!" he says, his words soft, but still a command.

Run? Are they running? Are they escaping too? "We should be with them!"

But he doesn't listen, just keeps yanking me along.

In a fair fight, no way are these shadow beasts guarding us enough to take Phantom, Onyx, and Dusk, but something tells me that they aren't about to fight fair. They're fighting for what they think is their freedom, for what they believe will stop all the death, and those are powerful excuses to put a good defense. But Dusk and Phantom and Onyx are fighting for their lives. *All* of their lives, even the ones fighting them.

So if my men dove into the darkness of the woods to pick them off one by one, that might not be the fair fight they would prefer, but it's most definitely smarter than taking them on out in the open. It's the only thing that will give them a chance to get away, even if they have to hurt or kill some of their brethren to do it. I just have to hang onto the hope that my guys can win.

Rayne pulls me through the forest, then down behind a boulder. It's confusing. Shouldn't we be ducking and weaving through the woods? Making noise to split the forces so they don't all go after my men? I want to be sure I'm helping in some way, but Rayne has his body wrapped around mine, a barrier between me and our enemies.

"Where are we meeting them?" I whisper.

Rayne doesn't answer.

"Shouldn't we be making more noise? Drawing their focus this way too so the guys can get away?"

He shushes me, and my anger boils.

"Talk, right this second, or I'm running right to the shadow realm!"

Rayne sighs then whispers, "They aren't trying to get away."

They aren't trying to get away? I feel the color drain from my face. *They're* the distraction. *They were only trying to get us to freedom while sacrificing themselves? Those idiots! Why the hell--?*

I push backward, using my weight against the boulder to move Rayne, but he's strong, stronger than I am, stronger than he was before he took Adrik's body. He holds me so I can barely move. "Let me go!" I struggle and shift and writhe.

"Stop, Ann! They're warriors. They don't need to be worried about you while they're fighting the forces of darkness." He's almost shouting at me now.

My anger changes. I hold myself still and feel a strange coolness flow through me. If I keep struggling against Rayne, I'm never going to get away, and with each second that passes, my men are in more danger. All those big warriors... they could easily kill them. But if our enemies have instructions to keep them alive and bring them to the shadow realm, they have a fate worse than death waiting for them there.

Rayne finally relaxes behind me. "If they get away, they'll follow our direction. You'll see this was the right choice. What they wanted."

Unfortunately, I know Rayne too well. It's in his voice. He doesn't think my men will escape. He sees them as already dead.

Angry tears sting my eyes. *I need to save my men. Not as a warrior. Just as me. Whatever I can do to help. Please. Please.*

Suddenly, I feel it. That strange and unexpected power inside of me. It blossoms, not like something I can physically touch, but almost like a memory. A forewarning of something to come. Hopefully, I can wield the magic without understanding how.

Feeling more confident, I slam my head back into Rayne's nose as hard as I can, then try to escape.

And fail.

A string of curses explodes from his lips, but instead of releasing me, he picks me up and tosses me over his shoulder. "Goddammit, Ann! Stop it."

I'm shocked, struggling against his rock-solid body as he races with me through the woods. *How many times do these idiots have to take off with me? At what point will they stop treating me like a child who needs to be protected and treat me instead like a partner? Someone who can help?*

Rayne slows, breathing hard. "They said they've lost. They just want you safe, Ann. And you have to know they wouldn't send you away if they thought there was any chance." He continues walking, brushing vines and weeds out of the way. "They want you to get to freedom. To be safe. If the shadow king gets his hands on you..."

I don't give a fuck what he has to say. I want to go back now. "If you ever loved me, you'll take me back."

He ignores me. "Rayne!" I'm screaming now, pounding his back, jerking my body back and forth, using the strength in my legs to no avail. I'm stuck until I can figure out how to get back to the fighting. How to save the men who mean more to me than anything else in this world or any other.

"I'll never forgive you if I lose them, if I had a chance to help them and you wouldn't let me. This isn't a threat, it's a promise."

His steps slow even more, but he keeps going. Further from the men who need me, even if they don't know it yet.

SIXTEEN

Onyx

THE WOODS around us are silent. Ominous. Even the shadow beasts who surround us are quiet. This isn't a win for them. It's a surrender. Almost like a man whose crawled through the desert for days, only to collapse, unable to go further. These beasts, these men, they can't go further. I understand. They don't have a mate to soothe the horrors of battle from their hearts. They've already lost anyone and everyone they've ever loved. Either they've had to kill them in battle, or the people they loved are slaves to the shadow king. Either way, they hit their limit.

It doesn't make me less angry at their betrayal, even though I sympathize with them. All I can be grateful for is that Ann is safe, that she escaped with Rayne, who will die to protect her. If I have to leave this world for the shadow realm, that's all that matters. That until the Void consumes this world, maybe Ann will have some happiness with Rayne. When the darkness sweeps these lands, all the animals and plants will die, but Ann and Rayne, I imagine, will survive as long as possible.

I only wish I could give her more.

We're bound once more, being dragged through the forest, taken to the shadow realm and this time, we aren't breaking free. I look over at Phantom. He's beaten and bloody. He took the worst of the onslaught that happened after our enemy shadow beasts won. His head hangs as if it's too heavy for him to lift, but it could be a ploy. At least I hope it's a trick to make them think they have him. It's why he's making them hold him under the arms and why he drags his toes in the dirt. Twice they've stumbled and twice he's groaned when they dropped him, not moving until they picked him up.

I just sincerely hope that he's faking it. Or maybe I don't. Maybe he should be out of it when we finally become his father's slaves.

Slade bumps my shoulder.

I look at the tired warrior with his dark hair and dark eyes. He signs, "Sorry." One of the few words he knows.

I'm not sure what to say. I can't even sign back with my hands bound with rope, but I don't accept his sorry, nor can I bring it in me to be nasty to him, so I just look away from him.

In the distance, I swear there's a disturbance. Dusk glances in that direction, but when our eyes meet, he just shakes his head. Some warriors are trying to find Ann still, worried the king won't be happy with just the three of us, even though she's our mate now. But I have a feeling that the disturbance wasn't one of the warriors, but Ann instead. And we don't want to give away her location.

She needs to stay gone. And if Rayne is half the man he

thinks he is, he needs to make sure she sees the logic in our decision, even if she doesn't like it.

The last thing she needs is to see what's going to happen once we're back in the shadow realm. How their father will force us to shift. How he'll control us once we do. How we'll cease to be who we are, even though we'll always be inside the beast, we'll always know what we've lost, who we are. Until we're crazy and only he can control what we become.

Dusk leans in a little closer so I can read his lips. "You okay?"

I nod.

He gives a small smile and mouths, "Who would have thought this was the way things would end?"

I did. I hoped it wouldn't end this way, and I didn't expect to be betrayed, but it seemed we were always going to lose against the shadow king.

We're drawing closer to the Void. I know it without seeing the Void yet. The darkness is closer here, closing in with every step, and the air is thicker though the trees are sparser here. Clouds swirl above, dark and black, and lightning splits the clouds even though the rest of the sky is calm and placid. It's not just a sign that we're close, but that the shadow king is closer to expanding his hold over this world. The Void hasn't reached this place yet, but I can feel the energy here. It's different. Darker and more dangerous.

I don't have to ask where the sliver is that leads to the shadow world, the little opening between our world and earth. I know. It's in the Void. The center of the black, looming cloud that we've named the Void. That we fear. That's an expansion of the king's world.

I only wish I could say something now, could hear my own voice, could hear the sound of the thunder and my impending doom. It's a stupid thought, but I can't seem to escape it.

And I'm probably pathetic for missing it at a time like this, at a time when I should be worried about breaking free or dying. But right now, with the clouds swirling and the thunder rolling, thunder I can feel rumbling through the ground not hear on the air, all I can think of is that I'll never hear myself again. I'll never hear the sounds of battle as I fight to save... everyone on Earth. I'll never hear the hiss of a fire, the flapping of leaves in a strong wind, the sound of Ann's passion as I take her, my name as a whisper on her lips, as a cry. It's just another thing this terrible journey has taken from me.

I glance at Dusk, at Phantom. In beast form, we'll suffer the same silence, privy only to the king's orders. The parts of us not useful to the king will die off. And there's not a fucking thing we can do about it, nothing we can do to save ourselves. The shadow king will kill the very essence that makes us who we are. He needs us to be moldable, amenable to his commands, unlikely, or more unwilling, to fight him. It's what the shadow king is counting on. It's how he breaks the wills of his people. Even though will doesn't matter when we're under his control. And he controls us all.

Or will. *Soon.*

Foreboding is more than a feeling. It's an actual state of being. Going through the Void and going back to our shadow world will destroy us. And there's no coming back once we're there.

Fate really is unkind. I finally found my mate. We all did. We found her only to have to give her up. To make the decision ourselves. Even though it's to save her, part of my soul is missing now. And it's more painful that I could've ever imagined. More crushing. I don't know that I can take the absolute destruction, but right now, I don't have a choice. We made our stand. Fought our fight. And lost.

The Void pulls me closer. I can feel its power now in a way I was only barely aware of before. Now it calls to me, demands I move. It's the beast responding to the shadow king's command. His power is deeper, bigger, stronger than ever before. It's frightening, sending a chill down my spine. It's almost a whisper of warning, like a snake's rattle before it strikes. Only, it's not a sound. It's a feeling deep in my soul.

Suddenly, we come to the clearing. In it we can see this side of the Void. A giant, swirling, looming black cloud. Only, unlike before, dark clouds, whispering of a storm, have spread all around it. A warning of the space that will soon be swallowed by our world. Never have I feared the Void more. Never have I had such a soul-deep sense that my fate is sealed.

I would panic if that was my way, but I'm a tower of strength, of courage. I'm the epitome of a man facing his destiny. And it's devastating.

Looking closer does nothing to calm me. But the choice is out of our hands. No one would choose this. Except the dumbasses who traded us for their "freedom." They'd damned well chosen this, even if they didn't know.

They force us forward, even though I feel like my legs are made of concrete. It's not just us slowing our procession though; our own captors are slowing. Moving toward the Void like men on a march toward death. But even though we move slowly, we're continually moving forward until we're standing just in front of it. Dusk says something to the men, something about this being our last chance, but I can read their answer in their faces. There's nothing any of us could say to change their minds, even if they're afraid too.

Slade's gaze meets mine, and then he forces me into the

Void while Flame shoves Phantom and then Dusk. The air crackles with energy around us and then everything goes dark. In seconds, we'll be back in the shadow king's world. Back where he can control us.

And so it begins.

SEVENTEEN

Ann

"RAYNE." My voice cracks, edged with tears.

He freezes, the darkness of the woods seeming to close in around us as he does. "Don't..." And he sounds just as upset as I feel.

"I know you want to protect me. That all of you do. But you can't do this. You can't use your strength to force me to do something I don't want to do. It's wrong. And if you carry me away now, mate or not, I will never forgive you. When you eventually put me down, I'll go right back to the Void, and I'll hate you. I won't want to, but I will." A sob explodes from my lips because I'm telling him the truth. I love him, but I'll never forgive him for this.

He takes a step forward, then stops again. "Ann, the other shadow beasts are probably hunting us as we speak. We need to get as far from them as fast as we can. At a certain point, they'll go back into the Void, and we'll be free."

"I don't want to be free, not like this." I wipe the tears from my eyes. "Please. I was able to help them before. I think I can now too."

"With your light?" He sounds doubtful.

"With my light, with my fists, it doesn't matter. I can help."

To my surprise, he slowly sets me down, and then we're staring at each other. "I'm fighting every instinct inside of me doing this. Losing you again... it'll break me."

"Which is how I'll feel if I lose them."

He drops his gaze to his feet. "I can't take you back there. I told them I'd keep you away. That I'd keep you safe. I gave them my word."

"Then, I'll go without you." I nod as if to tell myself that that's exactly what I'll do, even if it feels like by leaving Rayne, I'm leaving part of my heart behind.

I turn and push away the brush, trying to hurry away so he doesn't stop me, so that I don't stop. I have to do this although I have no idea where I'm going or how to get back to the spot where I'd left Dusk and Onyx and Phantom because I didn't pay attention when he hauled me through the woods like a sack of grain over his shoulder. But it doesn't matter. I should be able to find my way through the feeling in my heart as we fled the battle I left them fighting. Too strong to be a flutter, it pounds now at the thought of getting back to them.

I'm angry at Rayne for not listening to me and at Phantom, Onyx, and Dusk for deciding for me whether or not I should be there with them when they meet the king. These days have been so long, so exhausting, but I push forward, because I know they need me. Even if they think they don't. I might not entirely know how to control my light, but my new powers haven't abandoned me thus far, so why would they do so now when we need them the most?

Finally, Rayne calls out from behind me, "You're going the wrong way." So, apparently, he'd been following me. I want to be upset about it, but having him with me just feels right.

"How do I know you're telling me the truth?"

He sighs loudly. "I guess you don't."

Well, that's not helpful. I truly don't know if I can trust him to tell me the right direction to go. I *want* to be able to trust him and I want that with a desperation unrivaled before in my life, but he's also the one who pulled me away from them in the first place. Who, against my will, forced me to leave them there fighting, maybe even dying. And I don't know if I can forgive him.

I keep going, picking another direction.

"Wrong again."

Damn it. "Which way?"

"This way." He turns to what I think is the south and starts walking, without waiting for me to follow. Although we both know I'm going to. The further into the forest he takes me, the heavier the air, the stronger the pull to the men who occupy the bulk of the real estate inside my soul. I hope that means we're going in the right direction, but the truth is that I'm not sure.

When we get close to a small clearing and I hear voices, Rayne pulls me down behind a fallen tree that's almost taller than I am when I'm standing. "Listen to me, Ann. You can't just go running in there." He closes his eyes and breathes out his nose. "I have an idea. It's great in theory, but..." He shakes his head and sighs.

"What theory?"

He avoids my gaze.

"Rayne?"

His pale blue eyes meet mine. "Ask for help. Ask for the light to work."

I frown. "Like, out loud?" *And ask? Ask who?*

"Out loud, in your head, I'm not sure it matters, but ask for it. I have a theory that it'll work."

I don't completely understand it, but Rayne knows things that most people don't, so I nod, hoping that this might be the missing puzzle piece when it comes to my powers.

He takes my hands in his, brings them to his mouth, and presses a soft kiss against my knuckles. "I'm sure the guys will hate me for this, maybe I'll even hate myself, but I'm also ready to defend you."

"Thank you," I whisper, then kiss him softly before pulling away from him and standing up taller to look toward the Void.

The swirling mass looks different than the last time I saw it. Instead of it just being a dark cloud, it's like it's infecting the sky. All around it, dark storm clouds have gathered, stretching out in all directions from the Void, but not very far. Storms don't work this way. They aren't isolated the way this is. This is magic. Bad magic.

There are a few shadows beasts left standing guard, and I curl my hands into knuckles, not knowing how I'll take them down, but knowing I have to. The muscles in my legs tense. I bounce on them a little in anxiety, in preparation for what I'm about to do.

Then, three more shadow beasts come out of the woods and join the others.

"Shit," I whisper, kneeling back down, trying to keep an eye on them without being seen.

The men gather together, hug one another, speak in low

voices, and then they look at the Void. I don't know why, but the whole scene is heartbreaking. It feels like they're saying goodbye. Like they're preparing themselves to step off a cliff. I feel sorry for them, even though I'm angry about the betrayal.

And then, they step into the Void and disappear, and it's just me, Rayne, and the sense of impending doom.

As if to drive the point home, lightning splits the sky and thunder booms around us. The circling mass of clouds seems to swell, to expand, and I get the terrible sense that whatever the king is planning, it's about to be unleashed.

I stand up to my full height. Rayne is suddenly beside me. He links his hand with mine. "Can you do this? Seriously. Can you use the light again, or are we just heading to our deaths?"

Can I? It's the question of the day. I've asked myself the same thing about a thousand times. But since that's where my men are, I don't have a choice. Plan or not, control over my light or not, I'm going in. Releasing Rayne's hand I say, "I don't know, but I have to go."

"Then I have to go."

I almost tell him not to, that he already died once, but I stop myself before the words ever leave my lips. He's my mate. Just like I can't leave my shadow beasts in the Void, he can't let me go there alone, so why waste time by arguing about it? I climb over the tree like I'm some sort of wood sprite and then march toward the Void. The lightning crashes above us, more and more, and I see shards lighting up in all directions. My heart races, and it feels like I'm making the dumbest decision of my life, but I don't stop until I get to the swirling cloud.

Then I look at Rayne. "No matter what happens, I love you."

"I love you too," he says.

And we share a look. A goodbye. It's so similar to what we saw the warriors do that it scares me. If I don't do this right now, I might lose my nerve.

So, I dive into the cloud like there's an abyss behind the darkness, but there isn't. I land on my chest and the air whooshes out of me. Panic uncurls inside of me as I prepare to be attacked. Instinctually, I move into a crouched position and look around, expecting danger.

But no one so much as looks back at me because the Void is full of beasts and bodies and men.

A second later, Rayne comes in behind me, instantly falling into a crouch beside me. He's breathing hard. His eyes narrow. His hands curled into fists as if ready for battle. Even though, for this moment, we seem to be safe.

We're partially hidden behind some small boulders. It's enough that we're not like a flashing yellow sign, but we can also see what's going on. And none of it looks good. This place is just as horrifying as before. All darkness. A dark so deep that it seems impossible. And yet, the shadow beasts in their beast form glow like spirits in this world. Even their red eyes glow far more brightly than they did in our world.

Grave trolls carry torches all around the clearing we crouch on the edge of, bringing a brightness to this dark world that's almost blinding. Rot monkeys hide in the branches of blackened trees, their shrieks echoing around us, sending a chill down my spine. Here, we truly are surrounded and out of our element. But at least Rayne and I have an escape at our backs.

My men aren't so lucky.

"My king." Flame bows to the king.

The king's cloak moves behind him, like there's an unseen breeze, or some kind of evilness that has cursed even the clothes he wears. He inclines his head at Flame. Somehow the gesture being more mocking then respectful, but my eyes are glued to him. He emanates power and darkness in a way that seems impossible. It's an odd effect considering he's still partially burned from the light I spewed at him. His body is part glowing embers, part ash, part full-powered darkness. He's obviously still healing. As I watch him, part of the glowing embers reform as skin.

"My *loyal* servant," the king says, almost sneering. "I'm glad all of you have returned home. Returned to where you belong."

Flame bows even lower, and I can see the rapid rise and fall of his chest. The man is terrified.

"Servants, let us give our lost brothers a warm welcome back to the shadow realm!" the king says, spreading his arms out at all the beasts that surround them.

The shadow beasts, the ones in beast form rather than the men standing before him, glow like spirits, red-eyed anger in their faces. And they move in unison, as if controlled by a single thought, closing in more tightly around the small group of men and my mates. Something about the animals makes every hair on my body stand on end. Men, beasts, it doesn't matter, they aren't supposed to act like that. Even when they turn their heads to look at my men, it's in unison.

And I realize that the men in human form are shocked by this. Shocked more than I imagined they would be.

Flame stands taller once more, staring around himself at the beasts. His mouth is wide, his jaw slack. This is a man surprised by what he sees. As his gaze runs over them, it's obvious he's stunned by the beasts in front of him. It's as if he's seen his fate and wants to turn back. He's going to be a slave and it's just dawned on him that it's his own fault.

The faces of the men who came with him are mirrors of his own. Horrified. Intense.

"What's... what's wrong with them?" Flame finally manages. I think he knew they were serving the king. But the difference between the way the beasts behaved in our world verses this shadow world is night and day. Where before they seemed like soldiers, now they seem like puppets.

I wonder if that was why these men were so quick to the throw away their freedom. They didn't truly understand what that meant.

"There's nothing wrong with them. They're simply serving their purpose and serving their king. That's what all of you want too, right?" His words are slick, filled with cruelty. He knows damn well that the men are horrified by what they're seeing, and he's enjoying every second of it.

"None of us want this," Dusk says, drawing himself up taller, even though his hands are bound. His expression says, at least, that he hasn't given up. "In striving for power above all else, you've destroyed our people and our world. You're no king to me."

"Or to me," Phantom murmurs, then he coughs so hard I think he must be coughing up blood.

Onyx stands tall and silent, not that he can say much with his hands bound, but even from where I stand, I can feel his hatred of the king. His desire to rip the man to pieces. The only time he seems to waver from his hatred is when he glances at Phantom. And I know what he's thinking. The same thing I'm thinking. *Is Phantom really so severely injured? Or is this part of some plan?*

I pray it's a plan. The odds are already stacked against us. Without Phantom, I have no idea how we'll get out of here. How we'll have any chance at escape.

The shadow king steps forward. The ugliness inside of him has manifested in his features. But he was beautiful once. Like his sons. But not today.

He looks at his sons, at Onyx, and takes another step closer as one of his men delivers a black box. The king holds the box to his chest but doesn't move to open it. "It's time you bend a knee and shift." There's no mockery in his voice, just a coldness that runs down my spine.

Onyx shakes his head, Dusk glares, but Phantom is the one who speaks. "No."

The king sighs through a smile and shakes his head. It's as if he might actually be enjoying this. "And here I thought we could have a nice family reunion." Then, he looks at the other men. "Someone is missing."

Flame goes pale. "The girl ran away. We couldn't find her."

The king's gaze narrows into slits.

Another man says, "She was mated to your sons anyway, so she wasn't needed."

The king gestures to the man, and a minute later a rot troll tears his head right off his body. The troll throws the head toward the trees, which sends the monkeys screeching even louder, and the shadow beast's headless body hits the floor.

If the men were tense before, the tension is strong enough to cut with a knife now.

"I decide whether something is needed or not," the king says slowly, then smiles, a creepy smile. "Now, my men, shift into your beast forms. Your battle is over. You've won the war. You can relax. You can let me take control. There's nothing for you to worry about any longer."

"Don't listen to him!" Dusk shouts. "Look around you. Look what waits for you."

Flame turns away from the king and looks my men in the eyes. "I'm sorry."

And then he shifts. It happens over the course of a few seconds. Where once there was a man, now there's a massive creature, like a wolf, but it's pure black, and its fur seems to be made of smoke rather than fur. When he opens his eyes, they glow red, and he moves in a robotic way, joining the other wolves that surround the men.

One by one, the shadow beasts shift until there's no one left in the center. No one but my three men.

Terror throbs through my heart and I wish we could go back. I wish we'd left the forest instead of going back to the cave. But wishing won't do me any good now. I have to save them because without them, my soul is incomplete.

My heart races. *Please let me be able to use the light. Please let me use my powers to save my men.* And then, I whisper, "Please give me the power to use the light within me."

But I feel nothing. Nothing at all.

Was Rayne wrong? I close my eyes, even though the sound of the shadow beasts howling shakes the air. *Please.*

EIGHTEEN

Phantom

MY FATHER STANDS before his subjects, before the beasts who pace around us, who wait for us to make a wrong move so they can pounce on his command. And he *will* command it. I know that deep in my heart. If we don't shift, if we don't allow him to control us, our friends will shred us to pieces.

I also know that neither I nor my brothers will shift. We'll never allow ourselves to become his slaves. If this man wants us out of his way, he'll have to kill us.

"Shift," he commands us again, then he gestures to someone.

A rot troll moves forward with a sword and strikes, but rather than attacking us, he cuts our ropes away. Not that having our hands free will do much good. Without weapons, surrounded by our enemies, we're as good as bound still, and our father knows it.

Today, we're going to die. My only peace comes from

knowing Rayne and Ann are safe. At least until our world swallows their own. And that has to be enough for me right now. Something to cling to as I experience my last moments of life.

"Phantom." He says my name softly, like I'm a child breaking a rule. "You've always been too stubborn for your own good. Do what you should now. Do what's right."

It's strange. He looks like the man I once knew, the one who loved my mother, the one who cared for me and for Dusk when we were children, even with the damage from Ann's light still visible. But the shell of him doesn't tell the true tale. Not what I see underneath all the familiar things. His eyes are dead. His voice is flat. The father I knew is gone.

"Is there nothing left of the man who loved our mother, who loved his children?" I don't expect the words to have an effect on him, to make him consider his behavior, but I try anyway, for Dusk and Onyx.

I watch his face for any change, but his gaze doesn't even flicker at the mention of my mother. "Love is for the weak." There's no emotion left in him.

And I realize, *we* aren't going to make it out of here, but maybe Onyx and Dusk can.

A plan forms in my mind, and it's strange. For one moment the world seems to stand still around me. The shadow realm is dark, but I don't focus on that. Instead, happy images fill my mind. Ann's face when she agreed to complete the mating bond with us, the way her eyes looked, the way I sensed her heart connecting with mine. The way she moved when I touched her. The sound of her laugh and the way she brought joy and wonder to us all.

"It's time," my father says.

Yes, it is.

I look at Dusk and Onyx. Something changes in their faces, and Onyx shakes his head. They know I'm going to try something reckless.

"For Ann," I mouth, then I turn away from the panic in their eyes.

I have one chance to do this, to make it so my brothers have time to get away. I leap forward and grab my father, but as if he expected it, he's grinning. I try to ignore the look on his face and pull his dagger free, but it's caught in his shirt. I yank the material, shredding it, drawing the dagger and part of his shirt free. Around us, his beasts are going wild, but none of them attack, which I don't have time to think about.

Untangling the dagger from the shirt, I raise it above my head and stare at his chest. Then I freeze, feeling my eyes widen. My father's chest... it's wrong. In the center of his pale skin is a red jagged item, one that glows like the moonstone.

It's... a shard of the stone. Not just any shard, but the central part of the goddess's heart.

And now I know. I understand everything that I didn't understand before.

He's pierced his heart with the shard of moonstone. The power of it flows through him. It has given him the strength to do all the cruelties his inflicted on us all. But the moonstone changed the man we knew once into this one. It unleashed the physical darkness inside him. The one that has erased all care and love from his heart. Because man was not meant to hold the power of the goddess within him. This power was meant to allow our world to live, not to be stolen by one selfish man.

My realization only takes a moment, and then I'm pressing the dagger down, directing it toward his chest.

Toward the stone. But inches before it touches his flesh, my father catches my wrist in a grip too powerful to belong to him. Within seconds, he's twisted me so that the dagger is nearly falling from my hand, and I'm on my knees.

With his free hand, he takes the dagger from me like I'm a child and he flips it around, pointing it at my throat. I hear chaos behind me, probably my brothers trying to fight to save me, but I know they're struggling in vain. I didn't create the distraction I hoped for. I didn't hurt my father enough to distract him from the hold over his beasts so my brothers could get free.

The tip of the steel slices into my throat. "Say goodbye, son," he whispers, his smile filling his whole face.

"No!" I hear Ann's voice above the chaos.

Ann and Rayne—who have no business here in the shadow realm—jump from behind the crowd. She lifts a hand and points it toward us, emitting a light bright enough that I wish I could shield my eyes. I'm not in danger in my human form from being destroyed by her magic, but after the darkness of this realm, the light hurts me.

My father screams, "Stop her!"

A shadow beast hurls through the air at her and she turns to him, the light in her hands brightening. She aims the beam at him and within seconds, he evaporates into ash in a quiet puff not befitting such a torturous death. Many of the shadow beasts split off from the circle that surrounds us, racing toward Ann and Rayne. Rayne withdraws his sword and stands beside Ann, the look on his face saying he'll kill anyone or anything that tries to hurt our mate. I just hope he can. She rids the realm of several more shadow beasts while Rayne fights off a couple others. He's the easier target and they begin to descend on him, drawing Ann's focus from my father. Grave trolls roar and move toward them too, and the rot monkeys begin to race toward the battle from their dead trees.

She puts more and more of the beasts down while my father watches her. "She's extraordinary, isn't she?"

And that's enough to shake me back to what needs to be done. I smash his hand away, sending his dagger flying, then leap to my feet. His gaze snaps from Ann to me, and I grab him around the throat, bringing him so our faces are inches apart.

"Look at me, father," I command.

He chuckles like I've amused him, even though he shouldn't have the breath to chuckle.

I grit my teeth and squeeze as hard as I can manage, ignoring the way my body ached from my fight with the shadow beasts, ignoring the fact that the moonstone in his chest seems to give him uncontrollable power. Because this is all I have. This moment. And my two hands.

Behind me, Ann's glow grows brighter. Lighting our battlefield. Lighting beyond it. Spreading across our lands like the very sun.

But she doesn't seem ready to stop. The glow continues.

Brighter.

And brighter.

The shine is so bright, I can't look in that direction at all, but I try. Because I need to know she's okay. Because I need to know the brightness isn't because something terrible happened to her. I turn my head, just a little, to see her. And the instant I do, I'm glad. She's exquisite. So beautiful I can't breathe in the face of her light. "Ann." I whisper her name, and she looks over at me like I've screamed it to her.

"Phantom!" Her voice wavers as she reaches out to me, and her light shifts toward my father from the beasts surrounding her and Rayne.

My father surprises me by jerking me closer, putting my body between him and Ann, and I realize belatedly it's to protect himself from the light. She turns, briefly, to vaporize another shadow beast who made it around Rayne and was coming at them. Then she turns back to me and my father.

My stomach aches for her, to be near her, to see her safely away from this. I want to protect her and shield her from my father and this dark world, but I can't. I have to trust that she can survive without me by her side, at least until I can get back to it. So, I turn back to fight my father, ready to yank him into her light at the smallest sign of weakness, to blast him away, to end him in a way that means he can never hurt her again.

I don't see the shard in his hand until I feel it pierce my skin, until I hear the shallow scream erupt from my own lungs, until I look down at his hand. The pain is immediate but short and then I feel nothing.

NINETEEN

Ann

I CAN'T PULL it back in, I can't aim it or control it, but I can turn it, so that's what I do. I shift my focus so I'm looking at the king until he moves Phantom to stand between us. I would love to annihilate that bastard, to incinerate his ass with my power, but I'm afraid to hurt Phantom. My heart would never survive that. So I let my light fall over the grave trolls and watch as they fade away to ash, and I do the same when the rot monkeys descend on us from the trees. But in truth I'm barely paying attention to them. I'm watching the king and Phantom, waiting for my chance to reach the bastard who hurt my men.

As the rot monkeys seem to realize they have no chance against me and fall back, I slowly move my light toward the king. Phantom looks back at me as I do so, and my heart races. I want him away from that dangerous man. I want him back on earth, safe with me, and I'll do anything in my power to make that happen.

A movement catches my eye. The king's hand is spindly, thin, and looks brittle, but it's clawed and reaching inside the black box. I don't know what's in there, but I want to scream for Phantom to pay attention, to watch the king. But as I have the thought, the words die.

It's a shard.

"Phantom!" I scream a second too late, and the king plunges the shard into Phantom's chest.

The light inside of me dims, fades, and I can't do more than watch as the king takes Phantom away, disappearing in a puff of darkness.

"No!"

I need the light back. I need to find Phantom. I need to save him. I run from the crowd of shadow beasts left behind, probably filled with the order to kill me, but before I can get to the spot where the king disappeared with Phantom, Onyx grabs me by one arm and Dusk grabs me by the other while Rayne clears a path out of the realm with a sword he's lifted from one of the trolls who are now crowding into the space, embattled, ready.

Our enemies outnumber us by the hundred and I can't focus enough to make my light shine again, so I leave, running out behind Rayne as Onyx and Dusk pull me along. I instinctually fight, even though I know that staying behind is foolish, because I have to get back to Phantom. I have to find him!

"Phantom!" I look at Dusk. "He's there still. Somewhere! Let me go. We have to find him, before it's too late."

But I'm not fighting them. I just feel overwhelmed by a need to find my mate, and at the same time, there's the lingering knowledge that if we stay in the shadow realm, we'll die. We can't save Phantom if we're dead, so why does it feel so wrong to leave him behind?

And then we're at the edge of the shadow realm, staring at the dark wall that leads to our world. My men don't hesitate; they drag me through. And a moment later, we're back on earth. But they don't slow. Not yet. When we reach the edge of the trees around the clearing near the Void and realize no one is following us, we stop, although they don't let me go. Dusk and Onyx keep their fingers curled into my biceps like I'm mad and will dive right back into the shadow realm.

Which, to be fair, I just might. My head knows what's smart, but my heart is pulling me back, commanding me to return for the man I love.

"Let me go!" I yank and struggle, but these aren't mortal men. These are hulks who have muscles on top of their muscles and they're using them to hold me. My struggle does little more than wears me out.

"Please!" The terror is real. I shift to look at Rayne. "Goddammit! Make them let me go!"

He cocks his head and considers me. "So you can run back in there? So the king can take you? So you can die?" His lips purse and he looks at me, eyes dark, expression hard. "No."

It's a flat answer, one he has no right to speak. I jerk my body hard enough Onyx's hold tightens and the futility of it burns through me. But I can't let Phantom go. I just can't.

"Please, Dusk. Let's go back for him. He's your brother! He's my mate!"

He shakes his head, looking down and away, but continues holding onto me. "My father has him now."

It isn't an answer I can accept. "Please." My voice is weaker now because the fight is gone. The light is gone. Phantom is gone. And I don't know that I'll ever be able to get him back.

"He sacrificed himself to save us," Dusk tells me softly. "We can't let his sacrifice be in vain."

His words echo through me, and when they finally let me go, I collapse.

TWENTY

Ann

IT'S BEEN DAYS, weeks, and I have nothing to show for it but the few hundred moon shards we've collected. Yes, that's an accomplishment, but I'd trade them all in to get Phantom back. To even see him for a moment.

There's no doubt in my heart that these men are all my mates. Now, I have no idea how I was able to fight the pull to my shadow beasts for so long. Because now that I have Onyx and Dusk, they are like Rayne to me. They've buried themselves so deep in my heart that it isn't me and them, it's *us*.

And the loss of Phantom... it's like losing a piece of my soul. My entire chest aches all the time. It throbs like the shadow king ripped my heart from my chest when he took Phantom. The only reason I'm eating or drinking is because my men make me. The only way I can sleep is with them wrapped around me, with them holding me and comforting me every time I dream of Phantom and wake up sobbing.

Still, I continue on, because I'll never get him back if I give up. And I'll never be complete until I have Phantom with me once more.

I turn my head from one side to the other and roll my shoulders. "You should get some rest." Rayne lays his hand at the small of my back, his thumb caressing my skin lightly under the hem of my shirt. The touch is meant to console, to ease my thoughts. But there won't be any sort of consolation until Phantom is back with me. Where he belongs. Where I need him to be.

We're out again, but that's not strange any longer. We can't return to the cave that we had shared with Phantom. My men had explained it was too dangerous. Nor could we return to the main cave, not that we'd want to sleep in a place that's nothing but a reminder of all we've lost.

So, we travel. Every day. Not far. But enough so that the shadow king's creatures won't find us too easily. Most of our nights are spent in a couple of rough caves we'd stumbled upon. Places that were uncomfortable, but so far proved to be safe.

Today, however, night is almost upon us, so we're camping out in nature. We have a fire with food cooking and places where we all rested earlier, but we'll be packing up what little we have soon and going to the place we go every night. At least for a little while. At least to check, before we hide away from danger once more.

Rayne sits on a rock and pulls me back against him so I can feel his heartbeat against my spine. "Look at all those moon shards. It's impressive. Do you think we have enough to build our own moon, yet?"

I know he's just trying to lift my spirits, but nothing can lift my spirits now. I glance down. There are about three hundred of them, not quite a fourth of the original, from what Onyx and Dusk had told me, but enough to know the king won't be able to expand his realm without these. "It's something," I manage. "But not enough."

Enough? I don't even know what that means any longer. We have collected so many of them that the king shouldn't be able to expand his realm, but we no longer know what the king wants. He hasn't been back. We've seen no sign of his creatures or of Phantom. Whatever happened when he took my mate, his plan has changed. Maybe it was only adjusted, but it definitely changed.

"We're doing great," Rayne tells me soothingly.

Feeling weak, I lean back against Rayne, rubbing at the ache in my chest.

Dusk glances at me, sees the movement that tells him I'm hurting because of the loss of Phantom, and stands and walks away from the fire. But not before I see the look of utter pain on his face. As much as I feel this miserable emptiness inside of me since losing Phantom, I know Dusk and Onyx are hurting equally. He was their brother, their best friend, and had been a constant presence since they lost everything.

I kiss Rayne's cheek lightly, then pull away. "I should go to him."

He nods, knowing that I'm the only person that can soothe my men, even if it's only a little. And I walk away from him, following Dusk, wishing that I could hide my pain better, so that it wouldn't be a reminder to him of his brother.

Dusk stands at the edge of a rock formation that drops off into a cove below the forest. He's looking out and breathing slowly, as if he's just enjoying the view, but I can see the pain he's trying so hard to hide. Before I lay a hand at the center of his back and a kiss against his shoulder, he nods. "I should've killed him when I had the chance. Then none of this would've happened."

He's said this before. He's gone down this path in his mind so many times that it's horrible to watch. We all blame ourselves, but no one more than him. And he doesn't deserve that. Not my good, wonderful man.

"It's okay. We're going to get Phantom back," I tell him, and my voice comes out strong, because I mean it. We'll get Phantom back, even if I have to die trying.

His arms are crossed over his chest, and he stares into the distance that from here is nothing but sky, water, and forest as far as the eye can see. "Even if we do, there's no telling how much of him is left."

My men had explained a lot to me over the last few weeks. They told me more about the legend of their goddess. But what was more, since knowing their father placed a moon shard in his heart, they told me why they thought it ruined him. This power... it's too much for any person. Whether the goddess cursed her magic just to ensure this couldn't happen or the power pushed away all else, they felt that once the shard was placed in a person, that person was lost.

I disagreed. I told them that if this goddess of the moon was as good as they have said, her magic couldn't destroy someone like Phantom. He wasn't all darkness and cruelty like his father. He was a shadow beast with a heart of gold. I believed with every ounce of my being that we could remove the shard and get him back. Maybe he would have changed from his experience, but we'd help him find himself. I *knew* it.

I just wished they had the same faith as me.

"We have to hope for the best," I remind Dusk, stroking his arm. Hope is about all we have right now.

Hope and the shards, anyway, and I'd be damned if we lost either.

"Hope? What's that?" He's trying to sound sarcastic, but the words come out broken, edged with unshed tears. "We've been near the Void every night for weeks and there's nothing. No sign. No Phantom. If he was still himself, don't you think he would have found a way back to us by now?" His voice is flat, resigned to the notion that Phantom is lost.

"I know. But we have to keep believing that he's fighting to come back to us as hard as we're fighting to find him."

Dusk looks at me. "You saw him, Ann. You saw the light dim in his eyes as soon as the shadow king stabbed him in the heart." I did. But I also have faith that whatever his father is doing to him, we can undo with all the love and respect we have and whatever else he needs.

Reaching up, I touch his face, then leave a light kiss on his lips. "His heart belongs to me, and I'll get it back."

A sad smile touches his lips. "I want to believe you. I really do. But with every day that passes..."

"Every day that passes means there's hope for the next day." Then I stroke the stubble on his face. "You guys held out hope for me for a long time. You never gave up."

"We did," he says, his shoulders slumping.

"Did you?" I ask with a smile.

He sighs. It's deep and loud and from his gut where all his anguish stays. "Come on. We need to eat before we head back to the Void."

My smile falters. "I never gave up on you guys either. I just didn't realize it. And I think deep down, below all your pain, you haven't given up on your brother either."

He puts his hand over mine. "I love you."

It isn't an admission that I'm right, but at least it's something. "I love you too."

We hold hands as we walk back to our camp. His shoulders are still curved, his face still full of pain and loss, but he holds my hand tightly, and I know that means he hasn't given up yet. Even if he doesn't want to admit it out loud.

Onyx is waiting with food when we return. He smiles softly and hands me a plate. Since becoming his mate, so much has changed between us. The wall he was so good at erecting between us has fallen away. It's as if he's finally realized I'm the one person who will never willingly leave him now. That it's okay for us to love and care for one another. Which has allowed me to learn more about him. I've realized that Onyx is the quiet one, and not just because he signs. He's just a quiet man and probably was before losing his hearing too. He's softer than Dusk when he needs to be. Angry when he has to be. Sweet when he's walking with me outside the cave under the Earth's moon. Onyx is simply complicated and wonderful.

When we get Phantom back, I know this relationship between all of us will be beautiful. It will be everything I ever wanted in life and more.

At least in my mind.

We eat together around the dying fire. The food tastes like nothing, but that's how it's been since Phantom left. I eat because I have to. Not because it brings me any joy. I also eat because the less I fight eating and sleeping, the more my men seem to relax, and I want them to relax. I don't want them to have to worry about me on top of everything else.

"We're checking again today, then going to cave three, right?" Rayne asks, speaking slowly to make it easier for Onyx to read his words.

Dusk nods. "A quick check. Something about tonight... feels off."

Does it? I sit up a little straighter but feel nothing.

"Agreed," Onyx signs, then returns to eating.

Does he feel it too then? I want to ask, but don't. I'm not sure I want to know. This place is already creepy enough at night, I don't need a reason to be more afraid.

I finish dinner first, but Onyx is the one who cleans up. He tries his best to hide all traces that we'd camped there this day. And then we're off into the fading light of the evening.

We head to the Void and I have to slow my pace so as not to run to the Void. Every day is another chance to see him. To hope he's found his way back to us.

To be together again and fill the empty space in my heart.

We arrive at the Void together, but as always, we linger in the shadows of the woods. This might be the place Phantom can return to us through, but it's also the place our enemies can come through. And we all know it.

The rays of evening fade away as time passes and darkness swallows us. A wave falls over the forest, and the sound of crickets and night birds fills the air, but we all remain frozen, waiting. Each night we stand here around the Void, watching it as long as our hearts can take it, waiting. I've noticed the others seem to be wanting to leave earlier and earlier each night, but I don't want that. That feels like a step toward giving up our Phantom.

And that's something I'll never do.

As if my thoughts have power, *he* appears. *Phantom.*

My heart bursts with longing and emotion I don't know what to do with because as happy as I am to see him, there are differences in him that I can't deny. He's dressed all in black, head to toe, like the shadow king himself. He wears a dark cloak on his broad shoulders, and his gaze is sharp and cold as it runs over the woods all around us, as if he's searching for something he despises.

I want to go to him, but even I can see the danger in it. As much as every muscle in my body is aching to run to him, I wait. And watch. We all do. Searching for any sign that this is our Phantom. That there is something left inside of him outside of what the shard has done.

But there's no sign, just that cold look on his face. Just the strangest sense that this man is dangerous and different than the Phantom I love.

Oh God. Is he truly lost to us? This is worse than having him taken from me. This is the kind of aching pain I don't know what to do with. I'm tired. I'm angry. And now my heart is broken.

But maybe I'm wrong.

The shard in his chest brightens beneath his dark clothes, illuminating his chest in a way that might have been beautiful at any other time. Instead, it's chilling.

If I ever get close enough, I'm going to yank it out and crush it in my hand. I'm going to destroy every last trace of it so that it can never hurt him again.

Phantom moves away from the Void, slowly, circling as if testing something I don't understand. And I watch him, my heart in my throat. If he gets far enough away from the Void, we'll jump on him. We'll bind him up and tear that shard out of him.

I look at the others.

Onyx gives me a subtle nod, and I feel relief flow through me. We're still all on the same page. Even though he isn't the Phantom we remember, they're still with me. They still want to try to save him.

But the closer Phantom comes to me, the brighter the light from the shard is. And I realize after a few moments that that's what he was testing. To see if we were there. To figure out what direction I'm in. And I don't know if I should be happy or afraid.

He nearly reaches the edge of the clearing. His gaze moves up and connects with mine, even though I'm not entirely sure he can see me. And yet, the look in his eyes... it frightens me.

My stomach sinks and a whimper falls from my lips. "Phantom."

It's nothing but a whisper, but he grins. It's an evil grins that makes every hair on my body stand on end.

With one wave of his finger, trolls and rot monkeys pour from the Void. His voice, cold and cruel comes. "Find them! Kill them!"

Kill... us?

"Run!" Dusk commands beside me.

I know it's the right thing to do, but I hesitate, my heart not being able to understand what my eyes have accepted. Dusk doesn't hesitate though; he pulls me beside him, half carrying me away. My men move as one around me, guiding me through the woods with their much larger bodies, trying to move faster than the creatures that hunt us.

If that's even possible.

But my mind isn't on the danger looming behind us. It's on Phantom. On the look on his face. On the sound of his voice while he commanded his creatures to kill us.

Is there anything left of him? I feel tears tracking down my cheeks.

When a rot monkey wraps his fingers around my leg, Dusk lifts me like I weigh nothing at all, and then he zigs and zags through the forest. The trolls are no match for his speed, but the monkey are swinging from branch to branch overhead and for a minute I don't think we'll get away. But then we do.

The grave trolls roar in the distance. The monkeys shriek wildly in the trees far behind. But my men don't stop. Not until the forest quiets.

When we're safe in one of our hideaway caves, they draw a boulder over the entrance and start a small fire. My gazes run over my men, and the tears keep flowing.

"Phantom," I manage.

"Is gone," Dusk says softly.

I look at Onyx, and he avoids my gaze.

Then I look at Rayne. The truth is in his eyes.

I wipe the tears angrily from my face. "Maybe he isn't himself right now, but if there's any chance to get him back, we have to try. No matter what it takes."

Rayne surprises me when he speaks. "Agreed." When the other two look at him, he shrugs. "I came back from the dead. If that's possible, saving him should be too."

"We just need a plan," I say.

"Alright?" Dusk says, and then everyone is looking at me.

We just need a plan...

SHIFTERS' LOST QUEEN

STOLEN BY SHADOW BEASTS: BOOK THREE

ONE

Ann

The walk back to our cave is slower than I ever imagined possible, and with every step the bag tied around my waist containing the moon shards we'd collected feels heavier. Every one of us is limping, breathing far too loudly, and hurting. Although I'm two minutes from passing out, Onyx, Rayne, and Dusk look like they're struggling just to keep standing.

I wish I could say it was just because of our latest battle, but it's more than that we're exhausted from another night of fighting rot monkeys and grave trolls; it's that we're emotionally spent. We've just lost too much.

Phantom. Tears sting my eyes, but I try to push the thought away. *We haven't lost him yet. Maybe it feels like it, but we'll get him back from the Shadow King's hold. No matter what we have to do.*

Even though I thought by now we would have come up with a solution.

Onyx leads our group into a cave as the morning sunlight peeks through the trees. The filth of battle is thick in my clothes and hair, and I wish I could take a bath, but right now resting and eating are more important than that. With Phantom turned by the Shadow King into some kind of emotionless slave, we can't stay here for long. Not more than a day.

Unlike with our enemies, Phantom knows where we can hide, so nowhere is safe anymore. On our first night after losing him, he'd sent a team of creatures to kill us in our usual cave. We'd barely gotten out alive, but it was the moment when we realized this was really happening. Phantom was against us. And since then, we've found nearly every safe cave the guys were aware of destroyed by rot monkeys and grave trolls.

Phantom isn't just going after us, he's going for the *jugular*. Using the intimate knowledge he has of how we fight the Shadow King, how we've managed to stay alive, to make our lives even harder. Onyx seems to think it means there's nothing left of his best friend. I'm trying not to think that way, and I have no idea how Dusk and Rayne are processing this mess.

Our situation is worse than that, though, because Phantom is also smarter than his father, the Shadow King. It feels like he'll destroy us. It's only a matter of time. But we're doing everything we can not to make it too easy for him, to buy ourselves time to figure out how to save him, all the shadow beasts, and earth itself.

Yet, no matter where we go, Phantom attacks, and nothing stops him. His army of grave trolls and rot monkeys is stronger than we are and seems to have limitless numbers. His shadow beasts are ruthless, aggressive, and unrelenting. Every night is filled with me using my magic until I nearly pass out, and my men fighting until their bodies are battered and bruised.

We're slowing down. We're coming undone. It's an unsaid tension that hangs in the air, almost suffocatingly heavy and impossible to ignore, that we can't keep doing this.

And it's all the more painful because someone we love is doing this to us.

I toss the bag that's slung over my back with all my most important belongings onto the ground and then collapse next to it. The others all find spots around the cave and do the same, and then we're all taking a moment, sitting in silence. And it honestly feels like we're soldiers who just keep getting their asses kicked, but somehow manage to survive.

It's not the best feeling, but it's better than being dead.

"Good job with your light," Dusk says, speaking each word clearly so that it's easier for Onyx to read his lips, but his words are meant for me.

Looking at Dusk, I feel my heart ache a little. His long brown hair had been tied at his nape, but now so much of the strands had come lose that he looks like he'd stood behind an airplane engine. But that's nothing compared to the scratches on his face, his arms, even his neck. There are tears and stains all over his clothes too... clothes that were clean before this latest battle.

It's painful to see.

"You guys are the ones getting your asses kicked." I try to hide the guilt from my voice, but I can't. They're basically the brute force in our defense strategy. I'm hidden behind them, channel the light inside of me. I manage to do the most damage, but it doesn't change the fact that my men are our enemies' punching bags.

Yes, it's hard on me. It leaves me light-headed, exhausted, and weak, but it's nothing like they're enduring.

Punches from the trolls that crack their bones. Scratches from the damn rot monkeys. And worse. So much worse from Phantom and his shadow beasts. My men's brother and their friends, now our enemies.

"We're all getting our asses kicked," Dusk finally manages with a strained smile, then he reaches out and links his fingers through mine.

Just his touch eases some of the loneliness inside of me.

Rayne shakes his head. "We can't keep doing this. We can talk to the fae. If they knew our world was at risk..."

He's brought this idea up before, but doesn't seem to have accepted all the improbabilities of this plan. I'm a minor fae royal. I have lands, a manor, and people to watch out for... but I'm a no one to the other fae. And Rayne? Rayne died according to all the fae. He had a funeral. His body was buried. The man before us now doesn't look anything like that Rayne. Adrik has light brown hair, light blue eyes, and a much larger build than Rayne ever had. Taking his body meant Rayne was able to come back to me, but it also means that no fae will ever believe the powerful Bloodmore heir is still alive, just in a shadow beast's body.

Things like that don't happen every damn day, after all.

When I don't say anything, Onyx shakes his big head of long blond hair with a frown, then signs, "They still wouldn't believe you." Rayne's eyes have narrowed onto Onyx's hands as Onyx tries to sign more slowly for our sakes. "And we'll be dead by the time you get back."

Rayne lets his head fall back against the cave wall, looking grim. "I know. I know, okay. But this isn't working either."

He's right, but it doesn't help anything to say it aloud, which is exactly why Onyx has a grumpy look on his face. But Rayne is used to being a royal, being pampered, spending his days with his studies. He's not used to all of this chaos the way my shadow beasts are.

I mean, neither am I, but I've had more time to adapt.

"So, we just keep going?" I ask, and I sound so damn tired.

"Until something changes," Onyx signs, giving me a sympathetic look, those dark eyes of his holding mine. "Something always changes."

"But we need something good to happen," Rayne says.

Onyx shakes his head and goes to the remains of a fire we had from a few days ago. He builds up logs, and soon has a roaring fire going. Then he goes back to the cave wall and collapses, while we all watch the fire grow. We all know we need to gather herbs and vegetables for another soup, maybe even try to get a rabbit or two, but no one is ready to do that yet. Even if we're all starving.

I'm pretty sure I can make it out of the cave before I have to start crawling, but I try to mentally prepare myself. I know where there are some wild onions and some carrots. We haven't used them all, so maybe I can make it there and help get something to eat started.

In just a minute. As soon as my legs stop shaking.

Before I can take even a few breaths, someone comes stumbling in. We're all on our feet in an instant, in defensive stances, before we can get a look at the man. It's... the elder. Elder Auero, a man we thought had died when we couldn't find him.

He's much thinner than before, with clothes that hang off of him in tatters. He's emaciated. His face is swollen with deep purple that darkens his cheeks and jaw and under his eyes, and there's even a bruise across his forehead. Tufts of his white hair are missing, and pale skin shines where his scalp is exposed. As he moves, he holds his ribcage, and limps. When he stumbles, Onyx is there in an instant, carrying him and laying him down on a rock inside the cave.

"Lay," Onyx signs, when the elder struggles to sit up.

But the old man doesn't listen. He's desperately trying to sit up, fighting so hard against Onyx that I'm worried he's going to hurt himself. But my gentle giant seems to realize it so, with a frown, he holds the man up just a little. His big hands are almost impossibly soft on the fragile old man.

The elder winces and sucks in a short, sharp breath that he holds for a second then lets whoosh out. For a minute, he just sits there, pale, beaten, and looking far older than he'd looked before. We all exchange glances, on the edge of collapsing from exhaustion ourselves, but knowing taking care of this man is more important than our own needs.

But it's more than that. The guilt is as thick in the air as the smoke from the fire. We should've looked harder for the elder when the shadow beasts on earth turned on us. We were just so overwhelmed that we hadn't been sure if he was among those shadow beasts until it was too late. Then we'd searched for him, not knowing if he was in their world or on ours.

But the injuries on him right now are fresh, which means he was recently attacked by our enemies. If we'd found him sooner, we could've saved him this pain.

The elder coughs, struggling to pull in air, and I crawl to his side, my heart aching at the sight of him.

"It's okay," I tell him, sitting down beside him. I used a lot of my magic battling the shadow beasts during the night, but I'll use whatever I can to help him now. "You're here with us now."

The elder's head hangs, and his breaths come in quick, raspy wheezes like he's run miles to get here. He grabs my hand as he collapses back in Onyx's arms, and now, he's half on the rock and half on the ground of the cave. Only Onyx's body keeps him from completely falling.

The elder's thin, brittle fingers curl into my skin as he looks up at me, eyes wide. "I know what to do. I've figured it... out."

But before he can speak further, his head falls to the side.

TWO

Dusk

THE ELDER ISN'T GOING to live. Not without a miracle. And, luckily for us, we have Ann and her incredible powers. They've done amazing things for all of us in this terrible war, so healing him should be possible. Not *easy* after fighting against our enemies all night, but possible.

Luckily for Elder Auero.

Our beautiful light fae kneels down beside him, her expression worn. Those big blue eyes of hers are filled with worry. She tucks a stray strand of light blonde hair behind her ear, takes a deep breath, and closes her eyes. Within seconds, a golden light begins to illuminate her palms and then radiates out as she lets her hands drift just above his chest.

Rayne looks at me. "The Shadow King?"

I don't know what to say. We haven't seen the elder since Phantom was taken by the king. We'd assumed he'd died in the battle or gone with them. We had no way of knowing where he'd been or what he'd been through, only that someone had hurt him.

But I could assume. "Probably." I keep my voice low, not wanting to distract Ann.

Onyx signs, "Pray the Moon Goddess is with us."

"Amen," I sign back.

Rayne's forehead is wrinkled as he watches us, probably because our words aren't signs he's learned, but I don't want to take this time to explain things to him. It feels like we need to stay focused. Like Ann needs our willpower right now, because after using her light to kill our enemies all night, it's probably taking everything in her to use it right now.

But something seems wrong.

Her hands hover over a massive slash across his chest. But instead of it fading away like it'd never been there at all, it closes a bit, the bleeding slowing, but nothing else happens. Ann frowns, and sweat beads her forehead. She moves to the slashes on his stomach, and the same thing happens.

The elder breathes slowly, so slowly that it feels like any breath could be his last, and I find myself taking deep, even breaths to get him to match my own. My hands clench, and I wish I was more than a brute. More than a shadow beast. That I could help my woman right now, because being helpless isn't exactly something I'm used to.

Her teeth clench together so hard I hear the sound, and my heart aches for my beautiful mate. She reminds me of someone trying to lift a very heavy object, an object that they'll never be able to lift, but they try. With every ounce of their being.

I just hope our Ann is strong enough for this.

Her hands move back to his chest, and she leans over so

far that I think for a second she might fall, but her hands glow a little brighter. I swear in that moment I can feel her power like the sunlight on my skin. At any other time, I'd smile, I'd close my eyes and lose myself in that feeling, but I don't. I'm too focused on the elder as his chest seems to stop moving.

As he seems to stop breathing.

"Fuck, breathe!" Rayne murmurs under his breath, almost like he can hear my thoughts.

Suddenly, Elder Auero's chest expands and contracts slowly, and I feel a rush of relief. He starts to breathe more evenly, and with each puff of air, he seems to gains a small burst of visual strength.

"Incredible," Rayne whispers, and I have to agree.

For a guy I hated just a short time ago, he's certainly grown on me. But maybe that has less to do with his personality changing than the fact that I'm no longer worried about him taking Ann from us. Now we're on the same team, and it feels good, even now, to have that extra support.

Elder Auero opens his eyes.

I lean closer. "Elder?"

But he doesn't respond. He doesn't do anything, and Ann just keeps working, without pause. Trying to fix things in the old man that the rest of us can't. Even Rayne. He might technically be a light fae, or at least he was before his ghost took the body of a shadow beast, but even he can't do what she can.

Ann's body jerks a little, then her hands move to his head.

"Prince," he whispers, his gaze going to me. And nothing has ever made me so grateful as the sound of his voice, as this moment where he seems to be improving. It's a moment of hope in a time when I believed all hope was lost.

The old man begins to shake so noticeably that I want to reach out and hold him. To stop him from hurting, even though I logically know it doesn't work that way.

But it's not me that reaches out, it's him. He snags Ann's wrist. "Enough."

"But–" She looks confused and exhausted.

"I can't be saved... but I need to tell you, tell you what the shadows said."

Ann looks at me.

Slowly, I nod. One of the main powers of the elders is the ability to hear the shadows, to hear the whispers of the spirits who guide us. The spirits are everywhere: in the trees, the streams, and the air. But the most powerful ones are in the shadows, where we are born.

If the elder is saying this, I have to believe him.

But Ann doesn't stop. If anything, she looks more determined.

The elder's hand has fallen back down, so I lightly touch the top of her hand. "Enough. It's his choice. And he knows more than we do. Please listen to him."

Those big blue eyes of hers are begging me to do something different, but I don't waiver.

"Ann," Rayne whispers. "He deserves this respect at least."

And something about his words breaks her. The golden glow fades from her hand, and she drops it into her lap, tears in her eyes.

Later, I'll hold her. Later, I'll help her through this loss. But right now? Right now, we need to hear the message from the shadows. We need to see how they can guide us from here, when hope seems lost. Because if we don't, whatever the hell this man has been through, it'll be for nothing.

"Prince Dusk," he manages this time, and I hold my

breath, waiting for what he'll say next. But instead of saying more, I watch as his skin grows even paler and his wounds begin to flow with blood once more.

Fuck. Fucking hell. He's not going to make it.

We can't lose more people. We can't lose our last elder.

He coughs out blood that paints his lips, but then his gaze locks with mine, showing more strength than I thought he had left. "Y-Your father... took P-Phantom because, together, you all have the... strength to defeat him."

Of course, we did. Losing my older brother, *technically* my twin brother but older by just a few minutes, was a blow to not only our cause, but to our souls. When my father plunged that moon shard into his chest and changed him, made him his own little minion, the hell we were living in got worse.

I didn't even know it could get worse.

"Prince Phantom is a good man," he manages.

Yes, a good man. Unlike me. The idea that I had the chance to kill our father and stop all of this still burns within me. Then, I'd been too soft. People joked that I'd taken after my mother, and I had. I didn't like war, or death, or fighting. And so, when I had the chance to kill him, I stupidly thought he could still be saved. I hesitated, and everything that came after was my own damn fault.

If only I'd been more like my brother, everything would have been different.

I picture Phantom. He resembles our father more than I do. His long black hair hangs past his massive shoulders in the same way our father wears his. But it's more than that. The similarities extend to the green of his eyes, the span of his shoulders, the breadth of his chest.

And yet, he never had our father's cruelty.

Now, seeing him under the Shadow King's control, it all

feels hopeless. This war. This life. *Everything.* But I would rather die than let anyone see that weakness inside of me, those tears in my soul, and the worry that constantly flows in my veins. So, I try to hide that now too. I try to just listen and not reflect on all my fears and all the things I've lost, no matter how hard it is.

The elder coughs and more blood erupts from his lips. Droplets dot the shirt Ann is wearing and decorate his already destroyed clothes. She ignores it, but I concentrate on one of the little red spots because I need a minute to pull myself together. To focus on this moment and not the crushing weight of guilt and pain that I can't seem to rid from my shoulders.

His voice comes out soft but strong. "Only the father can remove the shard from the shadow beast's heart. That is the only way to get Phantom back. To win this war."

There are words I could say to express the anger his words bring, but I don't want anyone to know the depths of that anger. Because if there's one thing I'm sure of, it's that we'll never get my father to remove that shard. And if that's the only way, Phantom is lost to us.

Ann speaks, sounding heartbroken, saying what we're all thinking. "There's no way the king is going to–"

"No." There's force, stronger than the elder's last speech, but not much above a whisper. He's waning. Time grows short now. "The ghost man"–he means Rayne– "can enter the king's body, take control, and remove the shard."

My stomach flips. Does that mean Rayne would be trapped inside the king's body *with the king?* Because the only reason Rayne seems to be able to survive in Adrik after dying is because the warrior's soul had already left his body. In this case, the king would still be in his body, fighting for control, and Rayne would lose the safety of Adrik's empty body.

This plan sounds dangerous at best. At worst, an exchange of one life for another.

As if knowing my thoughts, Ann whispers, "If he does this, is Rayne going to be... will he survive?" For all her strength, the thought of losing Rayne is enough to make her falter, to put a crack in her voice, to make her blanch.

On a shaky exhale, he says, "I don't know but *all* will die if Phantom isn't freed." The elder's voice is less now than even a whisper, but it isn't really necessary. His message is clear enough. He isn't talking about only shadow beasts. He's talking about all the earth's inhabitants.

He closes his eyes and draws his last breath, leaving us with one more body to bury, and one more impossible task on our shoulders.

THREE

Ann

Dusk stands with a handful of dirt in his hand, looking like a lost little boy. My chest aches at the sight of him. *How much more can he lose before it's too much?* He's breathing hard, and I know it's not just from the work. He's just barely keeping it together right now, and I don't blame him for it. His handsome face is streaked with dirt, and his long, dark hair is tangled around his face. He's absolutely filthy, as are Rayne and Onyx.

But then, grave digging isn't clean work.

All of us stare at Dusk as he scatters the handful of dirt on the top of the freshly covered grave. "May you rest in peace with the goddess."

Onyx works silently to put the final touch on the grave before coming to stand with the rest of us. Next to me, he threads his fingers through mine, and our gazes catch and hold. Those dark eyes of his say a million things. That this is too much. That we can't keep going this way much longer. But then he squeezes my hand and looks away as he releases me, almost like he doesn't want me to see the secrets he tries so hard to hide.

And then a strange silence washes over us.

The elder's grave is marked by a stone with his full name on it, the marking Onyx had put into place. It sits in the center of a plot of about thirty others graves–shadow beasts who have fallen for one reason or another.

It's gut wrenching to see the graves stretching out all around us. So few of the shadow beasts were able to escape through the Void to earth before the shadow king took control of them... only to come here and lose their lives instead. Seeing how many of them died in their fight to protect earth from the same fate as their world makes my eyes fill with tears.

Every one of these men are heroes. Including the older man who went through so much just to give us a way to save our world and our people. Even if what he told us horrified me.

"He was a good man," Rayne says quietly. He doesn't know the customs of the shadow beasts, but he needs to say something, just like me.

"He was always kind to me," I add on, signing the best I can as I do so, then look at Dusk and Onyx, wondering if what we're saying is okay.

Onyx signs, and Dusk says his words aloud. "He was a hero in this life. And he will be a hero in the next."

They both bow their heads, so Rayne and I do too. Then, after a moment, they stand taller, staring out around themselves. Onyx looks defeated, but Dusk looks on the edge of losing all control. I don't blame them. I didn't know all these people, and I feel crushed looking at the depressing sight before me. What they're feeling... it's unimaginable.

Yes, I'd lost Rayne, at least for a while, and had never

thought a pain could be worse. But pain is not a competition. It's different for every person, as is grief. And they're definitely in pain and grieving right now.

Beside me, Dusk's shoulders start to tremble. "We can't keep doing this. We can't keep burying people." He shakes his head, but he's signing for Onyx as he takes a shuddering breath and continues. "We're all going to end up dead, so what's the point?"

The sky is darkening, casting everything in grey as evening approaches. There isn't even the brightness of a sunset to chase away the sadness of this moment.

So, I try to be that light for them. "As my father used to say, life is a series of valleys and hills. Right now we're in a valley, but one day we'll be at the top of the hill and things will be better."

"I hope so," Onyx signs to me, but Dusk just shakes his head.

Moving to my big warrior, I take Dusk's face in my hand and force him to look at me. "We'll get Phantom back. We'll fix all of this. There's a way, I know it."

His gaze holds mine and he leans forward and presses a light kiss onto my lips. But I think he's more trying to get me to drop this than because he feels better, which hurts. Still, I release him and glance at the grave one more time, trying to dig deep and hold onto my sense of hope. For me, as well as for these men who desperately need me.

Rayne places his hand at the small of my back, and then we all make our way back to the cave. There, they build up the fire once more and start a soup over the flames of mostly things they'd collected while we walked. It's the same thing we've had many, many times now, but I'm still looking forward to it. All this work with so little food is hard at times.

"They shouldn't be back tonight," Rayne says, and he's probably right. It takes the Shadow King a great deal of his energy to protect his creatures in this world because it's too light, and so when he sends over a lot of them, like he did last night, we're usually safe for a day or two.

We hope, at least.

It takes all the strength we have to journey to the river nearby and bathe, change our clothes, and tend to the guys' wounds from the battle. By then, night has fully fallen and the soup is ready, so we all sit in the safety of the cave, our light and smoke mostly hidden by the leafy branches we place over the entrance. Inside, the fire chases away the chill of the night and we gather around the fire and eat our soup in silence. Again, the flavor... mostly of mushrooms and herbs, some carrots and onions, isn't much, but I almost want to cry when it hits my stomach and I feel full for the first time all day.

Not much hunting has gotten done since Phantom was taken from us.

"Should we talk about the elephant in the room?" Rayne asks, ruffling his short, light brown hair awkwardly.

Onyx and Dusk frown and exchange a glance, then look at me. I actually smile. They probably have no idea what an elephant is. "He means we should talk about what the elder said," I explain, while trying to sign the words.

They nod but won't look at me or Rayne.

I understand. The Shadow King has an army and they're killing us. Literally. There's a fucking graveyard that proves it. But what the elder said... how can we possibly do that? How can we possibly ask Rayne to risk his life for all of us?

"He said there was only one way–" Rayne begins.

"But there could be others that we haven't figured out yet," I tell him without thinking.

Dusk stares at his hands as he answers me. "And you think we have time to waste?"

I feel sick. Of course, I know we're running out of time. Of course, I know that the fate of both of our worlds rests on defeating the Shadow King, his beasts, and fixing things with Phantom, but that doesn't change the way I feel.

Rayne sighs, and his light blue eyes meet mine. "I have to do this, Ann. The elder said…"

I shake my head because I just can't lose him again. "No, Rayne."

When Rayne died, a part of me died too. And when his ghost found a new body, and he and my shadow beasts accepted each other, I felt like I could handle anything life threw at me as long as I had them. This was love. This was the family I always needed.

I can't lose him again.

But I can't give up on Phantom either.

"The elder said if I don't go into the Shadow King, then you'll lose all of us." Rayne is the only one who can take over the king's body, and I know it, but I can't trade one of my men for another. Not Rayne. Not Dusk. Not Onyx. None of them. We have to find a different way to get the king to take the shard out of Phantom.

I glance at Onyx, and slowly he begins to sign, "I wish I could do this. I wish it wasn't up to Rayne. But he is a warrior, and I will not take away his right to decide for himself what he'll do."

A warrior. I see Rayne stare at the other man in shock. They really have come a long way, but to call Rayne a warrior is the ultimate compliment between these men.

Then, Rayne looks at me. "Right now, if things

continue, we'll be defeated. Maybe not tonight, but soon. And when we are, everything and everyone we've ever known or loved will be lost. Could I really live with myself if I let that happen?"

My stomach clenches and I tear my gaze from. He's right. But I hate that he's right.

"I can't give my blessing on this," I say, feeling so tired, not just from battle, but from this life. "I just want us all to be happy together."

Onyx taps my shoulder and gives me one of his rare smiles as he signs slowly. "We don't have to decide right now. We have the night, at least. We should eat and rest. We don't know how long we have before the next attack." I can't take my eyes off of him. There's something beautiful in that man's smile, something that eases a little of the ache in my heart.

"You're right. Let's not talk about it tonight. Let's just rest."

And Onyx... looks relieved.

We all arrange our bedding together, with me in the middle. We divide up the night in shifts, as we always do when we sleep at night, and then I snuggle together with Rayne and Onyx, while Dusk sits near the doorway on first shift.

Dusk gives me a little smile, and I let my eyes close. There's so much to figure out. The Shadow King's next move. Whether what the elder said was true or not. And what we will decide to do with that information.

But for now, we sleep.

FOUR

Onyx

Steam rises off the hot spring as I lower myself into the water. It's been two days since the elder died, and the Shadow King has been silent. My brother has been silent.

It's always a relief on the nights we're not overwhelmed by rot monkeys, grave trolls, and our fellow shadow beasts, but it's also not. Every day they don't come simply means they're building up their strength for yet another attack, and I'm not sure how many more attacks we can handle. I want to say as many as it takes, but I'd be lying.

But today, I've had enough of plotting and planning. Today, I want to relax. In the daylight, none of our enemies can attack. It's the only time we know we're safe from them, and that does bring peace, especially since my body has had a couple of days to rest.

I lay my head back against the earth and let the water wash over my skin, soaking away my aching muscles in the hot water. My mind flashes back to our shadowy world. I've missed what it once was before my father stole the Moonstone from the sky. We had hot springs like these, clean water, flowers that glowed at night, and even more trees and bushes that illuminated both the night and the day. It was paradise.

Perfect, except that it didn't have Ann.

Well, not perfect. I was lonely. My brothers were lonely. And the king was always a poor leader, even if his sons couldn't see it. But it was better than the dark and dead place that it is now.

Part of me wonders what we're even trying to save. Earth, yes, but is our world beyond salvation? Without the Moonstone to light it, no plants will grow, and no creatures will live beyond the ones who come from the dead realm. I know our creatures are capable of burrowing and hibernating, but for how long? Even if we could return the light, are all the animals dead? All our plants exterminated?

Our lives in our realm are over, either way. Now we're fighting to free our shadow beasts and save this world. A world that doesn't like us. That sees us as savage beasts.

Yet we still fight. Why?

I frown and splash at the water. This is not what I want on my mind. I want to focus on the goodness. On the little sparks of happiness that still exists. On my mate.

And then Ann comes to me. Like my want and need has summoned her. Like I have the power to wish her into being. It doesn't matter if it's my hidden talent or her wanting to bathe in the hot spring, she's here and I smile, watching her strip.

I would enjoy the moment more if not for the sadness haunting her eyes and the frown turning her lips down. She undresses quickly, her mind obviously far from here. I wait until she slips into the water beside me then cock an eyebrow. Some things don't need words or hand signs. Some things only require a look or a touch, a smile, a moment.

She closes her eyes for a second and I want to see them. The beauty in her face starts with her big blue eyes, and the light in them is so vibrant that I'm addicted to it. Every time she looks at me, she pulls me under. Makes me fall in love with her all over again.

When she looks at me, she sighs and the force of her breath makes a small ripple in the water. Instead of waiting, I slide my arm around her waist and pull her closer. Her slight body is warm and slick and I want to touch her, but for now, I'll simply hold her.

"We have to find another way to save Phantom." I smile, but not because of what she's saying. There's nothing amusing about that. I smile because she's saying it so well with her hands.

I nod.

"My magic should be able to help." And then she shakes her head and her hands move faster. She's an excited signer. "Or maybe...maybe the elder was wrong and there's another way we don't know yet."

I take her hands in mine to stop the frantic signing, bring them to my mouth for a quick kiss, then hold them for an extra second. She needs a moment to calm before I speak to her because what I have to say isn't going to calm her or make her feel better. I hate being the one to do it, but there's no one else but me to say it. Not right now anyway and now is when she needs to hear it most.

Releasing her hands, I sign slowly, "Using Rayne is our best chance at saving Phantom and defeating the king. We can't do it without him and Rayne is the only one who can take control of their father's body to remove the shard." She knows all of this. But hopefully, watching me say it will be enough to calm her, enough to make her see the reality of our situation.

"I know that, okay?" Her anger strikes bigger than her hands can move. She's not just simmering with it, she's on a rolling boil. "I just want..."

Her cheeks are rosy with color and her eyes flash with the fire that draws me to her. She's as beautiful now as ever and I am fascinated with the way her emotions are so clear to read on her face.

"You want to save all of us," I sign to her.

She calms a little, then signs back, "Yes."

I nod, completely understanding. In so many ways our Ann isn't built for war, but then, I don't think most people are. "If there's another way, we'll find it. But until then, we make a plan with this idea." My hands drop, and I wait.

"Okay," she finally signs, but her hands aren't excited, they're defeated. And so is her beautiful face.

"Until then, we have enough to worry about. We should take moments like this when we can." I finish my last sign and drop my hands again, watching her. Wondering if she'll spiral again or see the logic in my words.

"I know." I read the words on her lips as she turns to me and continues, "I just love all of you so much."

"We love you too," I mouth to her.

She smiles.

Like she knows I can't stop staring at her, she lowers her head under the water and comes up on a big breath that expands her chest, that draws attention to the swells of her breasts that are visible above the water. She's just so damn beautiful in every way. I want her in my arms, against my body, beneath me as I plunge my cock inside of her.

She quirks a brow like she knows what I'm thinking about, or maybe she can see the hard length of my cock under the water. I feel a wave of embarrassment. There's so much going on. She's been through more than most people can imagine. I shouldn't be thinking with my cock right now.

So, I duck under the water and scrub my long blond hair, trying to buy myself enough time to calm down, but my arousal doesn't fade. When I resurface for air, it's like my skin is too damn tight. I want something good, something that feels good. And Ann feels *so* damn good.

Our eyes meet again, and she slides closer to me in the water. I hold my breath as she lifts up taller, revealing those perfect breasts of hers, and she kisses me softly. Then, she rises up higher and straddles my lap beneath the water.

A shudder rolls through me as she slides closer and closer until she rubs herself against me. Her nipples are hard as they press against my chest. One of her hands slides into the back of my hair, and then she tilts my head and takes my mouth with her own, sliding her tongue between my lips at the same moment she reaches between us to stroke my shaft.

Desire explodes inside of me as a million sensations wash over me. This is everything I wanted and more. Her on me, touching me, stroking my cock until all I can think about is her and what I want to do to her. Even if shadow beasts are accustomed to being the ones in charge with sex, I can't find it in me to care right now.

I can let her have this moment of power. There's something even more seductive than usual about the energy she's radiating right now. I already know this isn't going to be a gentle fuck, and nothing about it will be *making love*. This is primal and raw and intoxicating. She's better than wine or ale.

As elusive these days, too.

I curl my hand around her ass, pulling her toward me, then break our kiss and lift her just a bit. Unable to help myself, I lower my head to take one of the pebbled peaks of her breasts into my mouth. Instantly, she stiffens and then I slowly begin to suck, worshipping her nipples just the way I always want to. She throws her head back when I let my teeth gently nibble, her breathing rough, given how fast her chest rises and falls.

What I miss most about hearing is the sounds a woman makes when in the throes of passion. I remember the symphonic nature to it, the hums and whimpers, the moans and squeals brought on by desire and excitement. And it seems a crime that I'll never hear those sounds from my mate, from my Ann.

But I don't want to focus on that right now.

Her lips part as she brings her head forward and twists her fingers harder into my hair. She gives a tug while her other hand strokes my clock in earnest and I hiss. Being with Ann is the most exquisite agony I've ever known. It's such a thin line between love and pain at all times, and yet, it's intoxicating. A drug I can never dream of quitting.

I slide one of my hands between us too and begin to stroke her. I sense the shock that radiates through her system as I suck one breast, then move to the other, all while rubbing her wet core. It's hot as fuck, but also allows me to gain a little control as I focus on her pleasure and not my own.

But then, she pushes my hand away.

I'm trying to catch my breath. Trying to figure out what to do next. Then she squeezes my length, and, fuck, I can't wait any longer. I *have* to be inside her. So, I turn us so she's beneath me. Her gaze locks with mine, and she spreads her leg wider, her expression that of a damn siren.

Keep your control. Keep your fucking control.

I brace my weight on my arms and slide my tip into her.

Even now, she's tight. Our light fae so much smaller than our shadow beast women that it's remarkable we fit at all. Slowly, I push myself inside her, watching for signs that it's too much. Watching to see if she's enjoying it.

When I reach my hilt, she gives a relieved nod and grasps my shoulders, which I know means she's ready for more.

Pulling back out, I don't hesitate, I drive my cock inside her. Her head tosses back, and then she wraps her legs around me and digs her nails into my shoulders. I pull out again, then slam back into her, over and over again. Our hips slap together as she meets every thrust with her body.

My body is coiled, ready to explode, and she's riding my cock, clutching and kissing me frantically. I sense her need to release, and I desperately want to do the same, because my blood seems to burn as passion and need build. But I wait. Wait for her release.

Her legs tighten around my hips and her head throws back revealing a long expanse of throat as I finally feel her orgasm. I kiss and suck her throat as she hangs on to me, riding her passion to the very last moment, and then my body tightens and I come, but still hold her against me as we ride the final waves of our orgasms.

Ann. The sweetness of her name is a sound in my mind only, but I hear it like a scream.

She collapses against me, and I hold her as her head falls to my shoulder. Gently, she kisses the inside of my shoulder at the base of my throat. Soft and sweet, just like her.

It takes a minute before we move more than that, but then she climbs out of the hot spring and starts to dress. When I climb out beside her, she smiles and runs her fingertips down my chest to my belly button and back up to my throat then across my lips.

She's smiling, but the haunted sadness is lurking in her eyes once more. This is hard for her. It's hard for her to think she might have to sacrifice one of her mates to save another, but eventually I think she'll realize that this will save us all. And that the risk Rayne would take would be worth it.

But it's a lot to ask of her. It's a lot to ask of her and Rayne. And we all know it. If there was a way to save her from this risk, this choice, any one of us, or all of us together, would do what it took, but this isn't a choice anymore. Not really. She'll come to see that. I hope.

And I hope it's soon.

I take her by the shoulders and turn her so she can see what I'm about to say and also so I can look at her one more time before we go back to the caves.

"I'll do whatever I can to protect Rayne. Not only for your sake but because he's one of us now," I sign, and I mean it. If Rayne does this, I'll be with him. I'll do everything I can to make sure he makes it back into Adrik's body. I'll treat him like I would my brothers, both because he's earned it, and because Ann loves him.

So, him doing this will be a risk, but not a guarantee that he'll lose his life. Which is much better than the alternative... that we just keep going until we eventually fail and everyone loses their lives.

Ann smiles, probably not aware of my thoughts, or she wouldn't be smiling. "Thank you."

And for some reason, I feel guilty.

FIVE

Ann

My dreams were filled with nightmares. Terrible images of losing Rayne all over again. Of losing Phantom. Of losing all the men I love. I swore I kept hearing a woman's voice in the distance reassuring me, but I had no idea who it was or why she thought everything would be okay when I wasn't even sure.

When I finally woke up, I felt shaky and off. *How much more could I take?*

We ate quickly, knowing that the sun was setting and soon we would need to be out once more, searching for moon shards and watching for more enemies. Because we didn't just have to be aware of attacks, we had to be prepared for their sneaky shit too. If they manage to plant enough moon shards on earth, they'll have the ability to spread the Void and take over our entire planet, turning it into a dark world of shadows, monsters, and no other life.

So, we hunt. Not just our enemies but the shards too.

"Ready?" Dusk asks as I finish putting my belongs in my bag and hoist it onto my shoulder.

I check to make sure the bag tied to my belt filled with moon shards is still there and securely attached, which it is. "As ready as I'll ever be?"

Rayne laughs. "Ain't that the truth!"

I smile at him. Bloodmores aren't exactly people known for saying words like 'ain't,' so I know he's trying to make me happy. Even though nothing my men do can chase away the emptiness in my soul where Phantom was, it means a lot to me that they keep trying.

Onyx and Dusk do their best to hide any signs that we'd recently been in this cave, and then we head out into the evening. The night animals are awake, filling the air with their calls to one another, and tonight there's at least a small sunset in the distance, painting the sky with orange.

"It's beautiful here," Rayne says.

Onyx signs, "We didn't have sunsets like this in the shadow world."

"How did anything survive?" Rayne signs back, while speaking aloud.

Onyx gives an almost-smile. "Life just has a way."

As we start walking, picking a path at random, everyone's eyes are on the ground. It's not as hard for them to find moon shards now that I'm with them, because for some reason they glow when I get close, but we still don't want to miss any. And, luckily for us, we find one right away. It glows that soft blue glow, even though it's partially concealed under a bush.

Onyx kneels down and reveals the sliver that looks like a glowing piece of broken glass, then he stands and hands it to me. For a second, I just stare at it in disbelief. If Phantom didn't have this one shard in his heart, he'd be *him* again. And if there are too many shards on earth, the Shadow King will take this world for his own.

How can such small things ruin so many lives?

"Ann?"

I look up and realize everyone is staring at me, but it was Rayne that spoke.

"Are you okay?" He runs his hand along my back as if he knows exactly what I'm thinking.

"I'm fine," I say, probably too quickly, then open the pouch on my belt and place the shard inside, trying to seem normal.

Rayne clears his throat, then glances at the other two men. I catch it all out of the corner of my eye, then look up at them with a frown. The shadow beasts used to do this to me when we first met, communicate silently, so I feel oddly left out. On one hand, I'm glad Rayne has been pulled into their little fold, but on the other hand, I hate that I'm not part of the silent looks.

We keep walking, but tension builds between all of us. They hang back a little, and I know damn well they're signing to each other, even though Rayne is still learning. I can feel their emotions, and I almost curse the mate-bond between us, because without it I wouldn't be as aware of the fact that they're having a serious discussion without me.

Finally, I spin around and snap, "What?"

They all stiffen and have the good grace to look embarrassed.

Rayne rubs the back of his head, then sighs loudly. "After you fell asleep last night, we talked."

My stomach drops. *Talked?* I'm pretty damn sure there's only one thing they have to talk about, and it's a discussion I should've been included in. But I wait. Letting these assholes tell me to my face.

Rayne's gaze meets mine, and he drops his hand, squaring his shoulders that way that means he's about to say something he knows I won't like. "The only person who should be able to decide what I do with my life is me, and I've decided that I'm going to do as the elder asked. Tonight, if our enemies attack, I'm going to go into the Void, find the king, and take his body."

"Rayne," my voice comes out too high, so I take a second to try to sound unemotional and practical, then continue, "we know so little about ghosts, about... what you are now. What if after you leave Adrik's body, it dies, and you have nothing to go back to? What if the king pushes you out and it accomplishes nothing? We'll just lose you *and* Phantom."

Rayne moves toward me and takes my hands. I yank them back, and he looks troubled, but continues. "This is a situation where every choice has its risks, so I made the choice I felt was best."

"And I, as your mate, don't get any say in it?" I feel desperate. I can't endure the heartache of losing another person I love. And even though that might make me selfish, I just can't. Not right now.

It's all just happening too fast. First with Phantom. Now with Rayne.

"Ann, if you could risk your life to save Phantom right now, would you?"

I would, of course I would. "That's not what we're talking about!"

"Answer the question," he says, his voice firm but also kind.

"If I went in there, Phantom would just kill me, or all of you. He's not himself any longer, so I can't save him." I feel tears prickling my eyes and try to brush them away.

"You're right. There's nothing you can do to save him, but imagine you could. Would you?" Those light blue eyes of his hold mine, refusing to let me dance around the question.

Damn him!

"Fine! Yes, you know I would!" I throw at him like an insult, even knowing I'm going exactly where he's leading me. Exactly where I don't want to go.

He nods. "But you can't. None of you can. But I have the chance to save him, and I'm going to."

"No," I deny, the pressure on my chest unbearable.

He takes a step closer, reaches for me, and strokes my hair gently... and I let him, moving even closer. Begging him with my eyes not to do this. "It has to be my choice and only my choice. I won't have you all living with this."

"But we have to live with your choice either way." My words come out a broken whisper.

He looks grim, but then just leans forward and kisses me. Hard. So hard that I find myself clinging to him when he finally breaks it, and then we're just staring at each other. "I love you more than anyone in this world."

"I love you too," I whisper, and hope blossoms in my heart. Maybe he's rethinking this. Maybe he's realizing that there could be another way. "We'll think. We'll figure out the best plan."

He kisses me again, then pulls away, but his hand slips into mine. We walk that way for a while, picking up a couple more moon shards. All of us are silent, probably lost in thought the way I am. My feelings bounce between hopeful and crushed.

I try not to think what would happen if I lost Rayne too. If I lost another man I love and still had to fight this war and find a way to save Phantom... but every time I think about it, I want to scream and cry and curse the world. So, I keep forcing my thoughts away from that painful topic.

Night falls fully, and we don't light torches. They're too dangerous now. And there's enough light from the moon to at least illuminate most of the spaces in front of us. Unfortunately, it's not just tripping over something that we have to worry about. When it's fully dark, our enemies can come for us, and after being silent for a few days, I have no doubt tonight they'll reappear.

Onyx leads our group, communicating with hand signals. We move slower, collecting another random moon shard and making our way closer to the Void. The massive black cloud has so many different directions that they can come out of on earth, but the back of it borders a massive canyon, so that, at least, helps limit them... a little.

Suddenly, Onyx motions for us to stop.

We do, but I peer slowly through the trees to the Void. The terrible cloud looms, even in the night, rolling and moving like storm clouds. Nothing seems to have emptied out of it, but I trust these men. They were fighting these creatures long before I came along.

Slowly, a grave troll emerges from the Void. The bastard is huge. Dusk had told me they were born in places of terrible pain and suffering, areas where people had died. Their bodies were made up of hundreds of pieces of dead people that come together to create a Frankenstein of a creature. This one is no exception, and as he stands, his nostrils flaring, his black sword thrown on his back like a club, my heart races.

The creatures always do that to me. No matter how many times I see them.

For one second, I think Onyx is just going to spring forward and fight it, but he remains in place. His hand raises, telling us all to wait. A dozen rot monkeys come springing out behind it. The bastards are almost completely pitch black and oily, with big red eyes, long teeth, and claws. They do this eerie chittering thing as they jump around, and I can see that each one holds a moon shard.

Now, now is the time for us to spring forward, before the monkeys race away into the woods, and we have to spend all night chasing them. But still, Onyx keeps that hand of his raised.

Two more grave trolls emerge from the Void, and my breath catches. *Three* of them? Three of them is a hell of a lot. We can handle them, but tonight will not be an easy night. Not that any is exactly. Still, I try to take deep breaths, to call to the weird magic inside of me that I don't understand... but the magic I have to ask to use, for some reason.

I feel it spring to life inside of me, waiting for release, but I look at Onyx. If I use my light before they start attacking, before they distract the creatures, they'll attack me. And, unfortunately, I'm not as good at handling a hand-to-hand fight as the guys. They've made it clear to me my magic has more value than my kicks and punches, but still, it's hard to always have to linger back.

At last, Onyx drops his hand. He moves back to us slowly and pulls Rayne into a tight hug, patting him grimly on the back. Dusk hugs Rayne too, although his hug is more friendly, and I wonder what the hell is going on. *Did the three grave trolls shake their confidence?* I know my emotions are far too raw after so many days fighting and so much loss.

They each hug me next. But Rayne hugs me the hardest, kissing my cheek and whispering that he loves me. Before I can say it back, he pulls away and then all the men withdraw their swords.

My chest aches. *Another battle? More wounds to my brave warriors? How much longer can we do this?*

But I don't say any of that. I just make sure my magic is ready and inch behind them as they move forward. They spread out, as they usually do, with Onyx remaining in front of me and the other two staying close, just in case, but to each of his sides. I keep my gaze on Onyx's back as the monkeys continue to chitter and the grave trolls snort and growl. Any second now, they'll follow the Shadow King's commands and begin planting the shards and searching for us, but we'll be on them before they can.

Then Onyx is out in front of them, attacking. It happens within a moment. Suddenly, Dusk is there too. A grave troll roars, the sound shaking the woods around me, and his sword meets Onyx's. Dusk is squaring off with one of the others, while the third tries to circle around to reach Onyx from behind. The rot monkeys keep leaping forward, but Onyx and Dusk are quick to kick them away.

Now, it's time for me.

I call my magic to me, asking it for help, and within moments golden light illuminates my hands before it shoots forward, blanketing the battle in gold. The rot monkeys hiss and screech and begin to turn to ash in front of my eyes. The grave trolls roar and fight harder, even as they begin to fade away to ash too.

Dusk and Onyx are still fighting, their swords meeting the massive swords of the grave trolls, but they're more confident now that the trolls are suffering and distracted. I'm trying to focus, to end this battle before they're hurt, but my focus falters for a second as I glance around, wanting to find Rayne. I need to know he's okay.

And then I remember the way he hugged all of us. The

conversation. The strange tension. *Did he go into the Void? Tonight? Already?*

My golden light begins to falter as panic awakens inside of me, but when I realize what I'm doing, I try to calm myself down. *I'll look for Rayne when the grave trolls are gone. Until then, I need to help my men.* I can't let one of them get hurt when Rayne might be fighting just out of my sight. When I might be overreacting.

Even if my gut is saying I'm not.

One of the trolls falls into a pile of ash, and I refocus my light onto the two that are left. They're almost gone. Almost defeated. It's taking everything in me not to leave my men to them and go to search for Rayne, but I manage to stay in place, teeth gritted together.

Suddenly, I feel a sharp pain on the back of my head, and everything goes dark.

SIX

Rayne

I'm breathing hard as I finish cutting the little rot monkey in front of me in half. It makes a strange sound like a shriek rolled into a gasp, then collapses into ash. The damn Shadow King had sent another group of them sneaking in from the side, but I'd been lucky enough to spot them before they got lose on earth.

Ann's light disappears as I race toward the others, happy to have dealt with the little assholes, but worried about the consequences of leaving Onyx and Dusk without my help. I might be the worst fighter among us, but Onyx had said every sword on our side was a good sword in battle. It wasn't praise exactly, and yet it made me want to be a sword he valued.

To my relief, in the clearing, all our enemies are gone. Ann's light worked its magic, leaving behind piles of ash that were once our enemies. I also spot the evidence of Dusk and Onyx's efforts, which are pieces of a few grave trolls scattered on the ground. Ann could turn them to ash too, but she's done what she needed to do. Her magic has limits, which we'd learned a long time ago, so using it for cleanup is stupid. Besides, we're more than good enough at burning grave trolls by now.

I see a few rot monkeys scattering and running into the forest, which sucks, but they'll return later to fight. For now, we have the upper hand and they won't stick around to join their friends in whatever afterlife is awaiting them.

Which means the big fight for the night is mostly finished, which is a huge relief. Some nights the fighting is worse than others. Sometimes there are clever plans, and sometimes, like tonight, it was just a rush of brute force. Probably just to see if they've weakened us enough that we won't be able to handle it.

A few of the rot monkeys come back, which, I guess, is better than having to track them down. Although it's annoying. I slash one across his chest and black syrupy soot oozes from the wound. Across the field of battle, Onyx rips the head off another and holds it in his hand as the body falls. Dusk has two on him and he's fighting hand to hand, hitting one then the other. It's a valiant fight for someone Ann once called *Fluffy,* a nickname I've been enjoying knowing ever since Ann told me about it. He looks like he's toying with them, but in the second it takes to have the thought, he ends one, then the other. And now, we're the last men standing.

Onyx moves to start a fire so we can burn the bodies of the grave trolls... or what's left of them.

Ann is still hidden, which kind of sucks. Some small part of me always wants to hug her after a battle, no matter how hard or easy. But I know better than to call her out of the trees. Onyx and Dusk have made it clear to her that they don't want her anywhere near the Void when she's weak and vulnerable after using her magic. And I don't think she's fought them much on it, because the smell of burning troll isn't exactly pleasant.

But still, I want to hurry and burn these trolls and get back to her. She's the only one who can shake this somber, exhausted mood after battle. Even if today's was fairly easy in comparison to the ones we've faced lately. She'll at least be happy, or somewhat so, that we've defeated more of the creatures fighting for the king.

Every enemy we kill is a step closer to our ultimate goal. That's how we look at it anyway.

"That wasn't too bad," I say as I drop a big log onto the other logs.

"I wonder if Phantom and father are getting tired of all of this," Dusk mutters, shaking his head as he kicks one of the grave troll's hands.

It's weird. They said the creatures could build themselves into grave trolls again if we don't burn them, but I'm not sure the body parts here would be enough for that. Not that I want to find out.

Onyx signs something I can't see very well in the dark. Luckily, Dusk's words put them into context as he gives a snort-laugh. "Yeah, you're probably right. It's unlikely."

We start up the fire, and within a short time, it's burning brightly. Together, we drag over the bottom half of one of the trolls and then toss it onto the fire, followed by the legs and crotch of the next one, and finally the lone hand. The smell of wood and rotted bodies burning fills the air, and I gag.

Onyx laughs, and I hate to say it, but I love his laugh. It's not quite a chuckle, but somewhere in between a belly laugh and a chortle. It makes it all the more special, somehow, that he can't hear the sound himself. And also, a bit sad. One day I'll have to tell him what a nice laugh he has. You know, when I'm not working so hard not to hurl.

"Just go find Ann," Dusk finally says, and I realize he's laughing at me too.

"Sorry, we didn't," I gag again, "burn trolls at the mansion."

Dusk, the ass, actually laughs harder. "No, I'm sure there wasn't troll burning time in between tea and dances."

I toss some dirt at him.

He grins, standing far closer to the flames than I could ever manage. "Just go."

"Fine, but you just remember that you're a prince too!" It takes everything in me not to loudly gag again as I retreat from the flames.

"A prince of the shadow beasts, not the delicate fae," he calls after me.

"I'm not delicate," I grumble, which would have been perfect if I didn't loudly gag again.

I glance back at them and Dusk signs something to Onyx, then they're both laughing their asses off. I give them the finger before turning around to look for Ann, but I'm smiling. This must be what it's like to have brothers, and although I love Esmeray, I'm kind of glad to have "brothers" now.

That thought fills my mind as I make it to the place that we'd left Ann. Only, she's not there. I understand that sometimes she has to adjust her angle or move deeper if the rot monkeys get too close, so I walk further into the woods, wondering how far Ann has gone, how deep into the cover of the trees she's ventured.

Maybe she felt the danger more acutely today. Maybe she wanted to get away from the sound of battle. Her light makes her sensitive to sound while she uses it. She's sensitive to many things, and vulnerable, which I knew she hates. Still, my Ann is a trooper. She always has been.

But after a few minutes, I start to worry. Probably unnecessarily. Not because I'm stupid and think she's safe out here, but because with her light she could vaporize anything that gets close to her. The concern for me is that I always thought she has to be close enough to see where she's directing her light, but I'm two-hundred yards into the forest, and I still don't see her.

Still. Don't. See. Her.

The last thing I want to do is call out and alert any lingering enemies that she's alone and vulnerable, but my stomach clenches. This isn't like Ann. I hope she's just sitting and tired. Maybe somewhere I missed. But something feels off.

Wrong.

I'm ten yards farther when I see them—the moon shards we'd collected earlier. She'd had them in the pouch she carries on her belt. She always keeps them there because she's the only one who can carry them without being affected. There's no way she would have left these on the ground. Not by choice, at least.

My heart races.

A flash of light catches my eye. Past the moon shards, a few feet farther away, her dagger sticks out of the ground near the stump of a fallen tree. I know it's her dagger because it's one I gave her from my personal stash. It's got an ivory handle and a blade that's sharp on both sides with a point on the end that could pierce a hole in a man without much force behind it. It's shiny and silver and she sharpens it every morning because she doesn't want to be caught off-guard. And somehow, someone caught her anyway.

Fuck.

There's no way Ann would have just dropped this all here. Panic builds inside of me, and I want to deny what I know because it's too painful.

But I can't.

Someone took Ann, and it isn't a big stretch to figure out who. My gut aches, and nausea builds as my heart twists. This is... worse than anything I imagined. We kept Ann far away from the Void. We handled the Shadow King's minions. Ann should have been safe.

I kneel down and gather the moon shards, then I collapse onto my knees and slowly pick up her dagger. Ann is... *gone*. Now, I can feel it deep inside. It's like part of my soul is missing. I try to picture her in that dark world with Phantom, how he is now, and the Shadow King, but the idea makes me sick.

If I thought the smell of the grave trolls would make me vomit, I was wrong. Finding my Ann gone though... bile rises in the back of my throat.

I won't rest until we have her back with us. Where she belongs.

And when Onyx and Dusk learn what happened, well, the king better be ready, because there's no wrath that compares with the wrath of the three of us. That bastard is going to burn, and our Ann will be back safely with us again.

I swear it.

SEVEN

Ann

I'm warm, wrapped in a dream of sweet happiness, cradled in strong arms on a comfortable bed under a soft blanket. And it's divine. I haven't felt so safe or protected in... I can't remember ever feeling so safe and protected.

If it's a dream, I never want to wake up. I never want it to end.

But like all good things, it does end. And when I look behind me to see who's holding me, my heart flips. I'm with Phantom, in a comfortable bed, with his arms and his scent wrapped around me. It's intoxicating. Everything I've dreamed of and more.

It's been so long since I've known comforts like these—a mattress, a blanket that doesn't smell like soot and ash, walls that aren't made of earth and roots, a floor not made of packed dirt. But that's not what matters to me now. I'm back with my stolen mate, and he looks like himself again as he smiles at me.

He's wearing a pair of silk boxers and nothing else. His body is as perfect as I remember—smooth broad chest, wide shoulders, sinew, and muscle—and my palm itches to run across the width of it. Instead, I spend a second staring my fill before I spot the small spot above his heart. Something crystal clear sticks an inch or so out of his skin.

A moon shard.

I reach for it, and he catches my hand. Slowly, I look up once more, and his smile widens.

"Good morning, my sweet Ann." His gaze is everything. Everything I remember, everything I need. Although, I have no idea how I came to be here with him.

But right now, it only matters that I am. That I have him back.

"Phantom." His name on my tongue is like a sweet berry. But I have so many questions I don't know where to begin.

Where are we? How did we get him back?

Is he... Phantom again?

He kisses my temple then smiles. The evil I thought I would see isn't visible. He's genuine. "It's me." The voice is the same, the gentleness of his touch, the reverence, even his eyes are right.

It's really him.

I've missed him so much I've ached with it, felt like part of myself has been missing. And here he is—flesh and bone—holding me. No signs of the ghost of a man he'd become. No signs of the man who had sent shadow beasts, grave trolls, and rot monkeys after us for weeks. It's just... Phantom.

And I don't know if I care how we got him back, only that my mate has returned to me.

Yet, I have to ask. And I *hate* that I have to ask. "What happened?" It's logical to ask, coherent even in a time where my thoughts are terribly incoherent. I can't understand how this is happening. He was lost to us. We've been fighting to get him back, but here he is, beside me. Gazing at me. Affectionate. Running his fingers through my hair.

The question isn't specific enough, but I can't think beyond it. My thoughts are slower here. I need to revise, but I'm still reeling, and I can't think of exactly what to ask.

"You've all misunderstood. You and Onyx and Dusk."

He sounds... not quite sincere, but matter-of-fact. And I want to believe him. *Has he just been pretending all this time to get access to his father? Or is the shard weakening and losing its control over him?*

"How have we misunderstood?" I ask, reaching up and touching his face, staring into those remarkable green eyes of his, desperate for an answer that makes sense.

"I'm not evil, Ann. I just understand how things are now." He leans down and kisses me, a kiss that sets my body aflame. A kiss that instantly brings me back to every time this incredible man ever touched me.

I couldn't say no to him before, less so when he turns us so his body is on top of mine and continues kissing me over and over again until my head spins and my heart swells. He gathers my hands and pulls them over my head, holding them there as he grinds his hips into mine.

It's harder than when we were together before, rougher than any of the others, but not wholly unenjoyable. When he touches me, it's like all my thoughts fade away. A small part of me thinks this might all be in my head, but I can't seem to care.

He releases me and pulls the long, white nightgown I'm wearing off. His gaze burns as it runs over me, and then he removes his boxers, tossing them onto the floor. Settling above me once more he kisses his way up my throat, catches my lips, and captures my hands, placing them back above my head.

My legs spread to accommodate him as he settles in lower, and then he begins to rub his length along my hot core. My body trembles. I feel myself getting wetter and wetter as desire rushes through me.

His tip pushes into my opening, and I gasp, pulling against his hands, but they hold me firmly in place. He's so big. Even after all this time, I haven't gotten used to the sheer size of my shadow beasts. Sometimes it feels like my body isn't made to handle cocks this big. Other times? Other times it feels like the most incredible thing to be so small and have men who are so well-endowed.

He plunges into me. It's harder than I expected, but I missed him so fucking much that I don't care. He keeps thrusting, and my legs curl around his back, allowing him to take me deeper, but then the way he thrusts gets uncomfortable. Too fast and too hard before I'm ready.

When I try to pull free, he clenches my wrists harder. I try to wrench away but he holds me, his eyes dark. "Fuck, Ann. You have no idea how incredible your pussy feels."

I'm not a prude at all, but his language surprises me. He's never been crude with me before. Maybe I was rubbing off on him. *Who knew?* Instead of worrying about it, I close my eyes and concentrate on the kisses he's trailing along my neck. They aren't tender, but the sensation is erotic. And even though he didn't say it, I suspect he's slowing down because he realized he'd gotten too rough.

My Phantom.

He moves down so he can nibble my breasts. His scruff scratches my skin a little, but the feeling isn't unpleasant. In fact, it keeps me present. Keeps me from simply being lost in his touch. He sucks my breasts harder and harder, and now my body feels better prepared for his massive length. His teeth bite a little, and I gasp, instinctually trying to lift my hands, but his grip keeps me in place.

Lifting away from my breasts, he returns and kisses my mouth once more, hard, before thrusting inside of me once more. This time, he's even more intense than before as he pounds his body into mine. The sensation is a thin line between pleasure and pain, but I try to focus on the pleasure, to match his rhythm, but all I can do is hang on.

He plunges in an out until I'm on the edge, then he pinches one nipple as he sucks the other, and my body flies apart. My orgasm hits me so hard that my head is spinning, and I'm barely aware of who I am or where. But he's not done yet. He drives into me harder and deeper, faster and faster, until he finally grunts and comes. I feel his hot seed as it spills inside of me, and it feels perfect. Perfect that we both came. That we're together again.

After a moment, he lets go of my wrists, panting hard above me.

My wrists are sore, and my fingers feel a little numb, which surprises me. I hadn't realized how hard he was holding me, probably hard enough that his grip will leave bruises, which is unlike him. Not bad. But not like Phantom.

In fact, something just feels... off about our love making. He was rough. Too rough. In a strange way. My men aren't exactly delicate in bed, but none of them have left me feeling anything but satisfied. This time though, I feel sore.

I shake off the thoughts because although our sex was roughly passionate, that's all it was. Not cruel. Not unpleasant. It's like I'm trying to ruin a nice moment with crazy worries, and I'm not about to do that right now.

He rolls off of me to lie on his back, arm thrown over his eyes. It's unlike Phantom, who typically loves to cuddle after sex, but I imagine he's as overwhelmed by all of this as I am. Or maybe I'm making this all into a big deal because I was stupid enough to have sex with him before asking him all the questions that seem to be haunting me. Most women don't want to sleep with someone when they have a bunch of things stressing them out.

"Phantom." He shoots me a side eye, peeking at me beneath his arm, and I smile. "You said we misunderstood. But what did we get wrong?" Maybe it's the after-sex euphoria that makes me brave, but I want him to tell me that he's coming back, that he let his father take him so he could destroy him himself, but instead, he gives me a smile that's so creepy it actually makes my breath catch.

"All life on earth is meaningless, Ann."

"What?" *He didn't just say that.*

"Ann, think about it. We can have everything we ever wanted here." *Does he mean live in a world with pure darkness, no plants, and just a bunch of half-dead creatures running around in it? That's everything we ever wanted?* "You just have to stop caring about *there*." He leans up on his elbows and looks down at me. There's possession in his gaze, ownership, and my stomach clenches.

I won't be owned.

"Nothing can survive like that. Maybe us, but not the humans, the fae, the shifters... not all of them."

He shrugs. "They don't really matter."

Oh, hell...

"And what about your brothers? They're on earth. They've been fighting the king and his men. Are they really going to be safe here?" I have to ask. They're fighting so hard to get him back. He should know how important he is to them, what they're willing to do, to sacrifice, although,

I'm not sure it matters to him or that he's going to care. Not the man who's sitting in front of me right now.

"Dusk and the other two can come here. They can be safe as our servants." His smile gets creepier by the second. "All you have to do–each of you–is accept that this is how it's going to happen. That this is our new world, with my father ruling."

He's so confident, actually smug, that I can't believe he's the same man we've been so desperately trying to find and save. More than that, I can't believe I was so fooled when I woke up to think he was the Phantom I had fallen in love with. Because the real Phantom would not want both our worlds to be like this one. And the real Phantom would know that there's no way Dusk, Onyx, or Rayne would ever serve him.

Still, I'm here, with him alone, away from his father. There might be a way to get him to see the truth. He might not seem to care about his brother or earth, but I think he *might* care about me still. "I don't want that. I want the shadow king to fall, for us to save both our worlds, and for us all to be together as equals."

He shakes his head and then stops and looks at me. "I promise, you'll change your mind." His confidence levels up as does the overall creepiness of his smile. "I can be very persuasive."

Before I can figure out what he means or how he plans to try, he rolls out of the bed, pulls on his boxers, then goes to the door, opens it, and leaves. While I'm sitting up trying to figure what the hell just happened, I hear a click of metal sliding against metal, which my instinct screams is more than a door latch. It's a lock.

There's something so final about the sound my heart twists in response, but I try to ignore it. Wrapping a blanket around my body, I run to the door and pull at it with all the strength I have in my body... but it doesn't budge. It's heavy and solid, like a prison door.

Accepting that the door is useless, I go to the window and look out, hoping to find a quick escape. Throwing open the window, I look down far below and gasp. It's like one of those fairy tales with a woman locked in a tower, only, it's worse. Because it's not just that I'm high up, it's also that this place is a nightmare.

Below me is a moat. A moat with black water that stands still like a mirror. Except with no light in the sky and no light across the dark lands, it's like looking into the waters of hell rather than normal water. All around me is nothingness as far as I can see, with the exception of torches that line the walls that surround us and more torches that seem to be being carried by trolls as they walk the dark lands around me.

And beyond the gate? I swear... yes, there are shadow beasts. *Everywhere.* Pacing outside the walls around the castle like hellhounds.

It all hits me at once. I'm *in* the Void. In the shadow world. I remember using my light to help my men, and then the pain on the back of my head. But until now I stupidly didn't put it altogether.

Reaching behind me, I feel the lump. *Do I have a fucking concussion? Hell.*

Phantom kidnapped me, brought me here, and made love to me... no, it wasn't love making. It was hard and rough and left me sore, unlike what it's usually like with my men. I had sex with the ghost of Phantom. A creature that looks like him but isn't any more.

And then I let him lock me in here. A high tower with no escape.

A sob catches in the back of my throat and I press my hand to my mouth to keep from crying. I hate that I allowed myself to be taken, that I left behind my men who need my light to keep fighting our enemies. I'm so damn angry at myself for being so stupid, but more than that, I feel dirty and sick. I had sex with that... that thing. That cold, cruel man who saw nothing wrong with using me and throwing me away.

I don't know what to do, but I know right now I can't escape, can't communicate with my men, and can't reach Phantom to try to shake some sense into him. So, I do the only thing I can think of, the most useless thing I can do: I collapse onto the ground and cry big, ugly tears while I wish that I didn't smell like Phantom.

If only this was a fairy tale, then my wishes might come true.

EIGHT

Phantom

The land is dark and dead. It's a cause-and-effect relationship and one I can see for miles in every direction
beyond the top of the castle tower where I'm standing.
Without the moon stone, our lands are no longer just dim
enough for us to survive and for the unique plantation and
animals to survive. Now nothing but the animals that hover
between life and death can exist here.

Before, I would've despaired about the lands and the
death in and around this place. But quite honestly, I don't
feel anything except a thirst for more. More power. More
land. More respect. More everything. I feel it deeply.
Strongly. It vibrates through me like an insatiable hunger.
It's a desire so powerful I can feel it in every fiber of my
being, and I know that I'll never be satisfied until it's
quenched.

If it ever can be.

My gaze moves to the outside of the walls that surround
our castle and goes to our people. Well, what's left of them.
Right now, there's no need for the shadow beasts to join the

fight against my brother and the others. No, we were wasting too many of them when right now we simply need distractions and for the moon shards to be planted on earth. Things that can easily be left to the creatures whose numbers are almost limitless.

Which leaves the shadow beasts bored. Perhaps even more miserable than when they're forced to fight their brethren.

They're huddled together in their beast-forms, camped outside the castle walls in groups, waiting, prowling, probably tasting the battle in the air, wishing, hoping for a good kill, a brave death. Wishing to be the one in power. Wanting it for themselves.

Or maybe that's just me.

Actually, it's probably just me. The moment my father took control of the Moonstone, he took control of *them*. Unfortunately for my people, they're not mindless animals, they've just given up inside the forms that are now their prisons. My father said that at first they tried to fight for control once more, but with enough time, they realized it was pointless.

It'll always be pointless. They will never have willpower again. My father is confident of that. But then, he's confident in everything, never showing an ounce of uncertainty, and now I understand why. The way I am now, I only feel that hunger for power. There's no room for anything else.

As I stand at the top of the tower looking out, the Shadow King comes to stand beside me, surveying the same landscape I am. I felt him coming, but didn't react. Because, why bother?

He smiles as he stares around us. This is his realm. He's strong here and powerful. His word is law. And he wants to keep it that way. Despite what my brother and his little friends want to happen. They're weak without Ann and I am stronger than all of them.

I. Will. Win.

Yet, there's no true happiness in my father's smile. It's strange, like a ghost of the smile I saw on his face as a boy. The knowledge used to bring me pain, but it doesn't now. His long brown hair, almost black like my own, is left loose, although no breeze stirs the air or ruffles the strands. He wears dark clothes and a dark cloak on his shoulders at all times, even though the temperature here is perfect. Strangely, he's less kingly than when I was younger, but more fitting for what he's become now.

"How did things go with the woman?" His voice is gruff and hardened by years, and his smile fades away as he waits for my answer.

I don't want to disappoint him. Not because he's my father. Not because I particularly care what he thinks. But because he's my king and pleasing him is essential to staying alive. The need to prove myself worthy burns inside me, but I don't have news that he wants to hear.

I sigh. "She won't agree with our plan." But I don't look at him. I can't. I don't want to see the disappointment I know is bound to be there. It's a hard thing to disappoint my king.

"She will. In time." He's confident. As a king, confidence is his birthright.

"Is this what happened with Shenra?" It isn't that I care about her, the woman who was my first love. It's that I want to know the details I've never been told. Knowledge, after all, is its own kind of power.

"Shenra was killed because she was unwilling to behave as a king's wife. She was unwilling to *become* a king's wife."

He'd forced her to become his wife anyway, so that is a moot point, and I don't need the explanation, just an answer to what happened to her. I never saw her body once they told me she was dead. I suspected the body in the moat was hers, but suspecting and knowing are two different things.

All I know for certain is that when she failed to bring him the power he desired, the power he thought bonding with her would give him, he erased her. How he did that... I still don't know.

I don't point out that he took her from me because he's my king and whatever he wants of mine is his by right and by rule. For some reason, I can't even remember why I thought otherwise.

"If your woman can't be controlled, she will need to be handled." His tone leaves no room for argument, reminding me that it doesn't matter what happened to Shenra, just what happens from this point forward to lead to our victory.

"Yes." The agreement is easy. Automatic, even. If she isn't amenable to helping, to being an asset, she has no purpose and she will be destroyed.

And he won't have to tell me twice.

NINE

Ann

After throwing myself a bit of a pity party, I went back to work trying to figure out how to escape. The first order of business was to get dressed. I found a variety of medieval-looking women's dresses in a wardrobe and reluctantly pulled on the simplest dress, a sky-blue gown. Then, I drank a lot of water from a pitcher left beside my bed before finally taking a deep breath, readying myself.

My men are out there, still fighting our enemies, and they need me. They need me to get out of here and help them kick some ass, to keep them going when everything seems dark. To use my magic to defeat more enemies than their blades can handle.

So, every minute matters.

Besides, I know deep down Phantom can still be saved, even if he'd broken a part of my soul with our heartless sex, and in some ways over and over again since his father plunged the moon shard into his heart. But what he is right now isn't his fault, and I'll never be able to save him if I stay trapped in here.

So, escape it is!

Unfortunately, the doors are still locked and no matter how much shoulder I put into it, the damned thing isn't opening. It's thick wood, probably made of a couple thousand-year-old oak trees, if they even have trees like oak here. Maybe it's some other weird kind of wood I've never heard of. Either way, it isn't budging.

Giving up on it, I start to circle my room, trying to see if there are any tools I can use to help my escape. The ceiling is tall, at least twenty-feet, and the bed is large enough to sleep five men the size of Phantom, at least. Neither of which is helpful to me right now. On one wall there's a wardrobe and a dressing table, uniquely styled furniture I've never seen the likes of, with carvings of the moon and a woman's eyes. There's also a fireplace and two nightstands beside the bed.

A doorway leads to an empty closet and nothing but darkness. Yet another doorway leads to a large bathroom, which appears to have modern plumbing, although I'm sure it's different from the ones the humans and fae use. Not that I intend to rip up the plumbing.

At least not until I get truly desperate.

Nothing in the room is particularly helpful, so I go back to the window and stare out across the landscape, this time in less of a panic. I'm being logical, trying to put together a puzzle of how I can escape, and this might be the answer.

Maybe.

All I can really tell about where they're holding me is that I'm in a castle with a massive gate surrounding it that's covered in torches and patrolled by shadow beasts, and that there's a moat far beneath the balcony. The dark waters call to me, and I wonder how deep they are. *Can I survive jumping into it?* Suddenly, I remember that it's the same moat where the Shadow King's wife's body was found after she jumped or was thrown.

Probably where they're going to find my body, too.

A shiver rolls down my spine, even under the thick dress I'm wearing. Jumping into that moat *has* to be last resort. Because if it kills me, I'm no good to anyone. At least trapped in here I have a chance at getting out.

With a sigh, I look down at the moat again. *Maybe I could knot the sheets and use them to climb down?* But the distance is too much and I wouldn't be anywhere close to halfway to the ground before I'd run out of "rope." A jump like that would kill me. Even if I somehow managed to land in the moat and not on the spikes at its banks.

There has to be something I can do. An escape. This can't be how my life ends.

Leaning further and further outside the window, to the point where I'm being stupid, I spot a window almost directly below mine. It's still a far distance from where I am, but *that* I might be able to reach with bedsheets.

If they'll hold me.

Racing across the room, I remove all the bedding and get to work tying it together as tightly as I possibly can. It takes a ridiculously long time, but I'm not able to hurry knots that are going to keep me from falling to my death. Then I test them, pulling and yanking as hard as I can, but they hold.

Success!

I tie one end around the foot of the heavy bed, knotting it several times, then sit back and look at my creation. It's long enough, most definitely, but I've never tried to hold my whole weight with tied sheets and blankets.

Is this stupid? Am I going to get myself killed?

Pushing aside the worrying thoughts, I tell myself this is

better than just sitting here, that *anything* is better than that, but the sweat on my forehead says otherwise. My legs are shaking as I go to the window and toss my "rope" down.

Peering as far over the edge of the window as I can once more, I double check that it'll get me to the window. It reaches, but staring down at the deadly drop does *not* help my confidence. In fact, the fake confidence I was trying to cloak myself with has even left me.

Calm down. Focus. This is the only plan you have.

"You can do this. You have to do this. For your men." I repeat the words over and over to myself until I feel calmer.

Then, before I can spiral again, I grab the sheet and take a deep breath. Part of me wants to look down again, but I don't. I just sit on the window ledge, my heart racing, and turn and start to lower myself down. It's strange, falling back into nothing. No, not strange, *terrifying*. It's terrifying to trust that I won't just fall and fall until I die, but I do it. I force myself into action.

My hands clench the sheet, and my feet scramble for purchase against the castle wall. Luckily, the big stones allow for a foothold between blocks, and then I feel a little less at the mercy of the sheets.

Which is exactly the moment the world seems to drop around me.

I'm falling. The sheet is falling. And it's by pure luck that my hands claw at the wall of the stone and catch. Then, I'm just clinging onto the wall, barely holding on. I feel the sheets and blankets strike my back as they fall all the way down, and I look to see them hit the moat and disappear into the dark waters.

This was a mistake. A terrible fucking mistake.

I'm sweaty, breathing hard, feeling terrified out of my mind. But the terror slowly clears enough for me to think, to realize that I can't stay like this forever. Already I'm tiring. I look down again and realize the window below me is far too far down from where I am. The crevices between the stones aren't trustworthy enough to work as a safe ladder. Above me, I just have to make it a short distance... a distance I'm not even sure I can manage, so there's no way in hell I can make it down.

It's a terrible feeling. That I might die right here, leaving my men to a terrible fate. That I made the wrong choice and it's going to end this way.

But even though I feel tears sliding down my cheeks, I slowly release one hand and reach up, running my fingers along the next crevice until I find a place that I think I can hold onto. I do that with my feet and with my other hand, lifting myself up higher and higher. Not able to focus on anything but that next secure spot.

When I reach the window, I barely notice until I've pushed myself up into that room and rolled myself onto the floor. There, I lie for the longest time, tears sliding down my face. My body is so tense and painful from being so scared, from climbing like that on the side of a building, that I feel like I just had another big battle.

What the fuck am I doing?

If I'd been faster earlier, I could've escaped out the door before Phantom had even had time to realize what had happened. But I'd been a fool. Too consumed with what I wanted to accept what was clearly right in front of my face.

I should've known when I woke up with Phantom that something was wrong. I should've remembered how I came to be here from the woods. If I didn't know things weren't right then, certainly I should've known when he used his body like a battering ram into mine.

He isn't the man who'd been taken from us. He looks

like him, sounds like him, even felt like him when I laid in his arms, but this version of Phantom is lacking the kindness, the care, the civility of the one I know.

And because I wanted him to be that man, I'm locked in a tower, useless to everyone I love.

It's a mistake I can't repeat.

If he enters my room again, I need to treat him like an enemy. I need to use whatever I can to escape, even if it means hurting him. Because if I hurt him to escape, he'll survive, and I can help the others come up with a way to free him. But, trapped here, I'm useless to everyone.

Damn it. I curl my hands into fists. *How can I possibly see Phantom as the enemy?*

A small voice whispers in my mind, *You don't have any other choice.*

TEN

Dusk

TODAY IS A FUCKING NIGHTMARE. Without Ann, there's just no goodness. It's like without our mate, we're already dead, and I hate the feeling. I hate it because it's *pathetic*. All I can do is stare at the fire and the soup cooking, gritting my teeth against the pain and wishing I had the ability to tear the world apart and find my mate.

But I can't.

The night before, we'd thought the battle was over. We'd thought we'd taken down all of our enemies. Ann's light disappeared, and then we were attacked by four grave trolls and dozens of rot monkeys. It was a lot given how worn down we were, and we didn't do our best. In fact, Onyx and I barely survived.

Only to discover from Rayne that Ann was gone, leaving behind nothing except the pouch of moon shards she held onto for us and her dagger. Still, we searched the area, hoping she got into trouble and hid. Or that whoever took her hadn't made it into the Void yet.

Even though the thread of hope we were clinging to was foolish.

We'd searched through the night and into the morning, when we should've been asleep and hiding from the roaming rot monkeys, but it was of no use. There was only one place she could be now. And it was the most dangerous place for us. A place completely controlled by our father and Phantom. A place teeming with dangerous creatures and with very little cover to conceal us should we try to infiltrate it.

But that's where she is.

So that's where we need to go.

My gaze meets Onyx's as he sits, carving wood into sharp points, the only thing he can do right now with his injured leg. He drops his tools with obvious frustration and begins to sign, "He probably has her in the castle."

I nod, then notice Rayne frowning, and I realize he probably doesn't know the sign for castle, so I sign as I explain, "Phantom has probably put Ann in his castle. That's what Onyx was saying, and I agree, that's the most logical place."

"And you're all sure," he begins then swallows, staring down at his hands for a moment, "he didn't just kill her."

Fuck. Is that why he's been so grim? Why he was demanding we go to the Void when we were all exhausted and injured?

"She has no value to him dead. They still believe in the prophecy," I explain slowly while signing.

Rayne looks relieved. At least a little bit. "But we still need to go there next. Right?" His gaze catches mine. "The sooner the better?"

I wince. Yes, that's where we should be going next. Where we should have gone already. The thing is, I don't think I can, and I *know* Onyx can't. Not without a little more time to rest. Rot monkeys had attacked my legs, leaving open wounds that are slowly healing, but painful even to shift. And a grave troll had punched me fucking hard. His big meaty fist had struck me in the chest and shoulder, leaving my body aching so badly that I don't think I could pick up a sword if my life depended on it. Without a doubt a rib is broken, probably more given my black-and-blue skin.

And I'm in better condition than Onyx. A grave troll had managed to kick him in the leg so hard that I'm sure it's broken. He'd strapped a branch to it, but the pain in his face is visible in everything he does. Even when he isn't moving, he looks miserable.

Without Ann's healing light, we need a day, at least, to get into fighting form. Shadow beasts heal quickly, but after so many days of fighting with almost no rest, our bodies are struggling to heal our old wounds along with our new ones.

If we go to the shadow realm like this, I have no doubt we'll be picked off so fast that Ann will never be saved. It kills me to know that, to accept that we are that weak, but it doesn't change the fact that it's true.

"You can't make it there, can you?" Rayne asks.

I don't want to fucking say it. "Tomorrow, perhaps."

Rayne doesn't say more, just looks away, and then we all get to work doing what we can to prepare to move to another location, but the tension in our camp is like another beast. It's impossible to ignore, so overwhelming that it isn't just my pain that makes it hard to breathe.

When our soup is ready, we all sit and eat in silence around the fire. I'm waiting, for what I don't know, maybe for Rayne to demand we pull ourselves together for our mate. But if I thought that was possible, I would have done it already.

He has to know that.

Suddenly, I sense movement outside of our little cave. I'm on my feet in an instant, sword in hand. My head spins a little, but I see that Onyx is on his feet too, swaying with his dagger held out before him. Rayne sees us, and after a second of confusion, he is standing too. We all stare at the cave entrance. I have a million thoughts running through my head, but the most pressing one is that none of our enemies should be able to attack during the day.

Could it be Ann?

Who else could it be?

Imara suddenly appears in the opening of our cave, looking filthy and exhausted. We lower our weapons, and Onyx collapses back onto the ground without a word. But I just stare in shock. When the battle with our father happened, and we were betrayed, I hadn't thought to look for the only female shadow beast among us. I just assumed she'd died or left with everyone else. And I'm so fucking angry with myself for not checking.

I failed the elder. Then Ann. Now Imara. I'm such a fucking mess.

"Are you okay?" I ask her, even though the second the question leaves my mouth I want to take it back.

She nods, moves to our fire, and sits down beside it, filling a bowl with our soup. Without speaking, she simply eats for a long time. Rayne looks at me in confusion, but I just nod, and then we're all sitting.

If she'd gone with the others, she'd be trapped in her beast form. The fact that she isn't means she didn't betray us. Anything beyond that we could figure out, after she feeds and rests.

She finishes her bowl in record time, drains a water pouch, then wipes off her mouth with the back of her hand, smearing the dirt on her face. Her dark eyes meet mine, and then she says, "The Void is spreading."

"No," I say. "We've been diligent. We haven't let them spread the shards..."

"On the other side, over the canyon."

Hell. "What would that even...? Why would they do that? They can't use that space."

If they came out of the Void above the canyon, they'd fall to their deaths, and expanding it as it hovers above the canyon couldn't have been an easy thing to do. They'd have to work a hell of a lot harder than expanding it here, and it'd only be useful when they made it to the other side and could expand onto the land there.

Or maybe they'd just kill everything in the canyon and expand their realm there. *Fuck. Maybe they don't even care about how usable the land is.*

"There's no stopping this," she continues, pushing her dark hair back from her face and looking around at all of us. "I thought maybe there was a way... but there isn't."

Onyx begins to sign, his face pinched in pain. "We'll find a way."

She shakes her head. "Perhaps you will, but I will not."

"Imara–"

She lifts a hand. "I have fought and fought. I have held out hope. But there is no more hope within me. I am going to the human towns and lands. I will find a way to have some peace before everything ends."

Rayne laughs and shakes his head. "Are you fucking kidding me? You're just going to let the world end?"

Her angry gaze pierces his. "My world already ended. I'm letting your world end now too." He looks like he wants to say more, but she turns back to me. "Your brother was taken?"

I nod, not knowing what else to say.

"Then *if* you defeat them, you will be king, and I hope this time you won't show any of our enemies mercy."

It's like a knife twisting in my gut. A reminder that I failed my people and caused all of this. "I won't make that mistake again."

"Even with your brother?" Her tone leaves no room for argument.

But I won't hurt him unless I have to. "I'll do what needs to be done."

She nods and rises. "I would suggest you all leave with me now."

"Imara—"

"Although I already know you won't." She tilts her head and studies the three of us. "May the Moon Goddess protect you."

"May the Moon Goddess protect you," I say, and then she turns and heads out of the cave, disappearing from view.

"So, she just came to tell us to fuck off?" Rayne asks in shock.

I shake my head. "She's a warrior. If I'd told her to stay, she would have. She came here to see if whoever was in charge would let her go, so she could leave honorably, and to warn us about the Void."

"Why didn't you tell her to stay? We need the help." Rayne sounds annoyed and I don't blame him. He doesn't know our ways. He doesn't realize that after all she's given to us, I would not be the one to tell her to spend her final days fighting for a cause she's already given so much to.

"It was her choice," is all I manage, and then that hollow emptiness where Ann holds my heart echoes inside of me, and I want to sleep and... I don't know what. But I want to do anything but keep feeling this empty and lost.

My words are met with silence, and then Rayne says, "And it's my choice too to go to the shadow realm today and try to get Phantom and Ann back."

I jerk my head to look at him in shock. "Rayne, you need us by your side. That world is too dangerous for you alone."

He glances between me and Onyx. "You need more time to heal. I don't. Besides, it'd be easier for me to go unnoticed if I go in alone."

Onyx frowns and begins to sign. "The fae is too soft. He won't survive there. We need to serve as a distraction so that he can take over the king and bring Phantom back to us, then rescue Ann."

Rayne must have understood most of what Onyx said, because he looks annoyed. "I'm not soft. I'm just different from the two of you. I spent a lot of my life alone, hiding, and know ways to go unnoticed. I know that I might not be able to fight the shadow beasts or the king, but I think I can stay unseen."

"And what if you can't?" I ask.

The fae gives a sharp nod. "I can."

Onyx signs angrily. "We're just going to lose him too. This needs to be planned out better. We need to be able to shadow him. There's no reason for us to stay here without Ann. One more day, that's all we need."

"I can't give you one more day," Rayne says softly, signing as he does. "One more day might be too late, for Ann, and for this world. We certainly can't fight them off if they attack again tonight, and I'm not willing to gamble any longer on Ann's life." He draws himself up taller. "When I said I was going today, I meant it. I'm not asking for permission, I'm telling you."

Onyx and I exchange a look. This is the kind of stuff that Phantom usually handles. The kind of stuff I handle wrong. But from the expression on Onyx's face, he's thinking the same thing I am... that we just have to let Rayne do this.

"Alright," I tell him. "But give us a few minutes to at least prepare you the most we can."

He agrees, and so that's what we do. Onyx works on a map. I explain to Rayne about our world, the creatures, the plants, and how to find our castle. He asks questions about where to find our father and the best places to hide Adrik's body when he becomes a ghost once more, and I do my best to explain things clearly to him. Even though I'm still not sure this is a good idea.

And then, that's all there is to say.

Onyx hands Rayne his map and Rayne holds it up in the tight roll, his expression a bit lost for the briefest moment, like he doesn't know what to say or do. Or maybe it's something more than that.

I look at both of them, and the words slip out, even though I wish I held them back. "Are you sure you want to do this?"

Wants don't matter so much right now, but if he changed his mind, I won't blame him. But we all know Rayne isn't about to change his mind. Ann is in there and he's going to get her back or die trying. And that's the part that worries me. But I don't say it.

"It's the best option we have."

He's right. I know it. But the apprehension in my gut is churning into a frenzy and bile rises in my throat. I swallow it back down, but the worry remains. Rayne is a good man, and while I'd risk my life for anyone I care for, I hate the idea of him risking his life for us.

But it's not just for us, it's for Ann.

Onyx reaches to hug him first and they hang on for an extra second, which is strangely nice to see. We have a bond, thanks to Ann. Thanks to all we've been through together.

When they part, I pull Rayne in for my own hug. "Protect yourself." He nods. "And her."

He smiles like he doesn't fear anything. "Always." He unrolls the map, glances down at it, then back at us before he salutes us. We salute him back, even though it feels silly, and then he turns and heads out of the cave, in the direction of the Void.

I swear neither Onyx nor I breathe until he's out of sight, but then my breath comes out in a rush. The Void was our home. Now, it's only a place of nightmares with death lurking around every corner. I still miss my home, but I don't envy Rayne right now.

Onyx stares at me for a second then signs, "You think he has a chance?"

I don't answer, because the answer wouldn't comfort either of us. But no, I don't think he has much of a chance at all.

ELEVEN

Ann

I've come to accept the only way I'm leaving this room is through that door, the *only* door out in my pretty cell. The window is pretty much certain death, so I sit on the edge of the bed, willing Phantom to return, no matter how much seeing him will tear out my heart. Because at this point just about anything is better than continuing to sit here like some damsel in distress.

Come on door, open... open.

I hear scraping outside my door, and it suddenly opens. I jump a little, heart hammering. For a brief moment I think my mind opened the damn thing, and then Phantom steps out of the darkness and into my room with all the grace of a king. He's wearing dark clothes, so much like his father's that it makes my stomach twist just to see. The only difference between him and his father is that rather than wearing a cloak, Phantom wears black fur on his shoulders and over part of his chest, reminding me of human Vikings from so long ago rather than these mystical shadow beasts. And I hate, absolutely hate, that he still looks so damned handsome, even while humming with his father's evil control.

It makes me sad, so much so I don't know if I can hide the way I feel even though I know I need to. Because one thing is for sure, I don't want him to see how I feel or how he affects me. I don't trust him. And it feels like any information, even my feelings, is information I don't want him to have.

His deep green eyes run over me from head to toe in a way that feels strangely possessive. "I see you found the dresses."

"I did, although I'd prefer my old clothes," I tell him, drawing myself up taller.

The thing is, after living in the woods for this long, my bar for what makes a decent outfit is pretty low. Anything clean seems to be good enough. Still, this dress is kind of ridiculous. It's long and simple, bright green and nearly the same color as Phantom's eyes, yet strangely form fitting until it flairs at my hips. So, basically, a pretty dress I can't easily fight in... or run in. And these shadow beasts seem to do enough of both that dresses seem like a waste of fabric.

"You're breathtaking," he tells me, but his words leave me feeling... empty.

It used to be that when he complimented me, there was a glimmer in his eyes that warmed my heart and made me feel alive. Now, his eyes are dead of all emotion and this all feels like an act. Like there's nothing left of the Phantom I love. Even though I pray that isn't the case.

"Instead of dinner in your room, would you like to accompany me to the dining hall?" he asks, his gaze trained on my face like he's carefully reading my reaction. And I'm kind of glad he's focused on me, because then he won't notice the bed that's missing all its linen.

Every muscle in my body stiffens. For some reason, I want to say no. I want to back away from this ghost of Phantom and forget all I've lost. But getting out of this room is my only chance for escape, so telling him no would be stupid. This is the chance I've been waiting for. And maybe if I play the part of a happy prisoner, he'll let his guard down, and I can escape and get back to the others.

Then come up with a real plan to save him and my world.

"That sounds perfect." I flash him my best smile, the one he used to love, and he takes my hand and brings my wrist to his lips, kissing the bruises softly. The ones he left behind on me.

Which feels... ominous, for some reason.

He puts my hand on his arm and leads me out of the room and down a circling staircase that seems to go on forever. And if I thought my room was cold and empty, it's nothing in comparison to this castle. The walls are dark grey stone on the inside, but they seem impossibly dark. Maybe because of how far apart the torches are on the walls, or how dimly they light the staircase. I can't tell for certain, but a frigid cold rolls off the stone so intensely that I can almost see it.

Like ghosts, haunting the empty castle. And after Rayne, I'd honestly be surprised if this place isn't haunted, since so many people have lost their lives here unjustly. It's a ripe location for the restless undead. Which is *not* what I should be thinking about right now.

We finally come to the end of the staircase, and my gaze darts in all directions around me, trying to memorize everything to help with my escape. One hall seems to lead to the outside, although I'm not entirely sure it does because it's just a dark doorway that seems to lead to nothing. He takes me past it though, and the halls widen until it feels like I'm walking through a castle rather than my prison.

Even if it's still my prison.

He stops us in front of two massive doors, and rot monkeys spring past us down the hall, opening the doors like creepy butlers. The oily black creatures regard me with tilted heads as we walk past them, their red eyes gleaming. A shiver rolls down my spine, and I dart my gaze away and to where we're going. Which is into a huge dining hall.

The place is strange. I bet at one time it was even beautiful. It reminds me of some of the oldest fae castles, with nods to medieval times: lots of stone, huge fireplaces, and silky fabric draping from the ceiling in the corners. But in this place, it's black material, a shade darker than the stone, but still not enough to brighten the place. Torches line the walls and both fireplaces are blazing, yet the flames do little to chase away the overwhelming sense of wrongness here. Of misery.

Phantom tugs on my arm, and I realize I was staring. "It's beautiful, isn't it?"

"It is," I lie.

Someone walks past us, and I stiffen when I realize it's the king, his dark cloak practically floating behind him. He moves to the far end of the table and sits at the head. A rot monkey is there in an instant, placing a glass onto the table in front of him with some sort of liquid in a glass. It could be a brownish-red wine with tannins floating in the cup or it could be water that desperately needs to be filtered. I don't know, and I'm not sure if I want to.

Phantom pulls out a chair for me beside his father, and I have to force myself not to flinch away from the horrible man. The man whose selfishness created all of this, who stole the Moonstone from the sky, who enslaved and hunted his people.

Who took Phantom from me.

He gives me a cold look as Phantom pushes my chair in. "Are you enjoying my world?"

I want to tell him to fuck off, but I manage, "Yes." It's not a great answer, but it's the best I can give.

"It's an incredible place, more than any other, and soon earth will be the same." He sounds pleased with himself. I eye my fork and wonder if these two could stop me before I put it through his eye.

Phantom pours my glass of... dirty-looking wine from a pitcher at the center of the table. I look, but I don't touch the brownish liquid. It seems to be the rule of thumb here to treat everything with caution. A rule I plan to stick to as much as I can. In fact, I'm going to check the water in my room again, if I have to go back there, because now I'm hoping like hell I didn't miss anything with something gross floating in it.

Ugh.

Phantom takes the chair beside me, then looks up at his father expectantly. It's weird, sitting between two people who don't feel like people. Who don't seem to radiate any kind of emotion. It's not quite... evil, just unsettling, even though I know the Shadow King is evil down to his core.

Sad, but evil.

"I trust you're finding your accommodations suitable?" his father asks, but it, too, is an act. He's no more interested in me or my comfort than I am in him or his. I want him dead. And he either wants the same for me, or doesn't give a shit about me. Either way, none of this is sincere.

But I can play this game. "They're lovely, thank you." *There.*

A side door swings open and a rot monkey comes out carrying two plates, followed by another monkey carrying a third plate. The stench of the monkeys comes a moment before they're close to our table, and I wrinkle my nose, resisting the urge to vomit. And by resist, I mean that I swallow the bile in my throat so it doesn't make this dinner any worse than it already is.

The king is served his food first, but doesn't seem to notice their strong scent. If anything, I think he might be pleased... you know, if he can feel pleased at all.

A monkey smiles at me as it climbs onto the back of my chair. No, it doesn't *smile* exactly, it flashes me its sharp teeth and then drops my food in front of me, his long, sharp nails clicking against the surface of the table as he does so. I jerk my gaze away from the filthy, stinking creature and look down at what I've been served.

Mistake.

The plate has slime on the edge, a dark brown slime that seems to be leaking off of the grey meat on the plate. *Grey meat? What the hell has grey meat? And what's left to eat here besides grave trolls, rot monkeys, and shadow beats?* Hungry as I am, I have standards and I would rather starve than eat anything prepared or served by such a vile creature.

Even if my stomach feels like it's going to cave in...

Both men begin to eat the meat, and I have to turn away or risk vomiting. There's no way that food tastes good. Food made by dirty rot monkeys from a world with almost no life. If I watch them putting that in their mouths... hell, I have to stop thinking about it.

A clank makes me turn my head back to the meal. The king has let his fork drop onto the table, and when he sees I'm looking at him, he folds his hands over his slender stomach. "You're not hungry?" He looks at Phantom, as if he's accusing him of sneaking me food, then back at me. "Rot monkeys are like any other creatures on this earth. They simply don't hide their vices... their desire for death and darkness. But, I assure you, what they make is quite sanitary." His grin is every bit as odious as his enslaved critters.

"If you say so," is all I can manage.

Instead of responding with anger, he throws his head back and laughs cruelly. "That's exactly it, Ann. It's as I say so."

Wow. Ego overinflated much?

I stare at my food as my stomach growls miserably.

"It's not earth food, but if you don't eat, you die," Phantom tells me softly.

I look at him, hoping to see concern or any sign he cares, but his face is blank. I realize he isn't trying to comfort me; he's just telling me facts. And as much as I want to yell at him and say to go screw himself, I realize he's right. If I don't eat here, how the hell will I have the strength to escape?

So, I eat, trying not to taste the grey meat as much as I can. It's not pleasant by any means, but it's not vomit-inducing. I take small bites, forcing myself to keep going until I've eaten as much of it as I can stand.

The king watches my every bite. "So, do all fae have the same powers?"

An alarm goes off in my head. One that says to proceed with caution. "No. We're all different."

I glance at him out of the corner of my eye. His expression is calculating. "Can others use their... light the way you do?"

"I'm not sure," I respond. The truth is, I'm not. I've never seen anyone use light this way before, but it doesn't mean it's impossible.

"And is it useful for anything else?" He leans a little closer as he asks the question, and I hate having him in my space.

"Not that I'm aware of," I say, not meeting his gaze.

"It can heal and kill," Phantom adds.

Super helpful.

The Shadow King makes a sound, like he's thinking. "Perhaps we should have Ann try her light in our dark world... see what it can do."

"Whatever my king wishes," Phantom says with a nod.

I'd call him a kiss ass, you know, if he wasn't being controlled by this monster against his will. If I didn't think deep inside the Phantom I love is still there. Yet, I'm careful, because this Phantom is his king's puppet.

"Maybe another time."

The king looks pissed, but then his expression relaxes and he sighs. "I guess you're inevitably waiting to help me until you get what you want. But not to worry, Ann, you'll be my queen soon."

Queen? Is that what he thinks I want? I stare at him. *When Phantom made love to me, was it part of this plan? I don't understand. What game are these two playing?*

Phantom turns to his king. "I thought since I had had her first you wanted our powers to unite, because you didn't want to risk angering the goddess by taking her after your son."

The king shrugs. "There are exceptions to that rule."

Exceptions like killing Phantom so that he can take me? Yeah, I bet. "Does that involve removing Phantom from the equation?"

"If it does, Phantom won't mind. Will you, son?" The king dares me with his eyes, even while he speaks to the man I love.

"Whatever my king wants," Phantom says, his response almost robotic.

It takes everything in me not to punch the Shadow King right in the face. "Why exactly do you want to marry me?" My question drips with anger.

He smirks. "You know why. The prophecy, of course." And then he takes another sip of his gross wine-stuff. "After the final battle, before I enslave your world and your men, we will wed, and all will be as prophesied by the shadows."

"You're going to bring me to the battle?" And I hate that even I hear the hope in my voice. Because that's what I'm focusing on—getting free and getting somewhere I can help my men, not the whole end of my world and the people I love thing.

He laughs. "So you can use your powers against me? No. But after everything is set into place and your powers can only be used to help me? Yes."

I look at Phantom, hating that he seems to lack all response. All awareness that everything the king seems to be planning relies on Phantom being dead.

How is it that Phantom can't see it? The king clearly has no intention of sharing power with anyone and that means Phantom isn't safe. *Could that shard in his heart really stop him from even seeing the most basic truth, that the king is using him for something and will throw him away when he's done with him?*

"Well." The king clears his throat, pushing back from the table. "We shall talk more. Another time."

I can't let this happen. I have to do something.

Suddenly, I spring to my feet. "*Actually,* I can show you my powers, if you like."

The king slowly lowers back into his chair and gestures

for me to go, and I hate that he seems pleased with himself. Like some cat licking its milk.

But I'm going to wipe that look right off of his smug, asshole face.

I smile, then hold out my hands, calling the goddess's power. My hands begin to glow brighter and brighter, and then as light begins to radiate from them, I point them at the king. He begins to brighten like lava, to turn to ash, just as he had before. It's so fucking satisfying to watch him dying in front of me, to know this is all about to end, that I'm swelling with happiness.

And then, I'm slammed to the ground.

I try to gasp in a breath, but the heavy body on top of me makes it impossible. Looking up, I see Phantom above me and his face is cold. "Try hurting my king again, and I'll remove your hands."

No, Phantom, I'm helping us! I'm saving you! I silently beg him as the need for air builds.

The king speaks. "Release her, son."

Phantom climbs off of me then offers me his hand as I'm sucking in breaths. I don't take it, so he grabs my hand and yanks me to my feet far too roughly. Before I even know what's happening, I'm shoved back into my chair.

"Bastard," I manage to gasp.

The king laughs, his face slowly returning back to normal until there's no evidence of my attack. "You, Ann, are powerful but stupid. Doing exactly what I expect of you at all times. It must have been pure luck that it took me this long to capture you at all."

He pushes back from the table and leaves as if he's dismissing us. His monkeys follow him in a rush, racing ahead of him to open the doors before he reaches them.

What the fuck just happened?

"You'll never defeat him, Ann. Save yourself some time and stop trying."

I look at my Phantom and my heart breaks. "Never." *I'm never giving up on you, no matter how hard it is to see how little of you is left.*

"Eventually, you'll learn," he says, then stares at the wall, his eyes vacant. "Are you finished eating?"

"Yes." I push the plate away and watch him for a second, remembering how it was before. Desperately wanting to see something in this man that reminds me of the person I loved so much. "I wonder how Onyx and Dusk are doing." He's never asked about them, but it occurs to me that maybe even if I'm not able to bring back the old Phantom, mentioning them might remind him of who he is. *Maybe.* "Don't you miss them?"

He shakes his head and shrugs like the time before he came here doesn't matter. "No." To Him the answer is simple. To me, it's heartbreaking. "Onyx and Dusk no longer hold value to me. I don't need their protection. All I desire now is their service."

I want him to be the man I knew so badly. And my hope is dying. "What about me? Do you still have feelings for me?"

There's a second of hope when he doesn't answer automatically, when he tilts his head and studies me. And then he dashes it with, "No," followed by another shrug like the words don't matter. "But I want to see what happens with the prophecy. And I want to see how you might be able to help my king."

"And you noticed he didn't answer about sharing power with you? Doesn't that make you nervous? And the way he spoke, it's like he's already decided he'll kill you."

Phantom pushes away from the table. "Whatever my king desires. Now, it's time to go back in your room."

It isn't my room, but I don't correct him. For some reason, I'm exhausted, and I want to save my strength for more than just arguing. Perhaps even escaping, if I find the right opportunity. Because who the hell knows how many chances I'll get to leave that room?

We take a different route back to the stairs. It isn't dark or as dank as the last one, but it's long and our footsteps echo off the walls. I don't know why he's taking me this way, maybe to confuse me, maybe because it's more convenient and he doesn't give two shits about whether it's a longer walk for me, but I don't care. I'm busy trying to remember everything I see, trying to figure out where I am, and trying to see if there's any opportunity for escape.

I glance to my side as we pass another hall. There's a door. It's big and probably heavy by the looks of it, definitely larger than what I'd expect to be used for another door inside. As I move slowly, peering down the dark hall, I realize it's opened a crack, and I think I can see the light from a torch from the wall outside. Which means it could lead to an escape. *If* I'm right.

This is my chance. Phantom is right ahead of me, not looking back, probably not expecting me to try anything. We're about to pass the hall, and then my chance to get back to Onyx, Rayne, and Dusk will be over.

Not giving it another thought, I take two steps and run harder than I've ever run before. So hard that it feels like my heart is instantly pumping as fast as my legs are, and the sound of my footfalls fill my ears.

When I get to the door, it is open wide enough I can squeeze through. Immediately, darkness surrounds me other than the light in the distance. I give my eyes one second to adjust because I don't want to fall into the moat, and then I keep running. I feel relieved when I feel wood beneath my feet and realize I'm crossing the moat, heading for the other side.

When I reach the other side, I look in both directions frantically looking for an escape and see the torches lining the massive stone fence on both sides of me. But more than that... I see a hoard of shadow beasts moving toward me from each direction. My instinct is to run, but there's nowhere to go. Just the moat, the fence I couldn't climb if I had all day, the castle behind me, and the shadow beasts to both sides.

No wonder Phantom didn't try to stop me.

My heart pounds in my ears and my feet are rooted to the ground. *This was pointless.* Even if I use my light, one of them will make it to me, and then it's over.

Growls rise up from all around me, and I know it, I know I'm about to be torn to shreds. Heart hammering, I move back toward the door. I'm half-crouching, ready to fight, even though I'm hoping it won't come to that. Maybe, just maybe, I can go back the way I came and find a less well-guarded exit.

Unlikely, but possible.

When I turn, Phantom is standing with his hands in his pockets, shoulder leaned against the doorframe. *Was he going to just stand there and watch them feast on me?* That's how it looks anyway. Although, I was brought here for a purpose, so maybe he would've called off his creatures.

But I'll never know because when I get close enough, he yanks me inside and shuts the door behind us, trapping me in the shadowy castle once more.

TWELVE

Onyx

We'd barely had time to sleep and heal, at least to the point where every moment wasn't pure agony, when they came. The rot monkeys. They'd poured out of the Void in a miles' long stream, suggesting that whatever final play the Shadow King planned, it was coming for us. I cut down as many as I could from one side. Dusk did the same beside me. But there were so many. Too many of them. And as the hours passed, we tired.

The night is long and full of death and darkness. Endless. Overwhelming. The thoughts haunted me as I fought until at last the monkeys slowed.

But if I thought that was the end of this night of fighting, I was wrong.

I'm engaged in battle with an aggressive grave troll right now. He's slower than the rot monkeys, which is usually my main advantage against their larger size, but tonight I'm slow too. I'm standing on a leg that moved past the aching stage and into sharp pain a few hours ago.

Trying to adjust my weight from my leg, I look away

from the troll for the briefest moment. He attacks faster than I thought possible, slicing my arm from shoulder to elbow. Blood pours out, running down my arm and painting the ground.

The pain is unbearable, but when the troll tries to severe my head from my shoulders with his sword, I manage to slip to the side and slice off his head before stumbling back, nearly crumbing to the ground.

My gaze catches Dusk's and his eyes widen. He finishes off the troll in front of him with a reckless move that was either going to kill the troll or get him killed, but he's making his way toward me. There's concern in his expression as he moves away from the Void. It's obvious that he knows what I've already come to accept.

We're losing. We can't keep going.

The smell of my blood attracts more of the damn rot monkeys, for some fucking reason. Probably hunger, the disgusting creatures, and I have to steady myself, to ignore the way the world tilts around me if I don't want them feeding on me. I fight off as many as I can, with my sword swinging wildly around me with my good arm, before I have to retreat because for every one I beat back, two come from the Void at me.

Dusk is suddenly there, stomping on the last few rot monkeys near me. Then, he takes something, lights it on fire, a fire that grows rapidly, and throws it toward the Void. It explodes into a sea of light, embers, and ash, and the rot monkeys race toward it.

"It's over," Dusk signs to me, then grabs my good arm and starts to run away with me. I think he's guiding me at first, but then I'm leaning harder and harder on him until he's almost carrying me. My sword drops. He stops and picks it up, then keeps going. The world around me is dark, darker than the night.

We make it into a cave, but my head is spinning so hard I don't recognize it. Dusk helps me around the corner, into the darkness, and then we're going down, clumsily. He stops and pushes me against the wall, before he leaves me. Unexpectedly, I fall and then just lie on the dirt, feeling lost and confused.

Then, light blazes to life and Dusk is standing over me. I watch him as he rolls a stone over the entrance, and then he puts down the torch beside me and signs, "You're going to be okay."

I want to say that I'm not sure, but my arms aren't working. He manages to get me back on his shoulder and grabs the torch with his free hand. From there, he drags me further and further down a tunnel until we come to a small cave underground. We've stayed here before. When, I can't remember, but he sets me down and builds a fire in the center of the cave, using the wood we always try to leave for emergencies.

Normally, I'd be helping him right now. But I try not to move, try to save my strength for what will be needed next. My mind goes to my sweet Ann, and I try to pull my thoughts away but fail. I miss my mate. I miss us being a team. Without her, I don't have anyone to heal me, and pain burns up and down my arm. Without her, it feels like I have nothing.

Nothing but the hope of getting her and Phantom back.

The light from the fire grows until Dusk moves away from it and looks back at me. His expression as his gaze runs over me is grim, but when he catches me staring, his face goes blank. He moves closer, kneels down, and studies my wound for a moment before pulling out his water and pouring it over my arm.

I'm pretty sure I hiss. I can't hear the sound, but my mouth forms it. Dots form in front of my vision, and I realize I'm taking rapid breaths, breaths that could lead me into a panic, so I force myself to breathe slower. It's a trick all soldiers learn and one I know I'll need to use if I'm going to get through what's going to happen next.

The water stops. Dusk stares down, then signs, "I can sew that up." He reaches for his bag and pulls out a medical pack.

He's not as gentle as Ann's light would be stitching up my wound, but it's better than bleeding out, so I don't complain. And he's talking like I can hear him, rambling like he does, at least according to the movement of his lips. But I'm not really focusing on the words his mouth is forming while I put all my effort into not punching him while he stitches me up.

At last, he finishes, and I collapse back. *Okay, alright. We're safe, for now. The shadow creatures are running wild on earth, but at least we're safe.* So, I turn back and focus on Dusk's rapidly moving mouth as he washes his hands.

"So that basically means we can't keep going like this. We need to focus on staying alive to help the others. But how? What's the best way? I mean, Ann should be safe because of the prophecy, but I'm worried about Rayne. Should we go in after him?" He shakes his head but continues speaking. "But if we leave now, no matter what comes through the Void, no one will be there to stop it. Yet, Rayne had no real idea what he'd face in the shadow realm... What if he doesn't make it back?"

Not surprising. Dusk has a soft heart. He likes to pretend he's as tough as Phantom, but in many ways he's gentler. I imagine he's wrestling with letting Rayne take this risk as much as I am. We are not people accustomed to other people fighting our battles for us, but as much as it pains me to admit it, we're needed here right now more than we're needed with Rayne. His is a task best left for one person who can slip in and out, and we're better at pushing back our enemies.

After we heal. Because we both knew even fighting tonight was a mistake, and we were right. In good shape, we could have handled what the Shadow King threw at us.

All of which I intend to tell Dusk. When I can take even breaths once more.

When Dusk is finished washing his hands, bandaging my wound, and washing his hands yet again, I flex the muscles just to be sure they still work. My arm and shoulder hurts like hell, but it's bearable, and I'm relieved. I'm going to need my arm to work if we're going to keep going.

"Thanks," I sign to Dusk, gritting my teeth when I realize moving my arm, even so slightly, hurts, but then I push on. "We have to have faith in the light fae. Keep our post and hope for the best." It doesn't sound like much of a plan. Faith is hard to come by these days and keeping post is easier said than done when there are trolls and slimy critters trying to murder us.

Dusk nods but then freezes. He's either heard something or lost his train of thought. I doubt it's the second thing, so I wait for him to tell me.

"Something's going on." He grabs the torch and heads out into the tunnel outside our cave.

I internally curse, slam my hand into the ground, and force myself to stand and follow him. My sore leg throbs and my arm screams, but I follow his torchlight to the entrance to the main cave. He's sliding the rock back a crack, and then he stands looking out.

Moving right behind him, I look out around him and freeze.

Holy fuck. A smoke dragon soars above the trees, smoke rising from its nostrils. On the ground, a troop of shadow beasts is spreading out, racing about like wild animals. And, hell, there are too many of them. Maybe the whole damn army of them.

For a moment I think things can't get worse. Then, rot monkeys with shining moon shards are suddenly running around the shadow beasts, planting moon shards at random. Creating the foundation to spread the shadow king's realm. Looking at the bag around Dusk's waist containing Ann's moon shards, I wonder if the king has enough without them.

My stomach sinks. Probably. *Fuck... this is worse.*

Dusk and I are alone without the benefit of our army of rogue shadow beasts—the few that were left. Phantom, Ann, and Rayne are gone, and we're injured. So, of course, this is the moment the Shadow King decides to unleash his army on us.

There isn't anything we can do to stop this. Not at this moment. All we'll do is get ourselves killed if we go out there, and it's painful to know that.

Dusk looks back at me, worry in his face, and then we crouch low to wait for morning. Hoping this world, and us, even make it to morning. He extinguishes the torch, so that we're waiting in total darkness. Only a sliver of light from the outside is there to show us the chaos the king is unleashing onto this world.

If we survive tonight, it's going to be a miracle.

THIRTEEN

Ann

I'm glaring out the open window, even though it's cold, and it's stupid to be standing here. Because not only am I still angry about Phantom tossing me over his shoulder, throwing me on the bed, and locking me back in this room, but I'm trying to figure out what the hell I'm going to do now.

Time is strange here without a sun or moon, but at some point I managed to sleep, take a cold bath, and change into the third simplest dress, a blue one with a low neckline and gems on the sleeves. Then I'd gone to the window and watched as creatures gathered outside of the gates. At last, Phantom and his father had emerged from the castle and led the shadow beasts out of the gates, giving them orders I couldn't hear.

I don't know what I expected then, but my stomach had sunk. The shadow beasts had rushed ahead of them, and the king and Phantom had ridden behind on what appeared to be skeleton horses, as if assessing their army at leisure. Behind them, rot monkeys ran too, avoiding the big, shadowy wolves. And in the distance, I was pretty sure there was another army of grave trolls.

None of which is a good sign.

But without light, the army fades away into the darkness, and I'm left staring at nothing. Cold. Alone. Trapped in a pretty room.

Frustrated, I decide to tear the room apart to see if there's anything I can use to get out. Yes, I'd done it before, but there's nothing else I can do, so at least it keeps me busy. I check the bed, the mattress and under it... There's nothing. I check in the nightstands, the empty closet, every crack of the bathroom. Nothing. Finally, I go to the wardrobe and stare. *Come on, please. I need this.*

I move the dresses out of the way to see if maybe there's something inside this thing, a loose nail, a screw I could twist free, anything that can help me get out of here. Behind a ball gown, almost tangled in the skirt, is a small wooden box.

Yes! Maybe all it has is a finger, or some other creepy thing that will fit this dark castle, but there's a small chance it'll be something helpful. So, I pull it into my lap and take a deep breath.

Come on. Come on.

When I open the box, I find a torn piece of paper with words scribbled across it in black ink. *Know your strength, find their weakness.* It's sound advice. Not particularly helpful, but I hope it gave whoever was stuck in here before me help.

I fold it and put it back. I'll know where to find it if I need the reminder. I move it to the side and find an old coin. It's American money from way back in the day, but, again, not helpful. The last item is a brooch. An ugly dragonfly with a yellow body and blue wings dotted with black. It's gaudy. But I don't care how it looks. I zero in on the pin on the back. It *looks* like it will fit into a door lock.

Yes! "So, now all I need to do is a pick a door lock. I've handled harder things." My voice sounds more hopeful than I feel, but whatever, I can do this.

Setting down the box, I go to the door, carefully holding the brooch. Straightening my shoulders, I shove the pin into the lock, jimmy it this way and that way, but that lock has to be made of some sort of super titanium unpickable metal alloy because nothing happens.

Or maybe lock picking isn't as easy as I'd hoped.

But I'm not one to give up. I pull the pin out, take a deep breath, and try shoving it in from another angle, twisting and shifting. I listen at the keyhole, hoping for some kind of sound to indicate I'm free. Again, nothing happens.

Frustrated, I sit back on my heel, glaring at the lock. *This has to work. What am I doing wrong? Is this even possible?* Suddenly, the lock clicks and I spring back in surprise.

Fuck! I didn't do it. I'm not alone here.

Leaping to my feet, I drop the brooch and assume a battle stance, hands fisted, feet spread apart, one to the front, one slightly behind me. I'm prepared and ready to shift my weight to make my punch more lethal, just like Onyx taught me. Then, I'll run. I'll run as far and as fast as I can to reach my men before it's too late.

But when the door swings open to a woman with long, white-blond hair, so pale it might as well be transparent, I don't attack. Even though the woman screams *warrior* through every inch of her leather-clad body. Because, frankly, I'm surprised. And because I'm not sure if she's a friend or foe.

Not that I'm putting my hands down until I know who she is and why she's here.

Her head tilts as she studies me, her hazel eyes strangely bright. "You must be Ann."

I don't want to tell her anything, but it's clear she already knows this. So... there's really no point in lying. "Yes."

Her expression isn't gentle, but it's not cruel either as she says, "I'm Shenra."

Oh.

Shenra. My men's first love. The woman who their father took, thinking she was the one in the prophecy that would lead him to great power. The woman everyone thinks drowned in the moat, or died on the way to it, is standing in my room.

So, either she's a ghost, or she's still alive.

What this means... I don't know.

She stands up straighter, so that I realize just how much taller she is than I am, and we just stare at each other for a minute. I can tell she's assessing me, so I assess her too. She has a dagger at her waist on a silver belt, and she's wearing... a long, black, leather dress-thing, although it's not exactly a dress, because in front it cuts all the way up to her belly, revealing black pants underneath. Her face is dirty, as are her clothes, and she's so thin it looks like she's missed more meals than I thought possible.

And yet there's no denying she looks strong. A warrior. That I'm sure of.

This ghost of a woman. This person who disappeared and let my men think she was dead. *Where has she been? And is she a friend or foe?* Part of me can imagine that she's been a prisoner in this castle all this time, and the other part wonders if she's just been quietly working for the Shadow King.

At last, those brilliant hazel eyes of hers meet mine again. "So, you're the woman of prophecy?"

I stiffen. Once upon a time the king thought she was. "I don't know."

She smirks. "Yes, you do. It was never me, and for some reason I feel like this would be the Moon Goddess's sense of humor... to bring some earthing, some fae, to save our world instead of me."

Okay... "Does that mean you're not working for the Shadow King?"

Fire leaps into her eyes. "I'd sooner carve out my own heart than help that cruel bastard. He took everything from me... starting with my freedom, my choice in a husband, then my men." She pauses, and some of the fire dims, but not as much as I might have hoped from a woman talking about my men like they're hers. "But nothing was worse than destroying this world, than enslaving my people. Do you know that his powers spread across the lands? Not just taking the people here but my own? Everyone I ever knew. My siblings. My parents. Every person I'd ever spoken to. They're all his slaves."

I don't want to be cruel, but I have to ask. Have to know. "I thought you died in the moat."

She lifts a brow. "I almost did. Rather than waiting to be rescued from this same room, I leapt. Broke my legs. Hurt myself. But I managed to crawl to safety only to see my maid throw herself too. I guess she decided that rather than face the wrath of the king, she'd die. The top of her body hit the ground, then slid into the water. It was... unpleasant to watch, but her body gave me the cover I needed to disappear."

Well, fuck, that's dark.

"That seems lucky for you and unlucky for her..."

"Or I had no choice." She gives me a pointed look. "Not all of us are willing to wait and hope to be rescued."

Pompous much? "Well, I guess it's good I didn't throw myself out the window, because if I did, your great woman of prophecy would either be dead or too broken to help anyone."

She looks like she wants to punch me, but she moves closer, erasing the distance between us. "Just be glad I took the risk for the both of us, or there would be no one here to release *you*. To bring *you* to your men and help to save both our worlds."

It takes everything in me not to take a step back as her wrath emanates off of her. "Agreed."

She moves back, her gaze sweeping over me again, sizing me up. "You're not much. Not at all what I expected. But it doesn't really matter. We need to go. The king has taken the wealth of his army to earth. They'll plant the shards, including the one in Phantom's heart, into the earth, and then the Void will spread. His power will grow, and he'll keep spreading it until all of your world is plunged into darkness. If we aren't fast enough, regardless of the prophecy, all will be lost. And he'll be too powerful to ever stop."

I knew everything except the piece about Phantom, even though the king had made it clear that Phantom wouldn't be ruling alongside him. "He's going to kill Phantom?"

She lifts a brow. "He was always going to kill Phantom. The Shadow King was never a good person, but his first wife tapered that evil. She gave him a reason to want more than just power. And then she died, and that terrible darkness inside of him overcame him. Even if he hadn't found a way to take the goddess's heart from the sky, he would have found a way to destroy this world. He needs to be stopped, regardless of whether it costs Phantom his life or not."

"No," I tell her, and she looks surprised. "We're going to save this world, my world, him, all of *my* men. I swear it." And this time, I'm the one who advances on her, glaring.

It's strange when she looks at me as if impressed. "Maybe you're not nearly as useless as I thought. Now, come on, I have our ride. But we're going to have to hurry."

She doesn't give me time to think, time to consider what we're doing. She just turns and heads out the door. It's maybe not exactly what I pictured, but I followed her, because this woman seems to be the one who will lead me to wherever my men are.

We race down the steps, and I hope like hell that we're fast enough. Maybe I'm not the person of prophecy. Maybe the prophecy is a lie. But I'll be damned if this thing doesn't end with me fighting at my men's side.

FOURTEEN

Rayne

Swallowing around the lump in my throat, I try to keep my breathing and heart rate even. I have no idea how refined the shadow beasts' hearing is, but if I give myself away, it's all over. Not just my chance to save Phantom, but *our* chance to save earth.

This is my role. My part to play in this war.

Even if just the idea of giving up this body makes me sick. *What if I can't come back? What if the body dies while I'm out of it? What if the king pushes me out and I spend the rest of my life as a ghost?*

Fuck. Those aren't good thoughts, so I try to force them away. To focus on the situation in front of me. Even though I've changed since dying, I'm still deep down a scholar, not a soldier, and right now I need to be a soldier. A warrior. Someone who stays calm and focused in a dangerous situation.

Someone like Phantom, Onyx, and Dusk. For some reason, I want to make them proud. I want to do this for them. Over our time together I've changed from someone they saw as competition to maybe... a brother. I already disappointed Esmeray when I died, when I pulled away from her. I didn't want to ruin this second chance by disappointing these men too.

So don't disappoint them.

And then there's Ann. This fucking king took her, or at the least, commanded Phantom to take her. He hurt her and created this whole mess, so I need to do this. For her. And for the men she loves.

I'm as close to the Shadow King and Phantom as I can possibly get, hiding in a patch of dead trees with a sizable boulder in the center of them. Luckily, the spot was close to where I'd crossed over, so I hadn't had to go far. I didn't risk peeking out at them as I heard their army approaching. There were too many eyes that could spot me. But I listened carefully as their sounds and voices got louder. Now, I can hear Phantom and the Shadow King like I'm standing beside them.

Although mostly the king has been busy tooting his own horn over the sound of the chittering rot monkeys, the growls of the shadow beasts, and the grunting of the grave trolls. Like now, as he finishes a string of compliments about himself, then releases a deep sigh. "This is it, son. This is the moment we've been waiting for."

"Your kingdom will expand," Phantom responds, his voice strangely emotionless compared to his father's. "Earth will be yours, and you'll have the power you deserve."

The sound of his dark creatures quiets so quickly from one moment to the next that it's eerie. I'm sure if I looked out now, they'd be all standing in silence, staring at the king, waiting for his command, having been silenced by whatever power the king holds. But I can't see them. All I can do is stay still and pray that Dusk and Onyx can handle what's coming their way. At least until I can save Phantom. Then, Phantom can help us take down his father, stop the shadow beasts, and end this war.

I just hope with him back, it's enough.

I try not to think about the fact that it wasn't enough to stop the king before, because those kinds of thoughts won't help me now. Whatever end game this monstrous man has worked out, it's about to happen, and the others need me. I'm their secret weapon. Their last chance to change the tide of this war.

No pressure, right?

Turning, I peek out just a little, and my stomach drops. This army... it's larger than I ever imagined, an unstoppable force of nightmarish beasts, and it's like the very world knows it. Trembles beneath their power, holding its breath. I wonder if their myth about the Moon Goddess is real, because I swear the dirt beneath my body feels... sad... upset.

The king speaks, his voice louder than before, meant to be heard by all his subjects, not just Phantom. He directs his army of beasts to cross out of the shadow realm, to attack anything that moves. But it isn't the speech of a moving leader, it's the command of a slave leader. Words that are simply meant to be heard and obeyed.

Howls from the shadow beasts fill the air. The grave trolls stomp and roar, and the rot monkeys squeal and race ahead of them all. Then, the army begins to move through the dark wall, disappearing from sight. It'd be a comfort if I didn't know Dusk and Onyx were on the other side. Because as incredible as those two men are, there's no way they can stop this army.

If they try, they're dead.

The king speaks more quietly this time, but his words

rise above the noise of the army moving. "Go with them. Command them." He smiles at Phantom, and it makes my stomach turn. "Bring me the heads of your brother and the mute."

I want to punch him for calling Onyx that, for enslaving his son and commanding him to end the lives of people I care about. I want to tear his head off and throw it to the grave trolls to feast on, but I swallow down my anger and stare at the two men through narrowed eyes. They're so damn close to me. Almost close enough to touch.

Should I try to take the king over now? I really fucking want to. I want to make this asshole pay.

Shaking my head, I will myself to be just a little more patient. My opportunity is coming, but not with Phantom staring right at the king. Not with his entire army surrounding him. I can't choose the wrong moment just because I'm angry.

"Show no mercy," the king says, then squeezes his son's shoulder, eyes flashing with an emotion I can't name.

Phantom nods like any mind he ever had of his own is gone. "I'll do as you say, my king."

As Phantom walks past me, I watch the king, and I find myself unimpressed. Yes, him standing in dark clothes, wearing a dark cloak, commanding nightmarish creatures gives him a frightening appearance. But when I actually look at the man himself, I see someone smaller than his sons, thinner and shorter. If he were wearing human clothes, I could picture him in a park feeding pigeons. Not that he's old exactly, just that beneath all his evil, he's just a man.

Or maybe I'm telling myself that because of what I'm about to do. I don't know, and I don't want to know. Whatever helps me.

The king waits until Phantom is out of sight, until his

army has faded from sight to earth, then whistles like he's calling forth a horse. I frown, feeling confused. I try to peer around without moving too much and risking him seeing me.

To my shock, a woman appears. I don't know if she melted out of thin air, or if I couldn't see her approaching until she was there, but she's terrifying in a way I never expected. Like for all my fears of the shadow beasts and the grave trolls, I never knew that this was the thing I should be fearing most here.

She's dressed in a scraggly black dress that drags on the ground and moves like the tentacles of an octopus in the sea. I can almost believe she's floating, but somehow, I don't think she is. It feels more like she's something so... wrong that she can't even exist in this dark world.

When she reaches the king, she lifts her head, and I almost gasp. I've seen ugliness before but she's a whole other level of hideous. She's wrinkled with bulging eyes, thin lips, and a long, skinny nose. It's as if she were a human forced to live until she was two or three hundred years old, but her body continued to disintegrate.

It seems impossible that her skin is still holding her bones together. Impossible that she can walk, or think. She's like a pumpkin left to rot in the sun, and I can only imagine what she might smell like if the wind shifted.

I wait for them to speak. I wait... I don't know for what. But she just stares at the king with cold eyes, not like Phantom, who seems emotionless, but like a dangerous creature forced into a cage. A shiver rolls down my back, and I find myself hoping that whatever figurative cage holds this woman, it stays there.

At last, the king speaks, looking down at her with an expression of pure intensity. "You saw my son?"

Her voice is thin and tinny as she says, "The one they call Phantom? Yes."

The king's smile grows as cold as her eyes. "I want you to use the shard in his chest and pin him to the Earth. It's the last piece. The most important piece. With it there, with him there, I can use him to be my conduit, to funnel my power and destroy earth." If ever there was a time that an evil laugh was fitting, it's now. I half expect it, but he simply smiles.

What will that do to Phantom? And can it be undone? I hate that I don't know, but what I do know is that if the king is right, that will be the end of earth, the end of life, and the end of everything and everyone I ever loved.

His smile expands as the witch turns away from him. "And when you're finished, bring me my bride from my tower, with her hands bound behind her back. We'll be wed immediately."

"Your wish is my command," she says, but there's something dark in her voice. Maybe even a warning.

Maybe because this asshole can only wed a woman who's tied up? My woman who could kick his ass, and he knows it?

The witch, and she can't possibly be anything else, turns back and bows to him, then heads to the edge of the Void. That strange gown of hers floats around her. Somehow her stride is powerful and sure until she disappears, following the army to earth.

Damn it.

Part of me wishes I would have already tried to take over the king's body, so I could have stopped him before he spoke to the witch, but the other part of me has no fucking clue how to do this and would rather try it without the added pressure of a witch watching me. Either way, it's too late now to stop her. I just have to hope that Phantom and the others will be okay. *My* job is to focus on what has to be done next.

This is my role. I have to do this. If I fail, we've lost.

Taking a deep breath, I watch the king for a few more seconds. I don't know what he's waiting for, but he's standing near, surveying the land, probably staying close to the battle, just in case. But, hell, I don't care what he's doing. This is the time. I have to act.

Closing my eyes, I do something I've avoided doing since taking this body. I search within myself for my soul, for whatever makes me... me. When I first entered this body, myself and Adrik's body felt like two symbiotic creatures, but as I search myself, I feel different. The separation between this body and me is almost not there. It's like this was always my body.

Relief rushes through me for one moment. If I stay in this body, I don't know if I'll ever lose it, and that's been something I've feared since the moment I came back. But then I remember what I'm doing, purposely stepping away from it, and my heartbeat suddenly fills my ears, my entire being. It's so loud it's almost like the harsh banging of drums. Overwhelming. Painful.

Every instinct inside of me says not to do this, but I force myself to untangle from the body. I'm shaking, or this body is shaking, I'm not sure which, but I keep extracting myself until I'm suddenly free. Separate. Hovering above Adrik's body, *my* body.

It collapses behind the stone, looking like an empty shell, even though the chest still rises and falls. I instantly want to dive back into the body, but I force myself to look away. To concentrate on the king. He stands with his fists curled, glaring toward the Void. Power radiates off of him in a way I didn't see before. And realize that it's taking an incredible amount of power and control for him to keep his army safe on earth from the harsher light. *So that's why he's here, close but not in the battle.*

My body wants to stay away from him, but I force myself to move forward. To stand in front of him. He looks through me, not aware of my ghost, and I take a deep breath, then force myself into him.

I expect it to be like when I took Adrik's body... I was wrong.

There's one second where it's easy. Where I simply glide into him and find, unlike Adrik's empty body, a bright, living soul inside of him. But the second I move to take control, everything changes. The Shadow King fights me. I don't know how he does it, but as I try to bury myself deep inside of him, in the places that allow me to take control, he's pushing me, shoving me. If I had a body, it'd be physically painful, but this is painful in a way I can't describe.

We fight and fight. We're both strong, but I think his uncertainty gives me an edge. I might never have done this before, but I know what's going on. He makes a strange wailing sound, and then I shove his essence... his soul... whatever the hell it is, away, creating a glowing box the color of my own bright blue soul around him. He crashes against it, and I sense each blow, but he can't escape the cage I've placed him in.

At least not right now.

He continues fighting my control for what feels like a long time before he finally stops. His grey color dulls, grows smaller in the box. He simply recedes into the darkness of his spirit, of the cage I've built for him, like he's given up.

Somehow, I know he isn't done, but I have to switch my focus from the king to the task I must do. Even though I'm hesitant to take my focus off of him, and if there was another way I would take it. But there isn't, so I accept it. I need to complete my task, but also be ready for anything he might pull.

Control of his body is mine, but keeping it isn't easy. Even when I open his eyes and stare out at the world. Even when I just take a step, I feel it. The king battles within himself and his body twitches, jerking unnaturally as he does what little he can. He's stronger than I hoped, but I still have control.

So, I better get moving while I still have it.

Just when I'm about to move toward the edge of the Void, Phantom returns, holding the severed head of the witch. Her hair in his fist is slick and dripping with blood. The tendons in her neck dangle, dripping blood with every step he takes. Her eyes are open and her jaw is slack, but the life has drained from her face.

He stares at me for a second before I remember that I'm in the Shadow King's body. When I remember I stand straighter, trying to act like the cocky king. Trying to make sure I can play this game until he gets close enough for me to pull the shard from his heart.

And as if the shard has a mind of its own, knows what I'm thinking, I see it glowing a light blue color beneath his shirt. Pulsing. Calling to me.

"The witch tried to kill me," Phantom says, tilting his head and studying me. "Did you send her for me?"

I don't know if Phantom is capable of being angry, of attacking the king, but I don't want to know. It's now or never. Maybe taking the shard out will kill him, maybe all of this be for nothing, but this is the only plan we have to save him, so I have to act. I know it.

"My son..." I begin hoping to sound like the king as I move forward.

He drops the witch's head, studying me as I get closer and closer.

"You see..." Then I leap at him, tearing open his shirt.

Phantom's eyes widen in surprise, but I can't focus on him. I look down and see it like it's the edge of a sharp, thin piece of glass. A piece that glows and pulses even brighter than before. My heart's in my throat as I reach for the edge and tear the shard from his chest, pulling the wickedly long, wickedly sharp piece all the way out until it comes free.

Blood trickles down his chest, but I don't hesitate; I toss the shard onto the ground, stomping on it until it breaks into pieces. But any satisfaction I felt fades away when Phantom's eyes roll back into his head. He falls to his knees then face first into the ground while I stare on in shock.

Fuck. Did it kill him?

I collapse in front of him and reach for his throat, trying to find a pulse. But... there's none. My mind starts working. I can't just focus on the man I care about, who's dying in front of me, I have to find a way to still save the others. To save Ann.

And it hits me... the one way I might still be able to save all of us.

But do I have the strength to do it?

FIFTEEN

Onyx

We're still near the opening to the cave when a passing shadow beast stops, lifts his head, and starts to sniff. I motion to Dusk, and we both move away from the opening, keeping the beast in sight. He circles a bit, and I have a moment of hope when I think he hasn't found us, and then he lifts his head and our gazes meet. He races to the cave opening, but it isn't large enough for him to fit through. Still, he starts to bark, growl, and dig at the dirt by the entrance.

All of which means we're screwed.

Dusk and I move further and further back. None of the shadow beasts can shift into their other forms while under our father's control, so they won't be able to get in, to move the boulder. But the grave trolls could...

The instant the thought enters my mind, I feel the earth shaking beneath my feet and know a troll is coming toward us. Dusk lights the torch once more, and then we head deeper into the tunnel. I'm limping, still barely able to move my arm, but we gain some distance from the opening before

I sense the ground moving under my feet once more, this time in a different way.

I look at Dusk, and he nods, confirming my suspicion. The boulder has been moved. Our enemies will come pouring in, and we'll die like cowards, hiding beneath the ground, being ripped to pieces.

Unless we can get to the other exit in time.

So, we run. Or, at least, I limp along as fast as I possibly can, passing the little cave Dusk had sewn me up in. We take a corner, choose one direction over another, and circle higher until we spot branches covering the exit. When we reach them, we put the torch out, and then Dusk leads us both out, moving slowly and cautiously. I can't hear if anything is on the other side, but Dusk seems confident, so I trust him.

These are the moment I wish, for the millionth time, to have that sense back.

We come out into the night... and into an army of waiting enemies. Shadow beasts with glowing eyes sit, as if patiently waiting for us. Grave trolls are behind them, and the rot monkeys are scattered around all of them.

Without speaking, Dusk and I withdraw our swords.

I don't need to ask him to know we can't go back into the cave. Our enemies are already there, and we can't run fast enough to avoid the shadow beasts. So, fighting is our only option. Even if fighting against such odds, in our condition, means certain death.

At least it'll be a warrior's death.

Taking a slow and steady breath, I look more carefully over the creatures around us. We're surrounded by every manner of killer the king could have sent our way— grave trolls salivating, thirsting for blood the king denies them to make them more vicious fighters; rot monkeys who hunger for entrails and are eyeing us like we're about to be a tasty treat; shadow beasts who are dedicated and loyal to a king that wouldn't think twice about killing them.

Two of us against all of them.

But then I see the Void peeking out from between a few of them. When Dusk glances in my direction, I nod toward it and his eyes widen. Only a few enemies stand between us and it... probably because they'd never believe we'd be stupid enough to run straight into it.

The thing is... right now it's a better option than any other.

I nod to Dusk. His eyes harden, and he nods back. Then, he holds up his free hand with three fingers raised. He drops one, then another, and finally the third. I start running, but he moves more slowly, running at my back, probably so he won't leave me behind.

Damn the honorable fool.

I zig and zag, cutting down a few rot monkeys with my sword as I breeze past. Gritting my teeth against the pain, I attack anything that moves around me, feeling their blood painting my face and body. Afraid of leaving my best friend behind, I glance back and watch as Dusk plunges his sword, lightning fast, into the eye of a grave troll, and then slashes a shadow beast that leaps at us. He turns to me with eyes wide and nods toward the Void.

It's right in front of us, and even though my stomach flips, I dive right in, wondering if our enemies will simply race in behind us.

We explode into the shadow realm, a place that is darker than the one we left behind. Slowing just a bit, I glance back at Dusk and see that he's covered in troll blood and monkey innards. He catches my gaze and gives me a look, one that says he's okay.

I slow a little and look at myself. My leg feels swollen and painful. I'm definitely covered in the blood of my enemies, and one stitch of my shoulder wound has opened, creating a line of blood that leaks down my arm. *Again.*

This time it's manageable. Ignorable. Especially because nothing is following us here. I'm guessing because those aren't the orders of that asshole Shadow King.

Dusk sheaths his sword, and I do too. For now. And then he signs, "Need to find cover."

I nod, then look around, searching for something that can work. Dusk takes the lead this time, and I'm grateful. He moves at a slower pace, a half-jog, and I can let some of my pain show knowing he can't see my winces with every movement.

We're more than twenty yards into the Void when I stop so I don't run into Dusk's back. So I don't crash into him. He slowly lifts a hand and points, and I shift to peer around him to see what's got him acting so strangely... when I find it. *Him.*

Phantom is lying motionlessly on the ground. He looks like he's dead, his body curled into a half circle, eyes closed, every inch of him whispering that he's nothing but an empty shell now. My gaze moves to his chest, but there's no rise and fall.

He's just... gone.

My heart beats so hard in my chest that it feels like everything around me dims.

I want to scream. My best friend... is dead. A man I'm proud to call my brother. A man I've fought beside my entire life. Gone. No more sparring. No more listening to him snore. No more stupid jokes he found in some paper edition of a book he "found" and kept in his travel pack.

But how? How is he dead?

His shirt has been torn open, and my gaze snaps to his pale skin. There's nothing but a trail of blood. A trail that starts from his heart and leaks down his body until it disappears into his clothes.

The shard. The shard was removed.

Movement draws my gaze to some trees. Suddenly, the Shadow King emerges, and our swords are in our hands in an instant. I level my blade at his chest, rage building inside of me.

But then the king signs, "It's me! It's Rayne," in frantic movements.

Some strange part of me still wants to kill him because all I can see is the face of the man I hate to my core. It's hatred from a dark place inside of me that knows deep inside it's Rayne, but *sees* the bastard who lied, who forced our people into his slavery, who effectively killed Phantom as soon as he put that moon shard in his chest.

But beside me, Dusk sheaths his sword and then rushes to Phantom's side. He kneels beside his brother, and I numbly put my sword away and come closer, standing over my closest friends. The men I see as family.

Rayne kneels down too, and I know it has to be him because of the pain in the Shadow King's face. "I thought he could be saved," he signs. "I thought it would work."

We all did. Damn it. We all did.

"No pulse. No breathing," Dusk signs, then he looks up at me, his expression devastated. His grief is potent enough that it entwines with my own.

Even though we already knew deep down.

My heart feels so broken it's hard to breathe. Rayne gets up, squeezes my shoulder, and I feel myself breaking. Falling into a thousand pieces that can never be pulled back together. It's a fragile item that will never be the same. I love Phantom. *Loved* Phantom.

This can't be happening.

A sob is building in my throat. Dusk drops his face into his hands, and I turn away from his grief, knowing that I can't handle it. If I see him breaking, I may as well lie down here beside Phantom and die too.

Or maybe I should. Ann is gone. Phantom is dead. The king's army has flooded earth. *What reason do I have to keep going?*

I wish Ann was here for so many reasons, but none as much as for the power of her light to save him. Because some part of me thinks the woman I love can save anything, even Phantom from death. She's just... that incredible. And our love for her feels like something that can overcome anything, even this.

I wish for so many things. Useless wishes. For a restart to our lives. For salvation. For... Ann. To have met her at a better time, a time when the Shadow King was no more and life wasn't fraught with danger at every sunrise and sunset. A world where all of us were together and happy.

Even though that life is impossible now. Some things, there's just no coming back from.

Looking back, I watch as Dusk puts his hands on Phantom's chest like he's trying to hold the blood inside his brother. Or maybe like he needs to feel his still heart and breath to know this is real, but it just seems so terrible. So heartbreaking to watch. And I wonder if the connection they say exists between twins is real, if Dusk is shattering even more than I am.

Is that possible? I don't know. I don't know anything anymore.

Rayne's hand drops from my shoulder and he steps

away from us so strangely that both of us glance at him at the same time. He's twitching, body jerking back and forth as he tries to maintain power over the king's body. I know that without him needing to tell me, because it truly looks like two people fighting for control over one body.

"The king is going to be in control again soon." He doesn't sign it, but I read the words on his lips and know it's true based on the pain in his face. Then he reaches down and rips open his shirt.

My jaw drops. The shard in the king's chest is massive, bigger than any I've seen before. It sticks out a couple of inches from his heart, but this piece pulses with a dull red light. Blood leaks from it, even as we're watching, and it creeps me the hell out.

"I think I should take the shard out of the king's chest," Rayne mouths, then reaches and places his fingers around the tip of it.

I stiffen. *What?* He's already learned that removing the shard kills the person. If he does that inside the king's body, I have no doubt he'll die too. At least I *think* he will, and it isn't worth the risk.

I shake my head no. Vehemently.

"I have to," he says, his spine stiffening.

Dusk rises to stand beside me, signing rapidly. "You might die, and we can't lose more. Please, don't do this."

My heart aches in agreement. If everyone we love is dead, will ending this war even matter? It's selfish. Earth needs us, but I can't... I can't lose Rayne too.

"If he dies, we win this war," his lips say, his expression open and vulnerable. "The world is saved."

I don't care anymore. "No," I sign, and our gazes hold.

He has to see it. To see that he can't kill himself for this war. That there's another way.

Dusk seems to know my thoughts, "Come out, then we'll kill him before he gains control again."

I see it in Rayne's face. He thought of that already, but knows that has a risk that we won't be fast enough. That the king will kill us, or run, before we can stop him.

Lifting my sword, I place it at the king's throat to show him I can do it quickly, the moment he leaves the body. There's no need to risk another person we love.

"You'd take the risk," he says, his mouth forming each word.

I would. But I wouldn't choose to lose him. But I can't say that. *What can I say?*

He doesn't give me the chance to figure it out. "Tell Ann I love her," his mouth says. Before I can stop him, he yanks out the shard, blood spurting from his chest as he does so.

His eyes widen. His express goes blank, and he looks at the massive shard in his hand for a second before it tumbles from his hand and he collapses. Eyes blank, body dead. Soul gone.

My lips move. Maybe I'm screaming. I don't know. But my sword slips from my fingers, and I stare and stare. Phantom. Rayne. The king.

Dead. They're dead.

Everything... has changed.

Is this over? This fight? Is there any chance Rayne is still alive? The horror on Dusk's face says no.

I don't know what to do. I'm lost. Drowning. Surrounded by dead people I love. I need... I don't know what, but I'm about to completely lose all control.

Dusk's head snaps to look in one direction. I do too, although I'm not sure what I'm looking for. In this dark world, I thought nothing good was left. Nothing of love and light. But I was wrong. Ann rides up on a skeleton horse with–I can't believe what I'm seeing, what I'm saying–with Shenra.

Ann pulls up to us so quickly that the horse nearly slams into us, but she yanks back on the lead and the horse rears. We spring back. The horse settles back onto all fours, and Ann slides off of the horse, rushes toward us, and freezes. Her gaze snaps from the Shadow King to Phantom.

I don't need to hear her scream to know that's what she's doing, and I wish like hell that I could have saved her mates. Saved the men I cared for. Protected her from this.

But as tears flow down her cheeks, I know I failed. Maybe we won the war, but nothing about this feels like winning.

SIXTEEN

Ann

I rush around the dead Shadow King and collapse beside Phantom. My hand goes to his chest and I hold my breath, waiting to feel his heartbeat... and feel nothing.

"I'm sorry, Ann," Dusk whispers behind me. "We were too late."

Ignoring him, I call for my powers. I beg them to save this man who I love so much. Instantly, my hand begins to glow, and then my golden light spreads over Phantom, lighting him almost from the inside out. I watch him with bated breath, pouring more and more of my magic into him.

But nothing happens.

I keep going, pushing myself as hard as I can. Crying. Begging for my magic to save him.

But his heart remains silent.

"Ann." I hear my name coming from Dusk's lips, and I try to block him out, but can't. "Rayne was inside the Shadow King when he died. He pulled the shard out of his heart. He saved us all, but..."

My hand shifts off of Phantom, and I feel blinded by pain and loss. I crawl to the Shadow King's body, and I place my hand over his chest, even though I belatedly realize it's covered in Phantom's blood.

"Don't!" I hear Shenra shout. "You'll save the king too."

She tries to pull me away, but Dusk grabs her and pulls her away. I turn away from them as she continues to fight him, and focus my golden light on the man in front of me. Knowing that the second Rayne is free, I'll kill him myself.

But nothing happens.

My light doesn't bring him back. Doesn't heal him.

"Maybe your magic doesn't work that way," Dusk says gently behind me, his voice filled with heartbreak. "Maybe once they're gone, they're gone."

I pull my hand away and scream and scream. "What the fuck is this?" I shout to the dark world. "You said I was prophesied to save the world! How can I save anything if I can't save them?" But I'm not done, I keep screaming into the silence. Demanding answers, even though it feels pointless.

And then that voice, the one I feel weaved with my magic says, "Use the shards. The shards are power." It's a soft whisper in my mind, like the wind. It makes no sense, and yet, I have nothing else. No other options.

Dusk brings Phantom, laying him down beside the Shadow King. I think he intends to make it easier to mourn, but instead, I focus on the two bloody shards on the ground, broken into pieces. I lift my hand and call my magic to me, and to my shock, the shards fly from the ground, then stop just inches from my hand.

Power flows through me. I wonder if it's the power the Shadow King felt that intoxicated him, because it is intoxicating to me. Like a drug. It rushes into my system, making my heart pump wildly, and yet, I know it's not enough.

Gritting my teeth, I call for the other shards. I *order* them to come to me, and the Shadow King's jacket opens. A small box emerges from it, floating in the air, and the top opens in a rush. Dozens of shards explode from it and join the ones hovering above my hand.

I'm sweating. Overwhelmed. The power radiating from them is mind-numbing.

But I know it's not enough. For what, I'm not sure, but I call for more. I command them to come to me. I'm their queen. I tell them that I'm the woman of prophecy, and they *will* obey me. They *will* do as I say.

Standing, I feel my body trembling, but not from exhaustion, from the power. The power before me and power coming to me. From out of the Void, brilliant blue glowing light, almost like stars, shoot toward us. A world's worth of power. The strength to conquer anyone and anything.

"What the hell?" Dusk mutters.

Shenra whispers, "May the goddess forgive us."

But I ignore them both. I don't know what I'm doing, but I know I need to do it. The shards shoot toward my hand, then stop, just as the others did. Together their light is incredible. It's truly like staring into the sun, or the moon if it was inches from you. And yet, I don't look away. I can't look away. The shards are changing, forming.

And... they become a heart. A heart of glass. A heart as large as a boulder, glinting and radiating with that incredible blue light. I can feel the energy coming off of it. Feel it calling to me.

Around us, plants spring from the dead ground. Pale green vines cover the land as far as I can see, and then blue flowers grow, open, and begin radiating more light, changing the world before my eyes.

Yet, it's not done. The heart begins to spin in front of me, and I know what it wants. I know its place is in the sky, and yet the power calls to me. It promises me that with it, I could save my men, that I could bring them back.

With this heart, I would be able to erase the pain of all that my stepfather did to me. I could erase the cruel words, the punches, the injuries that left me gasping for breath. Never again would I think of my days alone in my big manor, miserable, so desperately lonely that it felt like my heart was breaking over and over again each and every day.

I'd forget being alone at the Royal Fae Academy. I'd forget the fact that I'm plain-looking, that no one ever saw me or respected me. And the heart could give me more... I wouldn't hurt when I thought of losing Rayne the first time, or this time, or feel the terrible loss of Phantom's death.

The heart will give me more than I ever thought I could have.

I feel the tears that roll down my face, and I understand, I finally understand how a man with a dark heart could so easily be swayed by this kind of power. By the promise to forget what it feels like to lose someone you love. And as much as I want to forget that two of the men I love most in this world are dead at my feet, I can't erase those feelings, or steal this power to save them. No matter how much I might want to.

The heart must be returned to the sky. *Now.* Before it becomes part of me the way it did with the Shadow King. Before it finds a way to lure me into abusing this power.

Because my men wouldn't want to be brought back to a world that was dead. A world that can't survive without this heart. They wouldn't want to live in a world where I could no longer feel love, for them, or for anyone. And no matter how much I want to pretend that doesn't matter, it does.

To save this world, I have to give up what I love most. I have to truly say goodbye to Phantom and Rayne.

"The right choice isn't always the easy choice," the soft voice whispers in my mind, and I sob. "Return the heart to the sky. Command it and it will be."

I say goodbye. Goodbye to my men. Goodbye to ever being complete again.

And then... I give the command.

The heart soars above us, expanding, growing as it does. It flies into the sky, the light growing more and more brilliant as it does. The light radiating from it illuminates the lands all around us, and before my eyes, the trees turn green and golden leaves sprout from the branches. More plants and bushes and flowers explode from the ground, flowers that radiate their own incredible lights. Some blue. Some gold. Some green.

It's beautiful.

Casting my gaze above I finally see the heart stop. It hangs in the sky like a moon, and yet its glow is brighter, just a bit, giving the whole world a similar glow to that of a sunrise. A blue sunrise.

I fall to my knees, the tears flowing. I don't regret saving this world, but some part of me will always regret not saving my men. "I'm sorry," I sob as I look down at them. "I could save the world or you, but not both."

Suddenly, Shenra is beside me. She takes my face in her hands and turns me to her. "You have saved this world. The goddess will save them, all you have to do is ask."

I don't know if I believe her, but I pull away to look at my fallen men. Onyx and Dusk kneel near their heads, their gazes on me. There's hope in their eyes, but some part of me thinks I'm about to crush them all over again.

Still, I ask, "Goddess of the Moon, save my men. Bring them back to me." My words are broken, desperate. But I hold my breath and watch the two dead men in front of me.

But Shenra was wrong, because I asked. I did everything I was told. And they're still dead.

SEVENTEEN

Ann

I'm completely numb as I stand over two of the people I love most in this world, dead, unable to be saved. It's like I'm in a bad dream and I can't wake up from it, no matter how much I want to. My nails are digging so hard into my palms that I can feel blood running from them, but nothing changes how broken I am inside.

It's somewhere between numb and the most heart-breaking pain I ever imagined experiencing. *What do I do? How do I keep going?*

I... just don't know.

It feels like the moment couldn't get worse, until it does. A rumbling builds, shaking the ground, and we know. All of us.

Our group turns to the edge of this world, to the opening into the Void. The Shadow King's army comes pouring back into this world like a tsunami of death. The grave trolls roar, the shadow beasts growl, and the monkeys chitter eerily. All of their feet hit the ground with a vengeance that's similar to chaos from an earthquake.

It looks like the end of the fucking world.

Dusk grabs my wrist. "We have to go."

"Go where?" I ask him, whirling onto the man I care for so much.

He shakes his head. "The castle. The forest. Anywhere. If we stay here, it'll be certain death."

But before I can answer, the rumbling stops, changes. I turn back in shock and watch as the grave trolls begin to shriek. The sounds are so painful that I actually cover my ears. And then before our eyes, the trolls begin to melt. As do the monkeys. Only, instead of standing in place shrieking, the monkeys run for the half-dead forests.

It's eerie watching the monkeys. They're turning to ash as they run, some falling into piles, with nothing to indicate they were ever living beings. Others are half-burned, creepy-looking things that manage to find cover beneath the trees, although there's not a lot of cover there still.

The grave trolls all melt, well, collapse into ash, and an unseen breeze seems to ruffle the particles, stirring them into the air. It's horrific in a strange way to watch the creatures that have terrorized us for so long die, and yet, I don't know that I'd want anything to die this way.

The shadow beasts, however, don't turn to ash. They observe the scene before them and then begin to move again, this time more cautiously, toward us. Dusk and Onyx withdraw their swords. I hold out my hand, ready to call for what little power I have left inside of me... when Shenra grabs my wrist.

"No."

"Shenra, they're not our people any longer," Dusk says, his voice grave.

"They are," she says simply, "and without the king to

control them, they can be themselves once more. Someone needs only to remind them."

"How?" I ask, because the closer they come with their sharp teeth and claws, the more I want to run away from these beasts. To avoid being torn to pieces.

"Without Phantom, one of us should be their new leader. We just need to try to see if they'll obey our command. If they'll see us as an alpha. And once they accept us as their new alpha, we can allow them to transform into their other forms and remember what it is to be people. To remember who they are and that there's more to life than being controlled. Than living and dying for an evil ruler."

Fuck. She's right. As much as I want something to suffer for taking Phantom and Rayne from me, it shouldn't be them. They're victims in all of this too. They deserve our kindness, as long as it doesn't cost us our lives.

I let my hand drop. "She's right."

"And what if this doesn't work?" Dusk asks, and Onyx gives me a look that says he agrees.

"We can't just slaughter innocent people, or what did we even save this world for?"

My words are met with silence, and then both Dusk and Onyx drop their swords.

The shadow beasts are nearly on us when I decide to hell with it. "Stop!" I command. "I am your alpha, and you will obey me."

In response, they flash their teeth and growl. *So, okay, I'm not the alpha. I can live with that.*

Dusk is next, and my gut says he'll be the one, as the oldest remaining family of their line. "Stop. This war is over. I'm your new alpha, your new king, and you'll obey me."

They don't respond, just advance, closing in around us like prey. *Fuck.*

Onyx looks defeated even before he begins to sign, and then he says one word, too loudly, his tone a little off, but strong, "Stop."

Heads jerk toward him, but they keep going.

"Damn it." Okay, now it's definitely time to run, but I can't imagine just leaving Phantom and Rayne here. "We have to run."

And then Shenra moves to stand in front of us. As if this one woman could protect us from the dangerous pack of shadow beasts. "Stop, your queen commands it!"

I've never seen anything like it. *Felt* anything like it. Electricity moves through me raising goosebumps across my flesh, and every one of the shadow beasts stops.

Shenra looks back at me, those hazel eyes of hers wide in surprise, and then she looks back at the army in front of her. Her voice lifts, holding all the command of a true queen. "Our time of suffering is over. Our time of rebuilding is now. Go to the castle, and there we will remember what it is to be people. We will start over again."

The pack starts running again, this time heading in the direction of the castle. I cringe, but Onyx and Dusk are instantly around me, protecting me from the pack as they race around us with no regard. But none of them hurt us, they just run by, ignoring us as if we never truly mattered. And when I peek out between my men as the pounding of their feet eases, I see that sure enough they've run toward the castle.

They've obeyed her command.

My men move away from me, and then Shenra and I are staring at one another. There's longing in her eyes as she stares at Onyx and Dusk, there and gone again in a flash. "I guess... I'm their queen."

I nod, but then, and I don't know why, I move back to Phantom and the Shadow King's body. This war is over. The earth is safe, as is this world, and yet, it doesn't feel like we won. It feels like we've lost more than we ever imagined.

That soft voice that I've never fully understood comes into my head, gentle, but happy for the first time. "Saving the shadow beasts cost me my heart and my life a long time ago. It has cost you much too, but I will not let it cost you *them*. Not these two warriors who gave so much for my world. They can still be saved, if they return to earth, but none of you can ever return to the shadow realm again. I do not have the power for that. If they do, their lives will be taken the moment they enter my world."

All along it was the goddess speaking to me?

Part of me doesn't believe it, doesn't believe her promise. Part of me is angry with her because when I asked to save them before, she didn't. But if she's speaking the truth now, I don't care about any of that.

"Why now?" I ask aloud.

Everyone turns to me, but I ignore them.

"I had to know my people were safe, and they are now, with their queen, and with your mercy." Her words feel like they're saying more than I can understand, but I look toward the others.

"The goddess says if we return to earth with Phantom and Rayne, they'll live, but none of us can ever come back here." I release a slow breath. "Do you think it's true?"

Shenra answers, "The goddess wouldn't lie."

Dusk looks close to tears. "But our people need us. How can we just leave after all they've been through?"

"Because I'm here," Shenra says simply, drawing herself

up taller. "Technically, my marriage with your father never ended. I'm the queen. Our people obey me, see me as their alpha, and I know that I can help us find ourselves again. With them, I can return to my lands and try to save more than just the people here. I know I can."

I look at Dusk and Onyx. Either way, I'm returning to earth with Phantom and Rayne, because I have to try to save them, even if it's not a sure thing. But my heart would break if they stayed here, if we always had to live in different worlds.

Yet I can't take their people and this place they love away from them.

"Do what you think is best," I tell them, my voice cracking a little.

After a moment, Onyx signs, "I trust Shenra. I know that our people will be safe with her, but Dusk is the last member of his family, so I'll go with his choice."

Dusk releases a slow breath. "Once upon a time I made the poor choice not to kill my father when I had the chance, which caused our whole world unbelievable pain. As much as my soul wants to stay here and try to heal our people after what I did, that would be selfish, because it's clear the goddess has chosen Shenra as their leader. So, I'll return to earth with all of you, leaving my blessing with Shenra."

The woman smiles. "I promise I won't let you down."

I look at the bodies of the Shadow King and Phantom. "Does anyone know where Rayne's real body is?"

Because it isn't Adrik's body any longer, it's Rayne's.

They spread out searching for Rayne while I sit beside my men. At last, Onyx comes out of the woods carrying Rayne's body. He looks like he's in pain, but he holds the smaller man like he'll go to hell before he releases him.

"Are you sure that's him?" Dusk asks, staring intently into my eyes.

I look down at the Shadow King, then into the still face of Rayne. Both men are dead, but my heart knows the answer. "Yes, I'm sure."

Dusk picks up Phantom, even though he too looks exhausted.

I turn to lead them back to earth when Shenra touches my arm.

Looking back at the young woman with so much on her shoulders, I wonder if she's changed her mind. Instead, she says, "I can do a lot here, but I can't bring life back to this world."

Frowning, I shake my head. "I can't either."

She actually smiles. "You don't know, do you?"

Know what? But I just shake my head.

"The goddess who gave her heart to the sky... she was a light fae."

Dusk gasps behind me. "That's impossible."

Shenra grins. "I spent a lot of my time after my 'death' hiding in the library, trying to find clues about how to fix our world. I found old stories about the start of the world. In the beginning, she wasn't known as the Moon Goddess, she was known as the Goddess of Light. A fae with extraordinary abilities. That's why she was able to use you to funnel her powers. That's why she was able to connect with you."

I realize my jaw has dropped. It sounds impossible, but also, explains so much. "So that means... I can heal your world?" *More than just the space around me that the goddess's powers already brought life back into?*

"Just do what you've always done. Just ask the goddess to use you to accomplish what needs to be done. Otherwise, no matter what I do, it'll take these lands too long to grow crops, and we might all end up dead any way."

No pressure. "Okay."

Closing my eyes, I release a slow breath and ask the goddess. I ask her to fill these lands with life. To encourage them to grow. To bring back all the dormant seeds that have been waiting so long for light. And, it's strange. Different from before. It feels like light is coming from my every pore. Wind brushes against me, then grows stronger, before I feel the splatter of rain on my skin.

I open my eyes and watch as rain pours from the sky, then look around me in shock as I feel myself growing brighter and brighter. Suddenly, a pulse of light shoots out from me going in all directions. Everywhere it goes life awakens. Silver trees bloom with blue leaves, more glowing flowers cover the ground, along with vines, and light illuminates the land in all directions in a way that can only be described as... magical.

My glowing stops. My arms fall. And it's like my power is done. Spent.

Shenra is smiling, her face tilted up, letting the rain coat her skin. "It's not the same as before, but it's a start." Then she turns to me. "Thank you, light fae."

I'm about to say something, I don't know what, when a rumbling begins. We turn to see the wall separating this world from earth shaking. Dust rises from the ground, and I sense that something is changing, but I don't know what.

"Run!" Shenra screams. "The Void is closing. Soon, you might not be able to return to earth."

Panic awakens with me. Closing? We'll be trapped here? *Phantom and Rayne won't be able to be saved?* I look at Dusk and Onyx, and without a word, we all start running. We run as fast and as hard as we can toward the

Void, which, sure enough, is shrinking, fading before our eyes.

We reach the edge of the Void. I let my men go first, then look back. Shenra waves to me, a lonely woman beside her skeleton horse, and I hope that she can save this world. That she's the queen it needs, for her sake, and for the sake of all the creatures that have suffered here.

Then I take a deep breath and step through. Hoping and praying that the goddess was speaking the truth. That Phantom and Rayne can be saved.

I come through on the other side and, strangely enough, it's raining on earth too. Onyx and Dusk have laid Rayne and Phantom down on the ground, and they kneel in the mud beside them, heads bowed. A sob catches in my throat, but a massive rumble makes me turn... only to see the entire black cloud, the Void, disappear like the snap of fingers. It's truly as if it never existed anywhere but in my nightmares. I see a small sliver of silver in between the trees, but the danger seems to be gone.

The risk to this world is over. And yet, I don't feel relieved.

I kneel beside my men, but Phantom and Rayne still don't move. Don't breathe. Don't awaken. And it hits me: perhaps the goddess does lie. Or perhaps this was beyond her powers.

Tears prick the corners of my eyes as I feel the last shreds of my hope fading away. She promised. I did everything I was asked to do and more. *How can this possibly be how our story ends?*

Dusk and Onyx bow their heads even further. Their spines are bent. Defeat radiates off of every inch of their flesh.

"They were good men," Dusk begins, his voice broken.

But I shake my head. "No. No. She said they would survive. She said this was the answer."

Onyx looks at me, his eyes filled with sadness, then signs, "They're gone."

I'm shaking my head again, my stomach in knots. Reaching my hands out, I try to use my light on them, but no light comes. Rage builds inside of me. Desperation. *So, the goddess used me, lied to me, and then took her powers back?* I want to scream. I want to demand that she make this right.

And then, they both gasp in air.

Phantom and Rayne open their eyes, looking panicked and confused. I start to cry, but I want to be sure. *Is Phantom... himself again? Is Rayne... Adrik or himself?*

"Rayne?" I ask, and his name comes out no louder than whisper.

But he looks at me and smiles. "Yeah, it's me. And my dumb ass plan worked."

I laugh, hug him, and give him a kiss. Then, I turn to Phantom.

Those dark eyes of his find mine. He reaches up and touches my cheek, and I try not to shrink back. To remember the man he was with that shard in his chest. "Ann, I'm so sorry."

I break, wrapping myself around him, and then we're all hugging. Holding each other in the rain. Falling apart because of all that we lost, but also knowing that at last it's over. The Shadow King has fallen. The Void is gone. And we're all together.

In war there's never truly a victory, but this is as close as we can get.

EIGHTEEN

Ann

It's been months since that day in the woods, since Shenra and I rode in and found Phantom and Rayne seemingly dead. And things have changed in every way imaginable. I live in my mother's manor now, although she's retired to some place quieter and more tropical. I'm the *lady* of the manor. And the world is becoming what it used to be only better now that I have my mates with me.

It's perfect. Everything I ever imagined life could be and more.

I stretch and roll onto my side to look at Dusk. His smile spreads across his lips as he leans in for a kiss. On the other side of me, Onyx runs his hand down my spine, kisses my shoulder, then makes a soft noise, and I'm sure, falls back asleep.

Dusk and Rayne are next to them, completely out. Not even stirring with the morning light filtering through the curtains, probably because they were up late putting the finishing touches on the new room next door to ours. The room that whispers of dreams beyond any we imagined before.

I lie still for a while, surrounded by the men I love, a smile glued to my face. I sleep on and off as I dreamily think of my new life running my family lands. Because, apparently, after all was said and done at the Royal Fae Academy, they decided to pass me. I guess helping to save all of my kind means I have the skills to rule my own lands.

It's amazing lying between them, on a soft bed, with food in our stomachs. But after a while, I can't quiet my mind enough to slip back into sleep, and realizing my men have all gone back to bed, I slip out between the tangle of their limbs and go to the window and look out.

The landscape is lush and full. Flowers bloom. Leaves and grasses grow. People smile, *my* people, as they go about tending to our lands and working away in the little town just beyond the gates of our home. This place is like a fairy tale hidden away in the middle of all the human cities, and I love every inch of it.

I've almost forgotten how long I spent here, miserable, alone, and being hurt by my stepfather. For all the lives we've saved, I'm glad his wasn't and that he'll never be able to hurt me again. I still haven't asked for the details on how he died, but I know my men were involved.

Those grumpy guys would do anything for me. For *us*. For our family.

Happiness is making a comeback in my life, and I'm here for it, for *all* of it, and I'm never going to let it go. If that war taught me anything it's that no one is guaranteed a tomorrow, so we have to enjoy as much of our lives as possible. Not by throwing big parties or wearing fancy dresses, but by surrounding ourselves with the people we love.

And that's exactly what I've done. What *we've* done.

My body is changing with each day that passes, and I lay my hand over my stomach, smiling. There's only a slight bulge there, but it doesn't matter. I know that inside of me is so much hope. So much love. Everything we ever wanted and more.

I dream for the day this baby is born. For what she can be and how much we love her. Because I know in my heart that no child will ever be more loved that this one. By my men. By me. Even by Esmeray and her partners, who accepted all of this faster than I ever would have imagined, and who have plans to visit often.

"We're bringing you into a beautiful world full of love," I whisper to my belly, then press my hand over it. *Is that a flutter?* Probably not. It's probably too soon, but I imagine I feel the baby.

I never thought I would ever... feel such peace and contentment, such love. "Your fathers are going to love you unconditionally." I look down at the hand on my belly then out the window. The sky is so blue I think it must be painted and the trees are waving in a breeze that blows across the grasses and the flowers, too. We have so much to be thankful for. So much to love. "They're good and kind and brave. Heroes, every one of them."

"Yeah, we are." Phantom's arms slip around me from behind, and I jump a little, surprised, but then lean into him. He's warm and solid.

I turn in his arms to face him because I want to touch him, look at him, feel the solidity that is him. When he smiles down at me, his pec muscle twitches and I trace the silver scar just over his heart.

Our kiss is slow and sweet, sensuous.

"I think of them often, my people." I know. Sometimes, I see him staring, thinking, knowing he's torn between this life and that. "I know Shenra will be a good queen, that they'll follow her, and that she'll take care of them. But I still can't help wondering about them."

I nod. There's no doubt in my mind that Shenra is a woman of power, but that she'll wield it with mercy and grace. As hard as it is for my men not to be there to help, it was the right decision, for everyone.

He nuzzles my neck and kisses my throat. "You've saved me in every way I could've been saved."

I smile. He says this sometimes. Gets caught in the past. But I imagine it'll take some time for all of us to come to peace with what happened.

"I would've died without you," I tell him, trying to ease his pain. I could never live without them. Not then. Not now. "I love you."

From the bed, Rayne shifts, and I can see him over Phantom's shoulder, grinning. "What about me?" His voice is the husky rasp that I've always loved, and I still do.

Phantom lets me go, but I take his hand. Grinning at him, I pull him toward the bed so I can touch both of them at the same time. I'm spoiled like that, but luckily, none of them mind. "Oh, I love you, too. Don't ever doubt that."

These are the men I am never going to get enough of, never see enough of, never touch enough. That's just our kind of love. Fated. Meant to be. All the things that little girls dream of and more.

Rayne kisses the side of my throat as Onyx wakes again and lays his hand on my shoulder, squeezes gently, and pulls me backward. Then Dusk is there, his hand on my belly too.

"Everything okay with the baby?" Dusk grumbles.

Onyx smiles. He does that a lot now. The he gives me a

knowing look. Yes, my men are always worried about me and the baby. Even when half-asleep.

And then I can't help but laugh. I don't know what I did to deserve this, but every challenge I've faced, every hardship, it was all worth it since it led me to them.

IF YOU ENJOYED THIS SERIES, **check out another amazing series with a badass heroine, Dark Supernaturals.**

ALSO BY LACEY CARTER ANDERSEN

Stolen by Shadow Beasts

Shifters' Fae Captive

Shifters' Secret Sin

Shifters' Lost Queen

Their Reaper

Unlikely Reaper

Reaper Hospital: Code Possessive Boss

Reaper Hospital: Code Hot Nurse

Reaper Hospital: Code Stubborn Doctor

Guild of Assassins

Mercy's End

Mercy's Revenge

Mercy's Fall

Mercy's Rise

Revenge of the Blood Pack

Shifter Crimes

Wolf Laws

Monsters and Gargoyles

Medusa's Destiny *audiobook*

Keto's Tale

Celaeno's Fate

Cerberus Unleashed

Lamia's Blood

Shade's Secret

Hecate's Spell

Empusa's Hunger

Shorts: Forbidden Shifter

Shorts: Gorgon's Mates

Shorts: Harpy Rising

Dark Supernaturals

Wraith Captive

Marked Immortals

Chosen Warriors

Dark Supernaturals: Box Set

Wicked Reform School/House of Berserkers

Untamed: Wicked Reform School

Unknown: House of Berserkers

Unstable: House of Berserkers

House of Berserkers: Box Set

Royal Fae Academy

Revere (Prequel)

Ravage

Ruin

Reign

Lover's Wrath

Fallen Angel Reclaimed: Box Set

The Firehouse Feline

Feline the Heat

Feline the Flames

Feline the Burn

Feline the Pressure

God Fire Reform School

Magic for Dummies

Myths for Half-Wits

Mayhem for Suckers

God Fire Academy: Box Set

An Icelius Reverse Harem

Her Alien Lovers

Her Alien Abductors

Her Alien Barbarians

Her Alien Mates

Collection: Her Alien Romance

Steamy Tales of Warriors and Rebels

Gladiators

The Dragon Shifters' Last Hope

Stolen by Her Harem

Claimed by Her Harem

Treasured by Her Harem

Collection: Magic in her Harem

Harem of the Shifter Queen

Sultry Fire

Sinful Ice

Saucy Mist

Collection: Power in her Kiss

Standalones

Goddess of Love (Blood Moon Rising Shared World)

Falling for My Bosses

Beauty with a Bite

Shifters and Alphas

Collections

Monsters, Gods, Witches, Oh My!

ABOUT THE AUTHOR

Lacey Carter Andersen is a USA Today bestselling author who loves reading, writing, and drinking excessive amounts of coffee. She spends her days taking care of her husband, three kids, and three cats. But at night, everything changes! Her imagination runs wild with strong-willed characters, unique worlds, and exciting plots that she enthusiastically puts into stories.

Lacey has dozens of tales: science fiction romances, paranormal romances, short romances, reverse harem romances, and more. So, please feel free to dive into any of her worlds; she loves to have the company!

And you're welcome to reach out to her; she really enjoys hearing from her readers.

You can find her at:

Email: laceycarterandersen@gmail.com

Mailing List:

https://www.subscribepage.com/laceycarterandersen

Website: https://laceycarterandersen.net/

Facebook Page: https://www.facebook.com/authorlaceycarterandersen

Printed in Great Britain
by Amazon